VIGILANTE ASSASSIN

MARK NOLAN

To all the war dogs, police dogs, search and rescue dogs, service dogs and their hard-working K-9 handlers. Thank you for your service.

CHAPTER 1

Vigilante:
A person who seeks to avenge a crime by
taking the law into his or her own hands.
—Black's Law Dictionary

Pacific Heights, San Francisco

Lauren Stephens awoke before dawn with a sense of deep foreboding. She reached out to her husband, but Gene wasn't beside her.

She went to the kitchen and saw that he'd brewed a pot of coffee. She poured two cups and carried them to Gene's study, thinking he might be in there trading stock options online. It would be good to have coffee and a few minutes of conversation alone with her man before they both went to work.

Gene wasn't in the study, though the lights were on. Lauren

smelled something unusual—something vaguely disturbing. She wasn't sure what it could be or where it was coming from.

Had he already left for work? No, he usually ate breakfast with the kids—and anyway he would have sent her a text message if he'd needed to leave the house without saying goodbye. She checked her phone; no new texts from him. Where *was* he?

She walked down the hallway, and opened the door to the garage. His SUV was still there.

Maybe he'd gone for a walk in the dark before breakfast. He'd never done that before, but there was a first time for everything. She checked the alarm system, but the digital screen showed that the alarm had stayed on all night, just like always.

She blew out a breath. Gene had to be *inside* the house—but where?

She called his phone and it went to voicemail. Anxiety rising, she took deep breaths the way she'd been told to by her therapist. Her fears might be irrational, but ever since she'd become what some people called "rich and famous," due to her successful clothing company, she'd been getting hate email and online death threats from stalkers and trolls. It had made her paranoid, afraid to be in her own home, and she'd insisted on having an alarm system installed.

After the calming breaths, she called him again. This time she left a voicemail. "Gene, where are you? I'm getting worried." She wanted to raise her voice, but the kids were still sleeping.

The children!

Fear coursing through her veins, she ran down the hallway and threw open the door to her nine-year-old daughter's room. She found Chrissy in bed sound asleep, snuggled up with her softball glove instead of the teddy bear she'd favored for so long.

Lauren closed the door with a sigh of relief and went to the next room. She watched her son, Ben, her six-year-old, turn over in bed and mumble something in his sleep. He was a sensitive child with an active imagination and was probably dreaming about the bedtime story she'd read to him the night before.

Maybe Gene had been sleepwalking, and had fallen down and hit his head. Or maybe he'd had a heart attack or a stroke. He might be on a bathroom floor in need of medical help. She wrung her hands and wondered for the umpteenth time why they had bought this mansion. *Who needed all these extra rooms they never used?*

She searched the house. First, their bedroom. Gene's favorite shoes were still in his closet, but his house slippers were not. She didn't find his wallet or car keys on the dresser. Next, the exercise room—plenty of spouses had dropped dead on treadmills. He wasn't there. She then checked all the bathrooms, and the spare bedrooms. There was no sign of him. Every time she called his phone, she got no answer.

In the living room, Gene's overcoat hung in the coat closet. She checked the pockets. No phone. The coat smelled familiar, with a trace of his cologne, and she ached for him to hug her and say everything was okay.

Headlights cut across the room, and Lauren turned to see a car driving up the long driveway that divided the acre of front lawn. That would be Isabel, the nanny, coming to make breakfast for the kids and get them ready for school. Or, at least, it should be the nanny. *Who else could it be at this early hour?*

Lauren wondered if she should go to the master bedroom and get her pistol. She was somewhat afraid of guns, even though she owned one for protection.

Get a grip. With her palms sweating, she called Rod, the head of security at the high-rise building where Gene leased an office for his real estate firm. "Rod, this is Lauren Stephens. I've been trying to call Gene, but I think his phone battery is dead. Have you seen him this morning?"

"No, ma'am, he hasn't entered the building."

"I'm worried about him. When I woke up he was gone, but

his car is still in the garage and the alarm system has been on all
night without interruption."

There was a pause, then Rod said, "Would you like me to send
one of my people to your house?"

"Yes. Thank you." Lauren ended the call.

She turned off the alarm, opened the front door to let Isabel
inside, then closed and locked the door behind her. She
explained the situation to Isabel, who then went to the kitchen
and began preparing breakfast for the kids.

Lauren paced back and forth in the living room until another
set of headlights approached the house. The new vehicle, a white
SUV, had a bar of yellow lights on top, but they weren't flashing.
She was grateful that at least the neighbors wouldn't see
anything out of the ordinary to gossip about.

A young black woman got out of the car. She was dressed in a
light blue shirt, navy slacks, boots, and a windbreaker featuring
the security company logo. Lauren unlocked the door and let her
inside.

"I'm Mariah. Rod said you wanted me to search the house
and grounds."

"Yes. Thank you."

"Where have you looked so far?"

"In the bedrooms, bathrooms, and the garage," Lauren said.

"Does this house have an attic or basement?"

"An attic, no basement."

Mariah checked the attic and found nothing. In the garage,
she looked inside the cars and opened their trunks. Then,
retracing the steps Lauren had already taken, she searched the
house, looking in closets and under the beds.

Finally, she went outside and walked the perimeter of the
mansion, shining her flashlight in the dark.

Back inside, she told Lauren, "I'm sorry, ma'am. I've looked
everywhere except your kids' rooms. You should check those,

and if he's not there, contact the police and ask for the Missing Persons Unit."

Lauren felt a chill run down her spine. The reliable man who was the father of her children and her partner in life, a *missing* person?

She wondered who she might lean on for help. Her parents were both gone. She'd been an only child. Many of her friends had fallen away when she'd become financially successful. Most of the people she met these days wanted something from her.

As she caught another faint whiff of that strangely disturbing smell, she felt alone, afraid, and vulnerable to ... something.

CHAPTER 2

Jake Wolfe bolted upright out of a dead sleep, disoriented and sweating. Driven by survival instincts born from his years in the Marines, and later in the CIA, he reached for his nightstand and grabbed his pistol from a hollowed out constitutional law textbook about the Second Amendment.

He held the weapon in front of him with both hands. His eyes flicked back and forth, looking for someone to kill.

Then, he took a deep breath, as the remnants of a recurring violent nightmare about his covert paramilitary operations faded away and reality set in.

He was on board a boat, the *Far Niente*, out on the San Francisco Bay and anchored in a quiet spot. He was borrowing the motor yacht from his friend, Dylan, and he loved to spend the night on the water, away from the crowds and the problems of the city.

His adopted Marine war dog, Cody, came over to him and huffed, waiting for orders.

Jake scratched Cody behind the ears and whispered, "It's okay, buddy, I just had the dream again."

The dog, a yellow Labrador retriever and golden retriever cross, nodded and looked at Jake with wise eyes.

Jake got out of bed, and his body felt stiff with the aches and pains of old war wounds, especially in his thigh where he'd been shot and had nearly bled to death. The cool dampness of the Pacific Ocean air magnified the pain, but he loved being on the water so much it was a small price to pay.

His girlfriend, Sarah, was still sound asleep. Smiling, he gazed at her for a moment as she lay there; seeing the face of an angel, her beautiful bare shoulders, and silky dark hair on the white pillow. All that and a personality that pulled him to her like iron to a magnet.

Turning away, he found a pair of blue jeans and a T-shirt on the floor, put them on, went out the stateroom door and closed it behind him.

In the hallway, Cody sniffed Jake's thigh, sensing his alpha's pain. He whined and pushed his head against Jake's stomach.

"I'm fine, Cody," Jake said, and patted his dog on the back. He walked to the galley, opened the sliding door and let Cody out onto the deck.

Cody went to an area of artificial grass to relieve himself.

Jake walked back to the galley, which was close to the sliding door, brewed a pot of strong coffee and poured a cup. He opened a cupboard, grabbed a bottle of Baileys Irish Cream and added a shot to his coffee. He took a sip and nodded his head in satisfaction.

He put the Baileys back in the cupboard next to a bottle of Redbreast Irish Whiskey. Jake stared at the whiskey for a moment, shook his head, closed the cupboard and pushed that temptation out of his mind. He'd gone down that road once when his close friend, Stuart, had died of a heroin overdose. After that, he'd promised his family and friends he would steer clear of the *whiskey prescription* to dull the emotional pain that was his constant companion.

Cody came back into the galley and trotted to a water cooler with an inverted five-gallon jug on top. When he pressed his right paw down on a blue lever, water poured out of the spigot, down through a plastic tube and into a large bowl on the deck. Once the bowl was full, Cody took his paw off the lever and drank his fill, then raised his head and looked at Jake with water dripping off his snout.

Jake smiled. "You like that Stinson Beach spring water, Cody?"

Cody licked his nose, barked once and nodded.

"You're probably wishing there was a lever to fill your food bowl, too, huh?"

Cody raised one eyebrow, then sniffed his empty food bowl and gave it a lick.

Jake headed out onto the aft deck to do some fishing. It was still dark outside and a thick fog had blanketed the Bay. Visibility was minimal, but Jake could see the muted glow of the lights on the Golden Gate Bridge in the distance as he cast his line off the stern rail.

Cody sat close to Jake, as always, like his shadow.

Jake drank some coffee, and reveled in the freedom of being out on the water. He didn't need to travel very far from shore. The water was a natural barrier to the endless cars, people, and trouble. It offered a refuge from civilization, and it just felt so peaceful. Peace was what he wanted most in life right now.

He was thankful that his friend, Dylan, was letting him borrow the *Far Niente*. Dylan was one of those Silicon Valley software millionaires. He currently lived in Dublin, Ireland. All the large American software and internet companies had branch offices in Dublin. Although Dylan owned the boat, he never used it. He was a world traveler and a serial entrepreneur who only came home to California once or twice a year.

Jake patted Cody on the back. "This is the good life eh,

buddy? When I got fired from my job last month, it was a blessing in disguise."

Cody wagged his tail, and thumped it on the deck. Thump, thump, thump.

"But I still need to make a living so I can buy the essentials—dog food, beer, and fuel for the boat, right?"

Cody barked once and nodded his head. He'd been trained for three different jobs: as a Marine IED detection dog, then as a patrol dog, and finally, after he was retired from the Marines due to a lingering injury, he'd been retrained as a civilian service dog. He could understand over a thousand words, and more than a hundred hand signals and whistled commands.

On paper he seemed like the perfect service dog. The problem was that he'd once had to kill an enemy combatant while deployed overseas. He'd saved the lives of his Marine platoon, but now, much like his owner, he couldn't let go of his war training. He was too independent to be a normal service dog; only a former war dog handler like Jake could offer the firm leadership he required.

A foghorn sounded from the south tower on the San Francisco end of the Golden Gate Bridge with a low, drawn-out blast. There was a quiet pause, and then another foghorn answered with two distinctly different blasts from the midspan of the bridge. Each horn doing its part to help guide ships safely through the fog.

In the quiet stillness after the foghorns ended, Cody stood up and growled. His hackles stood on end and his tail stuck straight out as he sniffed the air while showing his teeth.

Jake paid close attention. He trusted Cody with his life; if his dog sensed that something was wrong, he believed him. Opening a tall storage cabinet, Jake grabbed a pump shotgun with an illegal Salvo 12 silencer attached.

The hair on the back of his neck stood up and the sixth sense that he'd honed in combat warned him of impending danger. He could almost smell it, like an approaching storm, if such a thing was possible.

He heard a little song in his head. He'd been told it was similar to the way some people with epilepsy heard a tune just before they had a seizure. It had started happening after he'd had a near-death experience.

Reaching into a drawer for a pair of night-vision binoculars, he searched the darkness. There—something was behind them in the water. An inflatable dinghy emerged from the fog and headed straight toward the glow of the *Far Niente's* running lights.

The boat was approximately ten feet long and powered by a quiet electric trolling motor. The lone man on board sat on the dinghy's rear bench with one hand gripping the motor's tiller handle, and the other holding a rocket propelled grenade launcher across his lap.

Jake felt a familiar anger burning inside his chest. Some of his best friends had been killed by RPGs. *Did the terrorists still have a bounty on his head, or was the man seeking revenge for somebody Jake had assassinated?*

One thing was certain—if an RPG hit the *Far Niente's* one-thousand-gallon fuel tank, the resulting fireball would destroy the boat and kill him, Sarah and Cody.

Cody stared at the raft and sniffed the air. One of his back legs—the one that had been injured in combat—trembled.

Jake whispered, "Cody, take cover," and gave the dog a hand signal.

Cody ducked down prone on his belly, out of sight. He kept his intelligent eyes trained on Jake, waiting for orders.

Jake aimed the shotgun at the raft and focused his thoughts. He had to make sure his target pointed the RPG downward. They weren't far from shore; a high shot could send the explosive round on a long arc where it might hit a boat, a house, an apartment building or a restaurant on the nearby shoreline and cause civilian casualties.

Jake shook his head. That was not going to happen on his watch. He would take whatever steps were necessary to stop an enemy combatant armed with a military weapon who was attacking America's coastline.

He flipped on the spotlight and red targeting laser mounted on the shotgun, and purposely blinded his opponent. "Drop your weapon or I'll open fire!"

The bearded man's eyes widened in surprise, but he ignored the warning as he stood up and raised the launcher.

Jake didn't hesitate. He fired at the man's hands, where they held onto the launcher. He shot down and to his left, shredding the man's left hand and knocking the weapon downward and to the side.

The man pulled the trigger with his right hand, and the rocket-propelled grenade fired into the water of the Bay. Moments later, there was a bright flash underwater as the RPG exploded. Dead fish floated to the surface, along with air bubbles that smelled like war.

The familiar scent triggered Cody's memories of battle and he let out a fierce growl, struggling to follow Jake's orders to take cover.

The man dropped the empty grenade launcher into the raft and groaned in pain, holding the wrist of his injured hand tightly.

Jake kept the red targeting laser trained on his enemy's chest. "Who are you? Who sent you?"

The man cursed in another language, and spat in Jake's direction.

In the years since Jake's first deployment overseas at the age of nineteen, he'd seen many men just like this one—and he'd killed them. "I should blow your head off, but I'll give you *one* chance to lie facedown and put your hands on the back of your neck."

The man just sneered, then drew a pistol with his uninjured hand and opened fire. Jake fired at the same time. He pumped a blast of buckshot into the man's chest, and then another. The man fell onto his back in the raft, which began to lose air.

Jake set the shotgun down on the patio table, pointing its powerful flashlight at the sinking boat, and then used his encrypted black phone to take pictures. He zoomed in to get a shot of the man's face before the raft went under. The assassin's legs were caught up in ropes and netting, and he was pulled down along with the deflated dingy by the weight of the electric outboard engine and the RPG launcher. Now the only visible signs of the battle were the dead fish floating on the surface of the water, and they would soon become shark food.

"That's a shame about those fish," Jake said.

Looking at the man's face on his phone, Jake took several deep breaths in an effort to calm his simmering rage and push back memories of dead friends killed by men just like this one. The fierce animal inside of Jake could rise to the surface at any given moment if it was provoked, but he tried to keep it under control as best he could.

Cody stood up on his hind legs and put his front paws on the aft rail, sniffing the air and growling.

Jake noticed that Cody's back leg was trembling again; it was a telltale symptom of his PTSD.

He gave Cody a command to stand by. The last thing he needed was for his dog to dive into the Bay right now, for no reason other than that he wanted to bite the throat of a dead killer.

He texted the photos to Secret Service Agent Shannon McKay. She worked at the White House, but was currently in San Francisco. McKay had requested a lunch meeting with him at noon. They'd originally had the meeting scheduled a month ago, but they'd had to postpone it until today.

With that done, Jake stood there staring out at the dark water and dark sky. No boats were nearby, so if anyone on shore had been staring out into the dark, all they might have seen were a few flashes of light. But there was a dead body in the water, and a fishing boat might pull it up in a net. He hadn't planned on killing a man before breakfast. *What should I do now?* The correct thing would be to call the cops, and sit here until the police boat *SF Marine 1* arrived. Jake knew Captain Leeds, and he was good man. But some over-eager rookie prosecutor in the DA's office might put Jake and Cody behind bars. Jake could end up in a jail cell, while Cody sat helpless in a cage at the dog pound, hoping to be adopted and avoid the needle. No, Jake would *never* let that happen to Cody.

Maybe they should just cruise away, avoid the government bureaucracy, and protect the most precious commodity in their lives—their freedom.

Cody looked at Jake and barked once.

Jake felt like Cody was reading his mind. He went inside the boat and heard water running. Thankful that Sarah was in the shower, he climbed the stairs to the bridge, manned the controls, raised anchor, and started the twin engines.

The sixty-foot motor yacht was large enough to be seaworthy and cruise the ocean, yet small enough that it could be handled by one skilled sailor. Jake always said it was a good vessel for a loner who liked people, but only in small doses.

He glanced at the GPS display and took a picture of it with his phone.

As he steered the vessel toward the yacht harbor in Sausalito, he tapped the contact "Grinds" on his phone and sent a text to his best friend Terrell Hayes. *I had a situation, but it's all good now. I'll give you a report in person.*

Terrell was a homicide detective with the SFPD, and an early riser who existed mainly on coffee, cigarettes, and the occasional sandwich from Molinari's deli. In combat, he'd sustained a traumatic brain injury, and now suffered a headache every day of his life. He often claimed Jake was the source of his headaches, not the TBI. His text in reply was a single word: *Sigh.*

Jake nodded when he saw the text. He often put his friend through a lot of trouble. But that's what friends were for, right?

His encrypted black phone buzzed with a reply text from McKay: *I ran the photos through Homeland's facial recognition system and got a positive ID. I'll tell you more when we meet at noon.*

Jake watched the sun begin to rise, painting the morning sky and water with brushstrokes of purple and gold. It was another beautiful day on the Bay, except for the fact that somebody had tried to kill him.

Would he ever have a normal, peaceful life? Or had fate doomed him to a violent struggle against the bloodthirsty killers of the world?

He had a strange feeling he was about to find out.

CHAPTER 3

Lauren Stephens stood in the kitchen of her Pacific Heights mansion, overwhelmed with doubts and fears. Had her husband run away and abandoned her? Had he gone for a walk and gotten mugged? Maybe he'd snuck out to have an affair and ended up having a heart attack in bed. Since the alarm hadn't been disengaged, none of those seemed possible, but he'd obviously gone *somewhere*.

She didn't really have anybody to turn to for help. If her mother was still alive, she'd say, *When the going gets tough, the tough get going*. Both of her parents would want her to soldier on, keep her chin up, and be strong and proactive.

She hadn't become a successful businesswoman by being indecisive. She closed her hands into fists and spoke to the nanny.

"Isabel, please get the kids up and dressed, and feed them breakfast. If they ask about their father, tell them he had to go to work early."

"Of course, Mrs. Stephens." Isabel's brow furrowed in concern as she walked quickly toward the kids' bedrooms.

Lauren turned to Mariah. "Can you stick around for a while?"

"No, I'm sorry; I have to get back to work."

"My company will hire you right now and double what you're making."

She shook her head. "That's generous of you, but my uncle owns the security firm, and I can't just quit on him like that."

"I respect your loyalty. Does the firm have somebody else they can send over here?"

"No, we only do security for corporate buildings. You want a firm that offers personal security to individuals, families, and homes."

"Is there one you'd recommend? I want the best."

"Executive Security Services LLC is the best in town. Let me give you their information." Mariah wrote down the company name and website on the back of one of her business cards and handed it to Lauren.

She glanced at the card. "Thank you. I appreciate it, and that you came over this morning."

Mariah nodded, said her goodbyes and left.

As soon as she was gone, Lauren locked the door and pulled up the website on her phone.

Executive Security Services LLC. A private security firm for high-net-worth individuals. Reliable. Discreet. Trustworthy. Providing you with maximum peace of mind. Call us when you demand the absolute best security that money can buy.

She called the number.

CHAPTER 4

The sunrise continued to paint the sky and water as Jake navigated the *Far Niente* across the San Francisco Bay and headed toward Sausalito. He opened a window of the enclosed bridge, letting the salty breeze blow through his hair, and feeling the unique joy of cruising on the open water. It was so much better than traveling on land. There were no painted lines, traffic cops, or commuter car lanes. He felt that freedom deep in his bones.

Upon arrival at the marina, Jake pulled into his boat slip and tied up. He went through the sliding door into the *Far Niente's* galley and salon area, heard the shower running and Sarah singing the song "Free Falling." He smiled, remembering the first night they'd spent together, four weeks ago, when he'd played the song on his acoustic guitar for her—and then they'd made love.

A beeping sound came from a security system speaker and Cody started growling. Somebody was approaching the boat. Jake looked at his phone and saw a CCTV view of a man walking toward the *Far Niente* as if he was planning to come aboard uninvited.

The man didn't appear to be a boater or a deliveryman; he looked like former military or law enforcement. He was dressed in a suit and tie and had close-cropped hair with a dash of salt and pepper on the sides. The man walked right past the signs that said *No Trespassing* and *Beware of Dog* as if they didn't apply to him.

Jake had seen that type of nonconformist attitude before. It was what he saw when he looked in the mirror. After what he'd already gone through this morning, he wasn't in the mood for any more surprises. He grabbed a pistol and gave a command to Cody as they went out the sliding door onto the aft deck. Jake then gave Cody a hand signal and they split up. The dog went to the port side of the boat and headed toward the approaching visitor. Jake went down the starboard side and around the bow to surprise him from behind.

The man began boarding the boat and said, "Ahoy, Far Niente —permission to come aboard?"

Cody blocked the visitor's path, baring his teeth while letting out a fierce growl.

The man stopped in his tracks and said, "Whoa now. Easy there, fella, easy does it."

Jake came up behind him. "Don't move. That's a war dog, and I have a pistol aimed at your spine. Raise your hands and stand perfectly still."

The man raised his hands. "I can explain."

"I hope so, for your sake. We've had a bad morning, and your surprise visit is making my dog's PTSD flare up. I'm not sure if I can control him right now. If you sneeze, he might sink his teeth into your crotch."

"I apologize."

"State your business and your reason for trespassing."

"My name is Howard 'Levi' Strauss. I own the Executive Security Services Company."

"I think you've got the wrong address. And who in the hell would name their kid Levi Strauss?"

"I'm a friend of Dylan Williams, the owner of this boat. He asked me to stop by because a burglar picked the lock on your door a while ago. I thought he was going to let you know I was coming by this morning, but I apologize if I misunderstood him."

"Dylan mentioned he'd call a friend, but that was the last I heard of it," Jake said. "Can you show me some ID?"

"Yes, I'm going to take out my wallet and hand it back."

"Do it carefully. My dog *wants* to hurt you. Look at him."

Levi glanced at Cody. The dog was growling and staring at Levi's crotch. Levi held his wallet out behind him until Jake took it, and then put his hands up again.

"Can you please tell your dog to stand down?"

"Maybe in a minute. I'm still looking through your wallet; lots of interesting stuff in here."

Levi let out an impatient breath but continued to hold perfectly still as Cody watched his every move.

Jake handed the man his wallet. "Your ID seems to back you up. Dylan said you used to work for the CIA, and you'd be getting in touch with me. But he didn't say you'd be coming aboard unannounced this morning."

"Sorry about that." Levi glanced at Cody and then slowly turned sideways toward Jake. He kept his hands above his head.

The two men studied each other with the eyes of trained professionals, appraising strengths and weaknesses, and deciding how they would defend or attack, if necessary.

Jake said, "My dog knows you're armed. He can smell your concealed pistol, your adrenaline and testosterone. He's standing by for orders to disarm or fight."

Levi nodded. "That is one amazing dog, and you obviously have a few skills you didn't learn in college."

Jake stared at him but didn't reply. He commanded Cody to

guard the man while he sent a text to Dylan, to verify the man's identity.

Sarah came out through the sliding glass doorway with her hair wrapped in a white towel on top of her head. She was barefoot and wearing one of Jake's button-down shirts with the sleeves rolled up.

She froze when she saw Cody on alert and Jake pointing his pistol at a man. Her years of martial arts training kicked in and she instantly raised her fists and assumed the on-guard position in the fluid style of *Jeet Kune Do*, the fighting system developed by Bruce Lee. Her knees were slightly bent, and she was ready to throw a straight-lead punch with her dominant right hand.

Levi caught sight of Sarah and stood very still. Now there was a dog snarling at his crotch, a man with a pistol aimed at his spine, and a woman who appeared ready, willing and able to fight him with some kind of martial arts.

Jake checked his phone and read Dylan's response, sent all the way from Dublin, Ireland where it was eight hours later than in San Francisco. He put his pistol away. "It's okay, Sarah; everything is fine. Cody, stand down. This man is a friend. Don't bite him."

Cody looked disappointed. He barked once but remained where he was, in between the visitor and the woman he would fight to protect if necessary. He never took his eyes off Levi's hands. Cody was known for being slow to give his trust. Jake told people that you had to earn the dog's trust and work to maintain it.

Levi turned to Sarah. "How do you do, ma'am? My name is Howard Strauss, but everybody calls me Levi. I apologize for stopping by here unannounced. It was a miscommunication about my appointment to install a better lock on that sliding door over there."

Jake said, "Sarah, meet Levi. He's friends with Dylan. Levi, this is Sarah Chance. She runs the best veterinary clinic in America."

Sarah blushed at the praise. "Good morning, Levi. Now that I'm semi-sure Jake isn't going to shoot you, may I offer you a cup of coffee?"

"Coffee would be fine, thank you," Levi said. He gave Sarah a big smile, which she returned before she went inside to the galley. Levi tried his smile on the dog, but didn't get the same results. Cody just glared at his crotch and bared his teeth again. Levi got the message: *If you bother this woman, it will cost you something irreplaceable.*

Sarah returned with three cups of coffee and set two of them on the outdoor dining table, holding onto one and taking a sip. "Jake, what were those noises I heard earlier when I was in the shower?"

Jake was thankful his shotgun had a suppressor attached. He shrugged his shoulders and lied to protect Sarah. "When I raised the anchor it clanged some and we also hit some wake and jumped a few waves. Oh, and we hit a piece of driftwood. It didn't cause any problems, just some loud bumps against the hull as it passed by."

Sarah looked doubtful, as if she were going to ask more questions.

Jake changed the subject by reciting a spiel about the *Far Niente*. "Speaking of jumping some waves, I just love this boat. She's a Horizon PC60 Power Catamaran with an enclosed skybridge. A seaworthy live-aboard vessel, sixty feet long, powered by dual 715-horsepower diesel engines. I can handle her all by myself without any crew, thanks to the ZF joystick maneuvering system and the fly-by-wire steering."

Sarah raised her eyebrows as he ran on, sounding like a salesman. The look on her face said she wasn't buying his explanation about the noises, but she didn't want to argue about it in front of their guest. She took another sip of her coffee.

"Right—well, you guys go ahead and talk about the fascinating diesel engines, joysticks, and door locks. I have to get ready for work."

After Sarah went inside, Levi looked at the two empty shotgun shells that littered a corner of the deck. He gestured toward them and said, "You mentioned having a bad morning."

Jake picked up the shells and tossed them in the gun cabinet. As he closed the door, he noticed Levi looking at the modified shotgun with its illegal suppressor attached. "I was doing some target practice," Jake said.

Levi looked off in the distance, toward the Bay. He wasn't surprised about the shotgun, or the fact that Jake was lying to him. He'd learned from Jake's CIA file that he had a strong protective instinct for women, children, and pets. Jake was like some kind of Good Samaritan with a gun. His file said it was one of his lethal flaws, a soft spot that could get him killed. The CIA had cut ties with him because he was a loose cannon who had his own set of rules and couldn't be controlled.

The file also said that one time, in a black ops battle far from home, Jake had killed a gang of terrorists known for beheading women who refused to be sex slaves. The terrorist cell couldn't be eliminated with a drone strike, because the young female hostages could have become collateral damage. Jake, who'd gone by the code name *Troubleshooter*, had gone in alone on a semi-authorized mission to hunt down those men in the middle of the night and take them out. Every terrorist in that group died that night, and the hostages survived and were now living in another country under new identities. A psychiatric evaluation in Jake's file said that he still had recurring violent nightmares about it, and he couldn't sleep through the night, but he'd do it again if there was no other option.

~

Levi said, "Jake, I won't mention the shotgun shells to Dylan. There's no need to worry him or anybody else."

"Agreed, and Sarah doesn't need to know about it either."

"I understand that you've faced some difficult challenges in life. I want to be upfront with you and tell you that I've accessed your Marine Corps records, and your top-secret CIA and JSOC missions files."

Jake glared at Levi and his gun hand twitched. "Is that why you're here? Do you think you can talk me into killing people for the CIA again? If so, you're wrong."

"No, I'm not here on their behalf."

"Why, then? You could've sent an employee to look at the door lock, but you came in person."

"I wanted to meet you. Dylan speaks highly of you."

"Why are you looking into my records? How do you have the necessary clearances to even do it if you're retired?"

"I was thinking of offering you a job at my security company, so I pulled a few strings and did a deep background check on you. I apologize if you feel I've invaded your privacy. Believe me, the last thing I want to do is anger a former government assassin."

Jake's eyes darkened. "Be careful when you stick your nose where it doesn't belong."

Cody barked several times as he noticed a change in Jake's body language and tone of voice. He moved closer to Levi and pulled his lips back, snarling.

Jake commanded, "No, Cody. This man is not a threat."

Cody's eyes never left Levi.

Jake said, "Cody, go to the grass and do your business." He pointed up the dock at the grassy area.

Military working dogs are trained to go on command, in case they need to ride in a truck or helicopter. Cody gave a final look at Levi that said *I'm warning you* in every language on the planet, no matter what living being gave the warning—but he obeyed the order.

Once Cody was trotting up the dock, Jake pointed his finger at Levi. "If you're going to visit this boat, please be careful what you say in front of Cody. That dog has a fiercely independent spirit and a lingering touch of trauma. He's been through hell and back, and he's barely under my control. Don't provoke him by raising your voice, or talking about war, unless you want him to eff you up."

"I'm sorry. I won't bring this up again. I know that Duke, your war dog, died. And Stuart, Cody's handler died too. But I'm glad you adopted Cody. That's good for both of you."

At the mention of Duke and Stuart, every muscle in Jake's body tensed, and his hands became fists. A shadow passed across his face. He took a deep breath and let it out.

Levi saw this and held his hands out. "I'm on your side, Jake."

Jake shook his head. "Those are polite words, but look me in the eye and tell me you understand that Cody is trained to proactively fight a threatening man like you to protect his handler."

Levi looked at Cody as the dog trotted toward the grass. He then met Jake's eyes. "I understand. I'll be very careful around him."

"If you'd drawn your pistol, Cody would've disarmed you by biting your wrist. Then, when you fought him in panic, he might have ripped your throat out."

"I'm glad I held perfectly still."

"He's a good dog, but both of his handlers died and he's very protective of me."

"Understood."

CHAPTER 5

Lauren called the security company. The receptionist went into a canned pitch that she'd no doubt spouted a thousand times before. "We offer a wide variety of security services and—"

"Tell your boss I want all of your services—right now," Lauren said.

"We have all kinds of options, ma'am: home security, personal security, child protection, bodyguards, armored vehicles with professional drivers, background checks on employees, surveillance cameras—"

"Send *every* available person to my house immediately. I don't care how much it costs. Charge the fees to my American Express Black Card."

"Uhm ... I don't know if we can do that, this is somewhat irregular. You'll have to talk to my boss. He might be able to reroute some assets to make it happen as soon as possible."

"What's your name?"

"Paula."

"Listen to me, Paula. If you get this done in the next fifteen minutes, I'll personally give you a bonus of five thousand dollars cash, delivered to you this morning by courier."

"Oh my gosh."

"And if you *don't* get it done, I'll see to it that you lose your job and never get another one in this city for the rest of your life. Do you understand me?"

There was a long pause. "Well, then I guess I'll try to get it done. And I promise that when I get your cash bonus I'll spend it wisely."

"Good plan, Paula. Call me back in ten minutes to give me a progress report."

Lauren ended the call. If she had a crisis, everybody else had a crisis too.

She went into the dining room and checked on her kids while they were eating breakfast.

"Where's Daddy?" Chrissy asked.

Lauren felt a knot in her stomach as she lied to her child. "Daddy had to go into work early today so he could help a family buy a house."

Chrissy gazed at her mother with the frank appraisal of a child. She paused to think about it, then nodded her head, innocently believing the lie—for now.

Lauren walked back into the kitchen. Sophie, her maid, arrived and started cleaning up the skillets from breakfast, giving her boss a long look as she did so. "Are you okay, Mrs. Stephens?"

Lauren spilled her feelings to Sophie. "I'm torn between wanting the children to have a normal life and wanting to keep them safe inside my house twenty-four hours a day under my constant watch."

Sophie nodded as she dried a plate and put it away. "You feel the same way as every other mother."

"Do you think I'm overreacting?"

"I don't know. I'd be going crazy right now, but I'm a serious helicopter parent."

"Should I send the kids off to school, like always?"

"Do what you need to do, but the school is a safe and familiar place for them. It's part of their normal daily routine. And there's a police officer at the school for safety."

Lauren heaved a huge sigh. "Thank you, Sophie, I can always count on you."

Sophie nodded and went out of the room. In the hallway, she looked over her shoulder and then tapped on her phone and sent a text message.

She's sending the kids to school.

CHAPTER 6

Jake led Levi to the sliding door on the aft of the *Far Niente*.

Levi studied the hardware. "This is a top-quality lock in perfect working condition. There's not a scratch on it. Whoever opened it without a key must have used a high quality locksmith's tool."

"He was an assassin, sent here to kill me," Jake said.

Levi stared at him for a moment. He pulled a chrome tool out of his pocket. It looked like a small, slender flashlight with a lock pick sticking out one end. "This is a Kronos electric pick gun. Go inside and lock the door, please."

Jake locked him out. Levi eased the pick into the door lock's keyhole, and pressed a button. The pick gun vibrated quietly and opened the lock in a few seconds.

"My team will install a lock that's preferred by people in law enforcement," Levi said.

"Thanks," Jake said, and came back out the door and onto the deck.

Levi's phone buzzed. He answered it and asked a few questions, looking more concerned as he asked each one. He ended the call. "I have a situation and need to go. My company just got a crisis call from a woman in Pacific Heights."

Jake took a business card out of his wallet and used a pen to cross out his former work number and email, leaving just his personal contact info. He handed the card to Levi. "Here's my number. Get back to me and we'll set up a time for the lock."

Cody returned to the boat from the dog area. Jake poured him a bowl of dry dog food which Cody began to devour, the dog tags on his collar jingling against the metal bowl as he ate.

Levi glanced at Jake's card. "Does this mean you no longer work at the TV station as a photojournalist?"

"Yeah, I got fired from my photography job. It happens to me a lot, but that's okay. I can go back to doing freelance work. Maybe I'll cruise the boat up and down the coast on photo assignments."

"If you have some free time right now, would you like to come along with me and assist with this situation in Pacific Heights? A family is in trouble. They could use some help from you and your dog. It'll give you a chance to see what we do."

"A family? How can Cody and I help them?"

"My client's husband went missing. When she called the police they told her to file a missing persons report and said they'd investigate as soon as they could."

Jake nodded. "The police are busy with violent crimes."

"Right, and she wants results immediately."

"So, were you hired as protection? Or to find her husband?"

"Both—she and her husband are wealthy and well known. There are business fortunes and reputations at stake. She also wants to protect her kids from the media."

Jake met his eyes. "The media might be a problem. I could make a few phone calls to my contacts at my former employer. Ask them to lay off."

"Mostly I was hoping you and your dog could search the house and grounds."

"We could do that, but past experience has taught me I should never volunteer for anything." Jake looked off in the distance and thought about the time he'd volunteered to help the CIA kill high-value targets.

"Understood. I read the psychology tests results in your file. Your empathy scores are off the charts. That's why you're a good dog handler—but that's also why you've volunteered for things you should have avoided."

"Now that you've invaded my privacy, be aware that the only time I'll volunteer is if Cody and I are needed to do search and rescue work—missing kids, lost hikers, natural disasters."

"This would be similar—a missing family member. But I'm willing to pay you for your time, so you wouldn't be a volunteer."

"Cody isn't for hire. If we helped you, would he be in any kind of danger?"

"None that I'm aware of. When you were a photojournalist, did you learn a lot about video equipment?"

"Of course. Why do you ask?"

Levi looked at one of Jake's security cameras, mounted on the boat. "I'm wondering if you could check the home alarm system's video and tell me if anything looks suspicious or has been tampered with."

"I could, but how would this kind of arrangement work? I don't want to go back to having a job and a boss if I can avoid it."

"I'd only be hiring you for one day. I'll pay you double whatever the TV station was paying you."

"Lucky for you, they weren't paying much."

"Okay then, I'll pay you the same as my highest paid and most valuable employee. She's very good and I pay her accordingly, but I have a feeling you and Cody are worth it; especially Cody."

Jake smiled. "Fair enough, but I'll work *with* you, not *for* you. I'll be an independent contractor, providing a service to your company for a fee. I can walk away at any time."

"We can treat it that way between you and me, but my team

operates under my private security employer's license. Didn't I see in your file that you're licensed?"

"Yes, as part of my celebrity photography work, I got licensed to do private security and act as a bodyguard. But I can't do any private investigator work. That takes five years."

"Then you're good to go. I just need you to sign an employment form so you're covered under our insurance."

"That works, but we'll have to ride with you because my Jeep is in the shop."

"No problem. Later today, I can loan you a company car if you want one."

"I should probably wear shoes, right?"

"At least," Levi said. "Everybody on my team wears a suit or a sport coat and slacks."

"That's another reason I'm not on your team. I won't be following your dress code. Wait here and I'll be back in a minute. Keep in mind, you're being recorded on video, and my dog doesn't like you very much."

Cody growled at Levi and stood between him and the sliding door.

Jake headed to the master stateroom, where Sarah was sitting on the edge of his bed, putting on her rubber-soled work shoes. Jake wished he could spend the morning with her. She thought of herself as plain looking, but he disagreed. She wore black slacks and a white blouse that accented her shape, horn-rimmed glasses, and her hair was tied back in a ponytail to keep it out of the way while she practiced veterinary medicine. Her purse was on the bed next to her, a book sticking out. Women who wore glasses and read books were Jake's weakness. In his opinion, Sarah was sexy without even trying to be.

Sarah stood and grabbed her purse, glancing at him as she did so. She started to say something, but stopped.

They'd only met a month ago, but their relationship was moving fast—maybe too fast.

Sarah's phone buzzed with a text. "My assistant, Madison, will be here in a few minutes. I asked her to pick me up."

"All right. Cody and I are going to assist Levi on a security job in Pacific Heights. A family there needs our help."

Sarah sighed. "Jake, why are you always taking risks for other people?"

"It's probably nothing risky. The wife just needs a SAR dog to find her missing husband."

"If the husband is missing, he might have been kidnapped or murdered. You have no idea how dangerous it could be, for you or Cody."

"I know you're stressed about Cody, but I'll protect him and take good care of him, I promise."

"I want to believe you, but you're often reckless, and Cody is so loyal he'd follow you into hell and fight the devil."

"We'll be fine; don't worry."

"But why *you*, Jake? Why do you have to be the one who does this kind of thing?"

Jake struggled with his answer for a moment. He felt conflicted, wanting peace and quiet, but unable to turn his back when a family was in danger. "Because it's the right thing to do. As the Irish philosopher Edmund Burke said, *the only thing necessary for the triumph of evil is for good men to do nothing.* I believe in being a good man, Sarah. I can't stand by and do nothing. If I did, my life would feel meaningless."

CHAPTER 7

Instead of leaving, Sarah crossed her arms and waited while Jake changed clothes. She noted the controlled, deliberate, and dangerous way his animal-like body moved. His muscular chest and back were covered with all kinds of scars. It was like a map of battle, pain and survival. He was six feet of solid muscle, with dark wavy hair, "devil-may-care" brown eyes and a jaded smile. He had a thing for nerdy girls who were kind to animals. He'd asked her out the first time they'd met, when she was giving first aid to Cody. She felt a strong attraction to him too, and she loved Cody, but Jake seemed to be a magnet for trouble.

Before he put on a fresh shirt, she noticed a bite mark on his shoulder. Her face flushed as she realized she must have done that to him in bed last night. That surprised her because she'd never sunk her teeth into a boyfriend before. What was it about this guy? He wasn't celebrity handsome but he had a confident, dangerous way about him that made her heart beat faster. That scared her a little bit.

She watched him grab a pistol and holster, plus two extra mags of ammo, then pick up his KA-BAR knife. It had a black blade, etched with gold letters that said Operation Enduring

Freedom. It looked like it had been through hell and back. He shoved it into a sheath and attached it horizontally to his belt behind his waist with velcro loops. There was no way that thing could be legal to carry around. Next, he pulled up his pant leg, and strapped a small pistol and holster to his ankle.

Sarah took a deep breath and let it out. She felt mixed emotions as Jake stood before her in his jeans and boots, black t-shirt and leather jacket. He looked like a rock star who could kill terrorists, and she knew he'd done so in his past. In her opinion he was a man with a good heart, but a lot of flaws. Most of the time he was a strong, in-control person who could handle himself in any situation. Yet he was still young and hot-headed, overprotective of women to a fault, and he had zero tolerance for cruelty to children and pets. Sometimes he could lose his temper and do things that were reckless, dangerous, and illegal.

He was rebellious, had a smart mouth and no patience for bureaucrats. Years ago a bureaucratic mistake had left him alone on foot in the desert, while hunted by terrorists who had a bounty on his head. Yet deep down, he also had a sensitive side. She'd caught a glimpse of that in the way he took care of his dog.

Sarah had given up on meeting Mister Right—the perfect man who didn't exist. She had to admit that she wasn't perfect either. It made her happy to have met a hot alpha male who found her attractive. Jake knew what he wanted, and he went after it. Right now he wanted her. She wanted him too, but he was always in some kind of danger, and she wasn't sure if she could learn to live with constantly worrying about Jake and Cody. It was a decision she'd have to make soon because she was falling for Jake.

~

On his way out the door, Jake stopped and stood close to Sarah. "Let's have dinner tonight."

She smiled at him but shook her head. "I think I'm going to take a night off to rest up. After work I just want to take a hot bath, have a glass of wine, and go to bed early for a good night's sleep."

"We could just relax, watch a movie, and get a pizza."

She rolled her eyes. "Netflix and chill? I know how that would end up. You'd be having your way with me on the couch. Hold that thought for *tomorrow* night, okay?"

Jake put his hand behind the small of her back and pulled her against his body. "I have no idea what you're talking about."

"Mmmm-hmmm," she said as he kissed her.

He smiled against her mouth, and she smiled back. Then she put the palm of her hand against his chest and pushed him away. "*That's* what I'm talking about."

Jake shrugged. They gazed into each other's eyes. Promises were made and agreed upon, without any words being spoken.

A horn honked in the parking lot and Sarah's phone buzzed. She headed toward the door with Jake close on her heels.

Jake locked the sliding door behind them, and everybody stepped off the *Far Niente*. On the way up the dock, Cody trotted along protectively beside Sarah as she made her way to Madison's car.

Levi moved toward his SUV, and Jake said, "Just one sec. I'm expecting something important in the mail." He stopped at the row of marina mailboxes and unlocked his box. He flipped through several more letters from collection agencies, courtesy of his former fiancée and her spending spree.

At the bottom of the stack was one envelope he'd been waiting weeks for: the admission packet from the California State Bar Association. He opened it and read the cover letter stating he had completed all the requirements for membership. It felt surreal to read those magic words.

"After you have forwarded the completed membership enrollment

card, which has the oath on the back, to the State Bar's Membership Records office, you are eligible to start practicing law."

Jake resisted the urge to yell in victory. He put the membership card and the cover letter into his jacket's inside left pocket and then stuffed everything else back into his box, closed the door and moved toward Levi.

The evenings and weekends of internet law school had finally paid off. He felt grateful that he lived in a state that allowed online law students to sit for the bar exam and become lawyers. He'd kept it a secret from his friends and family because he didn't want to hear their negative opinions and their endless lawyer jokes. Few people knew that most lawyer jokes started out as racist jokes, and people simply substituted the word "lawyer" for a racist word.

Sarah was still in the lot and was down on one knee, inspecting the stitches that ran along Cody's side. Satisfied, she gave him a hug, and then stood up. "Your stitches are in fine shape, but don't do anything that might pull them loose. Promise me that you and Jake will try to stay out of trouble."

Cody barked once at Sarah and pressed his head against her stomach. With a final pat, Sarah got into Madison's car and drove away.

Cody ran back to Jake, and they got into Levi's vehicle. As they sped toward the Pacific Heights mansion of Levi's new client, he briefed Jake about the situation. Levi was hoping it was only a case of a runaway husband.

Jake silently hoped so too, but he had a bad feeling that it could be something worse—far worse.

CHAPTER 8

As Jake was riding in the car, he received a text message from his ex-fiancée, Gwen.

Jake, I'm sorry. I apologize. Can you find it in your heart to forgive me?

Jake had no idea what to say, so he didn't reply. He thought of what Will and Ariel Durant had said when they were asked what they'd learned while writing the history of the world, "One of the lessons of history is that nothing is often a good thing to do, and always a clever thing to say."

Jake did the clever thing and said nothing. He hoped Gwen was doing okay in rehab, and he wished her the best in life, but their relationship was beyond repair. When he'd called off the wedding, she'd thrown a champagne bottle at his head. He'd then walked out, saying goodbye forever. Enraged, she'd called the police and falsely accused him of domestic violence. The next day she'd emptied his bank accounts and run up debts on his credit cards.

Levi's car arrived at a Pacific Heights mansion that was surrounded by a stone wall and high privacy hedges. The black wrought iron gate in front swung open on silent hinges powered by an electric motor and granted them entry to a sweeping driveway.

Jake was surprised at the size of the estate. The property went on and on, with an acre of perfect lawn in front of the home, and more lawn on each side. The artfully manicured landscaping included bushes that were trimmed into the shapes of circus animals. He'd been expecting something grand, but this was on par with the old mansions of San Francisco's gilded history—and now the more recent internet startup business millionaires.

Several of Levi's employees had already arrived and were patrolling outside the house.

Once they were out of the car, Jake dressed Cody in a service dog vest and clipped a leash onto his collar.

Cody looked around, sniffed the air, and pawed at the lawn.

Jake, like many dog handlers, could sense Cody's energy up and down the leash. He had a feeling there was something unusual going on here—far more than a runaway husband.

Levi tapped his phone. He waved to a woman, and she jogged over to him.

She was in her early thirties, wore a dark pantsuit, police-style shoes, and a starched blouse. The tell-tale bulge of a pistol under her suit coat told Jake she was equipped with a concealed weapon.

She tilted her head and glanced at Jake and Cody, curious.

Jake gave her a polite, respectful nod in reply.

Levi made the introductions. "Kim, this is Jake Wolfe and his search dog, Cody. Jake, this is Kim Buckley, the number one most reliable member of my team."

Kim reached out to shake Jake's hand. "We got the text saying not to pet the dog."

Jake nodded at her.

Cody sniffed the air and looked around the grounds. One of his eyebrows twitched.

Levi said, "Kim, I want you to drive the kids to school, and bring the nanny along for the ride. Take the armored Suburban, but just tell them it's a limousine. Keep in constant contact by phone. Stay alert and watch your six. We'll be tracking you via a beacon in the vehicle. If you see anything unusual, return here immediately."

Kim nodded. "Is there any immediate perceived threat I should be aware of?"

"No, we're simply operating on standard procedure. We're going to level-three security as a courtesy to our new client, until her husband is located."

"Understood. Will the mother speak to the nanny and kids first, so they know what I'm doing?"

"Yes, they're expecting you."

"I'm on it."

"Wait a minute," Jake said.

They both turned and looked at him.

Jake glanced at the armored Suburban. "Are you sure you want to send the kids off to school?"

"Yes, Mrs. Stephens requested it," Levi said.

"Kim, please give me your phone number," Jake said, pulling out his phone.

Kim turned to Levi, who nodded. She recited her number. Jake sent her a text, and her phone buzzed. "If you notice *anything* remotely odd on the drive to school, call me immediately, okay?"

Kim looked Jake in the eye. "Okay." She glanced at Levi curiously.

Levi said, "I'm giving Jake a lot of latitude. No time to explain right now."

Lauren came out the front door with her children and the nanny. As the two kids climbed into the brand new SUV, they acted as if they thought this was a fun change of pace from the daily routine.

Jake observed the nanny. She seemed doubtful, and

uncomfortable with this change in routine, but wasn't really acting secretive or guilty. She obediently climbed into the front passenger seat, going along but appearing worried and overprotective of the kids. Jake's impression was that she seemed bright, aware, and sincere. He intended to talk to her when she returned, to get her honest opinion about Lauren's husband.

The SUV drove away, with Lauren waving goodbye and smiling as if everything was just fine. Her body language told a different story.

Jake noted that Lauren was in her late twenties, of average height and weight, with wavy dark hair and smart eyes. Levi had told him she owned an apparel company that had become an internet sensation and made her a millionaire. Jake watched the SUV leaving, crossed his arms and frowned.

Levi said, "Kim is my most reliable employee, and she's well-trained as a bodyguard."

Lauren took deep breaths, bit off part of a manicured fingernail, and then quietly cursed.

Jake said, "I was impressed with Kim. I'm sure she'll take good care of your kids."

Levi introduced them. "Lauren, this is Jake and his dog, Cody, of our K-9 team. They're going to search your house."

Lauren looked Jake up and down with the appraising gaze of a boss evaluating her new employee. It appeared that she was about to give a speech.

Jake held up his hand and cut her off. "My dog has to smell your husband's shoes, to get his scent. Cody will then track his movements step-by-step until we find out exactly where he disappeared to."

Lauren's face went pale when Jake stated the cold reality so bluntly. She nodded.

Jake decided to set some boundaries. "If you agree to this search, I'm in charge of it. Please tell me you understand and agree; otherwise I'll leave now, and you can try to find another private K-9 team to help you on such short notice."

Lauren stared impatiently at him for a moment while she thought it through, and said, "Okay. You're in charge of the K-9 search. Everyone will cooperate with you for *one hour*, including me. I give you my word."

Jake scratched his dog behind his ears and then displayed Cody's assistance dog registration tag on his collar, issued by the San Francisco Department of Animal Care and Control. "And another thing—please remind everybody in your house they shouldn't try to pet my service dog when he's working."

"I've heard of that, and I'll pass the word," Lauren said.

"Prior to becoming a service dog, Cody served as a military working dog (MWD). He may be huggable-looking, but he's a former war dog. He was deployed overseas, where he once had to kill an enemy combatant. His training has made him one of the most intelligent animals in the world, but he has a mind of his own and he's overly protective of me."

Lauren took a step back. "Is it safe for him to come into my home?"

"Yes, unless you have an aggressive dog."

"No pets."

"Okay. Then we should be good to go."

"How did you come to own a war dog?"

"When Cody entered civilian life, he was retrained to be a service dog. He used to live with my friend Stuart, who'd served as a Marine dog handler, like me. When Stuart died of a drug overdose, I adopted Cody."

She looked at Cody and then at Jake. "I'm sorry to hear about your friend, and I'm counting on you to keep Cody under control while he's in my home. Is there something wrong with him?"

Cody barked twice at Lauren. It seemed as if he shook his head.

She looked at him in surprise. "Does he know we're talking about him?"

"Of course; we're saying his name. All dogs know their name."

Lauren stared at Cody for a moment and he stared back at her with his bright, intelligent eyes and raised one eyebrow. Lauren rubbed her arms as if she had goosebumps, turned away and walked toward the house.

They all went inside to the master bedroom where Jake gave commands and Cody sniffed the husband's shoes. After he got the scent he circled around the room. He went to the bed and alerted at an oblong, tube-shaped pillow.

"Electronics?" Jake asked.

Cody barked once.

"Leave it." Jake had seen that special kind of pillow before. It looked as if it was designed to go under the back of your neck, but he knew it was a hiding place for personal items—the kind that vibrate.

Lauren closed her eyes for a moment at this embarrassing invasion of her privacy.

Jake moved on without further comment.

Cody went to a nightstand next to the bed. He sniffed at a drawer and then pawed at it.

Jake opened the drawer and found a gun safe. He picked it up and saw a biometric fingerprint lock. Jake praised Cody and put the gun safe back where he'd found it.

Lauren said. "That's my husband's. Did it feel heavy, like his pistol is inside?"

"Yes, ma'am. I believe his weapon is still in there."

"I have one just like it in my nightstand."

Cody went around the bed and sniffed the other nightstand. Jake opened the drawer and found Lauren's gun safe. He lifted it to judge the weight, put it back and nodded at Lauren. "Both feel the same. Any other weapons in the house?"

"No, just the two pistols."

Jake didn't say that she might be wrong, but he had married friends who hid weapons from their wives—rifles, pistols, shotguns, knives—you name it.

Cody pulled on the leash and went over to a wall, then stood up on his hind legs and sniffed at a painting. Jake turned to Lauren. "Is there a wall safe behind that artwork?"

Lauren's face couldn't hide her surprise at how Cody was finding every secret detail of her life. "Yes, it contains jewelry, some cash, passports, and birth certificates."

"I need you to open it so we can see if your husband's passport is still in there."

Lauren blinked several times. She pulled on the painting and swung it open on hidden hinges, then tapped a combination into the digital electronic keypad to unlock the safe.

Jake watched her and memorized the combination. As he did, he asked himself why, and realized he was still feeling the influence of his brief stint as a CIA operative.

Lauren opened the safe's door and examined the contents. Her shoulders slumped in relief. "His passport is still in here, along with the cash."

"He doesn't own a private jet, does he?"

"No, he doesn't believe in buying a plane when you can just rent one, which we do quite often."

"We need to call that aviation company."

She nodded. "I authorize your firm to do it for me."

Levi took out his phone. "What's the name of the company?"

Lauren sent him a text, and he forwarded it to an employee.

Jake gave a command to Cody and they returned to the husband's shoes. Cody sniffed them again and looked at Jake.

Jake gestured toward the bedroom door. "Where did he go, Cody? Find him now. Seek, seek, seek!"

Cody followed the scent through the house, down the hallway, and into the kitchen. He paused at the coffeemaker and then moved on. He ended up in the husband's study, searched the room and stopped in front of a floor-to-ceiling bookcase. He sniffed all around it with an intense focus and then sat down.

Jake held up his hand. "Stay back. Cody is indicating he smells explosives of some kind."

Levi escorted Lauren out of the room and took her a safe distance down the hallway.

Jake caught the hint of a strange and frighteningly familiar mixture of aromas. He carefully checked the bookcase; everything on the shelves appeared to be normal, except for a fist-sized sculpture of a carved amber skull. It was fastened down, but he found that he could turn it if he applied enough pressure.

There was a quiet *click* when he slowly turned the skull counterclockwise. The tall bookshelf slid to the left with barely a whisper, revealing a hidden doorway and a flight of stairs that went down underground.

A disturbingly familiar odor rose upward from the closed door at the bottom of the stairs. He recognized the scent from combat, but it made no sense to find it here in this family home.

Cody alerted and growled, his hackles standing up.

CHAPTER 9

Jake patted Cody on the back. "Easy, now. Don't go down there."

Lauren walked back into the room, impatient with the delay. She glared at Jake and started to say something, but then stopped and stared at the secret stairway. She put her hand over her mouth in surprise.

Levi came into the room behind Lauren, and he let out a low whistle. "Whatever is hidden down there is probably not going to be good news."

Jake nodded. "Only one of us should go down there. Someone has to cover this entrance, for mission security."

Levi drew his pistol. "I'll cover you. I've got your back—no surprises from this end."

Fearing for his dog's safety, Jake put his hand on Cody's head. "Cody, I'm going down there alone to check it out. You stay here. I'll be back in a minute."

Cody barked twice and shook his head. One of his back legs began to tremble. He let out a low growl, jerked the leash out of Jake's hand and went down the stairs ahead of him—determined to protect his alpha from the nightmares he sensed on the other side of that door.

Jake whistled a command, and yelled, "Cody, hold your position. That's an order!"

Cody obeyed and waited for Jake.

Jake drew his pistol. Catching up to Cody, he scratched him on the nape of his neck and whispered, "We'll do this according to protocol."

Jake removed the clip from Cody's collar so he could go off-leash, and they descended together as a team. The smell grew worse with every step. At the bottom of the stairs, Jake reached for the doorknob with his left hand, while his right hand held his pistol up in front of him and ready to fire. He whispered to Cody, "Kill zone."

When Jake turned the knob and kicked the door open, the full force of the sickening aroma hit him in the face. They rushed in and Jake waved his pistol back and forth as he looked for targets. Nobody waited in ambush, but inside the secret room, something was terribly … wrong. Cody started barking, and Jake had to make an effort not to gag. He now understood the source of the smell. The room was like a scene from a nightmare.

Jake holstered his pistol and took out his phone to call Terrell. He was surprised to find that he had four bars, then noticed a cell phone amplifier next to a conduit pipe, among the high-tech equipment that filled up one wall.

When Terrell answered the call, Jake said, "I've got bad news, Grinds. Look at the pics I'm sending to your phone."

Jake took several photos of the room and sent them to Terrell. A moment later, he heard Terrell cursing. Jake knew that his friend was like many cops, considering the city he protected to be "his city." He represented the thin blue line. Nobody could commit a crime like this in his city and get away with it because he would move heaven and earth to hunt them down and put them in a cage where they belonged.

"Give me the address. I'm on my way," Terrell said.

Jake texted him the address. Next he sent the photos to Levi and wrote: *Confidential. This is a crime scene. Nobody can enter. The evidence has to be preserved for the police.*

He took some video with his phone, and then he and Cody left the room, pulling the door closed behind them. They quickly climbed up the stairs to the study, where they drank in deep breaths of clean air.

Lauren asked, "What did you find down there?"

Jake shook his head, refusing to describe what he'd seen. "The police are on their way."

Lauren appeared close to having a nervous breakdown. "Why did you call the police?"

"Because it's the scene of a crime."

"I insist on seeing what's down there, right now!"

"No, I'm sorry Lauren, but I can't let you do that," Jake said. "It's not safe, the police won't allow it, and if you see this—there is no unseeing it."

Her face flushed with rage. "I'm the head of a multimillion-dollar company. Nobody says no to me. When I say jump, people ask how high."

He stood firm. "I respect you, but I don't care about any of that. Please stay out of there. You'll thank me later."

She pointed her finger at Jake. "You work for me, and you will do exactly what I tell you to do. Otherwise you're fired, and you can leave right now."

Jake nodded. "No problem, I'm fired. But I still won't let you go down there."

"Get out of my house, at once."

Jake just stood there. Cody did too.

"Can't you make him listen and obey?" Lauren said to Levi. "He's your employee, isn't he?"

"He's an independent contractor, with the key word being *independent*," Levi said. "And, you just fired him. Now he's only an unpaid trespasser who is stubbornly trying to protect you from ... something."

Lauren glared at Jake for several more seconds, but when it became obvious he wasn't giving in, she said, "You have to understand that I'm under incredible stress here and I need some *answers.* Move away from the doorway. Please."

Levi held out his phone. "See this form you signed? You agreed that Jake was in charge and you'd give him your full cooperation for one hour."

"That is null and void now that I've fired him," Lauren said. She clenched her fists and cursed.

"I apologize, Lauren," Jake said. "Please trust me. I'll explain everything once the police get here. Until then I'm taking control of the situation for your own safety."

Lauren stared into Jake's eyes and saw understanding there. She took a deep breath and let it out. "As soon as the police get here, I insist on going down those stairs."

Jake held her gaze and shook his head. "I'd strongly advise against it, Lauren. If you do that, you'll regret it for the rest of your life."

Lauren heard the sound of police sirens coming closer to her home. She had so many unanswered questions. Where had her husband gone? Why did her house have a secret underground room? What was Gene hiding from her? Why wouldn't Jake let her see what was down there? And what in the world was causing that strange smell?

Shaking, she wrapped her arms around herself, wondering if she'd ever really known her husband. Maybe he was a complete stranger, a talented actor, and liar. Maybe he'd only been using her—but for what?

The police sirens arrived at her front gate, and then, in another area of the house, somebody screamed.

CHAPTER 10

Sophie, the maid, was collecting laundry in the master bedroom when a flying drone crashed against the screen of the open window. Sophie screamed and stood there in shock as the flying machine hit the screen again and again, like a giant buzzing insect that wanted her blood.

The drone was basically a shotgun with a top wing and two copter blades spinning above it. A camera was mounted underneath. It pointed a red targeting laser into the room and swept it across the wall toward Sophie.

Jake ran down the hall with Cody following him. They went into the master bedroom and saw the drone trying to enter the house.

He recognized it as a Russian shotgun drone. Drawing his pistol, he gave a command for Cody to take cover and protect the civilian.

Cody leapt toward the panicking maid and bit down on her

leather belt, pulling her onto the floor next to the bed. They hit the carpet, keeping the bed in between them and the window.

The drone then swept the red targeting laser toward Jake, who ducked down next to the bed just a moment before a shotgun blast shredded the window screen, hit the bed and the wall, and destroyed a large mirror.

The moment after the mirror glass exploded, Jake rose to a crouch and fired his pistol at the incoming drone. He shot a tight grouping of rounds, and one found its moving target. The drone spun in circles as it fell from the sky. Jake ran to the window in time to see that the drone was still flying with one copter blade, but at an awkward downward angle. It was listing to its side, on a crooked course toward the front of the house.

Jake cursed and gave Cody a command to stand still. He grabbed Sophie's arm and pushed her toward the door. "Come with us. We'll protect you."

It wasn't a question, and Sophie instinctively obeyed the person who had saved her life. Jake steered her into the hall, and then turned back and picked up Cody and carried him over the carpet littered with razor-sharp pieces of broken mirror glass. He set his dog down in the hallway and then pulled out his phone and called Levi. "The house is under attack by at least one armed drone. Lock it down, close the front door and secure every window."

"Roger," Levi said. He yelled orders and sent texts, and his people charged through the house to do his bidding.

Jake heard police sirens as several SFPD vehicles sped down the driveway and parked out front. He ran to the window again and saw a black SUV drive onto the vast lawn and head straight for the house, not stopping until it was near the front door.

~

Terrell Hayes jumped out of his SUV and looked around, assessing the situation with a frown on his face. He was a tall, rugged-looking black man with a body like a professional athlete and was wearing the same clothes he always wore: a dark suit, a white shirt, a plain tie, and perfectly shined shoes.

He received a call from Jake. "Watch the sky for a shotgun drone. I shot it, but it's still airborne and heading toward the front door."

Terrell growled some creative profanity in reply and grabbed his police shotgun out of the vehicle. He scanned the perimeter and saw that somebody had left the front door wide open.

The drone appeared in the air from a corner of the house. It was listing to the side as it flew toward the front door. At the same moment, inside the house, a frightened woman was running toward the door.

Terrell ran across the lawn with the pump shotgun held at shoulder height. He shot the drone out of the sky, like a duck hunter shooting his dinner. Fire—pump—fire—pump—fire. The drone crashed onto the lawn, and moments later, an attached grenade exploded.

Terrell reloaded the shotgun and then scanned the skyline and the airspace around the house for any additional threats.

Inside the house, the woman reached the front door and slammed it, nodding at Terrell in thanks as she did.

Jake walked down the main hallway and spoke in a low voice to Levi. "If the house is under attack, we have to assume the kids might be in danger. What's the status of your driver? I want to borrow one of your cars, rendezvous with her and provide backup."

Levi called Kim. "Report your current status."

"We're almost to the school."

"Negative, don't go there."

"Should I return to the house?"

"No, the house is under attack and the family is in danger. Code Red, take the kids to our secure location and protect them until we sort this out."

"Roger that. Code Red. Protect the children at all costs."

Kim pressed down on the gas pedal and made some evasive maneuvers to lose anybody that might be a threat. She took four right turns to see if she was being followed. Sure enough, she spotted a vehicle that had tailed her all the way around the block.

She drove the car like she'd stolen it. "Hang on tight kids. We're going to drive really fast now."

CHAPTER 11

In a penthouse apartment on the top floor of a tall skyscraper—one of San Francisco's most luxurious buildings—an exotic-looking brunette woman named Elena Savina sat at her desk studying a laptop computer and working a drone controller. She watched a spy camera video from her drone as it fired its weapon through the window screen of a mansion, and then a man in the room returned fire. The picture tilted and wobbled while she tried to fly the drone toward the front of the house. Then there was a bright flash and video feed stopped.

She ran facial recognition software on the image of the man's face, identified him as Jake Wolfe, and then cursed in Russian.

She made a call, and a mobile phone buzzed in Las Vegas.

The call was answered by a deep male voice, raspy from a lifetime of smoking unfiltered Russian cigarettes.

"*Da.*"

"Dmitry? It's me."

"Elena, my dear girl. How are you? You should visit here. I'll take you to some of our world-class restaurants run by celebrity chefs."

"I'm troubled. I need you here in San Francisco to exterminate a pest."

"Hmm, how much do you need me?"

"The usual amount."

"I've raised my rates. People here are willing to pay top dollar."

"Maybe I'll hire half a dozen local amateurs for a fraction of your usual fee. One of them will get lucky."

"Wait a minute, Elena. Humor me; what pest are we talking about?"

"A man who has disrespected the *russkaya mafiya.*"

Dmitry's warm tone of voice went cold. "What is the name of this disrespectful person?"

"Jake Wolfe."

"I've heard that name recently, and not in a good way. I'll be on the next plane to San Francisco. No extra charge. It will be my pleasure."

"Good man." Elena ended the call.

Her mentor and benefactor had not survived his rivalry with Jake Wolfe. But she'd hacked into some of her mentor's offshore bank accounts, and was hell-bent on revenge and becoming the crime queen of San Francisco.

She left her penthouse apartment and drove through the city, listening to the police frequency on a tablet computer.

Her plan required an attractive accomplice, so she called a friend who was as beautiful as she was dishonest. "This will be easy money for you, Trish. I'll pick you up on the corner in front of your apartment."

Minutes later, Elena stopped the car and Trish got in. Elena continued crisscrossing the city streets as she explained the con to Trish. They drove on, listening to the police frequency, until they heard a male voice say, "Ten-seven, for coffee at ten thirty-five Fillmore Street, at the Ethiopian Café."

"Male cop coffee break," Elena said. She drove to the address, stopped and found her target as he was parking his unmarked police SUV a block away.

"What if he won't talk to me?" Trish said.

"He will. If he's straight, show him the girls. If he's gay, talk about your wife."

"What if he's an old grouch having a bad day?"

"Ask his advice, get him to mansplain something to you."

Trish got out of Elena's car, and walked quickly down the sidewalk toward the plainclothes policeman.

She got to Ray Kirby just as he was about to enter the Ethiopian coffee shop, and she bumped into him. "Oh! Sorry about that," she said.

"No worries." Smiling, Kirby opened and held the door for her.

She gave him a big smile in return, her eyes innocent. "Thank you."

When they approached the counter, a kindly Ethiopian man took their orders. Trish turned to Kirby. "I've never been here before. What do you recommend?"

"I called in my order for some coffee," Kirby said. "It's enough for two—would you care to join me? I'm on a fifteen-minute break." He shrugged as if it was no big deal either way, but his eyes said he wanted to talk.

"I'd be happy to. I'm on vacation, and I was just walking around Alamo Square."

"If you'd like something to eat, they have bagels and sandwiches."

"Just coffee will do. I had a big breakfast," Trish said.

"Okay then," he said, then motioned for her to follow him. "Let's grab that table, over there."

They walked over toward the tall windows and sat down at a small table for two. Trish quickly sat in the seat facing the window, so Kirby had to sit with his back to it.

An Ethiopian woman with a cheerful smile brought them a

wooden platter that held a tall clay pot full of coffee along with a bowl of brown sugar, a small pitcher of cream, and a woven basket filled with popcorn.

Kirby poured two of the small cups. "Try the popcorn, and then take a sip of this coffee. It's amazing."

Trish followed his suggestion, and her eyes lit up. "What spice is that?"

"It's cardamom-spiced popcorn, and the coffee is house-roasted in small batches."

"It's delicious," she said, looking around. They play some good music here too, and I like the artwork."

Kirby smiled. "I stop here every day around this time. I'm glad we could share the experience."

"You seem like a very confident man, if you don't mind me saying so. What do you do for a living?"

Kirby straightened his back, and said, "I'm a Sergeant with the SFPD homicide division."

"Oh, I've never talked with an undercover policeman before. I'll bet you have some interesting stories about your work."

"You wouldn't believe me if I told you."

She asked to see his badge. He held it out to her and she touched his hand and stared at it in reverence as she leaned forward and displayed her cleavage.

Kirby was mesmerized.

Elena waited until Kirby was distracted by her accomplice and then got out of her car and walked up to the police SUV. She used an electronic handheld device to hack into the car, unlock the door, and turn off the alarm. She sat in the driver's seat, closed the door and glanced around. No one paid any attention to the woman sitting in the plain black vehicle.

She inserted a thumb drive into the car's dashboard computer, tapped out a string of code, and uploaded her virus. It was surprisingly easy, and she felt somewhat unsettled about her crime. With that done, she exited the SUV, walked back around the corner and got into her car, where she sent a text to Trish: *Time to go.*

∼

Trish felt her phone buzzing and checked the display. "I'm sorry, but I have to run. It was nice meeting you. Maybe I'll see you here tomorrow? Same time?"

"Sure. Let's trade phone numbers. I'll give you a call," Kirby said.

She wrote down a fake name and phone number on a napkin, then gave him a wink and walked away.

Kirby sat there and enjoyed the rest of his coffee, and the smile on his face seemed to say, *Once in a while, life is good—why can't more days be like this?*

Elena picked up Trish on the corner and drove several miles away. She stopped at a random busy street intersection so she could be sure nobody was waiting for her in ambush, and handed Trish an envelope full of cash.

Trish thumbed through the cash and smiled. "Let's do this again soon."

Elena nodded in agreement, but she didn't say what she was thinking: *Never cross me, or I'll kill you just as easily as I'd swat a fly.*

Trish got out of the car, and Elena drove back to her building. Once she made it back to her penthouse, she tapped on her keyboard. Now she had access to the police computer system and she could see the SFPD activity, as well as data trails she could follow from other law enforcement agencies such as the FBI and Homeland Security. She ran a search and noted some activity that mentioned the name Jake Wolfe. She gritted her teeth, and her blood pressure began to rise.

She sent a string of unusual, vicious malware code to Wolfe's phone. Hopefully the nasty, violent high-tech surprise might remove him from the chessboard, or at least make him rethink his participation in the game.

CHAPTER 12

At the mansion, Jake walked down the hallway when his phone vibrated with an incoming text. There was an image of a strange-looking symbol displayed on his screen. It appeared to be an ornate tattoo. His phone vibrated again, this time with a call from an unknown number—the kind you shouldn't answer. He was worried about Lauren's kids, though, so against his better judgment, he thumbed the answer icon and said, "This is Jake."

The phone went on speaker, the volume went up to maximum, and a shockingly high-pitched squealing tone blasted into his ear. It disrupted his equilibrium, his heartbeat began to flutter, and his eyes rolled back in his head. Seconds later, his knees buckled and he collapsed to the floor.

Jake dropped the phone, which continued to broadcast the horrific sound. He struggled to reach out to it and end the call, but he felt like he was moving in slow motion. His breathing became labored, his ears were ringing, his vision was blurred, and he felt as if his skin was covered with hundreds of crawling, stinging insects.

Cody was shocked by the sound. He began howling as his

sensitive ears heard four hundred percent more sound than Jake, and many more frequencies.

He pawed at the phone, trying to turn it off. He'd been trained to operate all kinds of controls, such as light switches and doorknobs, but he wasn't able to swipe on a touchscreen.

He managed to turn the phone over so the speaker was facedown against the carpet. He then pressed on the back of the phone with both of his front paws and barked at the top of his lungs to alert his "pack" to the danger.

Terrell ran up to them with his hands over his ears. He got down on one knee next to Cody, grabbed the phone and ended the call. "What the hell was that?"

Jake struggled to a sitting position on the hallway floor, with his back against a wall. He was groggy and his head hurt. He retched between his knees, but nothing came up from his empty stomach. He took deep breaths in an attempt to regain his equilibrium and then looked around for his dog. "Cody, are you okay?"

Cody barked once and came closer, pressing his face against Jake's. Jake hugged him and continued to breathe as his heart rate returned to normal.

A drop of blood trickled out of Jake's nose and dripped down his face. Cody licked the blood off Jake's chin.

"I'm all right, thanks to you, buddy," Jake said. He gave a silent prayer of thanks that his dog had not been harmed.

Terrell handed Jake's phone to him. "Turn that damned thing off until our tech officer can check it for malware."

Jake tapped the phone. "Roger, that."

"On my way in here, I shot down the drone that was trying to get in through the front door."

"Good work. I answered my phone and got my ass kicked by some kind of weaponized sound."

"What is this—an attack by a mad scientist?"

"I don't know, but there's plenty of scientific equipment in that secret room."

Terrell looked at his phone. "Roxanne Poole just arrived. If anyone can figure out the scientific part of this, our tech officer can."

Terrell reached out to Jake, clasped hands with his best friend and pulled him to his feet, then kept his grip and pushed him against the wall to keep him upright. He looked him in the eye. "You good to go?"

"Yeah ... I'm good," Jake said. He'd never had an older brother, until he'd become friends with Terrell in the Marine Corps. They'd gone through hell together in the Middle East, and had somehow survived. Now they thought of each other as a brother from another mother.

Terrell scowled at Jake. "Why are you at this fancy mansion anyway?"

"I let myself get talked into doing some security work for Dylan's friend, Levi. That former CIA guy."

"Not good," Terrell said. "The last time you worked with the CIA, you nearly got yourself killed."

"That's a fact. This guy's retired CIA though; he owns a private security firm," Jake said.

Working for the CIA and the JSOC could be highly dangerous. You didn't do it for the paycheck. You did it because you knew that somebody *had* to do it.

Terrell shook his head. "Being a good man is a thankless job."

Jake nodded in agreement and walked away on wobbly legs toward the study. Terrell and Cody followed him.

Terrell stopped and stared in amazement at the secret doorway.

Jake noted Terrell's defensive body language, knowing how his friend felt about being closed in. "Sorry, but the room is down those stairs, underground."

Terrell frowned. "Underground? You've got to be kidding me."

~

Terrell's irrational but all-too-real claustrophobic fears crawled in hot tendrils up his back. His heartbeat increased, and his skin became clammy.

He recalled a past life in a desert far from home, where he'd fought through a secret underground bunker that held chemical weapon missiles and prisoners who were being tortured. He couldn't fire his rifle or pistol because he might hit a prisoner or detonate a warhead.

He and his fellow Marines had cut the power lines after midnight, infiltrated the bunker, and killed the enemy up close, with their KA-BAR knives. They'd fought in hand-to-hand combat, in pitch-black darkness wearing green-lighted night vision optics. They'd won the battle and freed the hostages, but right then, Terrell had sworn he would never put himself in that position again. *Never.*

~

Cody stood in the doorway, sniffed the air, and growled. Jake patted him on the back. "I don't want to go down there again either, but it will only be for a minute."

Terrell's phone vibrated and he read the message, then turned to Jake. "Roxanne is coming inside now, along with the CSI team. They don't want anybody to go into that room, so we'll wait here."

"Roger that," Jake said. He noticed the look of relief on Terrell's face.

Terrell took a pack of cigarettes out of his pocket, stopped and looked around, and then put it back. "You sent me a text at dawn. What was that about? What happened?"

Jake turned on his phone and showed Terrell a photo of the dinghy and the dead man with the grenade launcher. "He was going to blow up the *Far Niente*, and kill Sarah and Cody. But I gave him a burial at sea, which is more than he deserved."

"If you shot him in self-defense, that works for me," Terrell said.

"You're right, international maritime law and universal jurisdiction allow you to take defensive action against pirate attacks at sea."

"It sounds like you're still reading those law textbooks."

"Maybe I'll surprise you one day and become a lawyer."

"Sure, in your dreams. You don't even have a bachelor's degree."

"There are ways around that. Besides, you'd think that after all the bachelor parties I've been to, those might count toward an honorary bachelor's degree."

Terrell shook his head. "We can get the FBI to run this through their facial recognition database."

"Agent Singer has Homeland working on it."

"I'll touch base with her."

"It made me wonder if there was still a bounty on my head."

"Cody had a bounty on his head too."

"Right, all the military war dogs were wanted by the terrorists. Remember the reward? Twenty thousand dollars for any MWD, dead or alive."

"Yeah, and I've seen you kill a man to protect your dog."

Jake nodded. "If those dirtbags try to come after Cody, it'll be the last thing they ever do."

Lauren came into the room. "Jake, the police have arrived."

Jake gestured at Terrell. "This is my friend Terrell Hayes with the SFPD."

"Hello," Lauren said.

Terrell gave her a nod. "Ma'am."

Lauren stared at the secret doorway, then turned to Jake. "Did you say the amber skull controlled the bookshelf?"

"Yes. I turned this counterclockwise, and the shelf rolled sideways." Jake pointed at the sculpture.

Terrell stepped closer and looked at the skull. While his back was turned, Lauren took a deep breath and headed down the stairway.

Jake realized what she was going to do, and tried one last time to protect her from the horrors that awaited her if she went down those stairs. "Lauren, please don't. The police have sequestered it as a crime scene, and you don't need to see it for yourself. The description in the report will be enough to give you nightmares."

"This is my house, and I have to know what's down there!" Lauren said.

～

Lauren hurried down the narrow stairs and opened the door at the bottom. She heard Terrell say, "Stay out of there, it's a crime scene."

A terrible, pervasive odor took her breath away. It reminded her of burnt meat combined with the acrid sulfuric aroma of discharged fireworks.

At first glance, the room looked like some kind of high-tech surveillance setup. On her left was a wall of electronic equipment. There were over a dozen computer monitors lining the wall. Some flickered with real-time stock market investment charts, but most were focused on the insides of homes, spying on the residents as they went about their daily lives. On one, a woman she didn't know was taking a shower. Another displayed a crystal-clear view of her own bedroom, in living color.

Along the far wall was a wooden worktable that looked

strangely out of place. It held a locksmith's key-cutting machine and all kinds of blank keys.

On her right was something that chilled her to the bone—a desk and a black leather office chair, where her dead husband was sprawled. She only knew it was him because she could recognize his bathrobe. His face was so mutilated there was no trace of the familiar features that she'd fallen in love with so long ago.

He was wearing headphones, and the ear covers appeared to be melted onto his skull. Both sides of his head were horribly burned and disfigured. Most of his facial skin was burned off, exposing the scorched skull underneath. His hands were gripping the headphones, and they were both burned to a crisp. His mouth was open in a silent scream, and his tongue was fried like bacon, sticking out between what was left of his lips. Worst of all, his eyeballs appeared to have burst.

It looked as if the headphones had fired blowtorches into both of his ears and made the flames shoot out of his eyes, nose and mouth—burning his skull from the inside out, while his hands were seared to the black plastic of the headphones in a desperate attempt to pull them off.

The room was a nightmare, hiding underground, beneath her happy home.

She screamed and staggered backward toward the door. Then everything became a blur and went dark.

CHAPTER 13

The Crime Scene Investigation Unit entered the mansion carrying the tools of their trade. Tech officer Roxanne Poole, a brunette with determined brown eyes, came into the study and approached Terrell, Jake, and Cody.

Roxanne had a brainy look on her face that said: *If you mess with a tech nerd like me you'd better change all your passwords, quick.*

She nodded at Terrell. "What have we got, Lieutenant?"

"Follow me, Rox, down those stairs. The husband is dead. The wife just now went down there and screamed at the sight of him."

"What's that awful smell?"

"Burnt magnesium, scorched skin and boiled blood. It reminds me of war, and I don't want to be reminded," Terrell said.

Roxanne recognized Jake. She used one finger to push her glasses higher on her nose. "Why are you here?"

"I'm working for a private security firm hired by Lauren Stephens. My dog found that hidden stairway, and I called the police."

Jake's phone buzzed. He looked at the display, then walked out of the room, with Cody close on his heels.

Terrell said, "Rox, I want you to check Jake's phone for viruses. Those could spread to my phone and others."

"No problem. I can do it in a minute."

They gloved up and wore shoe covers. Terrell went down the stairs ahead of Roxanne, clenching his teeth and holding his breath. Once he was inside the room, he stayed near the door; guarding it, but also staying close to the escape route.

He noted Lauren passed out on the floor a few feet away from the body, and cringed when he saw what was left of her husband. No matter how many times he saw death, he could never completely suppress that initial reaction. The room began to close in. Sweat broke out on his forehead, and his heart raced until he heard it pounding in his ears.

Roxanne noticed Terrell's discomfort. She was feeling something similar, but made an effort to appear calm in front of him as she snapped a picture of the dead husband. "Did his headphones electrocute him?"

Focusing on regaining control of his body by concentrating on facts, Terrell said, "If this is what I think it is, the headphones shot sizzling-hot magnesium shrapnel into both ears, that burned white hot like fireworks inside his skull."

Roxanne coughed in the foul air and shuddered. "What an awful way to die. How do you know about the headphones?"

"Last month in Las Vegas a wealthy man was killed this way by his cell phone. I heard about it from a contact at Vegas Metro."

"Couldn't the killer have used shotgun pellets instead of burning magnesium?"

"Yes, but this is more horrific and it sends a message."

"A message to who? Lauren?"

Lauren stirred on the floor and groaned.

Terrell felt the walls closing in on him. "I'll carry Lauren upstairs before she comes around and sees her husband like this again. I don't know how you can stand to be down here. It's like a burial crypt."

"It's all about mind over matter. If I don't mind, it doesn't matter," Roxanne said.

Terrell picked up Lauren, put her over his shoulder in a firefighter's carry, and made his way back up the stairs.

Roxanne was left all alone, underground, with the mutilated dead body. Only after Terrell had left did she allow herself a moment to express her own repulsion. She took a breath and coughed out the sulfuric air, then clenched her fists and closed her eyes for a moment.

After she'd gathered herself, she looked at the wall of high-tech electronics, and her eyes lit up. She tapped on the computer keyboard while watching the screens.

"Oh yeah, still logged in to all kinds of things. You're going to tell me everything you know."

CHAPTER 14

Jake stood in the mansion's living room talking to an employee of the security company when he heard footsteps behind him and felt as if someone was staring at his back. He turned as Roxanne approached him.

"I'm Sergeant Roxanne Poole, the tech officer. We've never officially met, but I feel like I know you because I saw everything on your phone when you were arrested."

"Which arrest? It seems like everything is illegal these days and I'm always getting arrested for one damn thing after another."

"The most recent one."

"Good thing I deleted some stuff off my phone before you got ahold of it."

She tipped one side of her mouth up in a half-smile. "I saw everything you deleted, too. It only took a minute to crack your password and extract your data."

"One minute?"

"Yes, I used a Cellebrite UFED."

"What's a UFED?"

"Universal Forensic Extraction Device."

"Huh. I guess I'll have to get a phone with fingerprint security."

"I can open those too; it just takes a little longer. I wanted to tell you I liked your nature photography."

"Thanks."

"And surprisingly, no dick pics."

It was his turn to smile. "Disappointed?"

"No." She shook her head and looked away, not meeting his eyes.

"You're welcome to keep copies of my nature photos."

"I already have some of them rotating as my screensaver."

"I'm going to be traveling soon. Is there anything on my phone that might cause excitement with Customs and Border Patrol?"

"The CBP might wonder why you have such an unusually high number of contacts."

"I worked in the media and I made it my business to know everybody in town."

"Okay, but why do your contacts include the chief of police, SFPD inspectors, FBI agents, Secret Service agents, and Congressman Anderson?"

"Maybe you've heard that Garth Brooks song, *Friends in Low Places*," Jake said. He tapped on his phone. "What's your number?"

"Why do you want mine?"

"We're working together on this situation. I might find a clue and pass it along to you. I do that with Terrell and his partner, Beth, and an FBI agent named Knight."

Roxanne thought it over for a moment and then recited her phone number.

"If you're the tech, can you unmask a number that texted me a photo?" Jake held out his phone and showed her the symbol.

She stared at it curiously and took a picture. "I can try, but first, Terrell said to check your phone for viruses."

Jake handed his phone to her. She pulled a device out of her pocket and plugged it into the phone. A minute later she handed the phone back. "You had some seriously bad stuff on there."

"Did it come from that image?"

"Probably, a picture text can infect your phone with a virus, allowing a hacker to take control."

"That's what happened, my phone's volume went up, and some kind of weaponized sound knocked me to the floor."

Roxanne blinked. "It's a good thing you didn't forward that image to anybody else. I'm going to grab some equipment out of my van, and I'll be right back."

Roxanne went out the front door, just as Terrell's partner, Beth Cushman walked in.

Beth was pale-skinned like her Scottish mother. She wore a pantsuit and cop shoes and had short, fiery-red hair and a personality that matched. She appraised Jake with her cool blue eyes. "Jake Wolfe, why am I not surprised?"

"Hey, Beth."

"What are you doing here?"

"Nice to see you too," he said with a smile. "I just dropped by to find a secret room and a dead body for the cops. I know you're busy, so I try to help out when I can. You owe me a donut."

Beth shook her head at Jake. He shrugged in reply. Jake knew she was concerned that he was dating her friend, Sarah, the veterinarian who took care of Beth's cat. His guess was that Beth was hoping he wouldn't break Sarah's heart, so Beth wouldn't have to break his arm.

Cody barked at Beth, and she scratched him behind his ears. She was one of the few people who could get away with that.

"Hi, Cody, I see you're still hanging around with this troublemaker," Beth said.

Suddenly, they heard Levi yelling, "Please put down the gun!"

Lauren said, "Not until you tell me who killed my husband,

why my home is under attack, and where you've taken my children!"

Beth drew her pistol, but Jake raised a finger. "Hold your fire, Beth. It's Lauren Stephens, the wife of the deceased. Let me try talking to her. It sounds like she's having a panic attack."

The sound of a gunshot boomed throughout the house and Beth held her hand out toward Jake with her palm facing him. "Shots fired. Stay back; this is a police matter now."

Jake gave a command to Cody and they both stayed in place. Jake took a deep breath in frustration as his high respect for Beth fought with his concern for Lauren.

Beth ran down the hall and Terrell came toward her from the other direction. She reached the door and said, "Police! Put down your weapon and raise your hands above your head!"

Lauren sounded panicked. "I'm sorry. It was an accident; I didn't mean to fire. I'm so sorry."

Beth nodded at Terrell, and they stepped into the room with pistols held out and ready to fire. She went left, and he went right.

Levi was sitting near the end of a long table, with his right hand holding pressure on his bleeding upper left arm. Lauren was sitting across from him, crying and wringing her hands, her Glock on the table in front of her.

Levi nodded. "It was an accident. Can you call the paramedics to patch up my arm?"

Beth holstered her pistol and called 911 while Terrell took a pen out of his pocket and used it to pick up the Glock by its trigger guard. He set the weapon down at the far end of the table, out of reach of Lauren. "Where did this pistol come from?"

"I keep it in a gun safe in my nightstand," Lauren said.

Jake came into the room along with Cody.

Terrell caught Jake's eye and pointed at the Glock. "Did you know she had this pistol?"

"Yes, Cody found it."

"Well, you should have told me."

"Sorry, Grinds."

Levi looked at Jake and said, "This is the first time I've been shot by my own client. Maybe it's a sign I should retire from this BS."

Jake noted that Lauren wasn't doing well and said to his dog, "Be friends, Cody. Comfort those in need."

Cody walked right past Levi and went to Lauren, who was rocking back and forth in her chair. He put his head in her lap and wagged his tail. She reflexively petted him and stopped rocking.

"What is it with your dog?" Levi said. "Why doesn't he like me?"

"You two just got off on the wrong foot this morning. He'll probably warm up to you eventually—maybe by this time next year."

Jake saw several large white linen napkins on the table. He picked one up and used it to bandage Levi's arm. "You were lucky. It's just a flesh wound. Looks like the bullet went right through."

Levi grunted in pain and gritted his teeth as Jake tied the bandage.

Lauren stared at Jake in surprise. "Those napkins are the highest quality Irish linen."

"Great. That one made the highest quality Irish linen bandage for the man you shot."

Lauren closed her eyes, grabbed a fistful of tablecloth in front of her, and took some deep breaths.

Jake approached her. "Are you on any anxiety meds?"

"Why do you ask?"

"You're under a lot of stress, I want to make sure you're okay. Should we call an ambulance?"

"I've taken my medicine and I'll be fine," Lauren said. "But I wish I'd trusted you and stayed out of that room."

"You want answers—I understand that," Jake said. "I'll tell you what I know, but most of it is still a mystery."

"Thank you, Jake."

"Sometime before dawn, your husband was murdered by an unusual weapon that was hidden inside his headphones."

"How is that possible?"

"Think about who could have switched the headphones for another pair exactly like it."

She turned her palms up. "I have no idea. The whole thing is just so bizarre. I didn't even know the room existed, much less what, or who, Gene was involved with."

"The police will suspect that you switched them, so help me find out who actually did it."

"The police will suspect me?" Lauren's face paled.

"Of course; you'll be the number one suspect because you're the spouse. Did your husband take the headphones with him anywhere? On business trips, to the office, maybe leave them in his car sometimes?"

"Yes, Gene used them when he traveled—on airplanes, at airports, in hotel rooms. When he was home he left them on the desk in his study."

"Did he usually lock the door to his study?"

"No, the door was left open so the maid could clean the room and empty the trash."

"Well, anybody you let into the house could have gone into his study and made the switch."

"But *why* was he murdered?"

"What did he do for a living?"

"He was a real estate broker, but he earned the majority of his fortune by buying and renting out high-end properties in the city. The rents in San Francisco are astronomical. He was cashing in on the housing crisis."

"My guess is his death had something to do with all of those spy camera feeds I saw on the dozens of TV monitors. It looks like he bugged the rental properties. Maybe he was blackmailing someone, or he saw something he shouldn't have seen and he had to be silenced."

"I saw my own bedroom on one of those monitors. Can you find the hidden camera for me?"

"Yes, it's a tiny pinhole camera, virtually undetectable, but I can find it with a spy cam detector."

"Are all of those cameras in the rental properties against the law?"

"Yes, they sure are. Unlawful video surveillance is a felony, punishable by up to four years in prison."

"If it's four years for each count, could Gene have gone to prison for forty years or more?"

Jake nodded. "I'll find the spy cam and remove it for you, and we'll check the rest of your house."

"Thank you."

"Somebody has to inform all of the people Gene was spying on, and remove the cameras from their homes."

"Will they all want to sue me?"

"Yeah, but if you hire Levi's security firm they could make up a story about a burglar who broke in recently and installed the cams. They'd need permission from you and each tenant before going in."

"You'd lie to the renters?"

"Not me personally, but yes, one of Levi's employees would lie to protect you—and to help the renters remove the cameras with as little fuss as possible."

"I'd feel bad about lying to the renters."

"Would you rather feel bad, or hold a press conference and invite the renters to sue you into bankruptcy?"

Lauren put her hand to her forehead. "If my husband was already dead, why did that drone attack the house?"

"Good question. It may have come here to kill the person who switched the headphones. To eliminate the witness."

Lauren's mouth went dry, and she took a drink of water from a crystal glass. "Where did your driver take my children? You said they were safe, but you didn't say where."

"When the drone attacked, we diverted the driver away from the school, and sent the kids to a safe house."

"What's the address of the safe house?"

Jake turned to Levi. "Send the address to our phones."

Levi tapped his phone and sent the texts.

Lauren's phone chimed a second later, and then rang. "It's my daughter." She thumbed the answer icon, "Chrissy, is everything okay?"

"Mommy, I'm *scared!*" Chrissy said.

Lauren's face went pale. "*Why* are you scared Chrissy? Tell me what's happening."

"We're driving really fast, and a car is chasing us."

At that moment Lauren heard the car slam against something with a loud thud, and then her daughter screamed.

"Chrissy? What happened? Talk to me!"

The phone went dead.

CHAPTER 15

Levi called his driver, Kim. There was no answer. He sent her a text message: *Report.* There was no reply. His phone made an alarm sound. He cursed. "I've lost contact with my driver, she sent out the distress signal, and the tracking beacon in the car has stopped working."

"Give me the last known location of the beacon," Terrell said.

Levi checked his phone and recited the cross streets.

Terrell called police headquarters and reported a possible kidnapping attempt in progress. He questioned Levi then relayed the car's license plate and the address of the safe house. He asked Lauren for the cell phone numbers of both of her kids and gave them to HQ.

Roxanne ran into the room. "Everything is being erased from the computer downstairs. I unplugged it from the internet, but a virus kept running so I shut it down."

Terrell ended his call. "Rox, assign someone else to the computer. The Stephens kids are in danger. I want you to go out in the surveillance van and track their phones. Beth, you drive while Rox navigates. Find that car and rescue those kids. I'll follow you."

Beth was already halfway to the door and Roxanne right behind her. "Copy that, we're on it."

Jake sent a text to Levi.

Levi's phone buzzed. He looked at it and shook his head at Jake. "No way. You can't be serious."

Jake pointed his finger at Levi. "Just do it."

Levi let out a loud breath and sent a text to one of his employees. "Done."

"And I need a car, right now," Jake said.

Terrell shook his head at Jake. "Not this time, brother. Let the cops handle it."

Jake frowned. "When Levi hired me this morning he said this family needed my help. I made the decision and commitment to help them and I'm going to follow through no matter what."

Lauren wrung her hands. "I appreciate that, Jake. Please do everything you can to help my kids."

"I have a friend at the FBI, Agent Knight, who owes me a favor. I'm going to call it in." Jake made a call and put it on speakerphone so Terrell could witness it.

When the call was answered, Jake said, "I need to speak with Special Agent Knight. It's an emergency."

"What is the nature of your emergency?"

"Two children are in danger and every minute you waste increases their risk. Please get Knight on the phone. Tell him it's Jake Wolfe calling."

"One moment, please."

Knight came on the phone. "Jake, what is it?"

"Is Agent Reynolds still assigned to your FBI bird?"

"Yes, she's in the helicopter right now."

"There are two children that have likely been kidnapped. I'm at their house with Terrell Hayes of the SFPD. Can you please divert the bird to the address of a safe house, then have the pilot work back toward an elementary school while Reynolds searches for their vehicle? I'm sending the info to your phone right now."

"Terrell, is this intel correct?"

Terrell spoke up. "Yes. I'm here with the mother of the children. The father was murdered this morning, and the house was attacked by an armed drone. Now someone is chasing the car that's transporting the children to a safe house. My people are in pursuit and are tracking their phones, but your helicopter will be a big help."

"I've got the address," Knight said. "Let me bring Reynolds onto the call in case she needs more information." His phone clicked and dialed. A phone rang twice and a woman answered.

"Reynolds," a voice yelled. The chop-chop-chop of a helicopter could be heard in the background.

"This is Knight. I have Terrell Hayes from the SFPD on a three-way with a credible tip of a possible kidnapping in progress. Two children are in danger. You can get there faster than anybody else in the city."

"Location?"

"I'm sending it to your phone."

"Intel received, we're on our way."

Reynolds left the call.

Terrell said, "Thank you, Knight. As you know, the highest odds of finding them is in the first hour after abduction."

Knight cursed under his breath. "I'm going out there myself, in my car. Keep in touch."

The call ended, and Jake turned to Levi. "I need a *vehicle!*"

Terrell held a hand up toward Levi. "No. We have enough people on this now. Jake will just cause car wrecks and confusion, and get himself arrested ... again."

"Speaking of that, the only way to stop me from searching for the kids is to arrest me," Jake said.

Terrell gave Jake a hard stare. Jake saw the conflicted emotions that played across his friend's face, but he knew that technically it was not illegal for him to drive around and look for the children.

Terrell turned to Levi. "You could lose your license."

Levi shook his head and cursed in Yiddish.

Lauren opened her purse and took out a Porsche key fob and tossed it to Jake. "Take my husband's—my *late* husband's—car." Fresh tears ran down her face.

Jake caught the smart key. "For the record, Lauren, you've employed me as a bodyguard on your private security team, and now you're asking me to search for your children—all in accordance with state and federal law. Is that correct?"

She glanced at Terrell. "Yes, I'm formally requesting to retain your firm for the purpose of finding my kids and bringing them home safely to me. No matter what it takes, or what it costs— just do it."

"Send pictures of your kids to my phone," Jake said.

Lauren tapped her phone. Jake's phone buzzed and he received several photos.

Jake gave a command to Cody, and they headed for the door. At the last moment before Jake left the room, he turned to Terrell. "I'm sorry, Grinds, I have to do this."

"I know," Terrell said, pinching the bridge of his nose. He reached into his pocket for some ibuprofen, and popped two of the pills.

Jake went into the garage and found the Porsche. It was a four-door SUV that looked like it was going fast even when it was standing still. There was a police evidence tag on the door handle indicating that the car had been processed. He removed the tag and pressed a button on the key fob to open the garage door, then he and Cody got into the car and sped away.

CHAPTER 16

Beth drove the surveillance van while Roxanne tracked Chrissy's phone. She took a sharp corner with a squeal of tires, then punched the gas pedal. "Which way now?"

Roxanne studied the computer screen. "Take a left at the intersection up ahead."

Beth raced to the intersection and took the turn. "How close are we?"

"Very close. Wait; it looks like they've stopped moving. We've got them!"

Beth's phone was in a mount on the dashboard. She tapped it and when Terrell answered she said, "Are you nearby?"

"Copy. I'm coming up on your six."

Beth glanced in the rearview mirror and saw Terrell's SUV approaching fast.

Roxanne pointed her finger. "There—pull into that parking lot."

Beth roared into the lot and the van was barely stopped before she and Roxanne jumped out and drew their pistols.

Roxanne held a device in front of her and studied it as she began walking quickly toward the building. "Cover me."

Beth followed alongside, with her pistol ready as she watched for threats.

Terrell pulled into the lot a few seconds later, and jogged after them, carrying his shotgun.

Once he caught up, Roxanne stopped and pointed ahead of them. "I think they're in one of those vehicles parked in the corner."

Terrell sprinted toward the corner of the lot. He pumped a round into the chamber of the shotgun and raised it to his shoulder.

Roxanne stared at him. "What the hell?"

"He served as a combat Marine and they always run toward the fight," Beth said. "Let's catch up with him. Come on, move!"

Beth took off running after her partner and Roxanne jogged behind them and kept an eye on the device in her hand.

Terrell arrived at the corner of the lot and went from vehicle to vehicle, looking in the windows, ready to neutralize any threats in order to rescue the kids.

Beth caught up with Terrell and checked the cars across from him. They silently worked as a team, the way they had done countless times before.

Roxanne walked past them as she studied the device. She went to a dumpster at the end of a row of cars and stopped. Her shoulders slumped, and she turned and looked at Beth and Terrell. She tried to speak, but no words came out of her mouth.

Terrell ran over to her. "The kids' phones are in there?"

Roxanne nodded.

Terrell cursed. "Beth, don't look at this."

Beth was the mother of a little boy named Kyle. As a parent, this was one of her worst fears. She gritted her teeth and shook her head.

Terrell flipped back the right half of the cover of the dumpster and looked inside. He saw several plastic trash bags full of garbage and the toe of a shoe. He flipped open the other half of the cover and pushed some of the trash bags aside. Then he saw some long hair. With a heavy heart, he set the shotgun on the ground and hoisted himself up and into the dumpster. He tossed bag after bag of trash out onto the parking lot until he uncovered two bodies.

Then he let out the biggest sigh of relief in his entire life. "It's the nanny and the driver, and they're both alive and unharmed and smelling like garbage."

The two women were hog-tied with rope and had duct tape over their mouths. Kim had a black eye. Terrell used his knife to cut them free and he carefully peeled the tape off their faces. "Are you Kim? I'm with the SFPD. Where are the kids?"

Kim took several breaths and blinked her eyes, appearing dizzy and disoriented. "Yes, I'm Kim. The kidnappers dumped us in the trash and shocked us with a stun baton."

"We tracked the kids' phones here. Do you have them?"

"No, not unless they tossed those in here with us."

Terrell searched and found two phones in a plastic bag. He handed the bag to Roxanne. "Are these their phones?"

Roxanne held her device close to the plastic bag. "Yes, that's both of them."

"Now we've lost track of the kids." Terrell picked up Isabel, the nanny. He lifted her over the edge of the dumpster and handed her off to Beth then did the same for Kim before climbing out himself.

Beth asked Roxanne, "Is there any other way to find the kids now?"

Roxanne looked off into the distance. Her eyes lost their focus for a moment.

Beth glanced at Terrell. He nodded and whispered, "I've seen her do this kind of thing before. She's the poster girl for nerdy-geek-hacker cops."

Roxanne held up her right hand and snapped her fingers. "Yes! We can put the recent travel history of these phones into

our system and then run that against the database of local
OnStar and LoJack tracking data. An overlay of all three
systems will find the one and only vehicle with a one hundred
percent identical pattern, *and* where it went from this point
onward."

Beth gave Roxanne a fist bump. "Back to the van."

A Porsche SUV drove up and stopped, and a golden-haired
dog stuck his head out of a back passenger window.

Terrell went over to the SUV. "Dammit, Jukebox, how did
you follow us?"

"Luck of the Irish. Now please tell me you found phones in
that dumpster, but not dead kids," Jake said.

"Affirmative, we found the nanny and the driver, alive and
well. Now we're going to track the kids another way."

"I'll tag along behind you, just in case you need a K-9 to help
you search."

"No, you won't. You're not a cop, and you don't belong here.
Listen, if you put a tracking device on my rig, I'm going to kick
your ass."

"I would never do that to you—so I had one of the security
people put it on Rox's van instead."

"Seriously? You bugged a police surveillance van?"

"It seemed like my only option at the time."

Terrell slammed his hand against the SUV. "Cody, why do
you put up with this idiot?"

Cody woofed, reached out and put a paw on Terrell's
shoulder.

Terrell scratched Cody behind the ears. "I should arrest your
dumbass master for this, but then who would feed you your
kibble, huh, buddy?"

Terrell, Beth and Sarah were the only other people Cody
would allow to touch him unless Jake ordered him to socialize.

Terrell turned and looked Jake in the eye. "When we find the
perps and the kids, there will be cops everywhere. SWAT might

show up and maybe the FBI helicopter. I don't need you two there. You might even get arrested again, or shot by accident."

Jake nodded. "Maybe I'll head back to the Stephens' house. The kidnappers will probably call Lauren and state their demands."

Terrell motioned toward the nanny and the driver. "Give those two a ride back to the house. And they might need medical attention for shock."

"Will do."

"If the kidnappers call, let me know immediately."

"Of course."

Beth drove up in the surveillance van and stopped next to the Porsche. Roxanne jumped out and said, "Jake, give me your phone. I'll unmask that unknown number."

Jake handed over his phone and she connected it to a handheld data extraction device. In a few seconds the device unmasked the number and she handed the phone back to Jake. "Got it, thanks. This could help us find the kids."

"You're welcome. And if that unknown number calls your phone, do *not* answer it."

"Right." Roxanne got back into the police van and Beth hit the gas pedal, sending the van roaring down the street.

Terrell ran to his police SUV, climbed in and drove after them.

Jake glanced at his phone and saw the unknown phone number she'd just unmasked. Several ideas crossed his mind about what he might do with this new information, but first, he had to get Isabel and Kim back to the mansion.

He and Cody got out of the car and walked toward the two women. Jake tapped his phone and made a FaceTime call to Lauren Stephens. Her worried face appeared on screen. "Jake, what's happening now?"

"The police are on the trail and they're getting closer. They found Isabel and Kim. Both of them are okay."

"Oh, thank God."

Jake held the phone so Lauren could see the two women. "I'll send them home to you in a taxi, so I can keep searching for the kids."

"Good idea."

"Your nanny should probably get a raise in pay, if she passes the police investigation."

"Yes, Isabel passed, but the maid was arrested and taken away in handcuffs. The police said Sophie broke down and confessed that she'd switched the headphones. Someone was threatening to kill her family. She felt she had no choice."

"Understood. If Isabel has time to do both jobs, you could pay Sophie's salary to Isabel on top of her own. "

"Isabel works part time and she asked for more hours, so if she wants to do Sophie's job too I'd have one less person to worry about."

Jake ended the FaceTime session, and he smiled kindly at Isabel. "You passed the investigation, and Lauren is going to double your hours and income."

Isabel gave him a hug, holding on far longer than he expected. Jake pried himself loose and turned to Kim. "Who gave you that black eye?"

Kim held out her hand and looked at her bruised fist. "Some dirtbag sucker punched me with no warning. He said he wanted a USB drive. I got a piece of him afterwards."

Jake's eyes darkened. "Describe him to me."

"White male, short, with a thick neck, brown hair and eyes. His nose looked like it had been broken in the past. There were symbols tattooed all over his hands and neck. He had a foreign accent, maybe Russian."

"If I happen to meet him, I'll give him your regards, in a way that he won't forget."

"Please do. Tell him I said hello."

Their eyes met in understanding.

Everyone got into the Porsche and Jake drove to a taxi stand where he gave some cash to Kim. She and Isabel chose a cab and drove away.

Jake sat in the SUV and looked at the unmasked private number again. He thought of the children, and his heart ached, they must be terrified. And Lauren, trying to be brave but living through a mother's worst nightmare.

He decided to try a different tactic. If he couldn't find the kidnappers, maybe he could make them come to him. It was a risky and reckless plan, but that had never stopped him before.

He thought about how to frame the lie he wanted to tell, and then he sent a text in reply to the one he'd received with the symbol.

It's Jake Wolfe. I have the thumb drive. I'll trade it to you for the kids. No cops. No money. Just you and me. Win-win scenario. You have 5 minutes to reply. After that I'll take this to the FBI.

Minutes ticked by and he feared that his bluff had failed. Four and a half minutes later, he received a text.

Drive to Alta Plaza Park, at the intersection of Jackson and Steiner. Wait there for further instructions. If you bring the police, you'll be killed, and so will the kids.

Jake wondered if this might be a fatal mistake, but he was determined to rescue the children. He texted a reply.

On my way.

He drove toward the park and as he got closer, he thought about the two frightened young children being held hostage by criminals who'd threatened to kill them. His anger flared, and he felt the violent, protective animal inside of him rise to the surface, willing to kill the evil to protect the innocent.

CHAPTER 17

Jake arrived at the park and drove slowly past. He lowered his window and studied the various people there, trying to profile any one of them as a professional criminal.

He saw an eccentric man walking a poodle. The man's hair was perfectly groomed and he had on a red bow tie and a green plaid sweater. The poodle was equally groomed and wore a matching bow tie and sweater.

Jake studied the happy, smiling people at the park and realized he'd forgotten what it was like to be that carefree. He'd felt that way in his past, before going to war and seeing his friends die. And before he'd avenged their deaths by killing high-value targets for Uncle Sam.

He thought of a college girl he'd been dating before he'd joined the Marines and been deployed overseas. They'd visited this park, tossed a blanket down and enjoyed a fun picnic lunch. Where was she now? Did she ever think of him the way he sometimes thought of her?

He shook his head. He had to focus on the kids, not on his past. Where were they? Who had taken them? Who would he have to fight in order to rescue them?

In the backseat, Cody growled, sensing Jake's darkening mood.

On the road, next to the driver's side of the SUV, a man suddenly stood up from where he'd been crouched between two parked cars and fired a Pneu-Dart CO_2 tranquilizer pistol at Jake.

Jake felt a sting on his left shoulder. He reached around and found a remote drug delivery dart stuck into his skin. He recognized it as similar to one he'd seen used near Lake Tahoe by the Nevada Department of Wildlife to tranquilize a bear that had gone into the garage of his parents' vacation home.

He cursed as his vision blurred and his reflexes slowed to the point that he was almost paralyzed. He yanked out the dart and pulled the car over into a bus stop zone. The car hit the curb, driving the two right-side wheels up and onto the sidewalk. Jake managed to put his foot on the brake and stop the car before it crashed into the bus stop shelter.

The doors on a nearby parked car opened and several men got out. Jake opened his door and staggered out onto the street, so dizzy and weak he could barely find the strength to open Cody's door.

When Cody jumped out, one of the men fired a Coda Netgun at him. The canister shot a fifteen-foot knotless net into the air, with four steel bullet-shaped weights on each of the four corners. It expanded open like a spiderweb and flew toward Cody.

Jake staggered forward to protect his dog. He was hit by the net and wrapped up in it. As he fell to the ground, he gave commands for Cody to escape and evade capture.

Cody barked in protest, but he obeyed the commands and ran away. Moments later, Jake's body went still from the tranquilizer, and the world faded to black.

~

Cody's Marine Corps training kicked in as he obeyed his alpha. He took off running, even though every fiber of his being wanted to stay by Jake's side and fight to protect him. He barely missed getting hit by a tranq dart and a man chased after him. Cody turned down an alley and ran around a corner. He waited there in hiding, sniffing the air and listening for the approaching enemy. He'd been trained to avoid capture.

He smelled the man who was chasing him and he heard his footsteps. *Closer, closer, closer ... now!* Cody leapt out and snapped his teeth at the man's face, slammed his body against him and pawed at his chest.

The man yelled in surprise and fell down on his back. He rolled over, jumped to his feet and ran away in panic. Cody snapped at his heels, barking and growling as he chased him into the street. An eighteen-wheeler truck hit the man square on and ran over him with its whole length.

Cody's war dog brain understood that he had caused a man's death. That made his PTSD flare up. He was a Marine and was following orders, but this was a different kind of battlefield. It was hard to tell the civilians from the combatants. Nobody was in uniform, but he would protect his pack from any and all attacks. He ran back toward Jake's location, and saw two men toss him into the trunk of a car and drive away.

Cody ran after them and though he couldn't keep up, he followed the scent cone and tried to make up some of the distance every time the car stopped at a traffic light. When the car turned right, Cody turned right. When the car drove several blocks, Cody followed. His paws were tough from walking on hot sand for several years in desert war deployments. As long as the car didn't go onto that place Jake called a *highway*, he might have a chance. His heart was beating fast. His training, instincts and loyalty drove him to rescue his alpha or die trying.

～

Jake woke up with a headache and nausea. He got the impression he was in the trunk of a car. His hands and feet were bound with what felt like plastic zip ties, so he moved his bound feet toward a back corner of the trunk and felt around for the taillight assembly. Once he found it, he began to kick it—over and over again. He hoped that if he could break it, or push it out so it was dangling by the wires, a police officer might notice it and pull the car over.

Soon, the car stopped, and the engine shut down. Jake heard a garage door rolling closed, and then somebody popped the lock of the trunk. He positioned himself to kick his feet at whoever lifted the trunk lid. When it opened, he kicked out but missed a man who was standing off to the side.

The man shocked Jake with a stun baton, making him shake like a leaf in a storm. He and another man pulled Jake out of the trunk and hauled him into the house.

Jake recovered from the shock and found that he couldn't see or move. He was blindfolded, his wrists were bound to the arms of a chair, and his ankles were secured to the chair legs.

A man leaned close to his face and spoke in a foreign language. It sounded to Jake as if the man was cursing him in Russian. He could smell his cigar breath and sweaty armpits.

Without thinking, he tried to head-butt the man with all his pent-up anger. He felt a lucky hit, and the man grunted, stumbled and landed on the floor with a thud. Jake tried to stand up, pulling the chair up with him. A fist hit him with a sucker punch to the stomach, knocking him backwards onto the floor.

Someone lifted him and the chair and dropped him back where he'd been before. Jake noted that now his feet were free; the zip ties must have slid off the chair legs when he had fallen backwards. He kept his feet close to the chair and hoped that nobody would notice.

Another man with a foreign accent spoke in English. "Give him the truth serum."

Somebody jabbed a needle into Jake's arm and he began to feel a strange buzz. His eyes fluttered behind the blindfold and he heard a sound in his ears like waves crashing on a beach. He felt as if he was floating in warm water, yet experienced random and surprising cold shocks when he least expected them.

It reminded him of when he'd been shot in combat and a corpsman had given him morphine, or fentanyl—whatever it was. But now he also felt like he was hallucinating, and something was making him grind his teeth.

Jake heard the scraping of chair legs on a hardwood floor right in front of him and smelled the cigar breath again.

"Jake, can you hear me? Answer my question."

Jake spoke slowly, slurring his words.

"I can hear you … asshole. How did you like that head butt?"

"You're going to tell me the truth now."

"The truth is I'm going to kill you soon."

"You want to answer my questions, don't you, Jake?"

"No. I want to slit your throat." Jake clenched his fists and strained his wrists against the bonds.

"Thank you for being so honest. Honest answers will set you free. Please continue. How do you feel?"

"I feel kind of … hungry."

"The truth is starting to come out. Tell us a secret."

"Bankers control the world. Politicians are their puppets."

"I mean a secret about yourself. Tell us a bad secret, one you're ashamed of."

Jake hesitated. He didn't want to remember it.

"Tell us, you have to."

"Come closer. I'll whisper it to you."

"What did you see at the mansion, in the underground room?"

"I saw—what I'd like to do to your face."

"You said you had the item we want. Give it to us. We've searched you and your vehicle, and we can't find it."

"I proposed a trade, but I knew you'd try to steal it from me, so I hid it somewhere safe."

"Tell us where it is, or I'll start cutting off your fingers one by one with these pruning shears."

Jake felt two cold blades press onto both sides of his left thumb for a moment. "Prove to me that the kids are alive and well. Let me talk to them first, before I trade what you want."

The other man said, "He's playing with you. Give him another dose."

"Another dose could kill him, or drive him insane. This serum is opiates mixed with nootropics, hallucinogenics, meth, and date rape drugs. That amount hasn't been tested on humans yet."

Jake heard someone racking the slide of a pistol, putting a round into the chamber.

"Test it now—on him. Give him another dose, or I'll test it on you instead."

There was some loud cursing, and somebody stuck another needle into his arm. "Don't blame me if the prisoner dies or loses his mind. I'm only following orders."

CHAPTER 18

Cody ran down sidewalks and streets, following the scent cone. He smelled all kinds of things—restaurants, bread bakeries, coffee shops, the ocean, trees and grass, garbage dumpsters, and the urine traces of dogs, cats, and rats. There were endless distractions, but he ran past them all and focused on his mission.

He lost the car's scent for a moment and paced back and forth. He held his head up high, then down low. He whined in frustration but kept searching until he caught the scent of the vehicle's unique burnt aroma. Then he started running as fast as he could.

After a while, the scent faded away and he stopped at a crossroads. He ran straight ahead but didn't find any scent. He returned to where he'd been, and then turned left. Nothing there. One last chance. He headed back, crossed at the intersection and went down the other direction. Just when it seemed that he'd lost the trail—there, he smelled the car he was seeking.

Cody took off running again. He cut down an alley behind some restaurants. A man in ragged clothes was sitting on a doorstep, drinking from a bottle. As Cody passed by, the man tried to grab him by the collar, but Cody snapped at the man's hand, almost taking off a few fingers. He snarled and continued on with his search.

A white van began following Cody. He couldn't read the words on the side that said San Francisco Animal Care and Control, but he could sense that the vehicle was stalking him. When the van came closer, he saw the driver staring, and they made eye contact. From the van's open window, Cody could smell scent traces left behind by a great variety of frightened dogs. He raised his sensitive nose and sniffed the air, picking up the fears of every confused animal that had ever been in the van.

The uniformed driver stopped and got out of the vehicle, carrying a catch pole with a noose on the end.

Cody didn't know that he'd been reported as a stray dog running loose in traffic. He only knew that he'd been trained not to allow anybody to take him prisoner. He was a war dog, and somebody in an unfamiliar uniform was trying to capture him. He'd fight if necessary. His combat training came back in a flash as the uniformed man advanced toward him and held out the pole in a threatening manner.

Cody dodged the loop, leapt forward and bit his opponent on the thigh, drawing blood. He then backed away, snarling.

The Animal Control officer cursed in pain, dropped the catch pole, limped to his truck and climbed inside.

Cody ran even faster now, as the scent trail was fading again.

A homeless man stepped out of an alleyway, whistled at Cody, and called out, "Hey, golden dog, where's your friend?"

Cody stopped and turned his head, recognizing the voice. He barked impatiently.

The man approached Cody, unafraid. He had long, straight black hair, and the facial features of a Native American. He wore faded blue jeans, a threadbare shirt with a red and black checkered pattern, and a small backpack. He walked with a slight limp. "Is something wrong, boy?"

Cody whined and pawed at the ground. He ran a few feet away, sniffed the air, and then returned and growled.

"Are you tracking your master?"

Cody barked once.

"Go on, then. I'll try to follow you."

Cody took off running.

The long-haired man jogged after him and did his best to keep up, in spite of the plastic-and-metal prosthesis he wore below his left knee.

Cody ran up a hill and into a higher-priced neighborhood. After taking several turns on a number of streets, he stopped in front of a two-story house. The car he'd been following was here; he could smell the scent from inside one of the three garages. Cody watched the front windows of the house as he ran up the driveway. He didn't see any movement. He sniffed all three garage doors and confirmed that the car he'd followed was parked behind the center door.

His ears twitched and he heard a sound from inside the house. His alpha had yelled something in anger, or in pain. Cody's throat tightened as he held back his growl. He quietly ran to a chain-link gate, used his nose to lift the metal latch and then put his shoulder against it. As soon as it swung open, he ran along the side of the house, stopping at every window he passed to listen and sniff the air. All the windows were closed, but scent traces escaped and he inhaled them and learned about the interior of the house.

He found a window at the back of the house that was partly open. He stood on his hind legs and put his nose up to the narrow opening, taking deep sniffs. He smelled cigar smoke, greasy food, weapons, nervous man sweat, and—his alpha.

The fur on the back of his neck stood up. He would get inside this building, even if he had to fight someone to do it. Nothing would stop him—this was war.

CHAPTER 19

Jake was sky-high on the experimental drugs, with no guarantee he might ever come down again. He tried to focus on his mission, but his mind was a jumbled mess.

The man with cigar breath said, "Jake, where's the thumb drive?"

Jake didn't answer.

The man in charge said, "Ask him some personal questions; get him to open up."

"Jake, do you have a woman?"

"Your mom liked it," Jake said.

Cigar breath hit him hard in the mouth.

Jake spat blood in the direction of the man's voice.

There was some foreign cursing and then, "Tell us a terrible secret, one you're ashamed of."

Jake hesitated and shook his head.

"Tell us. You have to tell the truth."

"Well …"

"Do it! You'll feel better afterwards. And then maybe you'll tell us about the item we're seeking. Yes?"

The second dose of the drug was making Jake's head spin. It

reminded him of a time, years ago, when he'd been prescribed painkillers that had made him feel incredibly good—until he came down, and the awful cravings for more of them had *almost* broken his willpower. This new drug gave him a similar high, but it seemed ten times stronger.

He tried to stop himself from talking, but the words spilled out in slow motion as he tilted from side to side in the chair.

"One time … I shot someone … and I regretted it."

"Who did you shoot? A friend? A family member?"

"No."

"Who was it?"

"I shot … a boy. It was an *accident*."

"Who was he?"

"I don't know."

"You shot a random boy?"

"He was tall, and dressed as a man—and he tried to kill my friends."

"Did you enjoy killing the child?"

"No. I felt bad, once I realized."

"Where did this happen?"

"At a war zone overseas—in a village where we turned a chow hall tent into a school for the kids."

"You were in the military?"

"No, I was there on vacation."

The man slapped Jake's face. "What did the boy do?"

"He drove up in a junker car, got out, and opened fire on us at point-blank range. Shot the canteen right out of Terrell's hand as he was taking a drink. He almost killed my best friend with a headshot."

"What happened next?"

"I shot him and he blew up."

"Exploded?"

"He was a suicide bomber, strapped with explosives. They sent him to kill the schoolchildren, specifically the girls. The terrorists hate girls. They buy and sell them as slaves, and they don't want them to be educated."

"Did the schoolchildren die?"

"No, we were protecting them. So the bomber tried to kill us instead."

"How old was this boy?"

"I don't know, maybe sixteen—old enough to drive a car without raising suspicion. Hell, I was only nineteen at the time. We send our teenagers to fight terrorists, you know."

"Did the car blow up too?"

"No, it was rigged with a bomb, but we stopped it in time, thanks to my dog."

"What did a dog have to do with it?"

"Duke was trained to find explosives ... he alerted me to the danger."

"You survived."

"No, I died."

The man punched Jake in the face. "Somebody died, yes?"

Jake strained his wrists against the cuffs. "Sparks, my buddy, died."

"Who was he?"

Jake swayed from side to side. "Radio man ... was lighting a cigarette and talking to command ... distracted for just a second, and got killed."

"Did the suicide bomber kill anyone else?"

"No, we were able to defuse the bomb in the vehicle ... jam-packed with badness."

"Tell me about Duke, your war dog."

Jake didn't answer.

"Tell me about the dog. Did he die in the desert?"

Silence.

The man leaned close in front of Jake's face. "Duke died, didn't he? You couldn't save him. It was your fault. Now we're going to kill your other dog—the golden-haired one—slowly and painfully while you watch. And that will be your fault too, unless you tell us where you hid the thumb drive."

Jake gripped the arms of the chair, leaned back and kicked both feet toward the ceiling. He put his legs around the man's neck and got him in a choke hold. The man grabbed Jake's calves and tried to remove them but had no luck. He tried to talk but only grunted.

Jake twisted his body to the side and used his legs to pull his enemy down. The man fell and hit his face on an end table, smashing through the glass top. A piece of broken glass went into his right eye, and he screamed.

Jake's chair fell over and his shoulder slammed into the floor. He squeezed the man's neck as hard as he could. "You want the truth? You're going to die now, just like I promised you would. That's the truth."

"Let him go!" the other man said, punching Jake in the face and shoulders.

Jake took the punches, ignored the pain, and focused on his murderous goal with all of his drug-induced anger. In just a few moments, he would crush the windpipe of his opponent.

The other man picked up the pruning shears. "Enough! Release him or I'll cut your Achilles tendons."

The door to the room opened. A young man wearing a blue hoodie entered and said, "I got the sandwiches."

Behind him, a golden-haired dog appeared in the open doorway. The dog jumped onto the back of the young man and knocked him down to his hands and knees, then used the momentum to launch himself off the man's back and into the air, barking and snarling.

Cody leapt straight toward the assailant with the sharp object in his hand, who appeared to be the most dangerous and immediate threat to his alpha.

Jake recognized Cody's barking and yelled, "Cody—*disarm!*"

The big man turned to face Cody. He tried to raise the shears in self-defense, but it was too little, too late. Cody was on him like a predatory beast of the jungle.

Cody snapped his teeth closed on the assailant's wrist and clamped his jaws down in a bone-crushing bite.

The assailant screamed in pain, dropped the shears, wrenched his injured wrist free, and ran out the door into the hallway.

The young man in the hoodie stumbled to his feet and cursed.

Cody's military training was in full force now as he went into battle mode. He ran straight at the man in the hoodie, snarling and snapping his teeth in attack. The young man screamed, ran out the door and slammed it behind him.

The man with cigar breath broke free from Jake's leg hold by ducking his head and rolling sideways in a desperate effort to escape. He got up and ran, seeing out of his one good eye.

Jake yelled, "Cody, *take down!*"

Cody bit the fleeing man on the right butt cheek and wrestled him to the floor, then ran ahead and blocked his path. The man lunged at the door, but Cody bit him in the crotch. The man screamed in agony but got free, and then ran around the room as the fast-moving golden nightmare snapped at his heels.

The fleeing man somehow made it back to the door. Just then it opened, and a stranger with long black hair walked in, holding a frying pan. The long-haired man took one look at the room and the screaming man who Cody was biting on the butt. He swung the pan hard and hit the fleeing man in the face, knocking him unconscious. He said a few words in the language of the Zuni people as he stepped on his enemy's chest and went over to Jake. He dropped the pan, grabbed the shears off the floor, and cut off the plasticuffs that held Jake's arms to the chair.

Once Jake's hands were free, he tore off his blindfold, snatched up an AK-47 from a coffee table, and stuck the end of the barrel against the chest of the man on the floor. "Wake up

and answer my questions. Where are those children? Tell me!"
He shoved the barrel hard against the man's ribcage.

The semiconscious man cried out. He drew a pistol from
behind his back and fired it toward the sound of Jake's voice.

The shot missed and Jake disarmed him, and then began to
beat him with his fists. "Here's some more truth for you. The
truth hurts, doesn't it?"

He knocked the man unconscious, and in a drugged stupor,
continued beating him, demanding to know where the children
were. Cody barked at Jake, drawing him back from the brink.
Jake's head was still spinning from the chemicals. He yelled out
Terrell's military call sign, "Grinds!" He got no reply.

Cody went to a coffee table and barked several times while
pawing at something. Jake saw his weapons and his phone there,
along with a bag of plastic zip ties and a holstered pistol.

"Good dog." Jake felt dizzy as he tapped on his phone to call
Terrell, and then turned to the man with long hair. "We've met
before—you're an Army Ranger. You lost your leg fighting
overseas. That's all I can remember right now."

The man nodded. "My leg is still in Afghanistan. When it got
blown off, one of the wild dogs the Russians left behind ran out
and took it for food." He smiled. "But lucky for you, I can jog
okay on my artificial leg."

"How did you find me?"

"I saw your dog tracking you, so I followed him." He looked
at the man he'd hit with the frying pan. "My friend's enemy is *my*
enemy."

Cody barked at him once. The man looked at him and
nodded in reply.

Jake shook hands. "That time we met, you never told me your
name. I'm Jake Wolfe. This is Cody."

"My Zuni name is Eagle Eyes, but most people call me Paul."

Jake looked at the pan on the floor. "Do you always carry a
frying pan with you?"

"I grabbed it from the kitchen stove when I came in. I would have tried to find a knife, but I was in a hurry," Paul said.

"You used to carry a knife. You tried to rob me, that's how we met."

"I only made that mistake once or twice. Father O'Leary has me on the straight and narrow path now."

"Are you still working at his soup kitchen?"

"Yes, but I'm worried because the church is running low on food lately."

Jake removed the holstered pistol off the table, and handed it to Paul. "Carry this weapon and cover my six."

"Roger that." Paul strapped on the belt. "Jake, you look like a homeless man I used to know, who dropped acid, snorted coke, then shot up heroin while drinking whiskey. He didn't live through it. Maybe we should get you to a hospital."

Jake shook his head and checked his phone. Terrell had let his call go to voicemail. He left a message, slurring his words. "Grinds, trace my phone, and send the police to my location. Hurry!" He added some creative profanity from their war deployments. Grabbing some zip ties, he used them to bind the hands and feet of the man with cigar breath he'd beaten into unconsciousness.

"We have to find those kids." He stumbled into the hallway with Cody and Paul following him. Everything appeared as if it was a shimmering, melting dream. He forced himself to focus on his mission. "Cody, search for hostages. *Search!*"

Cody barked once and ran through the large house. Jake followed him, trusting his dog with his life. He held the assault rifle up in front of him, ready to kill any threat his dog confronted. Cody stopped and sniffed the air. He growled and turned down another hallway. Jake and Paul ran after him.

Cody went to a door and touched the knob with both front paws, trying to open it. Jake reached out and tried the doorknob too. It was locked. He looked at his dog. "Are you sure you want us to go in there?"

Cody pawed at the door.

"Okay, we're going in. You know the drill."

Cody stepped to the side and watched Jake, who took several steps back and then ran and slammed his body against the door. It burst open and Jake found himself in a master bedroom. He pointed the rifle left and right and swept the area, ready to shoot any threats, but he only saw two frightened children sitting on a bed—a boy and a girl.

The girl had a shower rod in her hands, holding one end out toward Jake like a spear. Her little brother stayed behind her, looking over her shoulder with wide eyes.

Jake was impressed with their courage and resourcefulness. He turned to Paul, "Clear the other bedrooms."

"Roger." Paul went out the door.

Jake leaned his rifle against the wall and got down on one knee, empty-handed.

"Chrissy and Ben, you're safe now. We're here to rescue you. Your mother sent us."

The girl looked like she wanted to believe him, but she had doubts and fears.

Jake took out his phone and called Lauren.

"Yes, Jake?"

"Your children want to say hello."

"You found them!"

Jake held out the phone to the girl. She shook her head and continued to point the shower rod at him.

"I understand. I'll hold the phone for you."

Jake used FaceTime, put it on speaker and then held the phone so the girl could see her mother's face.

Chrissy's chin trembled as she tried hard to keep from crying. "Mommy?"

"Yes, Chrissy, Mommy's here."

"Two scary men and a golden dog are with us. Who are they?"

"Jake and Cody are working for me. I sent them to find you and bring you home."

"Say the safe word so I know you're telling the truth."

"Barracuda."

Chrissy dropped the shower rod, ran to Jake, put her arms around his neck, and cried on his shoulder. Jake held her and patted her on the back. Ben came over to them and Jake pulled him in for a hug too.

Jake handed his phone to Chrissy so she could talk to her mother.

Chrissy swiped at the tears running down her cheeks. "I was so *scared*, Mommy, but I tried to be brave for Ben."

Lauren's voice sounded as if she was choking. "You were *very* brave, sweetheart. It's over now. Jake is going to bring you home to me."

Jake nodded reassuringly at the kids, but he knew it wasn't over yet. Not even close.

CHAPTER 20

Paul returned to the room. "Clear."

Jake asked Chrissy to give him his phone, and then he spoke to Lauren. "Call the FBI. Tell them it's an emergency and you have to speak with Agent Knight. Tell Knight to trace my phone, find my location and send the FBI helicopter to pick up the kids. Hurry; we're not out of the woods yet."

"I'll do it right now." Lauren ended the call.

Jake said, "Cody, find the *garage*. Find me a *car*."

Cody ran into the hallway.

Jake and the kids followed him, with Paul covering their backs.

Cody stopped at a door.

"I'll clear it," Jake said. He opened the door while holding his weapon up and ready, and went into the garage. A few seconds later he yelled, "Clear!"

Paul came into the garage first, weapon ready. He confirmed that it was Jake who'd spoken, and he was not captured. Only then did he let Cody and the children through the door.

Jake nodded at Paul. They both looked at the stolen Porsche SUV parked there with the hood up and the back hatch open.

The floor mats and the spare tire had been removed and tossed aside. Jake checked the front seat and saw the key fob in a center console cupholder. "Everybody get in the car—hurry!"

He quickly made sure the kids were buckled in while Paul slammed down the hood and closed the back hatch. Jake pushed a button on the wall that opened the garage door, then jumped in the Porsche, started it up, and backed down the driveway into the street.

As he shifted into drive, a car careened to a stop at the curb in front of the house with a screech of tires. An angry man flung the passenger door open and ran in front of the Porsche with a pistol in his hand.

Jake yelled, "Duck down out of sight. Do it!"

The kids leaned over on their sides in the backseat and Cody crouched in the back cargo area.

Paul lowered his window and drew his weapon. The man in the street fired at the Porsche. His bullet hit Jake's driver's-side mirror and then slammed into Chrissy's door.

Chrissy screamed. Paul fired his pistol and hit the man in the chest. Jake stomped on the gas pedal, sending the Porsche charging forward like a rocket, running over the attacker, with the car's wheels thumping over the body.

Paul pointed his finger at the road ahead and Jake swerved just in time to avoid crashing into an oncoming car.

"Jake, you should let me drive," Paul said.

Jake shook his head. "It's too late. We can't stop."

The man who was sitting behind the wheel of the parked vehicle got out and started shooting at the back of the Porsche.

Jake ducked his head and drove blind for a moment. The back window exploded and a section of the front windshield splintered into a spiderweb of hundreds of tiny cracks. Jake lifted his head and found that he could only partly see out of the windshield. He stuck his face out his door window and barely avoided hitting an oncoming car. "Close your eyes and cover your faces with your hands."

Jake pulled over for a second, closed his eyes and used his pistol to knock the cracked safety glass out of the windshield. He opened his eyes, looked in his rearview mirror and saw the other vehicle in pursuit. He roared down the street, arrived at a main road, turned right, and sped up. Everything he saw looked as if it was extra bright, shimmering with movement and melting. His forehead was warm, and he felt smarter and better than the other drivers on the road. They were idiots—he was a genius. Why didn't the fools pull over and get out of his way?

Paul took off his seat belt, leaned out his window and methodically fired shots at the pursuing vehicle.

Windshield.

Radiator.

Front tire.

A black helicopter appeared overhead, and a loudspeaker crackled with a female voice. "Jukebox, follow us."

Jake flashed his headlights in reply and followed. A mile down the road, the helicopter landed in the empty parking lot of a restaurant. Jake pulled up in the Porsche and said, "Paul, leave the pistol in the car."

"Roger that." Paul took off the holster belt and dropped it in the footwell.

Everybody got out of the vehicle.

"Chrissy and Ben, hold hands with me," Jake said. He held hands with the kids and they ran to the bird and climbed inside. Paul and Cody jumped in after them, and the helicopter took off just as the pursuing vehicle came roaring down the street.

Jake helped the kids into their seats. "Put on your seat belts and tighten them."

The kids buckled up and looked around with wide eyes.

The helicopter was over fifty feet long and could normally

hold up to fourteen passengers, plus one pilot, but the inside of this one was custom-configured.

"Give me a rifle, and circle back around," Jake said. He was down on one knee in front of the open door, in an area where some of the seats had been removed. The wind blew in his hair as he held onto a strap and looked down at the pursuing vehicle.

The woman closed the helicopter door. "Stand down, Wolfe. This is an extraction, not a firefight."

Jake recognized her. "Agent Reynolds, I know you have a rifle. Give it to me."

"You're not in charge. I am. The police are going to capture those men *alive*, so they can be interrogated."

"Some of them are already dead."

"That's what I was afraid of."

Jake grabbed a pair of binoculars off a seat, looked out the window, and saw police vehicles arriving from all directions, with their blue and red lights flashing. "Are you sure we can't provide air support for the police?"

"Yes, I'm sure. Terrell Hayes and Beth Cushman are closing in on the targets."

The look on Reynolds' face told Jake she wasn't going to back down. He respected her for that.

Jake looked through the binoculars again, seeing a police SUV drive up and stop a few blocks ahead of the pursuing vehicle.

Terrell got out of the SUV holding what looked like a black duffel bag. He threw it underhanded like a bowling ball while holding on to one handle. It unfurled and rolled across the road, leaving a strip of spikes designed to deflate the tires of a vehicle.

The speeding car ran over the spike strip and all four tires burst, sending the car careening out of control and crashing into a light pole.

Terrell ran toward the car while Beth drove up in front of it, blocked the road, and got out of her police SUV with her pistol drawn.

There were flashes of gunfire from inside the crashed car, and Beth's pistol and Terrell's shotgun blazed repeatedly as they returned fire in self-defense.

Jake nodded his head. "Get some, Grinds." He then reached out and shook Agent Reynolds' hand. "Thanks for the ride. How did you know my Marine radio call sign was *Jukebox*?" He slurred his speech a bit as he talked, and he swayed from side to side.

"The FBI knows more about you than your own mother does —and we're just as disappointed in you."

Jake smiled. "You made a joke, Reynolds?"

She shook Jake's hand. Jake got the feeling she wanted to understand him but just couldn't do it. He'd seen that look before. The two of them had past experience of not seeing eye to eye. His guess was she never knew what he might do next and that unsettled her. He was a wild card, a loose cannon, full of surprises. She didn't trust him because he didn't follow the rules. But somehow he got results in his own crazy way. She had to grudgingly admit that much. He'd heard that speech in any number of meetings, and was past giving a damn about it.

After Jake observed her facial expressions and body language, he held her gaze and raised his eyebrows as if he'd read her thoughts.

Reynolds frowned. Her face went red, and she turned her back on him. She went to the kids and checked their seat belts.

Jake sat down in a seat but didn't bother with the seat belt. Cody sat on the floor and Jake petted him. He was relieved that the kids were safe in the helicopter, and he felt grateful to be alive. Waves of drug-fueled emotion made him feel lightheaded. His phone vibrated with a text message from Sarah, along with a picture of her holding a puppy.

Look at my new client. A cute Scottie dog! I think I'm falling in love with this guy.

Jake misunderstood her text and sent a drunk-on-truth-serum text in reply. *I think I might be falling in love with you too, girlfriend.*

Jake suddenly began swaying, and he felt dizzy and sick. He was surprised because in the Marines he'd never had any problem with airsickness, not even in an Osprey tilt-rotor aircraft. He felt so weak that he held his arms out by his sides as if he was crossing a rushing river.

Cody stood up and barked at him.

Jake's vision went blurry, and he fell forward, collapsing onto the floor. His breathing became labored, and he started turning blue in the face.

Cody pawed at Jake's chest while barking frantically at Reynolds.

Reynolds rushed to him. "Jake, what's wrong?"

He tried to speak, but was beginning to lose consciousness. "The kidnappers—gave me some kind of drugs—to make me talk." He let out a gasp. His eyes rolled back in his head, his breathing shut down, and his heart stopped beating.

CHAPTER 21

Cody barked at the top of his lungs and clawed at the Red Cross box mounted on the wall.

The children screamed.

Reynolds opened the first aid kit, grabbed the Narcan nasal spray and administered a dosage of the anti-opiate drug to Jake through his nostrils, then slapped him across the face several times.

The drug worked as it was designed to do, and soon Jake began breathing again. The color returned to his cheeks, and he sat up abruptly, sniffing at the unexpected medicine inside his nose. He looked around to make sure Cody and the kids were safe. Cody pressed against him and Jake gave him a hug. "What just happened, Reynolds? I think I blacked out for a moment."

"You were dying, reacting to an overdose of opioids. The drugs suppressed your cardiovascular system and your body shut down. I gave you Narcan and brought you back from the dead."

"Damn. It's a good thing you had that on hand."

"Everyone in law enforcement is carrying these. In case you hadn't heard, there's an opioid epidemic going on in America."

"Thank you, Reynolds."

"Remember this, Wolfe. I saved your life. You owe me now."

"I do owe you, but you should thank me too, because you finally got the chance to slap me around like you've always wanted to."

Reynolds scowled and turned away to secure the first aid kit.

Jake noticed she had a tight smile on her face, as if he'd spoken the truth about her wanting to slap him.

Once Reynolds had secured the kit, she gestured at Paul. "Who is this? You said he helped in the rescue."

"Allow me to introduce Paul. He's a homeless veteran and a trusted friend."

"How did he find you and the kids?"

"Cody led him to us."

"I'm going to have to check him for criminal records."

"No problem, I understand. When you're a hammer, everybody looks like a nail."

Reynolds ignored Jake's remark and turned to Paul. "Can you show me some ID?"

Paul shook his head. "No, ma'am. Sorry, but my wallet was stolen recently when I was passed out from drinking."

"Name and Social Security number?"

Paul recited the information.

Reynolds took a picture of Paul's face with her phone and then tapped the display screen several times.

Jake watched her and remembered what he'd heard about the FBI's facial recognition software.

The system found a match within seconds. "He's clean," Reynolds said, holding up the display.

Jake saw that Paul didn't have any wants or warrants. The only thing on his record was an arrest for public intoxication a few years back, and Jake figured that it had probably been BS. Any homeless person with a drinking problem could be considered "publicly intoxicated" every night when they slept outdoors.

"Not bad; that's better than my record," Jake said. He saw some bottles of water and grabbed one, slowly pouring water into his cupped hand so Cody could have a drink. "Thank you for coming to the rescue when I was taken hostage, boy."

Cody barked once and nodded. He held Jake's hand in his mouth, not biting it, just holding it. This was a behavior Jake had never seen in another dog. He believed it was due to Cody being a retriever, and something more, his unique intelligence.

Jake looked over at the children who were watching him and Cody. He handed them each a bottle of water.

Paul opened his small backpack and removed the bag full of sandwiches that he'd picked up off the floor during the rescue. "Does anybody want a sandwich?"

The kids shook their heads and stared at Paul as if they didn't know what to think of him. He looked like one of the homeless people they'd seen standing by highway off-ramps and holding cardboard signs.

Cody sniffed the air and stared at the food, then turned and looked at Jake.

"Of course; you definitely earned a sandwich, Cody." He turned to Paul. "Just meat and cheese, no onions, no avocado, no raisins."

Paul nodded. "Sometimes there are raisins or grapes in chicken salad sandwiches."

"Bad for dogs," Jake said.

Paul tore open a paper wrapper, removed the meat and cheese from a sandwich, put it on the paper, and set it on the floor.

Cody attacked the roast beef and cheddar cheese, devouring it.

Paul held out a wrapped sandwich toward Jake, but he smiled and waved it off. "My stomach is too queasy from the drugs."

Reynolds approached Jake, holding a tablet so he could see it. On the display, Jake saw a close-up police dash-cam video of Terrell stopping his SUV and rolling the sixteen-foot-long roadblock strip of tire-shredding spikes across the street.

The car that had been chasing Jake passed over the spike strip and its tires were instantly deflated.

From there the clip moved to the firefight.

"Yeah, I saw that through the binoculars. My bro Terrell doesn't mess around."

As they flew toward the mansion, Jake sent a text message to Terrell. *The kidnappers said they were looking for a thumb drive. You might want to have your K-9 unit search every inch of the Stephens mansion for electronic items.*

Terrell replied: *The K-9 team has already searched the house, and they didn't find any thumb drives. Good work rescuing the kids. How in the world did you find them?*

Jake texted: *It was the luck of the Irish.*

Jake's phone buzzed with a FaceTime call from US Secret Service Agent Shannon McKay. He'd talked to her recently and he thought she was a badass. She was wearing her trademark dark blazer, white blouse, and plain tie. There was a telltale bulge of a pistol in a shoulder holster under her left arm. The serious look on her face suggested that she was carrying the weight of the world on her shoulders. Jake had a lot of respect for her.

He remembered that McKay had traveled from Washington D.C. to San Francisco, and she'd requested to have a lunch meeting with him. But he'd been hoping to avoid it, and he'd blocked it out of his mind. His reasoning was that she was from the White House, and that usually meant nothing but trouble in his life. He'd already been through enough trouble on behalf of his country. *Thanks anyway, White House—carry on without me.*

Jake was starting to realize that once you did any black ops missions for the government, it might be nearly impossible to leave your violent past behind. You were nothing more than a valuable tool and deadly weapon to them, so why would they ever let you go?

He didn't answer McKay's call. Instead he called Lauren and said, "The kids are on the FBI helicopter, safe and sound."

Lauren cried in relief. "Thank you, Jake! Please let me talk to my babies." Jake handed his phone to the kids and looked out the window at the city below as he wondered what McKay was going to try to talk him into at the meeting.

CHAPTER 22

The FBI helicopter landed on the acre of lawn in front of the Stephens mansion.

Jake saw Lauren run out of the house with tears on her face.

Reynolds opened the helicopter door and helped the kids unbuckle their seat belts.

Jake scooped up Ben with his left arm and held him close to his chest. He reached out and held Chrissy's hand and then ducked his head as they ran beneath the helicopter blades, followed by Cody and Paul.

Lauren knelt down on the grass, not caring about her white pants for once, and hugged her kids tight. All three of them cried in relief. Lauren then stood up and threw her arms around Jake. He returned her hug and patted her on the back. When she let go of him, she said, "Jake, could you please come inside with us? I have some questions for you."

Jake nodded and turned to Paul. "Can you stand post, right here?"

"Good to go," Paul said. He stood up straight with his hands by his sides, looked left and right, and then studied the gated entrance to the estate.

Jake and Cody followed Lauren into the house. "You might want to feed these kids some comfort food."

Lauren called out for the cook, but she'd been questioned by the police and sent home.

Jake shook his head. "Don't trust any of your domestic employees until the police and the security firm say you can."

"I'll call out for a pizza delivery."

"Levi won't allow deliveries of any kind."

"Okay, I still remember how to cook. I can whip up some grilled cheese sandwiches and tomato soup for lunch."

"That sounds good, you're making me hungry," Jake said. "By the way, your daughter is a tough cookie, and you might want to enroll her in karate classes. I wish every girl knew some kind of martial arts."

Lauren opened a cupboard and found a container of tomato soup. "I'll look into it."

Chrissy asked, "Mommy, is Daddy home?"

Lauren's face went pale. "No, Daddy is away on a business trip that came up at the last minute. He's very sorry he couldn't be here."

She got out the makings for the soup and sandwiches and went to work as the helicopter could be heard taking off and flying away.

Jake got down on one knee, patted Cody on the back and spoke to him in a low voice. "You did good, buddy. Do you see that family? You helped them. Thank you, Devil Dog."

Cody chuffed and wagged his tail. It appeared to Jake that he felt like it was all in a day's work for him. Give him more missions; he needed the exercise.

Once the kids were eating lunch and watching a TV in the kitchen, Lauren turned on the dishwasher and motioned for Jake to come closer. While the dishwasher was making noise, she whispered to him. "I'm thinking of telling the kids that their father died in a car accident while he was on a business trip."

"I don't know if that will work. The media will have a field day with this in the news. Everyone in town will be gossiping. I can't give you any advice about what to say, but my sister Nicole is a psychiatrist, and she could be helpful."

"Does she make house calls?"

"No, but she'll do it for you if I ask her nicely." Jake sent a text message to Nicole, and received a reply. "Nicole said yes, she's on her way over here."

Lauren whispered, "What happened to those kidnappers? Were they arrested?"

"Not all of them," Jake said.

"Some got away?"

Jake looked out the window and didn't reply.

"You mean, they're … dead?" Lauren said.

Jake turned to her. "Several are dead, and others are under arrest. A few may still be loose on the streets."

"Was there a fight?"

"Yes, there was what my gunnery sergeant would call an unavoidable violent confrontation. The good news is, those dead men will never bother your family again."

"But what about—I just don't know—I'm not sure what to say." Lauren looked into his eyes and shook her head.

Jake held her gaze and nodded. "Somebody helped me today. A man named Paul. You might want to consider hiring him as your temporary gardener. That way he can also act as an additional security guard outside the house during the daytime."

Lauren appeared doubtful.

Jake went to the window and pointed out Paul. He was standing post on guard duty, right where Jake had left him.

Lauren furrowed her brow, surprised at his appearance. "Who is he? Can I trust him? I'm sorry, but he looks like a panhandler."

"He served as an Army Ranger and lost a leg in combat. One

of the FBI agents in the helicopter checked him for wants and warrants and criminal history. He came up clean."

"Sophie passed a background check, but she turned on me when someone threatened her family."

Jake sent a text to Levi. "Anyone can be threatened or bribed. I've asked Levi to run a check on Paul for you. The most important thing to know is that today Paul voluntarily risked his life to help save the lives of your children."

"What did he do?"

"He came to our rescue, uninvited, and started fighting the kidnappers. He hit one of them in the head with a frying pan."

"Oh my God."

"He isn't perfect, none of us are. He drinks liquor in the evenings so he can fall asleep and not dream of his violent past in the Army."

"I don't want a drunk man on my property at night," Lauren said.

"Of course not, he'd only protect your home during the daytime when he's sober and alert."

"Do you trust him?"

"Yeah, I do. My dog trusts him too, which means a lot to me."

"Well, if you trust him and he risked his life to help rescue my children, then I'll give him a chance. He can start work today as long as he passes the security background check and stays outside the house."

"Good plan."

"Does he know anything about gardening?"

"That doesn't matter. He's a capable guy who can figure it out."

Lauren stared at Jake.

While Jake was looking out the window, he saw a black Suburban SUV drive up and stop. The front passenger door opened and a man got out, wearing a dark suit, white shirt, plain tie, and shiny black shoes. His face displayed no emotion as he walked directly toward the front door with a purposeful stride.

Jake recognized him as a Secret Service agent named Easton. "Oh yeah, I'm supposed to be at a meeting right now."

Lauren looked out the window. "You're leaving?"

"Yes, but I'll be back soon," Jake said. He walked down the hall and went outside, with Cody following him. He spoke to Paul. "You just got offered a job, working as a gardener here. You'd also provide added security for the property during the daytime. What do you say?"

"An actual job with a paycheck? It's been a while. Sure, I'll give it my best try. Thanks."

"You'll have to pass a full background check, and then show up every morning without any excuses. I believe you can do it. I have faith in you, Eagle Eyes."

Paul smiled and shook Jake's hand. "Is there a liquor store within walking distance of this place? Later tonight I'll need to stop by and get my medicine."

"I'm sure you'll find one. Just don't drink until after work, okay?"

"No worries, only at bedtime. The terrorist attack that killed my friends and took my leg happened at sunset. I've had trouble sleeping ever since."

Levi came out of the house and spoke to Jake. "You and Cody certainly earned your pay today, and then some."

"I'm glad we could help."

"I want you to spend the rest of the day inside the house, acting as the family's personal bodyguard team."

"We can't. I promised to go to a lunch meeting with this gentleman." Jake gestured toward Easton who walked up to them and stood facing Jake.

"I'll triple whatever he's offering you," Levi said. "Lauren trusts you and Cody. She wants you here, and her kids do too. Money is no object."

Jake shook his head. "I'm sorry, I wish I could stay, but this meeting is with the US Secret Service. It's not something that can be rescheduled."

Easton showed his credentials to Levi without a word.

Levi raised his eyebrows. "That's … very interesting."

CHAPTER 23

Levi said, "Jake, can I tell Lauren you'll be back here before it gets dark? The kids asked if you and Cody would have dinner with them."

Jake stared at Levi for a moment. "Why don't the grandparents come over here and have dinner with the kids?"

"Lauren is an only child, her parents are deceased, and her mother-in-law has always hated her. Now she blames Lauren for Gene's death."

"Gene's mother is going to be surprised to find out that her precious son was a very bad boy. In fact, she might be subject to massive lawsuits from the people her son was spying on with his hidden cameras."

"Gene's actions weren't his mother's fault."

"True, but people will try to sue her anyway."

Levi shook his head. "Will they sue Lauren too?"

"Yes. There's no avoiding it. I'll ask Bart Bartholomew to give Lauren some advice. He's one of the best lawyers in town."

"You have a lot of connections. Can I talk you into full-time employment with my company?"

"Probably not," Jake said.

"The salary is negotiable. What would it take to get you and Cody on my team every day?"

Jake looked at the house. "Let's work together again tomorrow. We can take it one day at a time and see how it goes."

"That'll work." Levi went back inside.

Jake turned to the Secret Service agent. "Good to see you, Easton."

Easton nodded. "You and I are going for a drive in that vehicle over there. You promised to meet Agent McKay for lunch today, and you will be keeping your word."

"You're absolutely right, but I usually have a late lunch, so I'm still on schedule according to California time."

Easton turned away without any further discussion and walked toward the armored SUV, with Jake and Cody following him.

Jake recognized a woman in a pantsuit standing next to the driver's door of the SUV. "Agent Greene, how's that bump on the head? Getting better, I hope."

Greene shook hands with Jake. "Yes, it's going to be okay. My doctor said I'm a hard-headed woman."

"I could have told you that, and saved you a medical bill."

Greene smiled and shook her head at Jake. She then turned to Cody. "Hey there, you golden furball from hell. How are you doing?"

Cody woofed at her and wagged his tail.

They all got into the SUV and drove toward the restaurant. When they arrived, Greene remained with the vehicle.

Jake reached into a pocket of his jacket for a lightweight nylon service dog vest. He dressed Cody in the vest and brought him inside.

The head waiter seemed affronted by the dog and he shook his head in dismay as he showed them to their booth in a private corner, far away from everyone else. Jake handed the man a generous tip in cash, and his attitude improved significantly.

Agent Shannon McKay sat in the booth with a pint of dark beer on the table in front of her, along with an empty plate and three glasses of water. She glared at Jake.

"Well, if it isn't the infamous Jake Wolfe. You suggested we meet here for lunch, but you stood me up, so I went ahead and had lunch without you."

"Sorry, McKay, I was kind of busy," Jake said. "Don't worry, I never pass up a sandwich and a pint. I'm just fashionably late."

She rolled her eyes. "You're only here thanks to Easton. You were going to blow off this meeting, the same way you ignored my phone call."

Jake sat down and glanced at the pint with a thirsty look. Cody sat on the floor next to him. Easton took a seat next to McKay.

A blond waitress appeared at the table, her curious eyes on Jake. "What can I get you?"

"I'll have one of these pints and a toasted crab sandwich on sourdough bread," Jake said. "My dog will have a bone-in ribeye steak, cooked rare."

"Coming right up."

McKay said, "Cancel that order; we're leaving. Just bring me the check."

Jake said, "My dog rescued two children today, and he deserves a steak. I'm not leaving here without it."

The waitress smiled. "A rare steak won't take long." She walked away.

McKay stared at Jake. "Do you have anything you want to say?"

"Sure, let me say that the government owes me for everything I've done for my country. It's not the other way around. If you're not going to buy me a sandwich, feel free to write me a bonus paycheck in compensation for all the times I risked my life overseas for Uncle Sam. Be sure to spell my name right on the check, and add an extra zero for Cody's service too."

To illustrate his point, Jake reached out and grabbed her pint and took a drink. For some reason, he couldn't resist pushing the buttons of starched shirt bossy types from D.C.

McKay's eyes narrowed, and when Jake set the pint down half-empty, she reached out and took it away from him.

Cody growled at McKay.

Jake said, "Careful now, you don't want to get on Cody's bad side."

Jake grabbed Easton's glass of water and held it down by his side so Cody could drink from it. Cody lapped up the water, and then looked at Easton and panted, Ha-Ha-Ha.

Easton took Jake's glass of water and drank from it like this was no big deal.

Jake looked at McKay's beer again, and she pulled it back closer to her. Jake smiled. "Remind me, McKay, what was the point of this pointless bureaucratic meeting? Couldn't you just send me an official email that I'd never open?"

"The president has a proposal for you, about how you could use your past training and skills to serve your country again."

"No offense to you or the president, but I've already served my country more than enough. Whatever he has to propose, my answer is no. Find another person to do it."

"You might change your mind once you hear the details."

"That's what you desk warriors always say right before you ask the troops to volunteer and risk their lives for the crisis of the month. It's always a mission of very high danger for very low pay. Meanwhile, you sit safely in your office and fill out a spreadsheet on your computer, then go home to enjoy a peaceful dinner and watch TV with your family."

McKay set her phone on the table and tapped it a few times. It emitted a hissing sound, as an electronic countermeasure to listening devices. "Your life would be in danger, I have to admit," she said. "This is a top secret project, deploying off-the-books rogue personnel, so there is total deniability. Among the very few who have heard of it, we privately refer to this new counterforce as..." She turned her phone so Jake could read the words on the display:

The President's Operational Emergency Team. Code name: The POETs.

Jake shook his head. His guess was, being on this emergency team could get him killed. He reached out, grabbed McKay's beer, and chugged the rest of it down in one long drink.

CHAPTER 24

The waitress gave the check to McKay and a to-go box to Jake.

Jake saw her glance at his left hand to see if he wore a ring and he gave her some cash for a tip. "Thanks for the steak. Cody will love it."

She held eye contact with him and smiled. "It was my pleasure. He's a handsome and charming boy. I hope we see him in here again soon."

Jake got the message. He was tempted to ask her for her phone number. It was the obvious and expected thing to do in this situation, but in his mind he talked himself out of it. His heart was currently pointed toward a veterinarian named Sarah Chance, as if she were the North Star. He silently reminded himself that he was a "one woman at a time" kind of guy, then smiled at the waitress and told a white lie. "We'll definitely be back—see you soon."

Jake turned and went out the door with Cody by his side. As he walked to the vehicle, he felt a sense of hunger and emptiness. He'd forgotten to eat breakfast, he'd missed lunch, and he'd passed up the chance to date an attractive and friendly waitress.

There was also a gnawing in his gut from the mix of opiates and other drugs, calling him to feed the evil hunger again.

Most of all, he felt a longing to take the *Far Niente* out on the Bay and get away from it all. But instead, he had to endure a meeting where government people tried to talk him into risking his life. That was bad enough, but they also wanted him to risk Cody's life. He felt his heartburn flare up.

Easton got in the front passenger seat next to Greene. Jake and McKay sat in the backseat, and Cody sat behind them in the large cargo area with the third row of seats removed.

Jake opened the to-go container and turned to Cody. "You ready for your steak?" Cody barked once. "I'm tempted to take a big bite out of it first, is that okay?" Cody barked twice and shook his head. Jake laughed and set the container down.

Cody began chomping on the steak as if it was the first, last, and only meal he'd ever eaten.

Jake smiled. "You're off duty, Cody. This is chow time."

McKay took a tablet out of her purse, put an earbud into one ear, and tapped on the screen. "No, he has not been cooperative." She turned the tablet toward Jake so he could see it.

Jake saw the US Presidential Seal. Now they were going to put full pressure on him. His guess was there must be a high-value target they wanted dead, and Jake was one of their draft picks to go overseas and take care of the problem. "With all due respect, I'm a civilian now, with responsibilities." He reached back and patted Cody on the head.

McKay interrupted him. "You agreed to a private meeting, and we're going to have one right now, in this vehicle."

"Great, let's get it over with, and then maybe we can stop by Super Duper Burger for some takeout food. Easton, you like Super Duper—am I right?"

Easton said nothing. He rarely did.

Greene drove the SUV into traffic, weaving her way through

the city on an unpredictable route. She checked her mirrors every time she turned a corner.

McKay tapped some controls in the vehicle's backseat console to initiate a new privacy technology. "If you'd arrived on time, the president would have joined us for a conference call. Now he's busy in another meeting."

"Sorry about that." Jake turned and looked behind him. Cody had devoured the steak and was now chewing on the bone. "How was that lunch, Devil Dog?" He wondered who would take care of Cody, if he went off on some suicide mission ordered by the White House.

Cody lifted his head and let out a loud dog burp.

"Well, all right, then. I'll take that as a thumbs up."

Cody went back to gnawing the bone.

McKay said, "Jake, do you remember me saying that Congress has secretly granted a blanket letter of marque and reprisal for one specific small team of the Secret Service?"

"Yes, I remember. I thought it was quite an ingenious legal maneuver."

McKay read from her tablet. "It legally converts your private vessel, the *Far Niente*, into a naval auxiliary. You become a commissioned privateer with jurisdiction to conduct reprisal operations worldwide, and you're covered by the protection of the laws of war. In addition, you'll be operating under admiralty and maritime law, which gives you broad legal powers on the water similar to what the Coast Guard has."

"It's my friend Dylan's boat, not mine. I'm just taking care of it for him."

"Dylan is on board if you are."

"What's in it for me, besides danger and pain?" Jake asked.

"You'd serve your country."

"I already served. My mind and body have taken a beating. Somebody else can step up to the challenge. Maybe you could do it, McKay. What are your plans for this weekend?"

McKay ignored the question. "It's a great honor to be asked to join this team."

"Napoleon said something about how men will fight and die for a piece of colored ribbon. I'm past that stage, so you can keep your honors, medals and ribbons. Thanks anyway."

"You'd have the protection of the government when you get into trouble, the way you always seem to do."

"But the government would have control over me too. I want to live a life of freedom, without pushy bureaucrats bothering me. I'd rather work at a car wash if I could just have some peace of mind."

"Is this actually because you don't want to have a woman as your boss?" McKay asked.

"No, I have great respect for you. I just don't want a boss, any boss—least of all a government boss," Jake said.

"You'd have a lot of latitude. You'd be more of an independent mercenary and a troubleshooter."

Jake looked out the window, far into the distance. "McKay, have you ever *killed* anyone?"

She sat there staring at him for a moment. "No, never."

"Well, let's be perfectly clear. That's what you're asking me to do—to kill high value targets for you when the president gives the order. That's not normal. When will Cody and I ever live normal lives?"

Jake felt torn in two directions. He wanted to help protect his country, and he was like a fire horse who heard the bell and had to go into action. But he'd already done his duty, more than any of the people he saw driving in cars or walking down the street. When would it ever be enough?

They rode in silence for a while, then McKay nodded. "Most of the time you'd live in peace and quiet. The missions would be few and far between. You'd only be called upon in an emergency."

"For me to consider it, I'd have to see proof in writing that I have the option to say no to your demands. I want the right to walk away at any time I choose, with no repercussions. My lawyer would have to read it and approve it."

McKay sat up straighter. "That can be arranged. We can run it past your attorney. Bart Bartholomew, correct?"

"Really? You'd have to give Bart top-secret clearances."

"We're willing to do that."

"You want me bad, huh McKay?"

She shook her head. "No, we want Cody, but he'll only listen to you."

Jake smiled. "Good one. You and I might get along after all."

"Are there any other complaints or prima-donna demands?"

"Sorry for being difficult, but you know my history of getting screwed over by the bureaucracy I fought to protect."

"Most of your troubles were caused by your CIA case officer, Chet Brinkter. The man who recruited you to do black ops missions in war zones."

"Brinkter abandoned me behind enemy lines while bounty hunter terrorists were hot on my trail. If they'd caught me, I would've been tortured for days, and then beheaded in a video on YouTube," Jake said, looking her in the eye.

She nodded. "You'll be happy to know he's been reassigned and shipped off on an icebreaker to a listening post at McMurdo Station, Antartica."

Jake grinned. "Brinkter the sphincter is freezing his ass off at the South Pole right now?"

"Yes, where all twelve months have an average temperature below freezing."

"Who do I have to thank for that?"

"You have me to thank. I pulled some strings on your behalf," McKay said.

Jake's body language changed, his shoulders relaxed and he looked out the window. "That means a lot to me, Shannon."

McKay paused for a moment. He'd never used her first name before. "That's why I made it happen. And FYI, there's more to this mission than you acting as an assassin. We'd want you to help protect the harbors, the bridges and the coastline from foreign threats."

Jake thought that over. "If I was to join your team, I'd want Easton and Greene to get big raises in pay. And I'd want them to be available for me to call upon, if and when I get into a hopeless situation that you created."

"We can't have Secret Service agents at your beck and call," McKay said. "You'll be assigned somebody who will—"

"No."

"What?"

"No, I will not be assigned *somebody*. I want these two, or you can forget the whole thing," Jake said.

"They're two of my very best agents."

"Exactly. That's why I want them to cover my six when things get real."

"I thought you'd want some wild-eyed former black ops types."

"Greene fought like hell to save my life when a psycho was trying to shoot me in the back. Easton is calm in a crisis, utterly reliable, and always thinking two steps ahead. We all worked well together as a team once, and we could do it again."

"It's not a bad idea, but you're not running this show, I am," McKay said.

"Sorry, this is how I roll. What do you say, Cody?"

Cody stuck his head into the backseat area and barked several times.

Jake knew that his dog was feeling separation anxiety and wanted to be closer to him. Jake used Cody's interruption to test a theory on McKay.

"I think my dog is trying to say you're hiding something from us—so you might as well come clean now." He watched McKay's face for telltale clues. Yes, she was lying by omission. What potentially deadly details had she left out?

CHAPTER 25

McKay shook her head at Jake. "Your dog is not a person. All he's trying to say is that he wants us to pull over so he can pee on a tree."

Cody barked twice at McKay then tried to climb over the seat. Jake gave Cody a command, grabbed onto his collar and held him at bay.

"McKay, you have to watch what you say around Cody. Please don't insult him. He understands far more than you'd ever believe."

"Great. That will make him even better at his job when you two work on my team."

"Look, I admire you for what you're trying to do, but I should probably put this scheme of yours on hold until I have time to confer with legal counsel."

"Where's your patriotism, Jake?"

"Nice try. Don't lecture me about patriotism. I've *killed* for this country. I've also *died* for it and come back to life. I'm done being a disposable warrior. There are thousands of other war veterans who'd be glad to do these crazy missions for you."

McKay squared her shoulders and said, "Sometimes you have

to work with what you've got, and try to make the best of it. Greene, take us to the drop point."

Agent Greene drove for a ways and then pulled into an empty parking lot and stopped. Jake looked out the window and saw a brand new, shiny black Jeep Grand Cherokee Trackhawk sitting there. It reminded him that his own Jeep was still in the shop. He either had to spend plenty of money on further repairs or buy a new car.

McKay got out of the Suburban and motioned for Jake to do the same. When he opened his door, Cody climbed over the backseat without waiting to be asked. He followed closely behind Jake, sniffing the air and looking left and right for threats.

Jake observed his dog's body language and studied the scene. "What are we doing here, McKay?"

"If you agree to work with us, this Jeep will be your signing bonus." She held up a key fob and pressed a button. The back passenger door on the driver's side of the Jeep opened on automatic hinges. "That's a K-9 door, just like many police cars have. If a K-9 cop is threatened, he or she can open the dog door from a distance and unleash his partner on the criminals."

"Right. I've seen one of those. My K-9 cop friend Ryan has one for his dog, Hank."

"You can activate the remote door release from as far away as the length of a football field."

"That could come in handy."

"This particular device will also close the door. That function is dangerous and controversial, but your dog is smart enough to avoid getting his tail or a paw caught in the slamming door."

"Cody is smarter than most of the people you know."

McKay tossed the key fob to Jake. "Go ahead and take a look. I know you're curious about that K-9 door."

"I was planning to have one of those installed on my rig," Jake said. He walked over to the car and opened the driver's door.

Cody went to the K-9 door, sniffed the backseat and looked at Jake for orders.

Jake gave Cody a hand command and said, "Climb inside and check it out."

Cody jumped into the backseat and sniffed all around. He stretched out on the leather seats and seemed to be right at home. Jake sat in the driver's seat and checked out the dashboard and the interior. He liked what he saw.

McKay stood by the driver's window and read a list on her phone. "This vehicle is fully armored and equipped. It has *everything*. Bulletproof glass, run-flat tires, protection for the battery and electronics, reinforced suspension, tailpipe protection, reinforced pillars, operable windows, a heavy-duty brake system, emergency lights, a siren, a PA system, video cameras on all four sides, a fire suppression system, and a high-powered engine with plenty of horsepower."

Jake was amazed but he acted unimpressed. "No coffeemaker?"

"You want a coffeemaker? You've got it. And the Secret Service has installed some of our latest electronic technology. That dashboard display looks normal, but with the flip of a switch, we can turn it into a computer just like the police cars have. If you join us, we'll add satellite phone links, thermal imaging technology to see into other cars, hidden weapons, war dog equipment, and a few newly developed breakthroughs I can't tell you about unless you sign the nondisclosure paperwork."

"I might be getting a technology boner right now," Jake said.

McKay shook her head. "Well, then, this vehicle is having the desired effect on your bro brain. The first time we met I told you we needed your help on rare occasions. You were undecided, so I used an off-the-books black budget to pay for this incentive."

"Where does that kind of money come from?"

"One example would be what you did out on the Bay this

morning. There was a reward for the terrorist you killed. I'll put through a request on your behalf, listing you as a citizen asset I've cultivated. That cash reward will soon go into our budget and pay me back for what the Secret Service spent on this beast over the past month."

"Well, I'm glad I can pull my own weight. You mentioned needing my help on rare occasions. How rare would these occasions be?"

"It's impossible to speculate about future threats and—"

Jake held up a hand. "Forget the weasel words, McKay. Just give me a number."

She stared at him for a moment. "My rough estimate is that maybe once a month for the next year, you might be asked by the government to intervene in a situation that threatens the safety of the citizens of the United States."

"A dozen times, max? Either twelve ops or twelve months, whichever comes first? And then we'd part ways?"

"You'd have the option to part ways, or to continue doing the work you seem to excel at. The government will pay you for every mission. And of course you and your family and friends would be under the protection of our group."

"What happens if I'm arrested while serving my country in a secret operation? Will you disavow me and leave me to rot in prison?"

"We can't claim you, so yes, you'd be disavowed. However, we'd secretly pay for the best lawyers to help you. Bribes, threats, and blackmail would also be put into play. None of our team members are in prison. We intend to keep it that way."

Jake reached into his jacket and pulled out the U.S. Marshals badge. "What's my status after being deputized by Marshal Garcia? Can I use this badge to arrest people, or is it just for show?"

"You were deputized to capture one particular fugitive, but you're still on the books as a deputized citizen, and you have the power to capture wanted felons if you're participating in a task force."

Jake nodded thoughtfully and put the badge away. "If I worked with you, I'd need several new bulletproof vests for my dog. And an implanted chip that says he's protected by the government. It should say that if you find him, there's a large reward for returning him in good health—and if you don't, you'll go to prison for a very long time."

McKay reached a hand up and rubbed the back of her neck. "These details can all be negotiated. Are you in, or out? Decide right now, or the offer is withdrawn and you can give me back the key to this Jeep."

Jake pulled the key out of the ignition and held the fob out the window. "Here you go. Sorry I have so many questions, but I simply don't trust political types from D.C. all that much. No offense, McKay."

McKay turned her back on him and walked away. She looked over her shoulder. "Drive that beast for a while, with no obligation, while you make up your mind."

"Hey, wait a minute," Jake said. "Now that I think about it, you said the work I did this morning will pay you back for this Jeep. That means it's *already* mine with no obligation. Ha, this is great. Thanks for the Jeep!"

McKay didn't reply. She got into the Secret Service vehicle, and left.

Jake turned on the police lights, making them flash blue and red under the front grille and in the back window. He whooped the siren one time at the departing SUV. "Cody, be careful. I'm closing the back door." Cody sat up on the seat with his tail and paws away from the door. Jake looked at him in the rearview mirror to make sure he was in a safe position, and then pressed the key fob. The back passenger door slammed shut automatically. "I could get used to this vehicle."

Cody barked once and nodded.

"McKay knows me too well. This thing is hard to resist. She's using the puppy dog sales pitch. *Take this puppy home for a few days, with no obligation.* Next thing you know, you can't imagine life without the puppy. Or in this instance, the bulletproof Jeepzilla."

Jake started up the engine, and it made a deep growl. He drove through the city, getting the feel of the armored SUV. His route took him toward the office building of his attorney. It was time to complete the final formalities and become a lawyer.

High above the Jeep, a drone quietly followed. It was similar to the one Jake had shot out of the sky, and was similarly armed with a video camera and a weapon.

CHAPTER 26

As soon as Dmitry's flight landed in San Francisco, he rented a car and drove the city streets. On the seat next to him was a tablet that displayed a photo of Jake Wolfe.

In his opinion, this hit wouldn't be much of a challenge. The target didn't look impressive. He would shoot Jake in the head at close range and then walk away. Hopefully he wouldn't have to shoot the dog, that would be a shame. The only difficult part of this operation would be escaping without being caught—and he had plenty of practice at that.

Perhaps a drive-by shooting would be the best strategy. That might be blamed on one of the criminal gangs that plagued every big city around the world.

He took out his phone and made a call. A woman answered with one word. "Report."

"Elena, my dear girl, I'm here in your charming city of San Francisco. It can't compare to Las Vegas, but it's not bad."

"Vegas isn't a city, it's an amusement park."

"Perhaps, but I find it … amusing."

"Plans have changed. I'm going to take Wolfe's girlfriend as a hostage. Then he'll come to us."

"Does he have the item you seek?"

"I hope so, for his girlfriend's sake."

"Will you let her live after the exchange?"

"No, of course not, but if I get what I need, I'll make her death quick and painless. If I don't get it—she will suffer in creative ways."

Dmitry ended the call and shook his head. He could easily imagine the suffering she was referring to. He had suffered through it himself before she'd been born. When would it all end? As a child, he'd wanted to be a musician, but now he was a killer.

He didn't want to participate in the infliction of pain upon Wolfe's girlfriend, but the only way to stop it was to inflict pain upon the power-drunk woman named Elena. He couldn't win, unless he found the thumb drive and ended the life of Jake Wolfe. Then he'd be in charge of things.

That was the answer—find the drive and kill Wolfe while sparing everyone else a world of pain. He continued to drive through the city, intent on his mission of mercy.

CHAPTER 27

Jake parked his new Jeep on the street in front of Bart Bartholomew's law office.

He and Cody walked inside the building, and there was a new receptionist at the front desk who presented a serious and professional image. She was a young Asian woman, wearing a charcoal-gray dress suit and black pumps. Her dark hair was up in a complicated bun. She stared at Cody in surprise and said, "I'm sorry, but I don't think you can bring a dog in here."

Jake gave her a warm smile. "I'm sorry too, because I already did. He's a service dog. If you know the law, you're aware that you can't legally prevent me from bringing him inside your offices."

"I'm not a lawyer, but I can have one out here in sixty seconds."

"I'm not a lawyer either, but I'll become one sometime today. Please get Bart on the phone and tell him that Jake and Cody are here to see him. He's expecting us."

The receptionist picked up the phone and gave Jake a skeptical look, as if he was about to be kicked out of the building any minute now. "Mr. Bartholomew, there's a man here named

Jake—no last name given—along with a *dog*. He claims that he and his *pet* have an appointment with you. But I don't have him, or any *animals* whatsoever, scheduled on my calendar. Shall I call security?"

Her penciled eyebrows went up. "Yes, of course, Mr. Bartholomew, I'll send them right in."

She set down the phone and stared at Jake with a newfound respect. "Thank you both for your service, and congratulations on passing the Bar exam. The counselor will see you now. It's the third door on your right."

"Thanks, I visited that office in my youth, more times than I care to admit."

Jake walked into Bart's office and found him sitting behind his enormous oak desk talking on two landline phones, with one in each hand. The "ego wall" behind Bart featured an assortment of framed honors and certificates that memorialized how he had graduated from Harvard Law School and had been featured in media news stories.

Bart smiled at Jake and Cody and said, "I'll have to call you two right back." He put both phones down, stood up and held out his hand. "Jake Wolfe, future lawyer. Just look at you, and Cody too, soon to be a legal beagle."

Cody growled when Bart called him a beagle.

The men shook hands, and Jake sat down in one of the leather chairs.

Cody sniffed the air and went around to Bart's side of the desk. He sniffed a drawer and then looked at Jake for orders.

"Bart, do you have a pistol in that drawer?" Jake said.

"Yes. I think every lawyer should have one these days."

"Cody, leave it."

Cody returned to Jake's side, and Jake patted him. "Who's the smartest dog? You are, buddy."

Cody sat down and stared at Bart as if he thought he was

included in the meeting and was waiting to hear what the man had to say.

Bart smiled at Cody and then clasped his hands in front of him. "Do you have the oath card, young man?"

Jake took the card out of his pocket. "Yes, sir. I've got it right here, counselor." He handed the card to Bart.

Bart read the card while nodding his head in satisfaction. "This could change your life, you know. Don't underestimate the good you can do when you practice law."

"Is our favorite notary public ready to witness my signature?"

"Yes, she's been looking forward to it." Bart picked up a desk phone and punched a button. "Karen, our newly minted lawyer is here to sign his card."

A minute later, Karen came into the office. She had gray streaks in her hair and an air about her that commanded respect for her many years of experience. Karen set a big book on the desk and opened it to a page filled with signatures and rubber-stamped markings.

Jake read the card. The oath said:

I solemnly swear (or affirm) that I will support the Constitution of the United States and the Constitution of the State of California, and that I will faithfully discharge the duties of an attorney and counselor at law to the best of my knowledge and ability.

He signed the card, and Karen witnessed his signature. He thanked her, and she patted him on the back. "Good work, Jake. Make us proud, kid."

"I'll do my best. And does this mean you might finally go out with me on that dinner date I've been asking you about?"

"Hmmm, let's see," Karen said. "You've been asking me out to dinner since you were sixteen and got arrested for being a minor in possession of beer. No luck on the dating idea so far."

"Every police officer in America drank beer before they were twenty-one. When they had a beer, it was cute—when I had a beer, it was a major crime. Call the SWAT team."

"Save your smooth talk for your first jury."

"I'd always dreamed of trying my smooth talk on you at dinner, Karen. Are you telling me my hopes are dashed?"

"Sorry, kid, I've been happily married for forty-two years, and I'm a grandma. Dinner ain't gonna happen in this lifetime."

Jake put his hand on his chest. "Okay, fine, but my heart is breaking right now."

Karen laughed and walked out of the room, shaking her head and smiling.

Bart said, "Congratulations, Jake. All that's left to do is mail the card to the California State Bar and wait for them to record it."

Jake shook his head. "Can your courier take it there right now? After all these years of time and effort, I can't stand to just sit around and wonder when they'll get it in the mail and make it official."

"That's a splendid idea. I'll have a courier drive over there as soon as possible. He can ask to stand by while it's recorded."

"Thanks, Bart. I really appreciated your help while I slaved away with my law school studies these past years."

"I had faith in you. You possess a self-righteous sense of justice that I love to see in a young attorney. I think you're going to do great things."

"Now all I need is a client or two."

"I might be able to refer some clients to you from time to time. Our firm often turns away people who can't afford our fees, or who have a simple problem that could be quickly solved by a young lawyer such as yourself."

"I'd appreciate that. I have a referral for you too. A businesswoman named Lauren Stephens. I'll text you with her contact info."

"I've heard of her. What kind of legal help does she need?"

"Her husband was using hidden cameras to spy on his tenants

in dozens of rental properties. Somebody murdered him this morning. Lauren could use some asset protection advice."

"Yes. The vultures will be circling the widow before the sun goes down. I'll get in touch with her immediately. Thanks for the referral."

Jake's phone buzzed with a call from Dick Arnold, a television reporter. When Jake had worked as a cameraman for a TV news station and website, Arnold had been a rival, competing for scoops on news stories. Jake let the call go to voicemail.

Arnold sent him a text: *You're going to wish you'd taken my call. I'm doing a hit piece about Lauren Stephens—your new girlfriend.*

Jake's phone vibrated again with another call. He looked at Bart. "You know Dick Arnold, the reporter? He's threatening to do a negative news story about your new client, Lauren Stephens. Can I put his call on speaker so you're a witness to the conversation?"

"Yes, by all means. I'd be delighted to hear that fool put his foot in his mouth."

CHAPTER 28

Jake answered the call and put it on speakerphone. "This is Jake."

"Jake, it's Dick Arnold. Where have you been lately? Oh, that's right—you got *fired* from your job!"

"Thanks for stating the obvious, Dick. Is there a point to this call? If so, get to it. Otherwise I'll say goodbye now."

"Wait. How did Gene Stephens die? Did he have a stroke while doing the nanny?"

"Goodbye, Dick."

"Don't end the call, or I'll include you in the story. I have photos and video of you hugging the widow and driving the dead husband's car. That was very chummy of the wife to give you her dearly departed hubby's luxury automobile and wrap her arms around you too. How long had he been dead? A few hours? She didn't even wait for his body to get cold before she latched onto you."

Jake saw Bart scribbling notes on a yellow legal pad. He thought for a moment. "You're spying on the grieving widow's home? I'll alert the police to go from house to house until they find you and whoever's helping you spy on her and the kids. They'll want to see your photos and video, ask you a lot of questions, and take you to headquarters for several hours of interrogation. You might even have to stay overnight in jail."

Arnold laughed. "You think you're clever, but you're going to be sorry for that prank you played on me."

"Prank? What prank?" Jake said. "You know, I thought the one bright spot of being fired from my job was that I'd be free of your annoying presence."

"You were wrong, as usual."

"Don't ever call me again. I'm going to block your number."

"Fine, I'll run a story about how you're suspected of having an affair with Lauren Stephens. Gene died under suspicious circumstances. Hours later, Lauren gives her dead husband's Porsche to Jake, her lover boy, and clings to his muscled body for support in her time of need. You look like a murder suspect, don't you?"

"Be careful, if you run that lying slander and libel, Mrs. Stephens might sue you, your boss and your corporation for millions of dollars."

"Yeah, right. See you on television, loser." Arnold ended the call.

Jake cursed and made a fist. He looked at Bart's written notes. "Wow, that's a devastating list of torts you came up with."

"I recently filed a libel lawsuit, so I have all the tort law wording ready. If Lauren wants to sue, it won't take long to create the complaint."

"Whatever she decides, I think hiring your firm is a wise investment."

"Thanks, I appreciate that," Bart said.

"Speaking of hiring you, I need you to add something to my will." Jake patted Cody on the head.

"Ah, a guardian for Cody?"

"Yes, in the event of my death, I nominate Sarah Chance as the legal guardian of Cody. She's one of the few people Cody will obey, and I know she'd take good care of him."

"A veterinarian is a good choice." Bart scribbled on the legal pad. "And who is your second nominee if Sarah does not survive you, or lacks the capacity to act as a guardian?"

"Terrell Hayes of the SFPD."

"I have great respect for Terrell." Bart wrote down additional notes. "All right, Sarah is choice one and Terrell is choice two. You can change that order at any time with a phone call to my office."

"Thank you, Bart." Jake stood up and shook hands again. He and Cody left the room and went down the hallway.

The receptionist said, "Have a nice day, *Mister* Wolfe. And good luck with your new solo law practice."

Jake nodded. News traveled fast. He glanced at the name plate on the desk and saw that her name was Moon Hee. "Thank you, Moon, it was a pleasure meeting you. I believe your name is Korean, meaning *learned*. It suits you."

Moon tilted her head. "How in the world could you possibly know that?"

"I visited the Republic of South Korea once when I was in the Marines. The United States has been helping them protect their border from the North Korean Communists since before you and I were born."

"What did you do in Korea?"

Jake hesitated a moment. "I can't tell you; it's classified."

He and Cody walked out the door.

CHAPTER 29

As Jake drove toward Lauren Stephens' house he stopped by the auto shop to get some things out of his old Jeep. The repair guy seemed amazed to see Jake remove guns and ammo from unexpected hiding places.

Jake smiled. "You probably shouldn't watch this. That way you can't be compelled to testify."

The repair guy shook his head and walked away.

Jake dug out all kinds of stuff and put it into the new Jeep, including a Remington 870 Wingmaster 12-gauge pump shotgun he had stashed inside a long cardboard box with a big picture of a leaf blower on the outside.

He put a hand on the Jeep and pressed his forehead against it. "You were a good friend—the *best*. Now it's your time to retire and rest. Drive kids to school, parents to work, a family to a ball game. Be a good citizen. I'm going to miss you, but we'll always be friends." He patted his car on the hood and walked away with a sad look on his face.

Jake got in the new Jeep, drove to Pacific Heights, pulled up in front of Lauren's mansion and parked in front. He saw Terrell standing next to his police SUV, talking on the radio.

Jake pressed the key fob and opened the K-9 door.

Cody jumped out, pawed the grass and sniffed the air.

Terrell ended his conversation and turned to Jake. "We have two of the gang members in custody but neither one is saying a word."

"That doesn't surprise me."

"They were driving stolen cars, using burner phones, and that house was rented for cash with no paperwork."

Jake nodded. "Professional criminals."

Terrell pointed at the Jeep. "I want to take my car to your mechanics; they made your old heap look better than new."

"Agent McKay gave me this fine armored vehicle as an ethical bribe, but it does come with some strings attached."

"She's playing you like a fish—but how come I never get any ethical bribes?"

"You're too honest and superhero handsome. Nobody would believe you'd accept a bribe."

"That's just wrong. However as a law enforcement officer, I'm used to this bias, especially the part where I'm too handsome."

Jake laughed. "Yeah, that must be a tough burden to bear."

Paul walked toward them. He was wearing brand-new jeans, boots, and a t-shirt. Over that he still wore his old threadbare red-and-black-checkered flannel shirt—but it appeared as if it had been recently washed.

Jake looked him up and down. "You clean up good."

"Mrs. Stephens had some people come out to the house. They brought all kinds of clothes, and they tried to give me a … hairstyle." He shook his head.

Jake smiled and noticed that Paul's hair was still long, as usual, although it had been shampooed. "You didn't cooperate with the stylist?"

"I found some evidence while I was patrolling outside the house. Come on, I'll show you."

They followed Paul around to the back of the mansion. He

went into a pergola, walking through an arch and onto a walkway with trellises overhead and on either side that were covered with vines. He stopped near a park bench.

"I asked Lauren about this place," Paul said. "She told me her husband liked to sit on the bench under the shade cover and smoke a cigar in peace and quiet. The family would give him his space and privacy so he could think about business deals." Paul pointed at the row of round paving stones beneath their feet. "Look at these stepping stones and tell me what looks out of place."

Terrell pointed at one of the stones that had some dirt on it, although every other stone was clean. "The soil … maybe somebody lifted a stone and set it on top of that other one."

"Right, and do you smell fish?"

"Dead fish. Is it fertilizer?"

"Yes, that's why the police dog didn't find this. The fish concentrate was purposely used in that planter bed right there, so it would mask the smell of this hidden stash." Paul picked up one of the paving stones and set it aside.

Cody growled and sniffed a white plastic disc in the ground. Paul got down on one knee and leaned in along with Cody. He showed no fear of him. "I moved the stone and found this bucket lid. Look at what's hiding below."

Paul carefully pulled off the lid, revealing the inside of a five-gallon plastic bucket that was sunk into the ground. It contained one item—a hard black plastic case about the size of a loaf of bread. It looked like a small toolbox, with metal hinges on the back and latches on the front.

Jake stared at the case. "Grinds, that looks like the small cigar humidor you had when we were deployed overseas."

Terrell squatted and took a picture with his phone. He put on nitrile gloves, carefully picked up the case and set it on the grass, then used his knife blade to pop the two latches. Inside the box was a collection of personal items: earrings, bracelets, necklaces, lipsticks, cigarette lighters, sunglasses, etc.

"What is all that?" Jake said.

Terrell got a haunted look in his eyes. "It reminds me of the souvenir stash of a serial killer I saw once, but it only contained seven items. How many are in here? Maybe three dozen?"

Cody growled as he sniffed the box. The fur on the back of his neck stood up.

"All of those items belonged to women," Jake said.

Paul nodded. "I feel the spirits of many wounded souls here, crying out for justice, and for closure."

Terrell put the case into a plastic evidence bag. "Why didn't you tell the police about this sooner?"

"I just found it a few minutes ago, and I don't have a phone. I sold it to buy liquor."

Jake said, "Grinds, I know your K-9 team already searched the house, but Cody and I are going to do it again, right now."

Terrell nodded. "Cody has the best nose of any dog I've ever seen. I'll help you search and then it'll be official."

Paul replaced the plastic bucket lid and set the round stepping stone on top.

They all walked toward the front of the mansion. Jake sent a text to Lauren, and she met them at the front door.

She swept the door wide, motioning for them to enter. "Jake, feel free to search anywhere in the house. I'll be in the home theater room, watching movies with the kids and trying to keep their minds occupied."

Jake noticed that she had the look of a battle survivor. The thousand yard stare. He'd seen it plenty of times. "Don't turn on the news, Lauren."

She studied his face. "Is there something you want to tell me?"

"Good guess. I want to warn you about a reporter named Dick Arnold. He's been spying on your home. He has photos of us hugging each other, and of me driving your late husband's car."

Lauren frowned. "I've never liked that guy. His news reports are like mean-spirited tabloid trash."

"There are a lot of good people in the news media, but Arnold is planning to do a hatchet job on you."

"How do you know this? Do you two have a history?"

"Yes. He hates me, but I'm too busy to hate him back. My advice is to consult a good lawyer."

"I got a call from the office of Bart Bartholomew, attorney at law. A woman named Moon said you referred him to me."

"Yes, I did. I was in his office when Arnold called me about the story. Bart listened in on the call and took notes."

"What would Bart's fees cost me?"

"Some serious cash, but he's one of the best lawyers in town."

"I'll think it over. Maybe Bart could just call the president of the media company and have a talk about Arnold."

"Good idea. He could say he's preparing to sue, but he'd rather not—the same way Jennifer Lawrence did with Google."

Lauren locked eyes with him. "Forget all that for now. My kids are my main concern, and Ben has stopped talking altogether. I hope your sister gets here soon. How far away is her psychiatry clinic?"

"Nicole should be here any minute. Meanwhile, Ben seems to be fascinated with Cody. Let's go say hello and see if he responds."

CHAPTER 30

They went into the living room. Chrissy was talking to Ben, but, as Lauren had said, he wasn't answering, just watching a cartoon.

Jake stood directly in front of Ben and blocked his view of the TV. "Hey, Ben, how are you doing, buddy?"

Ben looked at Jake and held up his arms.

"Do you want me to pick you up?" Jake said.

Ben nodded.

Jake looked at Lauren. She nodded too.

Jake got down on one knee. Ben threw his arms around Jake's neck. Jake gave him a hug, picked him up and held him in the crook of his arm. Jake wondered if this was what it would be like if he was a father. He thought of his own parents. Most of their gray hairs were caused by him. What would they say in this situation?

"I'm here because I wanted to ask you a favor, Ben. It's for Cody. He might need you to pet him on the back, because he got scared today when he found you and Chrissy."

Ben looked at Cody. "He … did?"

Jake nodded. "Sure. Cody was brave, but it's perfectly normal to be brave and scared at the same time. I was scared too."

"You were?"

"Yeah, we all were. Isn't that right, Chrissy?"

Chrissy nodded in understanding, wise beyond her years. "I was *really* scared, even *more* than Ben."

Ben looked at her in surprise.

"And that's okay, we got tough and we got through it," Jake said. "That's what courage is—you're scared, but you keep going anyway."

"Is that what Cody did?" Ben asked.

"That's exactly what he did, and what you did too. Do you think you could sit on the couch and hold Cody on your lap and pet him for a while? That would help him feel safe and strong."

"Okay."

Jake set Ben down on the couch next to Chrissy. He gave a command, and Cody came over and put his head on the boy's lap. Ben petted Cody, while Lauren watched them.

"Cody's going to get up on the couch and lay on your lap now," Jake said. He gave a command and Cody climbed up and lay prone across the two kids' laps. He wagged his tail and shook his head so his ears flopped. Ben smiled for the first time since he'd been rescued.

Lauren pressed her wet eyes against the sleeve of her blouse and took deep breaths.

"I wish we had a dog like Cody," Ben said. "Mommy, can Jake stay for dinner?"

Lauren received a call and then spoke to Jake. "The security people said your sister has arrived."

Terrell escorted Nicole into the room and she gave Jake a hug.

"Nicole, this is Lauren Stephens," Jake said. "Lauren, this is my sister, Nicole Wolfe."

Lauren shook Nicole's hand and studied her face. "My goodness, you look so much like Jake."

Jake shook his head. "Nah, she got the looks and the brains. I got the gift for not knowing when to keep my big mouth shut."

Terrell nodded. "I can attest to that."

Nicole observed the kids and whispered, "How are they doing?"

"Ben was in shock, but Cody is helping him," Lauren said.

Nicole watched both kids happily petting Cody. "If your children respond well to Cody, why not get a dog like him? You could afford a trained service dog."

"I'll consider that. Jake, could you help us get the right dog?"

"My girlfriend is a veterinarian and knows people at the service dog organizations. There are waiting lists, but I'd suggest you pay the fees for several people who can barely afford a dog. That would help a lot of people, and shorten the list."

"My company donates to many local charitable organizations. I'd be happy to sponsor a dozen families that need a dog, if it moves our dog up the list for Ben and Chrissy."

Nicole raised her eyebrows. "You think big. You should check out some of the local service dog organizations."

"When I was growing up my parents didn't allow any pets. I had no idea what a big part of life a dog can be, but I'm starting to learn," Lauren said.

Jake went over to Ben and Chrissy. "Cody is a working dog, so he has to get back to work now. My sister, Nicole, wants to sit with you and talk about how brave you were today."

Jake gave a command and Cody got off the couch and followed him to the door.

Lauren motioned for Jake to wait for her and she followed him into the hallway. "You promised to find the pinhole camera in my bedroom. Have you done it yet?"

"No, but I'll take care of it for you right now."

"Thank you. One other thing, Ben asked if you and Cody could have dinner with us."

"I'd like to, and I'll try to, but please don't make any promises to the kids that I might not be able to keep."

"All right, but can you please try your best to be here?"

"If we can make it, we will."

Cody barked once at Lauren. She looked at him, and a surprised look came over her face when she nodded in reply to him, as if she and the animal had an agreement.

Jake noticed it and smiled. He tapped his phone and called Levi. "I need a spy cam detector, to check the master bedroom."

"I'll send someone from my team to meet you there."

Lauren went back into the home theater room. She spoke to Nicole. "Jake is so unusual. What drives him?"

"I'm still trying to figure that out," Nicole said. "I love my brother. He's a good guy trying to do the right thing. But even though Jake has a strong moral code, he breaks the law if it suits his needs to dole out what he considers to be justice. His past combat experience in the Marines explains a lot."

"Why? What happened?"

"Jake lost several friends who were killed in combat. And then the terrorists put a bounty on his head, and on his war dog, Duke."

"A bounty?"

"They ambushed his platoon and tried to kill Jake and Duke, for the money. Jake was seriously wounded and he nearly died. And Duke—well, he didn't survive."

"I'm so sorry."

"When Jake was healing up in the hospital and mourning the loss of Duke, he received a Dear John letter from his girlfriend back home, saying she couldn't wait around any longer. Next, came the news that Patrick, our grandfather had passed away. Then a CIA man named Brinkter talked him into doing secret black ops missions that he won't tell me about. All I know is he wasn't the same guy when he came home."

"That's heartbreaking." Lauren looked at her rescued children, and felt a lump in her throat. "I'm in his debt."

"He'll never collect on that debt. If you want to pay him back, follow through and donate money to that service dog organization."

Lauren tapped her phone and sent a text to her accountant. "Done."

CHAPTER 31

Jake, Cody, and Terrell walked to Lauren's master bedroom. A security employee met them and handed Jake a spy-cam detector, a black handheld device that looked similar to a monocular.

Jake held it up to his right eye, pressed a control to activate a ring of small IR LED lights, and began to look around the room.

As he got near one wall, the lights started blinking. The closer the device got to a wall clock, the faster the lights blinked, and then Jake saw a small red reflective dot on the clock that blended in with the number 3. When he removed the clock from the wall and turned it over, he found a wireless camera setup. "Gotcha."

Terrell took the clock and placed it into a plastic evidence bag. "How does that spy cam detector work, anyway?"

"The technical term is optical augmentation."

"I'll take your word for it, Professor Mofo."

"This particular device will find a camera even if it's turned off." Jake handed the detector back to the security employee. "Could you please use this to check the rest of the house?"

"Okay, I'll check every room," she said.

As they headed down the hall, Terrell turned to Jake. "That

was a long meeting you had with the Secret Service and you came away with a new Jeep. What do they want from you?"

"It was … interesting. I also stopped at my lawyer's office for a while."

"Why, are you being sued again?"

"If you really want to know, I was there because I passed the California bar exam. Today, I officially became an attorney."

Terrell grinned. "You're kidding me, right?"

Jake reached into his jacket pocket and took out the Bar Association cover letter. "I'm serious. Look what it says right here."

Terrell read the part about Jake being eligible to start practicing law. He shook his head. "No way. You don't even have a bachelor's degree. You joined the Marines to go fight terrorists instead of going to college. How could you possibly become an attorney?"

Jake smiled. "Thanks for asking. I have to say, your faith in me is touching."

Terrell raised an eyebrow. "What do you expect? You're full of Irish blarney. Everything you say is BS. Go ahead and explain your law school scam to me. I can't wait to hear this."

"California allows you to go to law school online—and that's exactly what I did in my spare time for the past few years."

"What about the bachelor's degree required to get into law school in the first place?"

"The college I attended lets you take CLEP tests in lieu of earning an actual bachelor's degree. I passed all the College Level Equivalency Program tests and went straight to the living hell known as One L."

"I find that hard to believe."

"Trust me bro. I know it sounds impossible, but feel free to look it up on this new thing I heard of called Google."

Terrell smiled and shook his head.

They walked into the kitchen and Terrell set the spy clock on a countertop. He opened a cupboard, removed some containers of tea, and started dumping the contents into plastic bags. "Where is this offshore diploma mill located? If I pay them ten dollars, will they give me a certificate that says I'm an ordained minister?"

"I enrolled in an affordable college here in California."

"What law firms would ever hire you?"

"Probably none of them, but I'm not looking for a job. I'll just start my own solo law practice."

Lauren came into the kitchen. "Nicole is so great with the kids."

"Yeah, she's good at her job."

"Did you find the camera in my bedroom?"

"Yes, it was in that wall clock." Jake pointed at the clock on the counter.

"Why would Gene put a camera there?"

"Hopefully, he only used it in the mornings, to monitor you when he was in the basement. That way, when he saw you waking up, he could run upstairs to his study."

Lauren nodded. "I hope so."

"We're going to search your kitchen for the thumb drive."

"Good luck, I'll be with my kids," Lauren left the kitchen and walked down the hall.

Jake began opening more drawers and cupboards. He gave commands, and Cody started sniffing along the kitchen floorboards.

They heard a helicopter flying overhead, and the thump thump of the rotor blades was all-too-familiar. Terrell leaned toward a window and looked up. "Is the FBI bird here again?"

"No, Lauren hired a private aviation company to do helicopter flyovers once an hour."

"I have Rox searching the underground room again. After she's done, let's have Cody search it, now that everything has been cleaned out and taken away as evidence."

Cody completed his patrol of the floorboards. Next he sniffed all the drawers and then stood on his hind legs and sniffed the countertops.

Terrell started opening bottles of vitamins and herbal supplements. He opened one and poured the capsules into a plastic bag. "The label says these pills are good for your liver."

Jake held out his hand. "Give me one of those."

Terrell handed him three capsules. "Take extra doses. Your liver probably needs all the help it can get."

"I'm pretty sure my liver ages in dog years."

"Of all the college degrees available, why did you choose law?"

Jake found a cupboard filled with bottles of spices. "Many degrees aren't worth the paper they're printed on. This one gave me the legal power to kick butt on anybody who bothers my family or friends. Someday you'll thank me for that, when I defend your ass from some BS lawsuit."

Terrell opened some more cupboards. He dumped out an open container of oatmeal into a large bag. "Licensed to sue. It's unbelievable. You'd better not become a defense lawyer, and work for the criminals I've arrested."

"That's not on my to-do list," Jake said. "There are a lot of honest and hardworking defense lawyers in this city, but I mostly just want to protect myself from the never-ending attempts to lock my ass up in jail. Now everybody can just kiss my lawyer ass instead."

"Maybe you could just stop breaking the law."

"I'll try my best, but everything is illegal these days."

Terrell opened a cupboard and found all kinds of coffee. "Yeah, I remember when you got arrested for taking a pee."

Jake held out his hands, palms up. "Good example. I walked out of a bar at one in the morning and peed on a bush in the parking lot while waiting for my taxi. Super Cop roars up in his car and says I'm going to jail for *urinating in public*."

"That's a rare thing. You seem to attract over-reactive psycho people to you," Terrell said.

"My theory is that my irreverent sense of humor causes uptight people to go crazy," Jake said.

Roxanne Poole walked into the kitchen. "Okay, Terrell, I went over that basement one more time with a fine-toothed comb. There was no thumb drive hidden anywhere."

Terrell waved her toward the cupboards. "Good work. Now give us a hand searching the kitchen."

"Why are we searching again? Our people already went all over the house," Roxanne said.

"We didn't know we were looking for a thumb drive on the first search, so we're going to do it again. The work all pays the same, Rox."

Cody got up on his hind legs, put his paws on the edge of the countertops, and sniffed the cupboards above. He alerted to one in particular and used his teeth to grab the knob and pull the door open. He sniffed inside, then turned his head toward Jake and barked at him.

CHAPTER 32

Jake went over to Cody, searched the cupboard and found a box of wooden "strike anywhere" matches, along with some candles. Jake dug through the matches, but he didn't find a thumb drive. He patted Cody on the back. "Good work. You found sulfur, potassium chlorate, and phosphorus sulfide. These matches are okay, but I'm going to put them on the highest shelf so the kids can't get at them."

Cody went back to sniffing the rest of the cupboards.

"He doesn't miss a thing, does he?" Roxanne said.

"He knows what you had for breakfast," Jake said. "Some dogs can sniff a house and find termites; others can smell your body and find out if you have cancer."

Roxanne stared at Cody.

Jake smiled at her science-nerd fascination with his smart dog. He began pouring out bottles of herbs and spices into bags, while Terrell poured out a bag of ground coffee. "Good idea, Grinds, check all the coffee."

"Yeah, some drug dealers hide their stash in coffee because it masks the smell from police dogs." Terrell opened another package and poured the coffee into a plastic bag.

Roxanne got down on one knee and pulled open the drawer below the oven. She removed it and set it aside, then pointed a small flashlight into the opening. She saw mouse droppings but nothing else.

Cody came over to her and sniffed the open space. Roxanne was caught by surprise. She held perfectly still. She'd heard the rumors about him. Cody finished searching under the stove and raised his head. When Roxanne and Cody were eye to eye, Cody sniffed her floral-shampoo-scented hair. Roxanne felt Cody's hot breath on her ear. Her mouth went dry and her heartbeat increased.

Cody stood up and he leaned his head under her stomach and helped lift her to her feet.

Roxanne just stared at Cody as he turned away to continue his search.

Jake noticed it and said, "Cody likes you for some reason. You should be glad. Just ask Levi, or Grinds."

Terrell threw a bag of coffee down on the counter. "Oh, sure, he's instant friends with the tech nerd cop. Meanwhile, I carried extra water on patrols in the desert, just so Jake's war dog had enough to drink, but do I get any respect from the canine community back home? Nope, nothing but attitude."

Cody panted, Ha-Ha-Ha.

The security system chimed and Jake looked out the window. Paul was dragging a man out from behind a hedge. He punched the intruder in the face, then grabbed him by the back of the neck and force-marched him toward the front gate.

Jake's phone buzzed with a texted security alert and he went to a TV display screen and looked at a grid of security-cam views of the property. In one of the square images, he could see Paul manhandling the intruder. Jake tapped the screen and zoomed in. "It looks like Dick Arnold was trespassing, and Paul caught him doing it."

Terrell looked at the screen. "You want me to have a uniform place him under arrest? A visit to jail might teach him some manners."

"No, he'd just run a negative news story about cops. The chief wouldn't like that."

Terrell scowled. "Let Cody loose on him. He'll bite into Arnold's butt like a pit bull on a pork chop."

Cody ran to the door, then stopped and looked over his shoulder at Jake.

"No, Cody. Maybe someday, but not right now," Jake said.

Cody returned to Jake's side, looking disappointed.

Jake texted the security cam video to Lauren. *Paul's doing a good job.*

He continued dumping out herbs and spices into bags but didn't find the thumb drive in any of them, so he went to the refrigerator and opened the freezer door. He carried a collection of frozen items to the sink, closed the drain, and then ran the hot water to thaw everything out.

Terrell held up a package of coffee and said, "Look at this expensive gourmet java that's past the expiration date. Rich people are weird."

"Just pour it into a plastic bag. I know it breaks your heart, but I'll ask Lauren to donate all the opened coffee to the food bank run by Father O'Leary."

Terrell started dumping out every kind of coffee. He picked up a package of what was said to be the world's strongest blend —a black package with a skull and crossbones, named *Death Wish Coffee*. It hadn't passed the expiration date but was getting close. He held it up so Jake could see it. "I hereby seize this under forfeiture laws. Now I'm going to pour some into that shiny machine and make a pot of strong coffee to help our noble search efforts."

When Terrell opened the coffee, Cody growled, observed Terrell and sniffed the air.

Jake studied his dog's body language.

Terrell poured the ground coffee into the filter basket and a lump dropped out along with the grounds.

Cody smelled something that didn't fit in and started barking at Terrell, standing on his hind legs and pawing at the coffeemaker.

Jake grabbed the coffee machine's cord and pulled the plug from the wall outlet. "Hang on, Grinds. Cody smells trouble."

CHAPTER 33

Terrell pulled the basket from the coffeemaker and dumped the grounds onto the kitchen counter, then pulled out his knife and pushed the grounds from side to side. "There's the thumb drive, inside a little plastic tube. Rox, get to work on this thing."

Roxanne just stood staring at Cody with her eyebrows raised in surprise. Cody had helped find evidence the police search had missed. That was something that didn't happen often, if at all.

Roxanne grabbed the thumb drive and looked closely at it. "This kind of drive has privacy encryption, but I'll use brute force attacks to hack the password."

Terrell nodded. "Be careful. You might find the virus from hell on there."

"I've got a sacrificial laptop I use for stuff like this." Roxanne walked outside toward her van while talking to herself.

Jake gave Cody a pat on the back. "Good work, buddy."

Terrell pointed at Cody. "Sometimes you are an amazing dog —although mostly you're a worthless fuzzball."

Cody barked at Terrell and pushed his head against his stomach in rough play. Terrell let Cody push him around and scratched behind his ears as he called him all kinds of profane terms of endearment he'd learned in the Marines.

Jake said, "Cody earned himself some grilled chicken. We're going to grab some food from my favorite taco truck, and then come back here. You want me to bring you anything?"

Terrell shook his head. "You need a taco truck intervention."

Jake and Cody went outside to the Jeep and drove down the long driveway. An unmarked police SUV was pulling in at the mansion. As it passed by, the driver glared at him. Jake frowned as he recognized Ray Kirby, the former partner of a policewoman named Cori Denton who had recently been hell-bent on destroying Jake's life.

"I sure hope he isn't blaming me for all the trouble Denton got herself into," Jake said.

Cody stuck his head out the open window and barked, showing his teeth to Kirby as the SUV drove past.

Jake headed toward his favorite food truck, his stomach growling with hunger. After a few miles, police lights flashed in his rearview mirrors from an unmarked SUV behind him that looked just like the one he'd seen Kirby driving.

Jake pulled over, taking his illegal sheath knife from behind his back and hiding it inside the car's center console. He wondered if he was legally allowed to flash the U.S. Marshals badge at Kirby and tell him to eff off. Probably not.

Ray Kirby and his new female partner walked up to the Jeep and he rapped on the driver's window with a nightstick. Jake opened his window an inch. "Hello Sergeant Kirby, what can I do for you, kind sir?"

Kirby gestured to the badge hanging on his belt. "I pulled you over for speeding. You were going thirty-eight in a thirty-five zone."

"You're kidding me, right? Why is a plainclothes homicide inspector making a traffic stop while carrying a nightstick?"

"You don't mind if we take a quick look in the back of your Jeep, do you?"

Jake knew it was a trick question. If you said no, they could take a look. "I do not give you permission to search my car."

"We have a report you performed work as a private investigator without a PI license."

"That report is mistaken. Who said that?"

"Lauren Stephens. I stopped by her house, saw you there, and asked her why. She said you were working for her as a private investigator."

"No, I was working for her on a private *security* team. Lauren hired Executive Security Services and signed papers that said private security. It never said the word investigator. It's all in writing, and it's all perfectly legal. Call Levi Strauss right now and he'll testify in my defense."

"Your witness is Levi Strauss, huh? He made great blue jeans, but he died over a hundred years ago. You can make a statement down at police headquarters."

"No thanks, I already made my statement right here. I'm sure you know that a lawsuit for false arrest could cost you and the city a ton of money in municipality litigation."

"Hiring a lawyer to file a lawsuit might cost you a lot too."

"I don't need to hire a lawyer—as of today, I am one."

Kirby laughed. "Now you're impersonating a lawyer too? That's great. Get out of the car."

"No thanks, I like it inside the car just fine."

"You're under arrest. If you don't get out of the car, you'll also be charged with resisting arrest."

"Actually, you're attempting to make a *false* arrest, Kirby. I'm not breaking any laws—you are. Trust me; I know more about the law than you ever will."

"I'll call a tow truck, haul your vehicle to impound, and use the Jaws of Life to open it. You'll go to jail, and your dog will go to the animal control shelter. Not to mention, if that dog tries to bite me, I'll have to shoot it in self-defense." Kirby put his hand on the pistol in his belt holster and gave Jake a challenging look.

Jake's eyes got dark, and his face flushed. He gripped the steering wheel and tried to control his anger. He took deep breaths as he felt the beast inside of him rising to the surface. "Listen, if you leave my dog alone, I'll cooperate with your illegal false arrest. Fair enough?"

"I don't make deals with criminals who are on their way to jail."

"Okay, I was just trying to reason with someone who will soon be suffering public humiliation, unemployment, and bankruptcy. But you win, Kirby—for now. I'm getting out of the car, slowly and peacefully. Hold your fire. You're being recorded on video, sent to the cloud as evidence that will end your career."

"Step outside, turn around and raise your hands above your head."

Jake closed his car window and gave commands to Cody to escape capture. He added, "Cody, go to Terrell's house, just like we've practiced. Understood?"

Cody barked once. Jake opened his door and stepped out. When both cops were focused on Jake, he pressed the button to open Cody's K-9 door. Cody jumped out, ran past the cops and disappeared. Jake stepped out, turned his back on Kirby, and raised his hands as instructed.

Kirby ignored the dog. "Put your hands against the car. Take one step back and spread your feet."

Jake obeyed the orders. "In the inside pocket of my jacket is a letter from Washington D.C. that says you can't arrest me unless you call the Secret Service first."

"Cover him," Kirby said, and he began to frisk Jake while his partner stood off to the side with her pistol in her hand.

Jake turned his head to the side and smiled at the other cop.

"Hi, ma'am, how's your day going? Sorry for this inconvenience. Ray is apparently holding a grudge against me because his former partner made some serious errors in judgment."

The woman shook her head at Jake, but looked doubtful as she observed what Kirby was doing.

Kirby found the letter from the White House and put it in his pocket. "Are you currently on the payroll of the Secret Service, or any other government agency?"

"No, not at the moment."

"Well, then, your magic letter is out of date and is no longer valid." Kirby continued frisking Jake and found the pistol in Jake's shoulder holster. "Gun!" He handed it to the other cop. He found a small pistol in an ankle holster. "Another gun!"

"Calm down, Kirby, I have a permit," Jake said.

"I'm going to cuff you now. If you resist, we'll use force to make you cooperate." Kirby grabbed Jake's right wrist, pulled it behind his back and slapped a cuff on it. He did the same with the left wrist, using far more force than necessary.

"You've always been a good guy, Kirby—don't change now," Jake said.

"You screwed over Sergeant Denton," Kirby said.

"No, she screwed the pooch all by herself. Where is she now, anyway?"

"In custody, undergoing psychiatric evaluation to see if she's mentally competent to stand trial. All thanks to you, asshole."

"Oh, it's my fault she's a psychopath? And you knew, but never warned anyone?"

Once Jake was cuffed, Kirby swung his nightstick and hit Jake behind the knees. The surprise strike caused Jake to trip and stumble toward Kirby.

"He's coming at me!" Kirby said. He began beating Jake with the nightstick.

Jake took several hits on his shoulders, back and thighs. As he struggled against his instinct to fight back, he heard Cody barking frantically from a distance away.

Suddenly the nightstick hit Jake on the back of the head, and the last thing he heard before he fell unconscious was Kirby saying, "That was for Denton."

CHAPTER 34

Jails have a particular smell—sweaty prisoners, moldy mattresses, bad food, toilets, bleach, and lost hope. Anybody who has ever been locked in a cage never forgets it.

Jake woke up and smelled jail. He'd been there before, and he'd hoped he would never return.

He was flat on his back on a thin mattress in the drunk tank. His guess was that Kirby must have lied and said he was drunk, not suffering from an illegal nightstick hit to the back of his head.

The overhead lights were bright, and Jake had a powerful headache.

A giant shirtless white male prisoner was saying something to him.

"Wake up, fresh meat. We need to have a little talk. Unless you'd rather just give up now, roll over and get used to being my new girlfriend."

Jake sat up and planted his feet on the floor. He took a deep breath and let it out. "And who might you be?"

"They call me Party Animal."

"What are you in for Mr. Party Animal, sir?"

"Dog fighting. We throw two abused pit bulls into a ring and bet on which one of them comes out alive. I must have won a dozen bets by now."

Jake glared at him in anger.

Party Animal clenched his right hand into a fist, took a step forward and reached out with his left hand to grab Jake by the hair on top of his head.

Jake decided to avoid being used as a human punching bag. He launched himself to his feet as he threw a punch in self-defense. He brought his fist all the way from his knees, and it shot forward like a baseball flying over the center field fence for a home run. He slugged Party Animal's throat so hard the man staggered backward, grabbed his throat with both hands and began wheezing for air.

Jake's hand felt like it had hit a brick wall. Next, he kicked the big man in the crotch. Party Animal dropped to his knees and swayed there. Jake gave him a *Jeet Kune Do* strike to the back of the neck. The man fell forward, Jake stepped aside, and his cellmate landed face-first on the concrete slab floor, just missing the toilet.

Jake was amazed to see that the big brute was still conscious. He grabbed a toothbrush from the sink and pressed the pointed end of the handle against the man's right eye. "I'm an abused dog who's been reincarnated as a man to find you and kill you. Say your prayers, because this toothbrush is about to be shoved through your eye and into your evil brain."

The man tried to yell for help, but it came out as a wheezing howl.

Jake dropped the toothbrush, sat back down on the bed and drew in deep, calming breaths. The calming part didn't work. His combat training told him to kill the enemy. He had to override his heated response with cold control.

He heard the sound of footsteps—shiny black shoes running in his direction. Two guards arrived at his cell, a black male and a white male. "Stand up and put your hands through the slot so we can cuff you," the white guard yelled at him.

Jake remained seated, and he gestured at his cellmate. "Mr. Party Animal tripped, fell down and hit his head. You should probably take him to the infirmary."

"Put your hands here, right now, or you'll be sorry."

Jake stood up. "Okay, but you might be sorry too—I'm a lawyer."

The guard laughed. "No, you're a loser."

Jake put his hands through the slot. "Maybe I'll file a lawsuit in self-defense, against Sergeant Kirby—and you, and your boss."

Jake saw the guard squinting at him—no doubt wondering if he really was a lawyer. He saw conflicting emotions playing across the guard's face. "Let me guess. Sergeant Ray Kirby told you a lot of BS about me, right?"

The guard put cuffs on Jake, opened the door and grabbed him by the bicep. "Get going, we're taking you to the holding pen with the other scum."

"When do I get my phone call, as required by law?" Jake said as he walked.

"There's a long wait to make a phone call. You'll get your turn eventually."

"Taxpayers pay millions of dollars, but you don't buy enough phones? Where does the rest of the money go? To the warden? Not into your paycheck, I bet."

"Shut your stupid mouth and keep walking."

"Sorry, but I'm kind of disoriented. Ray Kirby hit me on the head with a nightstick, from behind, while I was handcuffed."

The two guards exchanged doubtful looks.

"When my lawyer bails me out of here, I'll tell him to give each of you a hundred dollars. The sooner he gets here, the sooner you get your money."

"You can't bribe us—and a hundred is nothing."

"Five hundred dollars each if my lawyer is here within an hour. Two fifty each if it's two hours. One hundred if it takes three hours. Zero money and maybe a lawsuit against you and your boss if it takes any longer."

The black guard appeared to Jake as if he was the tall, silent type, but he put a restraining hand on the other guard's arm. "If you're really a lawyer, give me some free legal advice. My sister got arrested, and I don't have any money for her bail. It's a thousand dollars, and I'm flat broke until payday. My credit cards are maxed out, and I don't own anything I can pawn for that kind of cash. What can I do?"

"Is she in this same jail?" Jake said.

"Yes, in the women's wing."

"What is she charged with?"

"Drug charges—just for being at home when the cops came and arrested her stupid boyfriend. She had nothing to do with it. She's a good kid with bad taste in men."

"Something similar happened to my friend, Dylan. I'll make you a deal. Let me have my phone call *right now*, and I'll get your sister bailed out along with me."

"Seriously? And can you help her lawyer up and beat the drug charges?"

"I'll do my best, and I'll do it for free. But you have to get me in front of the night court judge so I can make bail and leave here immediately. Kirby threatened to shoot my dog, right before he hit me on the head. I have to find Cody and make sure he's okay."

"You've got a deal. But you'd better keep your promise and get my sister bailed out tonight, or there'll be hell to pay."

"I give you my word as a Marine. I won't leave here without her," Jake said.

The guard nodded at Jake. He held out his arm and showed a

Marine Corps tattoo of the Eagle, Globe and Anchor.
"Semper Fi."

Jake held out his cuffed hands. "I'm Jake."

The guard shook hands. "DeShawn."

They stopped to use the phone on their way to the holding
pen. The guards told the prisoners to stand aside, and everyone
grumbled and complained when Jake was led to the front of the
line.

Jake picked up the phone and tried to remember Bart's
number. The wound on his head was throbbing and he couldn't
think of the last four digits. He noticed dozens of paper notes
and business cards tacked onto the wall in front of him. One of
them was a card from Amborgetti's Bail Bonds Agency. The
owner was a cousin, and Jake had worked as a cook at
Amborgetti's Italian restaurant in his teens. He dialed the
number.

"Bail bonds."

"I need to talk to Anselmo Amborgetti."

"Sorry, Mo's not here right now."

"I don't care where he is. Get him on the phone. Tell him Jake
the Knife is in jail, and I need him to bail me out immediately."

"Jake the Knife? I've heard of you. Can you hold on a
minute?"

"I can hold for exactly thirty seconds."

Jake heard grumbling from the prisoners waiting behind him.
There were some static noises on the phone, and then Anselmo's
voice.

"Jake, what's going on, little buddy?"

"A cop hit me on the head and tossed me in jail."

"That's why you should work for me. I pay a couple of them
every month to leave my people alone."

"We can talk about that later. Please get me out of here, and
bring some large cash for my new friends."

"Of course. We all need friends. I'll come down there myself, right now. I know everybody at the jail and the night court."

"I'm not surprised. Thank you, Mo."

"You did the right thing to call your *family*. We are always on your side—always. *Capisci?*"

"*Capisco.*"

CHAPTER 35

Cody trotted to a bus stop Jake had taken him to several times. There was a crowd of people and he heard the sound of a bus engine approaching.

The bus stopped, its doors opened, and people got on and off. Cody waited until the way was clear and then climbed the steps onto the bus. The driver smiled at him. "Hey, Cody."

Cody woofed at him.

"Have a seat, buddy."

Cody went to an empty bench, jumped onto it and sat there looking out the window.

The driver spoke over the intercom. "Folks, this dog's name is Cody. Please do *not* pet him; he's a working dog, going to his job."

The bus passengers all started talking about Cody. They'd seen news videos of a dog that rode the bus in Seattle. Now they had one in San Francisco too.

After a few miles, the bus stopped and the driver said, "Here you go, Cody. This is your stop."

Cody barked once.

The driver opened the doors and held out his hand. "Have a good day."

Cody went down the stairs and onto the sidewalk. The passengers on the bus applauded. He ignored the distraction, ran down several streets, took some turns, and then arrived at a familiar home.

Terrell's wife, Alicia, worked as a teacher at an elementary school. Today, like most days, she got home before Terrell and spent a few hours of quiet time grading papers from her third-grade class.

The doorbell rang, and Alicia went to the front door and looked out the peephole. She saw Jake's dog, Cody, standing there on his hind legs with his face near the lens. As Alicia looked at him, Cody barked, dropped to all fours and tried to turn the doorknob with his mouth.

Alicia unlocked the deadbolt and opened the door. Cody came inside the house and barked at her while pawing the floor.

"What is it, Cody? Where's Jake?"

Cody howled and ran down the hallway and back.

"Oh dear, I'll get Terrell on the phone," Alicia said.

Cody barked once when he heard the word Terrell.

She shook her head. "You must be the smartest dog I've ever seen."

There was some barking from her own dog, a corgi named Boo-Boo.

"No offense, Boo-Boo."

Terrell answered the call. "Hey, babe, miss you."

"Hi, baby. Jake's dog, Cody, came to the house and rang the doorbell. I let him in and he's barking and trying to tell me something. There's no sign of Jake."

"Uh-oh, I'll be right there."

Boo-Boo barked and jumped around near Cody, wanting him to play like he often did, but this time Cody ignored him and observed Alicia as she talked.

She ended the call and looked at Cody, getting a weird feeling he was studying her. Jake had once said that Cody was always looking at your body language, listening to your tone of voice and smelling the scents of your body chemistry to learn what you might do next.

"Terrell is on his way here. I'm going to try Jake's phone now."

She wondered why she was explaining things to a dog. She called Jake, but it went to voicemail.

She sent a text. *Cody came to our house. Where are you, Jake?*

There was no reply.

"Cody, what happened to Jake?"

Cody barked and ran to the living room. He went to an eight-by-ten-inch framed photo hanging on the wall. Standing on his hind legs, he put his paws on either side of the photo, and growled.

Alicia followed Cody and looked at the group photo of SFPD cops doing a fundraiser for a charity.

"Did Jake get arrested by one of these cops?"

Cody barked once.

Alicia couldn't believe she was doing this, but she started pointing at the various faces in the photo.

"This person? No? How about this guy?"

When she pointed at Ray Kirby, Cody barked once.

"This man arrested Jake?"

Again, Cody barked once.

"Well, I'll be..."

The front door opened and Terrell came into the house.

Alicia called to him. "We're in the living room."

Terrell found them near the photo. "What's going on?"

"Watch this. Cody, is this the cop who arrested Jake?" She pointed at Kirby.

Cody barked once.

Terrell cursed. "I was afraid this might happen. Let's go, Cody. Jake's probably in jail right now. I'll check the computer as we drive over there."

Terrell kissed Alicia as if he was going away on a ship for a year. Cody barked impatiently. Terrell ended the kiss and playfully swatted his wife's ample rear.

She smiled and shook her head as the man she loved went off to rescue his "brother from another mother" … *again*. Jake was a high-maintenance friend.

Cody followed Terrell outside and jumped into the backseat of the police SUV.

Terrell checked the dashboard computer. Sure enough, Kirby had arrested Jake and charged him with a long list of fabricated BS. Terrell cracked his knuckles and said a few poetic curse words. He had great respect for most of his coworkers, but every organization in the nation had a few employees who were a pain in the rear—police departments were no different.

He drove toward the jail and called Beth to let her know what was happening. Beth might give Jake a ton of grief, but she knew that he'd always have her back. Jake had once said that if the cops were Terrell's brothers and sisters, they were his family too.

CHAPTER 36

In court, the judge recognized Jake. "Young Mr. Wolfe, what brings you here? I thought you were going to stay out of trouble."

"I apologize, your honor. It was a misunderstanding. How is your daughter these days? That was a beautiful wedding." The judge's youngest had been married the previous spring at his parents' winery in Sonoma.

"She's doing well. Enjoying married life. The winery venue was worth every penny, and thanks again for doing the photography at no charge." He set the bail and asked Jake to give his regards to his mother and father.

Anselmo showed up and posted bail for Jake and for the guard's sister.

Jake walked out of captivity with the young woman by his side, helped her into a taxi and said, "Please be careful and stay out of trouble. Avoid gang members and hard drugs. Promise?"

"Who are you?"

"I told you, I'm your lawyer."

She looked him up and down. "Seriously? You're the best my brother could do?"

"I got you out of jail, didn't I? But you're welcome to go back inside and wait for a lawyer to magically appear who's wearing a suit and tie."

"No, it's fine. My brother doesn't have any money; it all goes to pay his son's medical bills, so I figured my lawyer would be sketchy."

"Your boyfriend was sketchy. That's why you were in jail. Raise your standards from now on. You can do better."

A black limousine pulled up to the curb in front of Jake. The driver got out, opened the back passenger door, and stood at attention.

Two cops who were driving past the jail noticed the limousine and stared at Jake. He knew they were probably wondering if he had mafia connections. Who else gets picked up from jail by a limousine other than actors, rich people, rock stars and mobsters? And they knew he wasn't among the first three.

The limo driver recognized Jake. "You're in trouble again? What is it with you?"

Jake shook his head. "What can I say?" He turned to the young woman. "The cops will be watching you. Be careful to stay away from anybody who is buying, selling, or using hard drugs. Otherwise you'll be right back behind bars."

She stared at the limousine and the dangerous-looking Italian man. Her face and body language revealed that her attitude was gone, and now she was frightened. "How do you know my brother?"

"DeShawn helped me when I was in jail. Now I'm helping you —returning a favor."

"Will he be in your ... *debt*?"

"No, we'll be even, as long as you stay out of trouble. If you don't, he might end up in debt to these guys."

She looked at the limo driver and bit her lip, then nodded and got into the taxi.

As the cab drove away, Jake saw her staring at him through the rear window.

Anselmo, who had waited in the car after posting bail, got out of the limo and stood on the sidewalk.

Jake shook his hand. "Mo, thanks again for bailing me out."

"You're welcome. Speaking of bail, when are you going to do some fugitive recovery jobs for me again?"

"Bounty hunter work? Maybe when I have some free time."

"Get in the car, little buddy. We'll go have a drink at the restaurant. I've been saving an aged bottle of Barolo for a good conversation."

"I'd love to, but first I have to find my dog. That's my number one priority right now."

"He's lost?"

"When I was being arrested, I ordered him to evade capture."

Jake's phone buzzed with a call. He checked the display and saw that it was from Terrell. "Grinds, you'll never guess where I am."

"My guess is you're in front of the jail. Look to your right."

Jake looked down the block and saw Terrell standing next to his police SUV, smoking a cigarette. Terrell opened a back passenger door and Cody jumped out. Jake sighed in relief as the golden dog bounded toward him.

Cody barked several times and ran up to Jake. Terrell closed the car door and followed after him. Cody stood on his hind legs, put his paws on Jake's shoulders, licked Jake's face and barked at him.

Jake said, "Okay, okay—I missed you too, Cody." He acted as if this was simply a happy reunion, but he had a lump in his throat and he took deep breaths and let them out.

Cody ran in a circle around Jake and then stood at his side and pressed against him while looking around for anybody he might have to bite. Jake scratched Cody behind his ears.

The limo driver said, "I remember him. He's a good dog."

"When we met before, I never got your name. I'm Jake, and this is Cody."

"Yeah, I already knew you were Jake the Knife. I'm Vito."

Terrell walked up to Jake. "Cody came to the house—and get this—he rang the doorbell. Alicia answered the door and he ran inside, barking and trying to talk to her. I rushed home, and when I went in the house, Cody was in front of a photo, making a positive ID on Kirby."

Jake nodded. "Yeah, that sounds like him."

Anselmo said, "This is great. Now Jake can go to dinner at the restaurant. Let's get out of here." He stared at Terrell, challenging him.

Terrell stared back. "No, Jake and Cody are riding with me. I need them to help me with a police investigation." He turned to Jake. "Semper Fi, Marine?"

Jake felt himself being pulled in two directions, but the choice was clear. "Sorry, Mo, but when duty calls, I have to answer."

Mo looked back and forth between Terrell and Jake. He noted how Jake stood up straighter when he heard the Semper Fi motto. "Once a Marine … always a Marine?"

"That's how we roll," Jake said.

"You should join the Family and make it official. Once in … never out. You'd be good at the oath of loyalty until death."

Terrell crossed his arms and shook his head at Anselmo. His body language sent a message: *Don't push your luck or I'll eff you up.*

Anselmo just shrugged and smiled in admiration at Terrell, one of the many cops who could never be bought.

Jake said. "Mo, if I ever decide to become a made man, you'll be the first to know."

Anselmo gave Jake a bear hug and climbed back into the limo.

Jake watched the car drive off toward the restaurant and thought wistfully about how their waiting list was a year long.

His stomach growled as he and Cody walked alongside Terrell to the police SUV and he wondered if Terrell actually needed his help, or if he was just trying to keep him away from the organized crime branch of his family tree. That was just the kind of thing his Marine brother would do.

Terrell opened his car door and slid into the driver's seat. Leaving the door open, he lit another cigarette.

"Chain smoking?" Jake asked.

"It's been one of those days," Terrell replied.

"Yeah, it sure has." Jake opened the cardboard box he'd been given when he'd left the jail. He took out his two pistols and strapped on the shoulder holster and the ankle holster. He remembered that he'd left his knife in the Jeep.

"Is my Jeep in the impound lot being held for a hefty ransom?" Jake said.

"No, I have somebody driving it to us. He'll be here in a few minutes."

"How did you pull that off?"

"Cops help cops, at least most of us do. You're lucky I'm your friend." Terrell's phone buzzed, he looked at the display and thumbed the answer icon. "What have you got, Rox?"

"I hacked into the thumb drive," Roxanne said.

CHAPTER 37

Terrell had his phone volume up and was holding it two inches away from his ear.

Jake heard Roxanne mention the thumb drive. He asked Terrell, "Can you put your phone on speaker so I can listen in?"

Terrell thought about it and nodded. "Rox I've got Jake Wolfe in the car with me."

"It's your call if you want to keep him in the loop," Roxanne said.

"Show us what you've got," Terrell said.

The dashboard computer lit up and screen caps began to scroll across the monitor.

"Most of these file folders contain videos from the hidden cameras in the rental properties," Roxanne said. "Judging by the video names, Gene Stephens was using them for blackmail."

"Let me see some of the names."

"Here's one named *Payments*. It contains a collection of videos titled *Payments by Vanessa, Payments by Melody, Payments by Sharon*, etc."

"He made videos of women paying him money? Why?"

"No, not money—sexual favors. Gene blackmailed women into bed and recorded them on hidden video."

Terrell cursed. "How many names are in that file?"

"Several dozen. Take a look."

He studied the list. "Maybe that stash of jewelry and personal items we found are souvenirs from his sexual conquests—not from a serial killer."

"Besides the payment files, there are all kinds of blackmail files of activities that might be embarrassing or cause problems if they were made public."

A list appeared on the screen: assault, burglary, car theft, cheating husband, cheating wife, crossdressing, disability fraud, drug buying, drug selling, extortion, elder abuse, gambling problem, heroin use, insider trading, kleptomania, medical insurance scam, motorcycle theft, paying for prostitutes, stealing from employer, illegal weapons—the list went on and on.

Terrell said, "You never know what your neighbors might be up to."

Jake stared at the screen. "Rox, open that file about drug selling."

"I don't take orders from you, Jake."

"Cody found that thumb drive for you. Come on—can you return a favor?"

Terrell shook his head. "No, I found the drive in the coffee."

"You didn't find it; you were going to boil it," Jake said. "Cody found it and stopped you from destroying the evidence."

Terrell blew a stream of smoke out the window and then nodded his head. "Rox, go ahead and open the file. Jake and I both have a special hatred for heroin dealers. They caused the death of Cody's former handler, Stuart."

Cody growled.

Roxanne opened the drug-selling file. "One video is titled *murder at heroin warehouse*."

"Play that video," Terrell said.

Jake tapped his phone and aimed the camera toward Terrell's dashboard computer.

The video ran without any sound, and at a faster speed than normal. It showed the inside of a commercial warehouse. A yellow fork lift drove past, carrying a pallet loaded with clear plastic bags filled with white powder. Soon it passed by again going the other direction, carrying a shrink-wrapped pallet stacked with six-packs of bottled water.

Two men and a woman walked into the scene, pushing a third man ahead of them who had his hands cuffed behind his back. They made him stand on a large blue plastic tarp in front of a padded wall and he appeared to be pleading for his life. Both men drew their pistols and shot him several times in the head and chest. He fell dead, and they rolled his body up in the tarp and dumped him into a chest freezer. A forklift arrived, picked up the freezer, and drove away.

Jake tapped his phone and ended the video.

Terrell blew cigarette smoke out of his nose in twin streams. "Good work, Rox. You just found a large-scale drug trafficking operation."

"I guess Gene thought he could try to blackmail murdering drug dealers and somehow live through it," she said.

"The SFPD narcotics team has been searching for a gang that buys counterfeit AK-47s from China and trades them to terrorists in Afghanistan in exchange for opium. They turn the opium into heroin, smuggle it across our borders, and then sell it in America. The heroin kills a lot of people here, and the AK-47s are fired at our troops overseas."

"So the gang is making a killing, while they're killing Americans?" Roxanne said.

Jake interrupted. "This could be the same gang who sold the heroin to Stuart. What's the address of that warehouse?"

Cody continued growling and he pawed at the back seat. Jake reached back and patted him on the head, and thought about

Stuart and the sound of his loud laughter. They'd been best friends—two war dog handlers who'd understood each other better than anyone else. He wondered once again how his friend could survive Afghanistan and Iraq, and then die in the suburbs of California with a needle in his arm. Jake told himself he should have been there that night, to save Stuart's life. He'd been working on some stupid assignment for his employer and had missed his friend's call—his last call for help before he died. Jake thought about Norman at the news station and how he wanted to choke the man by the neck.

Roxanne said, "I don't know the address. Gene Stephens didn't own any warehouses. No commercial properties at all, only residential homes."

Jake spat out the window. "Heroin is the devil's drug. I hate the people who sold it to Stuart, and I need to find them, whoever they are."

Terrell nodded. "We had a meeting this week. Drug overdoses are now the leading cause of death among Americans under fifty."

"The supply of heroin coming into this city has to be stopped once and for all," Jake said. "I don't care what it takes."

Roxanne said, "Even if we put this gang out of business, other drug cartels will soon fill the void."

"Well, at least this would stop a supply line of AK-47s to the terrorists," Jake said. "Grinds, how many of our friends were shot by AKs?"

Terrell glanced at Jake and saw that his eyes were dark, his jaw was clenched, and he was staring off into the distance. "Rox will find the warehouse, Jukebox, but it'll be a crime scene for the police to deal with. Don't go anywhere near there."

"I can't just stand around and do nothing. If this is the gang that sold heroin to Stuart they have to pay for that. Cody and I are going to go out searching to see what we can find."

Terrell looked Jake in the eye. "Just remember to stay on the right side of the law. Don't cross the line to the other side. Agreed?"

"I'll do my best, but I can't promise anything. Where is that line, anyway? It seems like it's always moving."

A uniformed cop drove up in the Jeep and parked. He walked over to Terrell and handed him the keys.

"Thanks, Wilson. I owe you one. Hop in and I'll give you a ride back to HQ." Terrell gave the keys to Jake.

Jake and Cody got out of the car and walked down the street to where the Jeep was parked.

Wilson got into Terrell's SUV and they drove away.

CHAPTER 38

At the police station, Roxanne sat at her computer. She took a screenshot of the warehouse interior and uploaded it to Google Images. Thousands of results were displayed.

Beth sat next to her. "These warehouses all look alike."

Roxanne accessed the MLS database and searched for any warehouses that had been recently listed for sale in San Francisco. She studied the photos, but none of them matched the one in the video.

Beth shook her head. "This is like looking for a needle in a haystack."

Roxanne drummed her fingers on the desktop. "Maybe it's a leased warehouse." She checked some rental listings but still couldn't find it. She opened a spreadsheet. "Gene Stephens routinely copied the keys of homes that were for sale, and planted cameras in many of them."

Beth nodded. "Right, and each key was tagged with the home's address."

They both studied the spreadsheet. All the listings were homes—no commercial properties.

Roxanne entered each address into Google Maps and used

the satellite view to see what was nearby. Eventually she found one home located in a condo tower that was close to an area of warehouses. "Maybe when Gene visited this condo, he drove past a warehouse with a *For Lease* sign and stopped to look inside."

"I'll call Terrell." Beth tapped her cell phone.

"Hayes," Terrell answered.

"Rox found an area of warehouses near one of the condos owned by Gene Stephens." Beth recited the address.

"I'll drive over there and look around," Terrell said.

Beth ended the call. "Let's go through that file named *Payments*. Check every video of the blackmailed women performing favors. See if any of them were in a warehouse at the time."

"Why would Gene do that when he could have had his trysts in any number of million-dollar luxury homes for sale?" Roxanne said.

"Because Gene was effed up?" Beth said.

"Good point. Watching these videos is going to be painful."

"We'll put them on fast forward and only look at enough to check the location."

"Ugh," Roxanne said, and started going through the videos and taking notes.

Payments by Sharon — furnished home, seller's bed.

Payments by Val — empty home, on the carpet.

Payments by Melody — empty home, kitchen floor.

On the twenty-seventh video, *Payments by Marcia,* Roxanne found a warehouse. "Look at this."

Beth scooted her chair closer.

Gene appeared onscreen in the warehouse, wearing a business suit. Marcia was an attractive young woman, dressed in a short-skirt suit and heels. They walked through the empty warehouse, opened a door, and went into a hallway.

The screen went blank for a moment, and the next video was of the inside of an office, furnished with an oak desk, a black leather executive chair, a matching couch, and two guest chairs. Gene sat at the desk and Marcia sat on a guest chair, her long legs on display.

The office portion of the video had sound. They acted out a steamy office romance with a billionaire boss and his submissive secretary. Marcia asked for a raise in pay, Gene told her she would have to perform extra services for the extra money. Marcia stood up and began unbuttoning her blouse.

Roxanne cursed and stopped the video, then stood up and paced the room. Beth kept quiet and let her think.

Roxanne stood in front of a window and looked out at the city. "Marcia didn't seem aware of the camera."

"No, I'm sure it was a hidden spy-cam."

"Gene's computers were erased, but there has to be a third party with records of his tenants."

Beth tapped a pen on a pad. "We can try his bank and his accountant."

Roxanne went back to her desk, where she logged into Gene's business checking account and searched through it. "No records of rental payments received."

"Look for his accountant, or a property management company."

Roxanne scanned through the records and found a payment to an accounting firm. She looked them up online and called their number using the phone on her desk.

Beth picked up her own desk phone and listened in.

When a receptionist answered, Roxanne said, "This is Police Inspector Roxanne Poole of the SFPD. I need a list of every rental property owned by one of your clients."

"Our attorney will have to call you back tomorrow."

"I need this for a homicide investigation. I can get a search warrant right now if that's what it takes."

"Yes, Officer, that's what it takes. I don't make the policies, I just know that our attorney handles any law enforcement enquiries, and she insists on an official search warrant in order to protect our company from client lawsuits."

"I understand. Please have your attorney call me at her earliest convenience." Roxanne recited her phone numbers and ended the call.

Beth drummed her fingers on the desk. "Property management?"

Roxanne searched again and found a payment to a company that provided electronic lease services to landlords. She checked their website. They offered tenant screening, rental applications, lease agreements, and payment processing.

Beth looked at the display. "That's it. Nice work."

Roxanne called their Seattle offices. A woman answered the phone. "This is Inspector Roxanne Poole with the San Francisco Police Department. I need some information on the account of your client, Gene Stephens."

"What kind of information? I'm sorry, but we have a strict privacy policy on our website."

"I can subpoena you and your boss, but then your company might become famous in the online media as having aided and abetted a criminal. Why don't we avoid that, and you can just give me your dead client's password?"

"Dead?"

"Yes, your criminal client was murdered. You can help us with the homicide investigation, or you can risk being charged with obstruction of justice and subpoenaed to appear in court."

"Oh, uh, no problem—we're more than happy to help the police. I'll have to reset his password for you." She recited the new password.

"Stay on the line." Roxanne tapped on her keyboard and opened Gene's account. "Help me navigate your site. I'm looking for a tenant with the first name of Marcia."

"The database can be searched by name. Click or tap the green checkmark icon. That will bring up a list of tenants."

Roxanne opened the listings, took screenshots and sent them to the printer. She then searched for Marcia and found only one listing. It gave her full name, husband's name, address, email and phone number. "Got it. On behalf of the SFPD, thank you for your cooperation."

Beth gave Roxanne a pat on the back. "Let's hear what Marcia has to say."

Roxanne called the number. A soft-spoken man answered the phone. "Hello? This is Lucas."

"Sir, I'm calling from the San Francisco Police Department. I need to speak with Marcia."

"I'm sorry, that's not possible."

"Please get Marcia on the phone or I'll have to come to your apartment, right now. I know where you live." Roxanne recited the address.

"Officer, if you want to talk to Marcia, you'll have to visit her grave at the cemetery. My wife committed suicide three weeks ago."

CHAPTER 39

"I'm so sorry for your loss," Roxanne said. "I had no idea; my apologies."

Lucas took a deep breath and let it out. His voice wavered. "Marcia was active in our church choir, but lately she'd been missing recitals and staying home. People were concerned, me most of all. One night when I was out of town on a business trip, she took an overdose of pain medicine and drank a lot of vodka."

"Could it have been an accidental overdose?"

"No, she left a note." His voice cracked and he began to cry. "The note said, *I love you and I'm sorry for everything.*" He wept and took ragged breaths. "But I don't know what she meant. Sorry for what? We were happy. She was my angel, and meant the world to me."

As Lucas wept, Roxanne got a hunch about Marcia's use of pain meds. She searched through the file titled *Drug Buying* and found another video of Marcia, this time buying pain pills from criminals who appeared to be Russians. Gene's notes said that she'd become addicted to the prescribed pain medication and had soon required more and more pills, and he'd recorded drug dealer visits to her home.

Lucas stopped crying and took some deep breaths. "Why did you want to talk to Marcia? What's this about?"

Roxanne hesitated. He may have to know eventually, but not today. "I'm simply following leads on a case. Marcia is just one of the many people on a long list that I wanted to talk to."

"While I've been sorting out her estate, I found that her savings account was emptied out, and most of her jewelry was missing. What did she spend the money on?"

"I have some ideas, and I'll talk to you when I know more."

"Does this have anything to do with our apartment, somehow?"

"Why do you ask?"

"Before my wife died, she began acting strangely and saying she hated living here. She wanted to break our lease, give up our deposit, and move out of this building ASAP."

"Did she give you any reasons why?"

"Anything and everything—she didn't like the neighbors, the noise, the location, the traffic, the landlord—you name it."

"I'm investigating the landlord. Did Marcia have a specific complaint about him?"

Beth grabbed a pen and notepad and started taking notes.

"She said he was a jerk. One time he stopped by unannounced when I wasn't home and tried to get her to invite him inside for coffee. I got mad, called him on the phone, and yelled that he should never come over here again unless I was home, and only if there was a good reason."

"Well, he won't be bothering anybody ever again. He was murdered this morning."

"Whoa. Maybe a jealous husband did it. I hope I'm not..."

"Don't worry, Lucas, you're not a suspect. Thank you for your time, and again, I'm very sorry for your loss."

Roxanne ended the call and quickly scanned through the rest of the videos. She found one more where the victim was recorded in the warehouse and office. She repeated the steps on the landlord website to find the woman's contact information, then called the number and listened as it rang repeatedly and went to voicemail.

She left a message. "Nora, this is Roxanne Poole of the San Francisco Police Department. I need to speak with you immediately. Please answer or return my call. I'll keep trying until we connect. I get paid to do this and I'll never stop."

She hit the auto redial on her desk phone. After several more calls, Nora finally answered. "What's going on here? You're calling me at work. When I saw your caller ID I had to go into the restroom to take your call."

"Ma'am, the SFPD is investigating the murder of Gene Stephens and—"

Nora interrupted. "I didn't kill that scum, but I want to thank whoever did."

Roxanne paused and took a deep breath. This was good. An angry witness was a talkative witness. Nora was thrilled that Gene was dead. It was the perfect moment to ask her questions. "I know he took you to a building with a warehouse and offices. I need the address."

"I wish I could help you. He made me lean my car seat all the way back while wearing a sleeping mask. We drove around for a while, and then I heard the sound of an automatic garage door opener raising and lowering a door. It reminded me of my own garage, but it was louder and it lasted longer."

"Were you wearing the mask on the way out too?"

"Yes, I was. I have no idea where the building is located. If I did, I might burn it down."

"I've seen a few minutes of the video where you're inside the warehouse and then in an office. You weren't wearing a mask then."

"He made a video of that too? I should have guessed he would. No, I was told to remove the mask once we were inside the warehouse and the overhead door was closed."

"Think about what you saw inside. Did you notice anything that might help the police find the location? A company name, a vehicle, names on lockers, equipment, paperwork, anything?"

"The warehouse and most of the offices were empty. One office was staged with furniture, the way realtors do."

Beth wrote a word on the notepad and showed it to Roxanne. *Windows?*

"Were there any windows? Could you look out and see any neighboring buildings?"

"The warehouse had very few windows, but I remember looking through one and seeing a wall with some Chinese script lettering. There was also a drawing of a fish."

"I'd like you to sit down with our sketch artist and describe the letters and the fish while he draws them and tries to recreate what you saw."

"When will this nightmare ever end?"

"With your help, it will end very soon."

"Maybe I should take the Fifth Amendment and not incriminate myself. Gene blackmailed me for something I did that was against the law."

"You'll be given immunity from prosecution in exchange for testimony," Roxanne said.

Nora cursed. "All right, I'll meet with your artist after work when I get home."

"Great, let me know what time."

"I get off in a half hour."

"We'll come to you," Roxanne said.

"Thanks. I'd prefer that. These days I live in fear. I go to work and come straight home. My mother buys my groceries and brings them to me. I lied and told her I have agoraphobia."

"I'll see you when you get off work. Let me know if I can bring you anything."

"I appreciate that. This never would have happened if I hadn't become a kleptomaniac. I have thirteen stolen red vacuum cleaners I've never used, thirteen pairs of red pumps I've never worn, and twelve red blenders in their unopened boxes. I desperately *need* one more red blender to make it thirteen. It's a strange addiction and difficult to break."

"But you managed to quit at twelve blenders? And you're doing better now?"

"Yes, I got help. But Gene found me when I was at my most vulnerable, and he blackmailed me."

"The SFPD has a victim's counselor named Dr. Lang. She's good. I'll bring her with me if that's all right with you."

"That might be okay. I'll let you know. See you soon, and could you please bring me a double cheeseburger, a chocolate shake and ... a red blender? The number twelve is driving me crazy."

"Any particular brand?"

"No, just as long as it's red. I'll steal it out of your car if you don't mind," Nora said.

"No problem." Roxanne ended the call, looked at Beth, and shook her head. "Where's the nearest place to buy a blender?"

CHAPTER 40

A wealthy British criminal known by the code name "Chairman Banks" was riding in the backseat of his brand-new limousine. He was looking on his phone at some of the San Francisco restaurants he wanted to try. Pressing a control and lowering the window between him and his driver, he said, "Abhay, be a good lad and get me a dinner reservation at this restaurant." He held up his phone so Abhay could see the display. "I want to try their wood-grilled octopus as an appetizer. For the main course I'll have roasted baby goat, along with calf's brain ravioli in a lemon cream sauce, and some crusty slices of rosemary and olive bread. For dessert they offer an intriguing dish made of pig's blood cooked with dark chocolate to create a mousse that is layered between slices of white cake, drizzled with blackberry sauce and served with a cup of Turkish coffee."

"I'll do my best to get you a table on such short notice, sir," Abhay said.

"Money is no object. Bribe the maître d' with an outrageous sum if you must."

"But of course, sir."

Banks was surprised when his encrypted phone vibrated

with a call. Hardly anybody had the number, and most of those who did had died recently and quite violently. It was from an unknown caller so he let it go to voicemail. No message was left. Moments later, he received a text.

Hello, Mr. Banks. You're being followed by the FBI. A black helicopter is above you, and a matching SUV is behind you. Answer my call if you wish to avoid being arrested and sent to a federal penitentiary. My guess is that you have less than three minutes to decide.

Banks used a silk handkerchief to mop the sweat from his brow. His phone vibrated again, and he reluctantly thumbed the answer icon. "Hello?"

"Look out the back window of your vehicle. Do you see a black SUV, five cars back, behind a silver Benz?"

"Yes."

"That's the FBI. Their helicopter is above you. Look up through your moonroof."

Banks looked up at the sky above and saw the helicopter flying there. "How do you know this?"

"Because I've had a drone following you for some time now."

Banks gripped his phone tighter. "May I politely inquire as to why?"

"I was planning to kill you, but now I'd like us to work together. No hard feelings."

Banks felt his blood pressure rising. "Is that so? And what sort of work do you propose?"

"Making money from criminal enterprises, of course—what you do best."

"Flatterer. May I ask to whom I am speaking?"

"I'm Elena, the friend of a mutual friend."

"And what is the name of this mutual friend?"

"He was killed by a man who has meddled in your business and mine."

"I need names. Your full name, our mutual friend's name, and the name of the man you claim is meddling."

"Jake Wolfe is the man who killed our mutual friend, and he's the one meddling in our affairs," Elena said. "That should tell you what you want to know."

Banks hesitated a moment. "I don't believe I've ever heard that name."

"Liar. I'll let you go now. It will be fun to watch on my drone cam while the FBI agents arrest you."

"Now you're going to tell me there's only one way it can be avoided, and you hold the magic key to my escape."

"You're a bright boy. Do you want to hear the idea?"

"Not especially, but tell me anyway."

"You'll drive into an underground parking garage, switch cars, and drive out. I'll make the FBI believe that you're still in your limousine, and involved in a shoot-out."

"You expect the FBI to swallow that?"

"Yes, because the video will be shown on their own dashboard computers in their vehicles. It will show your limousine being shot by hundreds of rounds and bursting into flames."

"That might offer some convincing visual stimulation," Banks said.

"After you exit your limousine, two of my associates will pour gasoline all over it and shoot it with automatic weapons loaded with tracer rounds."

"I imagine they'll cause quite a flaming mess of my car."

"They'll transmit a video of the scene, and I'll route it to the FBI computers as if it's coming from security cams at the parking garage," Elena said.

"And you believe the federal agents will rush to the fire, like moths to a flame?"

"Yes. They want to take you alive, interrogate you and send you to prison."

"You might be leading me into a death trap."

"Look up at the helicopter again. It's descending to the pinch point, where you'll be stopped and arrested."

Banks looked up and saw the helicopter approaching fast. He looked out the back window and saw the same black SUV, but now there were no cars between it and his limousine.

"You can't really believe I'd abandon my limousine and get into a strange car based upon a phone call from an unknown person."

"Enjoy prison life and your new friends there. If you change your mind, you'll find the coordinates on your phone."

Elena then texted a code that only Banks and his former paid killer had known. The code to send payment to one of the killer's secret offshore bank accounts.

Banks stared at the code in shock. She'd hacked the dead assassin's bank passwords? That meant she had millions of dollars at her fingertips. The call ended. He received another text, showing a map and the address of a hotel that was three blocks ahead of his current location.

The SUV following him came up close on the limousine's bumper. The helicopter appeared above and in front of his car and hovered dangerously close to the street and buildings.

Abhay said, "Sir, a vehicle is closing in on us from behind, and a helicopter is dropping into attack position ahead."

Banks took a deep breath. "Be a good lad and look for a hotel parking entrance up ahead on the right." He recited the address.

Blue and red lights began flashing from behind the front grille of the SUV, and a voice crackled over a loudspeaker. "Attention, driver of the black limousine. This is the FBI. Stop your car, open your door, and put your hands behind your head."

Banks was sweating in fear as he said, "There's the garage. Turn in and go down to the second level. Go!"

Abhay obeyed, and the SUV followed behind them. As they

passed the first level, a pickup truck pulled out behind the limousine and blocked the path of the following SUV.

"Go quickly now," Banks said.

They roared through the garage with tires squealing. A man waved at them and pointed at a white four-door family sedan.

"Stop the car, Abhay."

"Sir, I suggest that we—"

"Sorry, but I'm leaving this car behind now. I invite you to come with me and continue to be my driver, but as of this moment, you are under no further obligation."

Abhay raised his eyebrows, but stopped the car and got out. He opened the door for his boss and gestured toward the other car. "Let's be on our way, sir."

"Good lad, carry on."

They got into the family sedan. Banks found a white blanket in the backseat that matched the white interior color scheme. "Brilliant."

Abhay looked on the dashboard and saw a baseball hat, glasses, an ugly sweater, and a stick-on mustache. He put on the disguise and drove up to parking level one.

Banks stretched out prone on the backseat and covered himself with the blanket.

They exited the hotel's underground parking area, just a few minutes after they'd entered. An FBI agent looked at the car as it drove past, but the vehicle and the sole occupant didn't match the descriptions on his dashboard computer.

In the garage, the limo was in flames and being fired upon by tracer rounds. All the FBI agents saw it on their car computers and phones. They raced to the burning car and used fire extinguishers to put out the flames. The men who'd driven the pickup truck and fired the tracer rounds were nowhere to be found.

After the flames were extinguished, the car remained sizzling hot, smelling like barbecued meat. An agent managed to get a back door opened, and they all saw a burned and smoldering carcass, prone on the backseat.

Upon closer inspection, one agent said, "That's a side of beef. Somebody played a trick on us."

CHAPTER 41

Elena called Banks. "I'm pleased you went along with the plan instead of going to prison. Here's video of your car in flames, with the FBI agents surrounding it."

"A ghastly scene."

"I have a stock tip to help further our new business relationship." Elena texted a stock chart to his phone.

Banks studied the chart. "What am I looking for?"

"The price of that stock is going to drop like a rock today, and most of tomorrow. Then it will make a recovery and shoot up to new highs."

"How can you be sure?"

"Because I'm working hard at stock manipulation."

"Impressive."

"Yes, it is."

"And your particular method?"

"One you'd appreciate—the accidental death of a few key people."

"Ah, yes, I've used it myself in the past."

"Keep an eye on that stock. Sell short, then buy low and watch it rise."

"I'll use stock options on this bet. *Puts and calls.*"

"Good idea. Less risk and more leverage."

"And what do you get out of this?"

"A percentage of your profits. You have vast sums available to invest. Your profits will be staggering."

Elena ended the call and studied her laptop. Her plan for the "accidental death" of key people began moving ahead on schedule.

A vehicle struck a pedestrian when he crossed the street. Sandeep was a humble genius engineer with a new theory of an internet algorithm profit model that might provide free Wi-Fi to the entire world while still earning millions from advertisers. He worked on the secret project in his home office, and kept a backup copy on a USB drive he carried with him everywhere.

A woman ran up to Sandeep as he lay on the pavement, dying. She acted as if she was trying to help, but she secretly reached into the coin pocket of his jeans and removed the small USB drive.

A few blocks away, an accomplice broke into Sandeep's apartment and stole his computer. In a few minutes, the young genius was dead and his work had disappeared—until one day in the future when a corporation would "invent" it, again.

Moments later, in Presidio Heights, a woman sat out on the back deck of her hillside home, with a latte and a laptop. She made her living by investing in local start-up companies.

San Francisco was a city of dreamers with big ideas. Billions of dollars in funding were available to promising new start-ups. Yet out of every hundred companies, there might be five success stories and ninety-five flameouts. It was high-stakes gambling with incredible risks, and astronomical financial rewards to the fortunate few who bet on the right idea.

She was one of the few. The ventures she invested in earned healthy incomes, and were often bought out for giant sums of money. Many went broke later, but she didn't care. One person's loss was another's gain.

Suddenly, she heard a strange mechanical whine and saw what looked like a remote-controlled toy fire truck rolling toward her. The bright red RC truck was about the size of a shoe box, with four fat black tires. The strange thing stopped in front of her, and a mechanical arm rose up and fired a shot.

She was surprised to be hit with a dart, and she felt like she was having a heart attack. Her heartbeat increased and her blood pressure shot up. She began shaking as she tried to use her phone, but instead she bit down on her tongue and foamed at the mouth as she experienced a heart attack and a seizure.

The toy truck approached her and the mechanical arm reached out and plucked the dart from her body. The truck then retreated and drove away, back the way it had come.

The woman went into convulsions, fell over onto the deck and rolled into the swimming pool. She died as she spasmed and inhaled the chlorinated water.

In the affluent Sea Cliff neighborhood, a man slept late, and when he awoke with a hangover, he remained in bed as he turned on the big-screen TV to watch the financial news. He saw Elena's face instead. She glared at him in anger and said, "Try to change the channel."

He pressed the remote, but her angry face was on *every* channel.

"You're a bright boy. If you look closely at the remote, you'll see why it doesn't work."

He stared at it closely, and it blew up in his face, spraying a liquid polymer onto him that resulted in a thick plastic-like coating over his face, nose and mouth. He tried to pull the mask off, but it hardened in seconds and stuck to him like glue. He choked to death, while trying to scream but only making a muffled sound as his eyes pleaded for life.

Elena's image on the TV screen cackled with laughter as she watched him suffocate and die.

CHAPTER 42

On their way to buy a red blender, Beth drove the police surveillance van while Roxanne tapped and swiped on a tablet.

"I've got something," Roxanne said. "This is new and unproven tech, but it says the computer that sent the weaponized sound to Wolfe's phone is located in a nearby building."

"Location?" Beth said.

"The corner of Market Street and Montgomery."

Beth turned on her lights and took side streets and shortcuts to avoid traffic as she drove toward the financial district.

Roxanne continued typing as her software searched for an individual computer connected to the internet.

"It's one of these high-rise towers." Roxanne pointed. Take a left at the next street. Now keep going, two more blocks. Pull over—it's that building on the right."

Beth stopped the car in front of a glass-and-steel skyscraper. She parked illegally in a loading zone and tossed the police parking permit onto the dashboard.

Roxanne got out of the van. She held a device up in front of her and thumbed the screen as she walked. Beth followed behind and scanned the street for threats.

"This might be wrong, but it says the targeted computer is located at the top of this building," Roxanne said.

They badged the doorman, and as they went inside he tapped on his phone. Getting into an elevator, they held the side rails as it rocketed upwards, making their stomachs drop. When they arrived at the top floor and stepped into the hall, a sign read: Penthouse Suites. Roxanne walked down the hall, stopping in front of a door. "This is it."

Beth pounded her fist on the door. "San Francisco police! Open up, I have a search warrant!"

Nobody answered the door. Roxanne looked at Beth in confusion. "What warrant?"

Someone inside the suite was cursing in Russian.

Beth motioned for Roxanne to stand aside. "It sounds to me like someone in there is calling out for help." She backed down the hall several yards, got a running start and slammed her shoulder and body weight against the door.

The door burst open and Beth saw a brunette woman wearing the kind of "wingsuit" that helps you fly through the air like a kite.

The woman gave them the finger, then jumped off the balcony into the air and dropped out of sight.

Beth ran out the open sliding door and looked down. The fugitive was flying between high-rise buildings like a bird or a paper airplane.

Roxanne appeared by Beth's side, grabbed her by the arm and yelled, "Get out! Run! *Now!*"

A laptop computer sat on the dining table, and an automated female voice said, *"Self-destruct initiated. Explosion in ten ... nine ... eight ..."*

"Go!—go!—go!" Roxanne said as she pulled on Beth's arm.

They ran to the stairwell and pounded down the steps to the

next floor. There was a tremendous thunder clap and the building shook. Roxanne stumbled, tripped and almost fell headfirst down the stairs before Beth reached out and caught her. Concrete dust rained down on both of them.

Beth used her handheld radio to call for backup and firefighters.

Roxanne cursed. "I have to get inside that penthouse before the evidence burns up." She ran up the stairs, grabbed a fire extinguisher from the stairway wall, and opened the door to the top floor a few inches. Flames rushed into the stairwell, but she stood behind the hot metal door, the heat radiating to her shoulder while she sprayed the fire extinguisher through the narrow opening. Flames licked her hair and singed her shirtsleeves but she continued spraying until the canister was empty.

Once she had partial control of an area of the hallway, she ran in and grabbed the fire hose from the wall. Flames were crawling up the walls, but she sprayed them with a torrent of cold water.

Beth appeared behind her. "Good job. Now spray into the apartment."

Roxanne blasted water through the open door of the apartment and onto the carpet and furniture.

"Give me the hose—you find the evidence," Beth said.

They entered the living room as Beth began spraying the floor, walls, and ceiling.

Roxanne held her sleeved elbow over her mouth, darted down a hallway, and found the master bedroom. Thankfully, it wasn't as damaged as the living room. A docking station with various devices being charged sat on a nightstand next to the bed.

She grabbed a pillowcase and began tossing items into it. She opened drawers and dumped them out, lifted the bed mattress and looked underneath, and checked the closet, inside pockets of jackets and coats, and behind furniture. Next she searched the bathroom.

When she finished, she ran back to the living room and left the apartment along with Beth as they coughed due to the foul smoke from burning sheetrock, plastics, and carpet.

The fire department arrived and insisted that the police leave the penthouse floor while they put out the flames.

The elevator wasn't working, so Roxanne and Beth hiked down scores of stairs to the ground floor.

Terrell Hayes met them there with a first aid kit and bottled water. "Let me see your hands." He cursed when he saw the scorched spots. "Drink this water, take deep breaths and hold these cold packs on your burns."

"Yes, Mother," Beth said, smiling.

"What the hell were you thinking?" Terrell said.

"Rox made me do it. She's a bad influence."

"Hmmm, it's always the quiet ones."

Roxanne drank from a bottle of water and said, "I grabbed some tablets and phones, and a hard drive."

Terrell patted her on the back. "Good work, Rox."

Beth coughed. "Rox saved my life. My little boy almost lost his mom up there." She vomited in the gutter at the thought of her son, Kyle, growing up without his mother.

Terrell handed her a piece of spearmint gum. "Here, this might help settle your stomach."

"At least I'll have minty vomit breath."

"Smells like victory."

Roxanne started crying as the shock wore off. She hugged Beth for saving her from falling down the stairs.

Terrell gave Roxanne a piece of gum and said, "To quote a line from a movie, Tom Hanks said there's no crying in baseball."

Roxanne smiled and gave him a punch on the shoulder.

While driving, Jake saw the top floor of a skyscraper explode. Glass and flames shot out of one side, debris rained down and a cloud of smoke rose into the air.

Cody started barking and Jake punched the gas pedal, sending the Jeep roaring down the street. He saw somebody in a wingsuit flying through the air between skyscrapers. Cars began to stop as people stared at the building and the flying human.

Turning on the Jeep's police-style lights and siren, Jake chased after the person in the wingsuit.

The flyer looked down at Jake and flew over a one-way street, flying against traffic. Jake turned and drove to a nearby two-way street and then turned again, racing in the direction the flyer had gone. He looked down each street he crossed, but didn't see the suspect.

He ran a red light, with siren wailing, turned and drove back to the one-way street. On arrival, he stopped in the intersection and looked for the flyer. Gone.

Jake drove in a crisscross search pattern. It was too late, the flyer had disappeared. He cursed, drove back to the bombed building, and parked on the sidewalk. There were fire trucks and police cars everywhere. He put the badge on his belt, opened Cody's door and kept him in the backseat as he outfitted him with an orange-and-black vest that said SEARCH DOG on both sides.

"We're going to search for survivors, Cody. Let's go."

Cody barked once, then hopped out of the car and pawed at the sidewalk, ready to roll.

Jake pressed his key fob to close the canine door, leaving the Jeep's flashing lights on. He put on a windbreaker that said Search and Rescue on the back, clipped a leash onto Cody's collar and walked to the front door of the building.

A uniformed police officer stopped him. Jake showed him his badge. "U.S. Marshal. Is your K-9 team here yet? If not, I'd like to do a quick search for anyone who might be injured or trapped."

"Go for it," the cop said.

The elevators were off. Jake walked past them to a stairwell, picked up Cody, and carried him up the stairs to the penthouse floor. His leg muscles were burning when he reached the top. His phone buzzed with a text.

Terrell: *Did I see your dumb ass run into the blown-up building?*

Jake: *Who—me? Nah, I'm at a 7-Eleven buying beer and cheese puffs.*

Terrell: *Dammit, Jukebox.*

Jake and Cody searched the top floor. Cody whined as he went past the bombed apartment, and then alerted at one down the hall. Jake told the firefighters, "Coming through, please. Search dog doing his job."

They went into the living room that was soaking wet with water from firehoses. Cody strained on the leash and headed down the hallway toward the furthest bedroom. He went inside, sniffed the room, stopped in front of a closet, and pawed at the door.

Jake grabbed the warm doorknob in his gloved hand, opened the door, and found a frightened little girl hiding inside. He spoke in a calming voice. "You're safe now, the search and rescue dog found you."

The girl looked at Cody and started crying in relief.

Jake thought of his father, who'd been a firefighter. He'd spent his career putting out fires in smoke-filled buildings like this one.

A firefighter came into the room and gave the child a big smile. "I'll carry you outside to the fresh air, okay? You'll get to wear my hat and sit in a fire truck!"

The stunned child nodded.

The firefighter scooped her up and put his hat on her head. He spoke to Jake as he passed by. "Jake Wolfe? How's your dad?"

"He's enjoying his retirement from the fire department, keeping busy at his winery."

"Tell Connor we miss him down at the station since he retired."

"I will."

"He'd be proud to see you helping us firefighters." The man walked out the door.

Jake got down on one knee and petted Cody. "You did good, buddy. You saved a child's life. Let's keep searching."

Cody wagged his tail and resumed sniffing the ground and the smoky air. He sneezed and turned his head from side to side as he tried to find human scents among the burning chemicals. Jake coughed and spat on the smoldering carpet.

Down on the street below, the firefighter came out the front door on the ground floor carrying the girl. They were filmed by the news media.

A reporter named Dick Arnold asked, "How did you find this child?"

"Jake Wolfe and his dog found her."

Arnold frowned and looked up at the top of the building.

CHAPTER 43

Jake and Cody searched the rest of the penthouse apartments but didn't find any people or pets. Several firefighters arrived and ordered Jake to leave the area now that he'd cleared it.

He led Cody slowly down the stairs, floor by floor. Halfway down, he picked Cody up and carried him the rest of the way, his muscles straining to hold the large dog. They arrived on the ground level, and he set Cody down.

Jake looked out the front windows and saw Dick Arnold and his cameraman, along with lots of other local media people.

Arnold spotted Jake inside. His cameraman began taking video while Arnold provided commentary saying Jake had no business being in that building right now.

Various news cameras began broadcasting video and images of Jake and his SAR dog. Jake's hair and jacket were dusted with debris. Cody's fur was too.

Some of the first responders asked Jake questions about what was going on. He stood there and directed traffic for a while, pointed out stairway doors, answered questions, and tried to help out. "So far, it looks like nobody was injured, thank God."

A female paramedic stopped, smiled at Cody, and gave Jake a

fist bump. Cody woofed at her. She handed a bottle of water to Jake. "Is this the dog who found the child?"

"Yeah, that's him."

"I have a Chocolate Lab. She has that same smile as your dog."

"Thanks for the water," Jake said. He got down on one knee, took a plastic bag out of his pocket and slowly poured some water into it while Cody lapped it up. Cody drank, coughed several times, and drank some more.

Pictures and videos of Cody began to appear on television news programs and media websites.

Out in front of the building, one of the onlookers approached Dick Arnold and told him he'd taken video with his phone before the news vans had arrived.

"Good work," Arnold said. "Let me see what you've got."

He showed him the video. Arnold saw Jake and Cody hurrying into the building, acting as if they were some kind of rescuers instead of an unemployed bum and a dumb dog. "Email me a copy of that." Arnold recited his email.

A woman walked up to Arnold and handed him an eight-by-ten manila envelope. "You've been served." She vanished into the crowd of onlookers.

Arnold opened the envelope and found documents that said he was being sued for millions of dollars by the law offices of Bart Bartholomew, on behalf of Lauren Stephens. His boss was also being sued, along with the news corporation and the board of directors.

Rival news crews broadcast Arnold's angry face, and the legal documents in his hand.

One of Jake's friends at his former employer ran a story about how Arnold had spied on Lauren Stephens when she was grieving her husband's death, and smeared her with a hit piece about her and Jake Wolfe. She said Arnold was now being sued for libel. Meanwhile Lauren had donated to a local service dog school, and Jake had helped rescue a child from a bombed building. The news story showed Cody in his vest, Jake wearing the U.S. Marshals badge, and a firefighter carrying a child to safety. The reporter had called Arnold's employer with questions, and she'd been told that Arnold was no longer employed at the company.

Somebody sent the news video to Arnold and he watched it on his phone. He turned and glared at the building, but Jake and Cody were gone.

His phone rang and he got a call from his boss. "Sorry, Dick, but the board voted to eliminate your position. Please come to the office, turn in your equipment and clear out your desk. You're fired."

CHAPTER 44

Jake and Cody walked to the Jeep and got inside. He sent a text to Terrell.

Jake: *Was that explosion related to the Stephens case?*

Terrell: *Yes, Beth and Rox found the IP address of the computer that sent you a weaponized sound.*

Jake: *I chased somebody who was flying through the air in a wingsuit, but they got away.*

Terrell: *That was the perp.*

Jake: *I'll send you a video from the Jeep's dash cam.*

Terrell: *Thanks.*

Jake: *Are Beth and Rox okay?*

Terrell: *Yeah. They almost got smoked but they're doing fine.*

Jake looked over at the smoldering building and shook his head. "This has to stop, and I'm going to do whatever it takes to end it."

Cody stuck his head between the front seats, put his paws on the center console and growled at the building.

Jake looked at the contacts on his phone and found a Russian woman he'd once dated, named Luba. He hadn't talked to her in a long while, not since she married a young millionaire who owned an internet startup funded by his rich dad.

Jake looked off into the distance, remembering the past, and he made the call.

Luba answered. "Jake, you promised you'd never call me again."

"I'm sorry, Luba. I'm not calling about … us. I need your advice regarding a problem."

"Girl trouble? Why am I not surprised?"

"No, Russian mafia trouble."

"Are you crazy? Stay far away from them. I should end this call right now."

"Wait. You and your family and friends are all such good people. Where did these violent gang members come from?"

"The *russkaya mafiya* here in San Francisco came from Russian prisons."

"Prisons?"

"Some time ago, the US government allowed Russians to apply for political refugee status and seek asylum. That's how my family made our way here—and we all work hard and pay our taxes. But someone in the KGB or FSB saw it as an opportunity to empty Russia's prisons and send their very worst criminals to the United States."

"Did all the criminals settle here in California?"

"No, but one particular gang chose San Francisco as their rendezvous point. The gossip on the street is that most of them are violent criminals who were serving long prison sentences for murder, rape, and assault."

"And now the Russian government doesn't have to spend money feeding them prison food for decades to come."

"All of my friends and family are afraid of the gang members. We avoid them like the plague."

"So, your community wouldn't be upset if the gang was put back in prison or run out of town?"

"No, we'd be thankful."

"Is there anybody I could talk to who might have useful information about how to make that happen?"

"No, Jake. Nobody will talk. It would be too dangerous for their loved ones."

"I understand."

"No, you don't, or you wouldn't be asking me these questions. Think of your family, and your dog."

"How did you know about my dog?"

"I don't remember. Maybe somebody mentioned it at church."

"The folks at your Russian Orthodox Church talk about me and my dog, huh?"

"I'm *afraid*, Jake. One of the *russkaya mafiya* who was in prison for murder now drives by my home every night and stares at my front window."

Jake's voice went cold. "Who is he? What's his name? Do you have his license plate?"

"No, Jake. Don't."

"Tell me, Luba."

"I have to go now. I've said too much."

"Say one more thing. I need a *name*."

"I can't."

"I'll put a camera on your building and get a video of him driving by. I'll find that man, no matter how long it takes, and then I'll—" Jake took an angry breath and let it out.

"Please don't ever call me again, Jake. You are my ... how do you say it? *Weakness*."

"Goodbye, Luba. Promise me you'll have a happy life."

"Bye, bye, Jacob." Luba started crying and she ended the call.

Jake looked off at the horizon. He thought about what might have been. Luba had wanted to marry a man with money. He hadn't been that man—yet. Her impatience had ended their promising relationship. He hoped she'd made the right choice when she married the dull guy with Daddy's cash, and he wished her all the best in life.

CHAPTER 45

A cargo van drove slowly past Sarah Chance's pet clinic, circled the block and drove by again. Two men sat in the front seats, and two more men and a woman sat on the floor in the empty cargo area.

The woman got to her feet in a crouch, looked out a window and studied the clinic as they passed by the second time. "Park over there. Let's do this."

The driver parked, and both men in the front seats double-checked their pistols.

~

Sarah sat at her desk, finishing up some paperwork. Her desk phone chimed and her assistant said, "I have a call for you from the law offices of Bart Bartholomew, on line two."

"Thank you, Madison." Sarah pressed a button. "This is Sarah Chance."

"Miss Chance, my name is Moon Hee and I'm calling on behalf of attorney Bart Bartholomew."

"I owe Bart a favor. How may I help?"

"Our client, Jake Wolfe, has updated his will and named you as guardian of his dog, Cody, in the unlikely event of his death."

Sarah paused for a moment. The thought of Jake being dead and Cody all alone was unsettling. "So, if Jake died, I'd adopt Cody?"

"Yes, you'd be named legal guardian. Do you accept this nomination as guardian, and the potential responsibility for the lifelong care of Cody? It's my duty to inform you that he's apparently a retired war dog who may have PTSD, behavioral challenges, and lingering war injuries to deal with."

"Yes, I accept. I also have a power-of-attorney form Jake signed regarding Cody."

"Could you please scan that form and email a copy to me, for Mr. Wolfe's file?"

"Yes, of course. I wish all my clients would provide for their pets in their wills."

"Well, Mr. Wolfe is an attorney, so I'm sure it's something he was taught in law school."

Sarah's brows furrowed. "No, Jake isn't an attorney. He's a photojournalist, or was until recently."

"Oh. I hope I didn't spoil a surprise. Well, it was nice talking with you, Sarah. Goodbye."

The call ended, and Sarah sat there thinking about Jake. If it were anyone else, she'd dismiss the idea that he might have become an attorney without ever letting on, but Jake was full of surprises. You just never knew what he might do.

"Speaking of surprises…" Sarah took her phone out of her purse and read Jake's text for the umpteenth time.

I think I might be falling in love with you too, girlfriend.

She shook her head, bewildered by men. The male species just didn't make any sense. One minute they would be an EUM —emotionally unavailable male, and the next moment, they might act self-aware and say something like this. Had Jake enjoyed a liquid lunch today? Was there going to be a full moon tonight?

Maybe she would change her mind, accept Jake's dinner invitation after all, and try to figure out what he was thinking.

She got up from her desk, grabbed her coat and purse, and walked into the front lobby. She set her purse on the counter and spoke to her assistant. "Okay, Madison, that's it for today. Let's get out of here."

"You're leaving work on time for once? Why? Do you have a date with that hot guy again?"

"I'm thinking about it, although I should probably go home, enjoy a glass of good wine, and go to bed early for some much-needed sleep."

"Oooh, is bad boy keeping you up late at night? Tell me all the sexy details."

"That's … not going to happen."

Madison laughed. "I'm sorry, but I just ended a relationship, so I'm hoping to live vicariously through yours."

Sarah shook her head. "I wouldn't exactly call it a relationship —not yet anyway."

"Is that what you're hoping for?"

"I don't know. My wish list for an ideal man would be a homeowner with a college degree and a secure job who wants a marriage and kids, likes salsa dancing, and is amazing in bed. Jake certainly qualifies for the last one, but none of the rest."

"Salsa dancing? Seriously?"

"What? I took a free lesson once, it was fun."

"Didn't you say he owned a condo?"

"He used to, but he put it up for sale when he broke up with his ex."

"Is he going to live on that boat full time, then? Would you ever consider living there?"

"Slow down. That talk is a long way off in the future. I have mixed feelings about Jake. Recently he answered a call from his ex-fiancée's mother. She wanted to tell him she was sorry he wouldn't be her son-in-law, and she had some questions about how to handle her daughter's rehab."

"Why would he care?"

"He told me he owed it to the mother. She was a good person."

"You don't think he still has feelings for his ex, do you?"

"I hope not. The call worried me, but it also warmed my heart at the same time. Jake is a walking contradiction. I never know what he might do next. Maybe that's part of the strange attraction I feel for him."

The television up in the corner of the waiting room was broadcasting the early evening news on low volume. Madison pointed at it. "Isn't that him on TV?"

Sarah looked at the television and saw photos of Jake being featured in a news segment. She grabbed the remote and turned up the volume.

The news report was by Dick Arnold. The headline said, "Rumors of foul play in wealthy realtor's mysterious death."

Arnold's breathless commentary provided lurid details as he showed a photo of Jake hugging the widow in front of a mansion. Another photo showed him carrying the widow's little boy and holding hands with the young daughter. A third photo was of Jake driving the dead husband's Porsche SUV. The last photo showed Lauren's white pants, green at the knees with grass stains. The subtitle asked why she'd been on her knees when Jake was there.

Arnold said that it all appeared very suspicious to neighbors and *unnamed sources*. "How did the husband die? Why was Jake Wolfe stepping into the man's shoes only hours after his death? Stay tuned for further details from our ongoing investigation to find the *truth*."

Sarah felt a headache coming on. She knew Dick Arnold had a grudge against Jake, and this was probably a smear campaign.

Yet it still made her heart ache to see Jake with his arms around another woman.

The photo of him with the kids struck a nerve. Did Jake want marriage and children? Was that what he'd look like if they had a family? Did she want kids, or was she content with the four-legged fur babies of her veterinary clinic?

Madison put her hand on Sarah's shoulder.

Sarah took a deep breath and said, "With Jake it's just one damned thing after another."

The clinic door opened, and a bell chimed as two men walked in. Madison turned to them and said, "I'm sorry, we're closed for the day, but the twenty-four-hour pet hospital is always open."

One of the men charged forward, backhanded Madison across the face and knocked her to the floor.

Sarah dropped her coat, reached into her purse, drew her pistol and aimed it at the man's chest. "Get out, now!"

The other man near the door was suddenly holding a pistol and pointing it at her. "Not so fast. We want your help with something, and we'll pay you a lot of money."

"I said get out. Do it!"

Madison staggered to her feet on trembling legs. The man who had hit her reached out and grabbed her arm. He pulled her close, held a knife to her throat and told Sarah, "Drop your weapon, or I'll kill your friend."

A voice came from inside of Sarah's purse, "Nine-one-one, what is your emergency?"

Sarah yelled, "Armed robbery, send the police!"

The man with the knife cursed. "Turn off that phone."

The other man with the pistol glanced at his accomplice for one second, and that's when Sarah shot him in the head. He fired his weapon as he fell backwards and died, shooting a hole in the ceiling.

The man with the knife turned and shoved Madison toward

Sarah, using her body as a human shield. He held the knife out in front of him and pointed it at Sarah as he moved toward her.

Sarah used her martial arts training as she evaded the sharp blade. She aimed her pistol and shot the assailant's foot. He cried out and charged again. Sarah sidestepped and tripped him, and then grabbed his knife hand by the wrist as he fell down.

Madison twisted out of the man's grasp and crawled away from him.

Sarah put her pistol against his shoulder and fired point-blank. He roared in pain and let go of the knife, and then kicked sideways at Sarah's legs, tripping her.

Sarah fell to the floor and landed hard, dropping her pistol.

Sarah and her opponent both got to their feet. Her assailant's right arm was hanging limp and useless, but he came at her with his one good arm raised, his left hand balled up in a fist and ready to break her jaw.

Sarah unleashed her most vicious attack of *Jeet Kune Do* martial arts. All of her training came to bear on this one life-or-death scenario, and she went for the kill.

Sarah deflected her opponent's attacks, using intercepting stop hits and blocking kicks. She punched him hard on the sternum and then kicked his knee. He roared and charged at her again, but she evaded his attack and delivered two wicked punches to his eyes. He threw his fist at her ribs, but she deflected it and hit him as hard as she could on his injured shoulder. He threw his head back and screamed in pain and Sarah used his throat as a punching bag, delivering multiple rapid hits with both of her fists. He went down on his knees, struggling to breathe, blinking his eyes in shock.

Sarah was about to deliver a knockout blow to her attacker's head when a woman appeared in the doorway wearing a thin black stretchy nylon mask. She fired a Taser, and Sarah fell to the floor, jerking and writhing in pain from the electric shock.

The injured man picked up his knife, crawled over to Sarah and raised the weapon above his head.

In a daze and unable to move, Sarah saw the knife and heard the woman say, "No, you fool."

Then came the sound of two suppressed rounds, and the man fell dead onto the floor.

Sarah was barely conscious when the masked woman picked her up and carried her over her shoulder to a waiting van that sped away into the night.

CHAPTER 46

Madison sat on the floor of the clinic with her back against the wall. She pulled her knees to her chest and wrapped her arms around them.

She was still sitting there, rocking back and forth and crying, when the police arrived.

Sirens and flashing lights filled the street in front of the clinic as SFPD black-and-white cars parked outside. Several uniformed cops came through the door with their guns drawn. They found Madison there with two dead bodies.

A female officer said, "Show me some ID. Are you the person who called 911?"

Madison shook her head. "No, Sarah called."

"Where is Sarah?"

"They took her away."

"Who took her?"

Madison pointed up at an upper corner of the room, near the ceiling, where a video camera was recording them. "It's all on video. Check the computer and you'll see everything."

"We have to search you now, and take you outside so we can secure the premises."

"I understand."

The female cop lifted Madison to her feet and searched her. "She's clean." She walked with Madison out the front door and onto the sidewalk. "I know it was all recorded on your office video cameras," the cop said. "But tell me what happened. I want your version."

Madison took a deep breath and let it out. "Two men came into the clinic. I told them we were closed. One of them hit me and knocked me down. He threatened to kill me unless Sarah did what they wanted."

"What did they want?"

"They never said exactly what it was, only that they'd pay a lot of money for it. Sarah shot one man in the head. That's legal self-defense, isn't it?"

"Yes, it's legal under castle doctrine law, if you have a reasonable fear of imminent death from armed intruders."

"The fear was more than reasonable—it was terrifying."

A male officer came outside. He wore blue nitrile gloves and held a phone in his hand that displayed a photo of Sarah. "One of those men had a photo of your boss on his phone—the same photo as the one on the wall in the clinic. He probably got it from your website. This wasn't a random robbery. You were targeted. Do you have any idea why?"

"No idea whatsoever," Madison said.

"Do you know this man?" He held out the phone again and displayed a different picture.

"Yes, my boss is dating him. His name is Jake Wolfe."

"What can you tell us about Mr. Wolfe?"

"Not much. Sarah's mentioned that he's best friends with a homicide cop. Terrell something. I don't remember the last name, though."

"The only cop I know named Terrell is Lieutenant Terrell Hayes. I'll give him a call."

"That's him," Madison said. "Were there any other photos on that phone? They didn't have my photo, did they?"

"No, just a dog."

"Wait—let me see the dog."

"What?"

"Let me see the dog!"

The officer held out the phone so she could see the picture.

When Madison recognized Cody, she started crying again. "I need to use Sarah's phone, so I can warn Jake about the threat to his dog."

The male officer said, "Sarah's phone is being tagged and bagged as evidence, but we'll let you borrow another phone in just a minute." He turned and walked away.

The female officer held out her phone. "Here, you can borrow mine to make the call."

"I don't know Jake's number. It's in Sarah's phone. Wait, it's also in the office computer. He's a client."

The officer escorted Madison back inside the clinic. Madison checked the computer and called Jake. She got his voicemail and left a rambling message. "Jake, it's Madison at the pet clinic. Sarah has been kidnapped! You and Cody are in danger. Armed men came into the clinic. Sarah shot one of them, but they Tasered her and took her away. Their phones had pictures of Sarah, and of you and Cody. The police are here and I'm safe. Make sure you and Cody are safe too. Please, Jake, don't let anything happen to Sarah or Cody!"

Sarah felt groggy from the aftereffects of the Taser. Her head was spinning, but she was aware of being on the floor of a cargo van that was driving and taking turns. Her hands and feet were tied. A woman wearing a black nylon mask stood over Sarah with her head bent to avoid the van's ceiling. "Hello, Sarah. Soon you're going to wish you had never met Jake Wolfe."

"You're the one who's going to regret this," Sarah said. She kicked her legs toward the woman's ankles as hard as she could.

The woman fell down and hit her head. She cursed in pain and used a shock baton to knock Sarah unconscious again.

She gave orders to an accomplice. "Sarah killed a member of our team tonight. Give her combat-level security."

A man with a short, thick neck and symbols tattooed all over his hands said, "You're afraid of this little woman?"

"Not afraid, just well aware that she could kick your ass with one hand tied behind her back and never even break a sweat."

"I don't think so."

"Well, I don't pay you to think, do I? You have two choices: obey my orders, or die." She drew a pistol and pointed it at his forehead.

"No problem. You're paying, so it's your party."

"Keep that in mind. Don't forget it."

They drove to a huge house and parked inside one of the three garages. The man with the thick neck carried Sarah to a room, put her on a bed, and tied her hands to the headboard posts with rope. He smiled as he gazed at her unconscious and helpless body. Picking up a piece of leftover rope, he wound some of it around each of his fists, leaving enough in between to strangle Sarah.

As he reached for Sarah's throat, the door opened behind him, and the masked woman entered the room. "I warned you about this."

He snarled at her. "Get out. She killed my friend."

"You're a liability." She drew a pistol with a suppressor attached and shot him three times in the heart. He dropped dead to the floor. She checked to make sure Sarah was breathing and the ropes weren't cutting off the blood flow to her hands.

"My apologies, Sarah. This will be over just as soon as your boyfriend is dead. The problem is, the stubborn man refuses to die." She walked out of the room and closed the door behind her, leaving the body on the floor.

A few minutes later, Sarah woke up and looked around. She found her hands tied to a bed, and there was a man on the floor with blood on his chest.

She clenched her teeth to stop herself from screaming, and frantically rocked the bed from head to foot, trying to break the headboard apart from the bed frame.

CHAPTER 47

After giving Wilson a ride to HQ, Terrell's police radio crackled and the dispatcher said there had been a murder/kidnapping at Sarah Chance's pet clinic. Sarah had been abducted.

Terrell turned on the lights and siren, stomped on the gas pedal, and raced toward Sarah's clinic. He called Jake as he drove.

Jake answered. "Did you find the heroin warehouse yet?"

"They've kidnapped Sarah. I'm on my way to her clinic."

Jake cursed at the top of his lungs. "Did they leave a ransom note?"

"No, but they must think you have the thumb drive."

"That's my fault. I told them I had it. Now they'll want me to trade it for Sarah."

"Maybe Rox can make a self-destructing copy for you if it comes to that."

"Ask her to make a fake copy, loaded with killer spyware, malware and viruses."

"We'll get Sarah back unharmed, I promise. The entire SFPD will be looking for her."

"Thanks, but I'm going to formally ask Anselmo Amborgetti to have everybody in the Family searching the streets," Jake said.

"Oh man, that could turn violent really quick," Terrell said.

"Yeah, whoever grabbed Sarah has no idea of the hornet's nest they've kicked. Debts have to be paid. It's a matter of honor, respect, and retribution."

"Jake, listen to what you're saying. People might die, and others could go to prison. You don't want to do either of those things."

"Those evil dirtbags kidnapped my girl. I'll stop at nothing until I know she's safe, and they're … not."

Terrell popped two ibuprofen pills in his mouth and drank some bottled water. "I don't suppose you could talk the Amborgetti Family into holding off on their vendetta until our cops have a chance to do their jobs."

"No, just the opposite. Sorry, but they'll want to get there before you do and end this the old-fashioned way. They have to send a message demanding respect. Otherwise they could appear weak and lose control of their financial interests."

"I guess the only good news is that they'll probably find Sarah faster than we can."

"You're right. Cops threaten people with jail, but the Family offers people the choice between a large cash payday or a painful death."

"I can't beat that offer. What are you going to do?"

"I'm going to work on the painful death part of the equation."

Terrell cursed. He arrived at the clinic just as Jake drove up.

They went inside and Cody searched back and forth, growling. The fur on the back of his neck stood up. He found Sarah's coat on the floor, sniffed it and barked several times.

Jake wore the U.S. Marshals badge around his neck on a lanyard. He and Cody went into Sarah's office. Jake tapped on her computer, scrolled through the recent video and watched Sarah fighting the criminals. "That's my girl." When a slender person in a mask ran into the clinic and stunned Sarah, Jake felt a tingling at the back of his neck.

He sent a copy of the video to his phone, and to Terrell and Anselmo. "Let's go, Cody." They walked out of the clinic, got into the Jeep and drove away.

His phone buzzed with a call from Terrell. Jake thumbed the answer icon. "Don't try to talk me out of it."

"Listen, if you and the Family find yourselves in a situation, call me and I'll send the cavalry," Terrell said. "No questions asked."

"Thanks, but the situation I'm thinking of involves me killing some foreign gang members who should have stayed home in their own crappy, corrupt nation instead of coming here to screw with American veterans."

Jake heard Terrell take a long breath and exhale. "I didn't hear that. Your call is breaking up. Semper Fi, Jukebox."

Jake closed his eyes for a moment and remembered battles from his past, in foreign lands, where he and Terrell had fought side by side. "Semper Fi, Grinds ... my brother."

Jake opened the center console, took out his KA-BAR knife and small-of-the-back SOB sheath, and attached it horizontally to his belt behind his waist. It was time to go hunting.

He called Anselmo and told him that his girlfriend had been taken hostage. She'd put up a fight and had shot a man. Jake texted him photos of Sarah.

Anselmo started cursing in Italian about how he would kill the *bastardo* who had given the order. He switched back to English and said, "I'll put everybody in the city on this. We'll get her back—I swear. Whoever took her is a dead man."

Jake drove through the streets of the city, intent on finding the people who'd kidnapped his girlfriend—so he could kill them with extreme prejudice.

CHAPTER 48

Anselmo arrived at the restaurant, stormed inside, and went to his private soundproof office in the back. He used a secure phone and began making calls and giving orders. People all over San Francisco would soon be looking for Sarah, or anybody who might be holding a woman against her will. He said to spread the word that the Family was offering a large reward for Sarah's safe return—no questions asked.

There was another reward for killing whoever had taken Sarah. Those kidnappers had a contract out on them. Anselmo invoked the dangerous word *vendetta*—the ancient Italian word for vengeance and a blood feud.

This could start a war against another organization, but he was willing to wipe them off the map if need be.

All across San Francisco, Italian men answered their phones and then packed their briefcases with weapons. They kissed their wives and girlfriends goodbye and drove through the city, searching for someone who was now under the protection of the Family.

A number of women answered the call as well. They had an

advantage because many people were clueless that they might be "connected," and be incredibly dangerous individuals.

One of the women was tall, with a toned body from working out at the gym. She was nicknamed "Razor," because she'd once posed as a barber and had slit the throat of a targeted man while giving him a shave. She'd killed nineteen enemies of the Family so far and was hoping to make it an even twenty soon.

The word was soon out on the street. Cash money was being paid to waiters, taxi drivers, doormen and security guards to keep watch for anything suspicious and to report it immediately.

The secret orders were that you were to bring this woman back alive and kill anybody who stood in your way. You would be rewarded and protected. If you died in the line of duty, your loved ones would be taken care of. Failure was not an option. This was a matter of *honor*.

As the sun was setting, phone calls started coming in to unlisted numbers. A taxi driver had seen something suspicious. A hotel maid had heard a woman yelling in a room. A security guard had noticed a questionable van driving into his building's garage.

A tip was privately reported to a policewoman named Tammi Martinelli, who secretly belonged to the Family. She parked her SFPD black-and-white in front of a run-down apartment building and went inside on an unofficial visit. The sight of a uniformed police officer caused several loiterers to scatter. Tammi walked along a hallway and heard a woman cry out. There was a loud noise, as if something had hit a wall, and then silence.

She put on nitrile gloves and knocked on a door.

A man answered, wearing a wife-beater t-shirt and an angry scowl. "Get out of here. You hassle me and you'll be sorry." He slammed the door.

The door hit Martinelli's black boot and stopped. She then

shoved the door as hard as she could and sent the drunken man sprawling backwards onto the floor.

Martinelli entered the apartment, closed the door behind her, and drew her pistol. "You assaulted a police officer. Stay on the floor, lie facedown, and put your hands behind your head. You're under arrest."

The man sneered at her and got to his feet. "Thanks for coming inside. Now I can destroy your face, and it's all legal." He pulled a heavy leather glove out of his back pocket and put it on his right hand.

Martinelli recognized that instrument of pain. It was an illegal sap glove, filled with tiny metal beads. When it hit you, it felt like a lead weight. She glanced at the woman and saw a face that had been beaten by this glove many times. The woman's nose looked like it had been broken more than once. Martinelli felt her heartburn beginning to churn. She spoke to the wife.

"Does this man physically abuse you? Tell the truth, and I'll protect you. This is your one and only chance to put a stop to it. Be brave. Stand up for yourself."

The wife wrung her hands, finding the courage to speak. "Yes, and he said if I tell anyone, he'll kill my children." She began to cry, feeling something she hadn't felt in years—hope.

Martinelli raised her chin, looked down her nose at the man, and purposely baited him. "Bring it, dirtbag. Try to punch me with your special girl-hitting glove. Show me what you've got, loser."

The man's eyes sparkled with violent hatred. He flexed his muscles. "Holster your pistol, unless you're afraid of me."

Martinelli holstered her pistol and held her hands out by her sides as she egged him on. "You're a loser, a punk, and a bully who likes to abuse people. Go ahead; I dare you to try taking on someone your own size. I'll kick your ass down the street and back."

He gave her an evil smile, licked his lips, and came at her like a bull charging a matador. He swung his gloved fist at her head and put his entire body weight into it.

Martinelli waited until he was totally committed, then stepped aside and kicked him hard in the shin.

He flew headlong and smacked his face into the hardwood floor.

Standing on the balls of her feet, Martinelli motioned for him to come at her again.

He got to his knees, shook his head, and turned on her with an animal-like snarl.

The wife put her hand over her mouth and moaned in fear, as if she'd seen this look on his face so many painful times before.

He grabbed a ballpoint pen off a coffee table, and said to Martinelli, "I'm going to shove this into your heart." He ran at her with the pen protruding between the two middle fingers of his gloved fist.

Martinelli drew a small untraceable pistol from inside her coat and shot him three times in the chest. He staggered on his feet but somehow kept on coming at her. She then shot him in the thigh. He dropped to the floor and screamed profanity as he began bleeding to death.

Martinelli asked the wife, "Should we call an ambulance? Are you heartbroken, or thankful that he's dying?"

The woman began crying and crossed herself. "I thank Jesus, Mary, and Joseph for answering my prayers. Please shoot him in the head to make sure he's dead."

"*You* have to shoot him," Martinelli said. She put the small pistol into the woman's trembling hands, and helped her aim and squeeze the trigger.

The wife sobbed as she shot her abusive husband. The look on her face was of both shock and relief.

Martinelli took the pistol away from her and dropped it on the carpet. "Your statement will be that you had to shoot him in self-defense—with his own pistol that you found in his sock drawer. I witnessed you do it."

"Oh my God. I'm not good at lying."

"I'll be the one who takes your statement, and I'll act as your witness. But you can never speak of what really happened here. Understood?"

"I overheard two young men say that your organization was searching for a missing woman named Sarah. You thought I might be her, didn't you?"

Martinelli looked her in the eye. "Do you know who you're dealing with?"

"Yes, and I'm in your debt. Thank you. If I can ever repay the Family, just tell me what to do."

Martinelli gave the woman some cash and called an unlisted number. "This is Razor. I had a situation. It wasn't the package we're looking for. I need another cop to corroborate my report." She recited the address.

An Italian woman said, "We only have one other police asset in San Francisco—the SFPD is nearly impossible to infiltrate, but he's in your area and I'll send him to your location. ETA five minutes."

CHAPTER 49

Sarah's wrists hurt from the rope cutting into her skin. She ignored the pain and continued to quietly rock the bed until the headboard finally came loose. The metal bed frame collapsed with her weight on top of it. She was relieved that it landed with a quiet thud onto unseen items that were stored under the bed.

Her heart was beating fast as she got off the mattress and carried the headboard with her and squatted down to search the dead man. She found a knife in his pocket and used it to cut the ropes off her wrists, then set the headboard aside, closed the knife, and put it in her pocket.

She continued her search of the body and found a pistol in a small-of-the-back holster. The dead man had a wad of bills in his left front pants pocket. She took that too. There was a card in his wallet with some phone numbers jotted on the back. She put that in her pocket with the cash. Next, she searched his jacket and found his phone. She dialed 911, and when the operator answered, she whispered, "This is Sarah Chance. Send the police —murder—kidnapping." She left the call open, put the speaker on mute, and shoved it into her back pocket.

She checked the pistol to be sure it was loaded, and took a

deep breath. Now she was ready to attempt an escape, but she had no idea what she might be up against on her way out. She walked to the door with pistol in hand, turned off the light switch, quietly opened the door, and peeked out into the hallway.

A tall, muscular man with broad shoulders stood in the hall at the top of a stairway. His shaved head slowly turned in her direction.

Sarah was faced with a fight-or-flight decision. There was a window to her right at the end of the hall. It was dark outside but she could see a tree close to the house. Maybe she could climb down the tree. But if she ran for the window her odds of being shot in the back were high, unless she took out the guard first.

She sprinted down the hallway toward the guard. Alerted by her footsteps, he reached for his pistol. Sarah leapt in the air and kicked him in the throat, silencing any cry of alarm.

The man grunted in pain. Sarah then kicked him hard on his right knee, hyperextending it sideways and causing a sickening *crunch* sound. The man started to scream, but Sarah kicked him in the throat again, with all of her body weight behind it. He crumpled and fell down the stairs, noisily rolling head over heels and landing at the corner of the stairway.

There was commotion from below and someone called out in another language. Sarah lay down on the carpet at the top of the stairs, aimed her pistol, and listened to the footsteps coming across the hardwood floor below. Feet thumped on the stairs, and moments later a man came striding around the corner. Sarah shot him in the chest and the head.

She jumped to her feet, ran and opened the window, ripped through the screen and climbed onto the windowsill.

More footsteps pounded up the stairs. She took a deep breath and jumped out the window into the night air.

A shot rang out in the hallway. Window glass shattered

behind her, but the round missed; she was already flying down and forward toward the tree. She landed on a bushy branch and desperately grabbed onto it with her arms and legs.

The branch bent but held her weight and she crawled along it toward the tree trunk. Hidden behind the leaves, she shimmied down. Another round zinged from the window and thunked into the tree trunk a few feet above her. She guessed the shooter would work his way down, so she scrambled around to the backside of the tree.

Rounds chewed up the bark in the spot where she'd been just moments before. One came so close it tugged at the hem of her pant leg. She kept going down the tree as fast as she could, desperately trying to keep her grip and avoid falling.

Below her, a door of the house opened and closed with a slam. Somebody was running and cursing in what sounded like Russian. Sarah drew the pistol out of her pocket and stuck it into her front waistband. When she reached the bottom branches of the tree, she held on with both hands, lowered her legs, and then dropped the last few feet to the grass.

A man came running toward her. She stepped behind the tree trunk and drew her pistol, then peeked out from the side. When the man got close, she fired three rounds at him. One found its target, and he spun sideways from the impact to his shoulder, causing him to trip and fall.

Sarah made a dash toward a stone wall. Shouts came from several directions and she was suddenly surrounded by half a dozen armed men.

One of them aimed a rifle at her face. "Drop the gun."

Sarah tossed the pistol onto the lawn.

The man called out, "*Idi syuda*, Elena!"

A woman approached, with a Taser in her hand. "Hello, Sarah. That was an impressive escape attempt."

"So, your name is Elena. Was that man speaking Russian?"

"You're a clever girl, and he's an idiot. Now, lie down and put your hands behind your back, or I'll have to stun you again." Elena aimed the Taser at Sarah.

Sarah crossed her arms. "If you stun me, it means you're a weak coward who can't fight a woman."

Elena sneered at Sarah and yelled, "Take her!"

Four large men pounced on Sarah and held her down. She was pinned by over eight hundred pounds of solid muscle and one of the men held a knife to her throat. "Which body part do you want me to cut off first?"

Police sirens sounded, causing a flurry of movement.

"Evacuate and meet at the rendezvous," Elena said.

Someone put a black bag over Sarah's head, and handcuffed her hands and feet. A man picked her up and carried her over his shoulders, jogging to a car and tossing her in the backseat like a bag of potatoes.

One of the men's voices sounded different from the rest. He spoke with a British accent. "I was favorably impressed by your display of violence, Sarah. But if you try anything like that again, I'll wring your neck like a chicken meant for the soup pot. Is that understood, my dear?"

CHAPTER 50

Jake arrived at the Amborgetti's restaurant and was met by Vito. They went down a hallway to Anselmo's office in the back.

A powerfully built man guarding the door gave Jake an assessing once-over, but when he saw Cody snarling at him, he dialed it back.

Vito sent a text message, and Anselmo called out in Italian from inside the office. The guard opened the door with a look of relief and Jake and Cody stepped inside. Vito followed them in and closed the door.

"Have a seat, Jake," Anselmo said, gesturing at a chair. "We're about to get a visitor who claims to know something useful."

Moments later, a man was escorted into the office. He got down on one knee and put his right fist over his heart. "Don Amborgetti, it's an honor to serve you."

"Thank you for your respect," Anselmo said. "Take a seat and tell me what you know."

The man sat up straight in a leather-upholstered chair. "Recently the boss of a Russian gang asked me to work as a truck driver. I would take deliveries to and from a warehouse for high pay in cash, but if I ever spoke of it, I'd be dead by sundown. I inquired about the cargo, but he refused to tell me. I asked him to promise me it would not be hard drugs or human trafficking, but he wouldn't promise, so I turned him down."

"You did the right thing. Who is this man? Where can we find him?"

"His name is Pavel. He owns a dance club in SoMa." He recited the address, and texted a photo of Pavel to Anselmo's phone. "I asked around and heard rumors he's dealing in heroin and has a new partner in crime, a woman named Elena."

"Thank you," Anselmo said. "I owe you a favor now. I'll be in touch."

The man nodded and left the room, closing the door behind him.

Anselmo texted the photo to Jake.

Getting up from his chair, Jake studied the photo. "I'll go have a talk with Pavel."

"Take Vito with you," Anselmo said.

"No, Cody and I will handle Pavel alone."

Anselmo noted the look on Jake's face. "Understood, everyone else will steer clear of Pavel. How can I be of assistance?"

"I could use an untraceable pistol, with a suppressor."

Anselmo got up and went to a file cabinet, unlocked a drawer, removed a shoe box, and handed it to Jake. "That's a nine with a silencer and two extra mags, no registration."

"After I deal with Pavel, I'll need help with the warehouse."

"What kind of help?"

"I'll need a large flatbed truck loaded with a twenty-foot shipping container. Plus half a dozen steel road plates that are one inch thick, four feet wide and eight feet long. And a metal fabrication shop that can start welding the plates immediately." Jake drew a rough sketch on a piece of paper.

Anselmo looked at the drawing and nodded. "I'll get people working on it right now. Anything else?"

"Once I deal with Pavel, and the truck is ready, I could use a dozen of your best soldiers, armed with assault rifles. You'll all be handsomely rewarded, in cash, if you don't get killed."

Anselmo looked skeptical. "Did you fall into a pile of Benjamins, or do you have a reason to believe there might be money at the warehouse?"

"I have a strong hunch about a large amount of money and where to find it. If you help me, we can split it fifty-fifty. Are you in? I can do this alone, but I'd be forever grateful if you'd help me wipe out this drug ring."

"I'm in. My people will assist you in any way they can. On one condition—you have to take the *omertà*."

"The oath of secrecy? If I have to, I will," Jake said. For years he'd carefully avoided getting too deeply involved with the Family, but now he felt he had no choice.

"It's non-negotiable if you want the Family's help with what you have in mind."

"Fair enough. If I'm right about my hunch, you'll be a far richer man after tonight." Jake described how he wanted the welding done and explained the plan of attack on the warehouse.

Anselmo nodded. "That might actually work, but I never thought I'd see you planning a heist."

"My plan is to stop the heroin dealers, take their money, give their drug supply to the cops, and make sure the gang members are all arrested or..."

"Arrested, or put out of business permanently."

Jake nodded. "Have you bailed out any Russian criminals lately who skipped?"

"Yes, I have one guy," Anselmo said.

"Assign me as your designated bail recovery agent for him. That way I have legal jurisdiction to investigate any Russian in town, and I can do the breaking and entering and all that quasi-legal bounty hunter stuff."

Anselmo tapped on his computer keyboard and pointed at the display. "I sent this to your phone. Sign it."

Jake tapped his phone. "Done."

"You are now authorized and contracted to investigate, surveil, locate, and arrest the bail fugitive," Anselmo said, reciting from memory.

Vito said, "Jake, the oath keeper is here. Anselmo and I will be your witnesses to the *omertà*."

There was a knock on the door and Vito opened it, letting in an older man, bent with age. The man carried an ornately carved wooden box, the size of a loaf of bread.

Anselmo stood and paid the man respect, speaking to him in Italian.

The man set the box onto Anselmo's desk, opened the lid, reached his arthritic hands inside and removed a knife, a candle, a sheet of parchment paper and a black fountain pen. He stared at Jake with dark eyes. "Read the oath out loud, and then sign your name at the bottom."

Jake read the ancient words that were first spoken in nineteenth century Sicily, and passed down from generation to generation. When he was done speaking, he signed his name with the fountain pen.

The oath keeper picked up the knife, held the tip against his thumb and nodded at Jake.

Jake accepted the knife, pricked his thumb with the sharp tip, and pressed his bloody thumbprint onto the oath he'd signed.

Anselmo picked up the parchment and read it. He nodded and handed it to Vito, who studied it and handed it back to the oath keeper.

The oath keeper lit the candle, stared at the paper for a minute and then held it over the flame. The paper caught fire and he held on until it was ready to burn his fingers, then dropped it into an empty metal trash can.

"Welcome to the Family," Anselmo said.

Jake nodded. "Thank you. Get to work on that truck." He left the restaurant along with Cody.

Anselmo picked up the phone and began giving orders.

CHAPTER 51

Jake drove to the dance club and saw a long line of people in front, waiting to get inside. He stopped for a moment and observed the club doors opening and closing as people went in and out. Loud music was thumping and flashes of a synchronized rainbow of colors from spotlights and neon-tube lighting spilled from the doors each time they were opened.

Jake drove on past, went around the corner, and parked in an alley behind the club. He and Cody walked to a back door.

A guard was selling drugs to a woman. She handed him cash and he gave her an envelope. When the guard saw the furious look on Jake's face and his hand reaching for a weapon, he fired a suppressed pistol at Jake, missing him.

Jake shot him in the right shoulder. The man jerked sideways and dropped his pistol. Jake slammed the butt of his pistol into the man's head, knocking him out. He dragged the unconscious guard behind a dumpster, and found a key on a lanyard around his neck.

The woman stared at Jake in fear, like a deer caught in the headlights. He pointed toward the street. "Go home. Never come here again."

She ran away and didn't look back.

Jake used the Guard's key to open the door. He and Cody went down the hallway, finding a private elevator with a lock. The key opened the elevator, and they stepped inside. There was only one button—the penthouse.

He pressed the button and the elevator rose to the top floor. When the doors opened, Jake came out with his pistol up and ready to fire.

An armed guard charged at him, drawing his pistol. "You're dead."

Jake shot the guard in the head and then shot Pavel in the shoulder. "Where have you taken Sarah Chance? To the warehouse?" Jake said.

Pavel held his injured shoulder, gritted his teeth and sneered. "I know who you are. I'll have your family and friends killed."

Jake shot Pavel's left foot.

Pavel cried out, cursing.

"That was the wrong answer. Where is Sarah? Give me the address." Jake said.

"Speaking of girlfriends—I know where your former girlfriend, Luba, lives. I drive past her place every night. After I make her mine, I'll kill her along with Sarah, your mother and father and your dog."

Jake's face darkened. He shot Pavel in the left kneecap. Pavel fell off the chair, landing on his butt on the floor, screaming in pain. He took ragged breaths. "If I tell you where they've taken Sarah, they'll kill me." He gestured at the window and the city lights, then pulled off his belt and used it as a tourniquet on his leg.

"You have it backwards. If you *don't* tell me, *I'll* kill you. But first, I'll order my dog to rip chunks out of your face with his teeth. One of your men will talk—one who's smarter than you and wants to live."

Pavel hesitated. He put his hand on the desktop and tried to pull himself up. Jake shot his hand, and Pavel cried out in agony.

"The next shot is to your crotch." Jake fired a round into the floor between Pavel's legs, barely missing his body.

Pavel's face went pale. "You're a psychopath!"

"Desperate times call for desperate measures," Jake said. He held up his phone and displayed a video. "Does this warehouse look familiar? There *you* are, committing murder. Tell me the address, or I'll send this video to the police."

"Okay, you win. I'll make a deal. Yes, Sarah is at the warehouse. If you let me go, I'll tell you the address, and then I'll leave town and never come back."

"You've got a deal, but the next words out of your mouth had better be the address."

Cody barked and snapped his teeth.

Pavel started to say something, but looked at Cody and stopped. He glanced out the window and shook his head. "The warehouse is on Selby Street, underneath the Embarcadero Freeway overpass." He recited the address.

Jake held up his phone again and showed a photo of his friend, Stuart. "Do you know this man?"

"I can't help it if that loser bought heroin from me, until he overdosed on a bad batch." Pavel's right hand reached for his ankle, drew a small pistol and fired it at Jake with a shaking hand.

The bullet missed Jake, and he fired at the same moment, hitting Pavel in the forehead.

Cody growled, and looked at Jake for orders.

Jake took a deep breath and let it out. "Sorry, Cody, but he was going to kill both of us. He's the man responsible for Stuart's death. I've been looking for him." Jake had always felt partially responsible for Stuart's death too. On that fateful night, Jake had been at a club. The pounding music had been so loud that he'd missed a call from Stuart. Later that night, Stuart had been found dead from a heroin overdose. Jake blamed himself for not answering Stuart's call in his time of need. Perhaps now, with the heroin dealer dead, he could find some peace from the heartache.

Cody lifted his leg and peed on the dead criminal.

"Attaboy." Jake looked around and found Pavel's mobile phone on the desk. It was locked with a Touch ID fingerprint sensor, so he used the dead man's thumb to open it.

"Maybe I'll mail this phone to Roxanne, with no return address." Jake put the phone into a plastic zip-top bag, along with the pistol he'd used to kill Pavel. "Now let's go find the warehouse and finish this once and for all."

They exited the building and got into the Jeep. As Jake drove off he saw the guard wake up, get to his feet and stumble toward the building while looking at Jake and yelling into his phone.

Jake took an evasive route in case some of Pavel's gang might come after him. His phone buzzed with a call from Anselmo. He thumbed the answer icon. "Update?"

"The plates are welded onto the truck; I had a group working on it," Anselmo said. "The shooters you asked for are standing by. Just give the order and they'll go into action."

"Let's do this." Jake recited the address of the warehouse and gave further details.

"You're a crazy SOB."

"You say that like it's a bad thing."

CHAPTER 52

Jake drove to the warehouse and parked nearby on a side street. He reached into his pack for dog equipment and outfitted Cody with a K-9 Storm Intruder vest—a Kevlar-lined tactical flak jacket with integrated camera and communication system.

He strapped it onto Cody and adjusted a wire that stood up from the dog collar like a little periscope. There was a tiny camera on the end that could see and hear whatever Cody saw and heard. The feed was sent to Jake's phone. A similar wire extended next to Cody's left ear, with a speaker on the end that gave Jake a way to speak commands to his partner and hear his response. The vest was also equipped with a bright flashlight, but Jake didn't turn it on.

He put an earbud into his ear and spoke softly. "Can you hear me, Cody?"

Cody nodded his head.

"Let's go. Quiet, now."

Jake gave a command. Cody ran toward the warehouse in stealth mode, keeping to the shadows.

Jake followed, doing his best to stay out of sight. He sent a text to Vito, who was driving the container truck.

In position?
Vito replied, *Yes.*
Stand by. We're going in.

≈

Cody ran down an alley along the left side of the building and found a closed door. Next to it was a window that was open a few inches. He got on his hind legs and sniffed the draft of air coming out of the window.

There was a row of fifty-gallon drums below the window. Cody leapt up onto the drums, walked quietly along the top of them, looked in the window and tasted more of the air from inside.

He smelled all kinds of things: rats, gun oil, ammunition, foreign foods, numerous men, and … Sarah.

≈

Jake saw on his phone display what Cody was seeing—the alley, the drums, the windows—and an empty hallway inside. He whispered, "Cody, do you smell Sarah?"

Cody nodded. The camera feed on Jake's phone moved up and down.

Jake's heartbeat increased as he caught up with Cody and tried the doorknob. It was locked so he climbed up on top of the row of drums behind his dog.

The casement window was hinged on one side and opened outward like a door. It was only open a few inches, but that was enough for Jake to reach inside, cut through the screen with his knife, and turn the crank until the window was fully open.

Jake whispered, "Cody, you're going in." He grabbed the handle on the back of Cody's vest, carefully lifted him through the window, and lowered him to the polished concrete floor. "Open, Cody. Open the door."

Cody turned the doorknob with his teeth. The lock button popped against his tongue as it unlocked.

Jake went inside and quietly closed the door behind him. He patted Cody on the back and whispered, "Search for Sarah. Search and *protect*."

Cody sniffed the air and the floor, making his way down the hall toward a stairway.

Jake followed behind and held his pistol up in front of him—ready to kill.

~

Upstairs in the main office, a man spoke to Elena. "Take a look at this security camera feed. A dog ran past a corner of the building and disappeared." He held out a tablet.

"Was it a stray dog, a pet, or a working dog?"

"It looked like a police dog, wearing some kind of electronic equipment."

Elena glared at the image and cursed. "That's Jake Wolfe's dog. We're about to be attacked. Give the order for battle stations. Secure all doors, and bring the hostage to my office."

Throughout the building, the lights blinked on and off repeatedly. People started running, grabbing assault rifles and taking defensive positions.

~

Jake heard people yelling, feet stomping and weapons being racked. He sent a text and alerted Vito. *They're onto us. Start the mission NOW. Go-go-go!*

Vito replied, *We're rolling. Impact in one minute.*

Cody continued down the hall, sniffing along the floor, and

then raising his head to smell the air. He climbed the stairway to the office area and began sniffing the carpeted hallway. He stopped at a door, smelling the doorknob and then the open space below the door. He turned to look at Jake.

Jake whispered. "Do you smell Sarah?"

Cody nodded once.

"I'm going to open the door. Be ready to *protect*."

Jake reached for the doorknob and quietly turned it.

Outside the warehouse, a flatbed truck carrying a shipping container arrived and backed up fast toward the metal roll-up door. The truck crashed into the door, tearing it off its mounting and sending it flying onto the floor. The truck screeched to a halt, then shifted gears and pulled out until only the back end was blocking the doorway.

Several men inside the warehouse fired automatic weapons at the back of the truck, but the rounds ricocheted off the one-inch-thick steel-plated doors and rear sides.

Ricocheting rounds zipped back and forth inside the warehouse. One man cried out in pain and went down.

As soon as the roll-up door was removed, Vito opened his driver's door of the truck cab and tossed three flash-bang grenades over the truck and into the warehouse. He closed the truck door, shut his eyes and put his hands over his ears.

There were three blinding flashes like lightning, and three loud bangs like thunder.

After the third explosion, the back doors of the shipping container opened and a dozen men jumped out, firing weapons and killing the enemy gang.

A hallway door opened and several more gang members ran into the area firing weapons. There was another gun battle and the Italians killed everyone. Three of their own men were shot.

They were helped outside and into one of the many cars that were arriving and then driven to a highly paid doctor who didn't ask questions.

Vito gave orders. One of the men got into a forklift, picked up a pallet of shrink-wrapped packs of bottled water, and loaded it into the shipping container. He continued working, loading three more pallets.

Shooters stood guard with their weapons ready. Nobody went toward the pallets stacked with kilos of heroin. The order was that if you tried to take it, you'd be killed and you'd bring dishonor upon your loved ones.

Jake observed Cody as he heard explosions and weapons fire and smelled gunpowder. Cody let out a low growl and his right rear leg trembled.

Jake patted him on the back. "Easy, now." He opened the office door, raised his pistol, and entered what appeared to be a meeting room. There wasn't anyone in the room, only a long conference table with chairs around it.

The wall at the front of the room displayed a battle plan and a collage of intel. There were photos of SFPD Police Chief Pierce and his wife, Joyce, and their kids, a map with their street address, and pictures from real estate websites showing the interior of their house. A few images showed the kids getting out of a car at school.

There was an assortment of additional photos and maps targeting other law enforcement officers and city officials. Jake also saw sections that profiled Beth, Roxanne, Terrell and Alicia, as well as Sarah, Cody, himself and the *Far Niente*.

Jake cursed and used his phone to take photos of the wall.

Cody sniffed a closet door, alerted and sat down in front of it.

Jake opened the door and saw a collection of assault rifles, including AK-47's, AR-15s, and lots of ammo.

"Leave it," Jake said

Cody continued sniffing the room. He stopped at a chair, then whined and pawed at it.

On the floor near the legs of the chair, Jake saw two zip ties that had been cut apart. "Was Sarah here?"

Cody nodded. His nostrils flared, and the fur on the back of his neck bristled.

Jake turned toward the door. "Find Sarah, Cody. Seek-seek-seek!"

Cody went out of the room and down the hall, with Jake following close behind him.

～

Sarah was being force-marched to the main office, with her hands bound behind her back.

A powerfully built Russian man held a tight grip on her upper arm as he presented her to Elena.

Sarah watched as Elena talked on her cell phone. She overheard part of the conversation and it sent chills down her spine.

Elena ended the call, set down her phone and picked up a pistol. She told the man, "Bring that chair over here and tie her to it."

The man let go of Sarah and walked toward a heavy wooden chair that sat against the wall.

The moment the man's back was turned, Sarah attacked Elena with a fierce kick to the throat.

Elena fired the pistol as she fell to her knees, choking and gasping for air.

The shot missed, and Sarah kicked Elena's hand, making the pistol fly onto the floor.

The big man turned and came at Sarah, swinging his fist. She dodged the attack, kicking him in the knee and hyperextending it backwards. The man screamed and fell down.

There were knives and stun weapons on a desk. Sarah turned her back, picked up a knife with her bound hands, and frantically cut off the zip tie from her wrists. She dropped the knife on the carpet and grabbed a stun baton, shocking the injured man as he crawled toward her.

Sarah heard her martial arts instructor's voice in her head, saying, *Once you get the enemy down, make sure he stays down. No mercy—your life depends on it.* She held the shock device against the back of her opponent's neck until he collapsed, dazed and temporarily paralyzed. She then raised the stun baton above her and brought it down hard, striking a blow to the back of his head and knocking him unconscious.

Elena staggered to her feet, gasping for breath. She ran and crashed into Sarah, knocking her down and sending the stun baton flying out of her hand.

They got to their feet and Elena began fighting with some kind of martial arts Sarah had never seen before.

The two women circled each other, punching and kicking at every opportunity.

Sarah threw one kick too high, leaving herself vulnerable for a second, and Elena leaped forward and head-butted her. Sarah saw stars but struck back with all of her fury and landed a hard blow on Elena's face.

Blood sprung from Elena's nose. She tasted it on her lips and gave Sarah a cruel smile. "You've seen my blood, now let's see yours."

CHAPTER 53

Sarah tried a desperate gambit and threw herself onto Elena, wrestling her to the floor. They rolled on the carpet and fought for dominance.

Elena got lucky and came out on top. She started choking Sarah with both hands.

Sarah fought to get free, but black dots appeared in her vision as she gasped for oxygen. She used the last of her strength to throw a right jab to Elena's injured throat.

Elena gasped and lost her grip on Sarah. She grabbed the knife off the floor and held it over Sarah's chest. Her voice was hoarse. "I'm going to stab you in the heart; just like Wolfe did to the man I loved."

Sarah planted her feet on the floor and thrust her hips upward as hard as she could, twisting her body and rolling free. She grabbed the stun baton and shot Elena full of volts.

Elena writhed in agony, screaming as she got a taste of her own medicine.

~

Chairman Banks and Abhay entered the room from an adjoining office. "I'll get Elena's car keys, Abhay. You bring Sarah along for leverage … hurry!"

Abhay rushed toward Sarah, who held the shock baton up in front of her. His gaze took in Sarah with her weapon, Elena on the floor, and the unconscious man with the twisted knee. He drew a pistol and aimed it at Sarah. "Impressive effort. Now drop your weapon, turn around and put your hands behind your back, or I'll put a bullet in your head."

The door flew open and Jake and Cody appeared in the doorway. Jake saw Abhay aiming a pistol at Sarah and shot him three times in the chest, sending him staggering backwards and onto the floor.

Banks turned and ran for a door.

Jake said, "Get him, Cody!"

Cody rushed forward, got between Banks and the door, and bit down on the man's crotch, shaking his head back and forth.

Banks screamed in agony, and slapped at Cody's face with both hands. Cody let go and chomped down on Banks' right hand. Banks cried out and tried to run, but Cody pulled him down to the floor.

Banks fell facedown, and Cody sank his teeth into the man's left butt cheek. Banks cried out in pain and drew a small pistol out of his pocket. He rolled over and tried to aim the pistol at Cody with his injured hand. "Die, you filthy animal!"

Jake dove onto Banks, grabbing his hand and twisting it in another direction as the pistol went off and shot a hole in the wall. Jake head-butted Banks, removed the pistol from his grip, and then sat on his chest. He began punching him in the face, over and over. With each punch, he said a few words.

"This is for Stuart. And this is for Sarah. One for Lauren. One for Chrissy. One for Ben."

Cody barked at Jake and pushed his head against him.

Sarah said, "Jake, stop it—you'll kill him."

Jake took a deep breath, then raised his fist up high and said, "One more, for trying to shoot Cody." He brought his fist down and punched Banks in his side as hard as he could, breaking a rib. Banks grunted in pain and fainted.

Jake reached into his pocket for some zip ties, then rolled Banks over onto his stomach and bound his hands and feet.

He went toward Abhay, intent on tying him up next, but the man bolted up and ran for the door.

Jake said, "Cody, takedown!"

Cody ran and bit onto Abhay's thigh, wrestling him to the floor. Abhay got onto his hands and knees and Jake kicked him in the stomach like an NFL kicker going for a field goal. Abhay collapsed with the wind knocked out of him.

Jake put zip ties on Abhay's wrists and ankles, then bound the two together so he was hog-tied. He put a zip tie around the man's neck and then used a few more to bind his neck to his hands and feet.

"Bulletproof vest, huh?" Jake said.

Abhay groaned. "The best vest money can buy."

"Hold still while my dog guards you." Jake gave a command to Cody who stood near Abhay and snarled at his face.

Abhay closed his eyes, gritted his teeth and held still as he felt the dog's hot breath on his ear.

Jake went to Sarah and put his arms around her.

Sarah hugged him tight. "Thank God you found me, Jake." She clung to him, her body shaking now that she was free.

Jake took a deep, ragged breath and held onto her possessively, relieved that she was alive and well.

After a moment, he held her at arm's length. "Are you hurt? Do you need to go to the hospital?"

"No, I have a few bruises, but I just want to go home, soak in a hot bath and drink a glass of wine."

"I'll take you home right now."

"Jake, what was this all about? That woman said you killed

the man she loved. I overheard her talking about using the millions in his offshore bank accounts to wage war on the police."

Jake's eyes got dark. He glanced around and saw a purse on a desk. "Sarah, can you check Cody to make sure he hasn't been injured?"

"Yes, of course." Sarah got down on one knee and gave Cody a quick checkup.

While Sarah was preoccupied, Jake put on gloves, opened the purse, and found Elena's wallet and phone. He put her phone in one of his coat pockets, then reached into another and took out a plastic bag that held Pavel's phone and the pistol Jake had shot him with. He opened the bag and dumped the phone and pistol into Elena's purse.

In the hallway, Vito said, "Jake, it's Vito. I'm coming into the room—just me, nobody else." He added a few code words in Italian.

Jake stepped in between Sarah and the door, drawing his pistol.

Cody turned and watched the door, ready to fight.

Vito entered the room alone and looked around at the captured prisoners. He nodded at Jake. "You've been busy."

Jake lowered his weapon. "Sitrep?"

"All targets are down. The escort cars have arrived, the truck is loaded with the water and we left the heroin for the cops."

"Tell everyone to clear out, but I need you to stay here and help me secure the prisoners."

Vito sent a text to his team in the warehouse. Their cars could be heard driving away, escorting the truck to a hidden location.

Jake and Vito began securing Banks to a heavy chair.

Banks regained consciousness and said, "Wait, I'll make you rich if you let me go. Name your price."

"My price is you going to prison for a long time," Jake said.

CHAPTER 54

Jake walked into the hallway, along with Sarah, Cody, and Vito. They went to the meeting room that held the photos of cops who had been targeted.

Jake used a burner phone to send a text to Roxanne. He attached pictures of the wall that had photos and maps targeting Chief Pierce and his family, along with other cops and city officials.

Once he'd sent the pics, he called her.

"Who's calling?"

"Rox, don't say a word; just listen. This is Jake Wolfe. I found the warehouse you're looking for. I'm going to give you the location, but only on one condition. If you understand and agree in principle, say *I'm listening*."

There was a long pause and then Roxanne said, "I'm listening."

"Did you look at the photos I sent just now?"

"Yes."

"There was a gang war at the warehouse with a high body count. You're the tech, *you* found the address and *you* solved the crime. The one condition is that I'm your protected source. My name and the names of my associates can never be mentioned, even under oath, and we all have immunity from prosecution. If you and I have a deal, say *okay*."

There was another long pause. Roxanne cursed.

"That was the wrong four-letter word, Rox," Jake said. "There's millions of dollars' worth of heroin at the location, along with a phone containing enough evidence to solve dozens of crimes. You'll have to go there immediately, before every criminal in the city tries to steal the drugs."

Roxanne let out a loud breath. "Okay!"

Jake recited the address. "You found the warehouse by working your sources, putting the word on the street, and then receiving an anonymous phone call from a burner phone. This will always be our secret, agreed?"

Roxanne hesitated for a moment. "Agreed. What is the current status of the situation?"

"It's a morgue, filled with dozens of dead foreign gang members, except for three prisoners who are alive for questioning."

"Only three are left alive?"

"There was a gang war. I hear sirens. You'll have to hurry to be the first on the scene."

"I'm on it, and … you're crazy, but … thank you for the intel."

"It's all in a day's work. Cody needed something to keep him busy." Jake ended the call.

Cars began arriving in front of the warehouse with the sound of screeching brakes and slamming doors. Jake looked out a window and saw men getting out of the cars, holding assault rifles. "It looks like another gang has come to steal the heroin."

Vito looked out the window. "How'd they find out about it?"

"I don't know but I'll be damned if I'll let them spread that poison all over the city."

"Jake, give me your monocular."

Jake handed it to him. "Who are they?"

"I recognize one of them. Those are members of a Serb gang."

"I heard about that gang when I was working in the media, but I thought they operated out of Sacramento."

"They're spreading out to other cities. Now they'll steal the Russian gang's heroin and use the profits to spread their Serb gang's influence to San Francisco." Vito handed the monocular back to Jake.

Jake turned to Sarah. "Vito will drive you home. Cody will stay with you and protect you."

"No, Jake. You can't fight a gang all by yourself."

Cody barked at Jake.

Vito shook his head.

Jake pointed at Vito. "Anselmo put me in charge. I'm giving you an order. Take Sarah home, park in front of her building and protect her."

Vito nodded. "If those are your orders, that's what I'll do."

"Do you have any more stun grenades?" Jake said.

"I kept one in reserve," Vito reached into a coat pocket and handed a grenade to Jake.

Sarah gasped when she saw Jake slip the grenade into a jacket pocket.

"Thanks, Vito. Now get out of here."

Vito walked out of the room, motioning for Sarah and Cody to follow him. Cody growled at Jake.

"Cody, protect Sarah. That's an order."

Cody barked once and followed Sarah as Vito pressed a protective hand on her shoulder and kept her walking toward the back stairs.

Jake opened the closet and grabbed a suppressed assault rifle, along with extra mags of ammo. The weapon reminded him of the M4 carbine he'd carried in the Marines. It felt familiar in his hands. He went back to the meeting room, opened all three windows, and took the night vision monocular out of his pocket.

Several more cars arrived and the armed men were

assembling in a group. Jake began firing warning shots at the cars, shooting their engines, radiators and windshields full of holes. One man fired a wild spray-and-pray burst of rounds at the second floor, shattering the windows.

Jake kept his head down until the glass shards stopped flying past. He then popped up in the far-right window and shot the man who was spraying bullets at the building. Before the man even hit the ground dead, Jake ducked back out of sight as bullets zipped through the windows and riddled the ceiling with holes. He crawled to the center window and removed the stun grenade from his jacket pocket.

CHAPTER 55

Jake left the grenade on the floor near the center window and commando-crawled to the far end of the room. He fired some rounds from the far-left window at the gang members on the ground and then went to the far-right window and did the same. He repeated the moves several times from different windows, trying to give the impression there was more than one shooter.

While everyone on the ground was firing up at the second floor, Jake heard the roar of a military-type vehicle nearby. He risked a quick peek out the window with his monocular and saw an armored SWAT truck arriving, along with Terrell in his police SUV. Several men in the gang below began shooting at Terrell.

"Oh, hell no." Jake pulled the pin from the grenade, waited three seconds as he cooked it, and then tossed it into the crowd below.

~

The SWAT team's vehicle came roaring up the street.

Terrell's police SUV was right behind it, with lights flashing and siren wailing.

Terrell saw muzzle flashes from dozens of weapons lighting up the dark area in front of the warehouse. A gang of men were firing at him. It looked like an ambush by cop killers. Rounds hit the SWAT vehicle, and several bounced off of Terrell's bulletproof windshield, leaving stars on the glass, right in front of his face.

A gang member reached into his car trunk, pulled out what looked like an M72 LAW rocket launcher, raised it to his shoulder and aimed it at Terrell.

Suddenly a bright flash illuminated the scene, followed by an incredibly loud bang. Many of the shooters staggered and fell down, stunned. Several men on the periphery of the area continued firing at the police and at the building.

Terrell saw weapons fire coming from the second floor. An individual was being shot at by the gang members, yet he was gunning them down one by one with military precision. The man with the LAW rocket launcher aimed at Terrell was the first to die.

Terrell grabbed his radio mic. "Looks like two rival gangs in a shootout. SWAT, you go in first."

"Copy. We're rolling." The SWAT team's armored vehicle crashed through the collection of parked cars and screeched to a stop. The weapons fire from the second-floor window ceased. Cops dressed in black jumped out of the SWAT vehicle and began yelling and firing weapons.

Soon, most of the criminals had surrendered and were facedown on the pavement, wearing handcuffs. A few tried to fight the SWAT team and were shot.

Terrell looked through binoculars at the second-floor windows. He saw a door closing as someone left the room.

∽

Jake moved from window to window, dodging incoming rounds as he fired his rifle the way he'd been trained in the Marine Corps School of Infantry. This was war and those criminals were the enemy.

When SWAT rolled in, Jake dropped the rifle and left the meeting room, closing the door behind him.

He went down the back stairs, out a door and into an alley. After checking for cops and gang members, he took off sprinting. At the next street he took a right, ran half a block, turned into another alley and kept running. He repeated a random zigzag pattern, avoiding intersections, until he was far from the scene.

Then he hailed a cab, giving the driver Sarah's address. "Drive fast. I'll give you a hundred-dollar tip." He opened his wallet and pulled out a Benjamin.

"*Da, spasibo,*" the driver said. As he drove, he glanced at Jake in the mirror, and then looked at his phone. He smiled and sent a text message.

Jake watched him and got a bad feeling. He looked at street signs. They were driving along an odd route. "I asked you to get there fast, not take me on a tour."

The driver punched the gas and roared down a side street, past some commercial buildings. The garage door on one of the buildings was rolling open.

Jake drew his pistol and pressed it against the driver's head. "Stop the car."

"*Stoy? Ochen horosho.*" The driver skidded into the garage and stopped. Jake saw someone cutting into a car with a torch. Auto parts were stacked everywhere. The garage door began to close, and the cab was immediately surrounded by several men with their weapons drawn and aimed at Jake.

"Sorry, Wolfe" the cab driver said.

An angry man who looked a lot like Pavel opened Jake's door and aimed a sawed-off shotgun at his head. "Well, if it isn't the great Jake Wolfe who killed my brother. Drop your gun or I'll blow your face off."

The other back door opened and one of the men aimed at Jake with a TEC-9 machine pistol that had two magazines taped together. The man said, "Go ahead and shoot the taxi driver, so I can comfort his widow."

The driver cursed at him.

Jake gritted his teeth. There was no escaping the cloud of lead from the shotgun at this close range, and the TEC-9 could fire thirty-two rounds into his back. He set his pistol down in the footwell and put his hands behind his head.

The man with the shotgun yelled, "Tie him up!"

Several men grabbed Jake, dragged him out of the cab, and stood him up against the side of a tall mesh cage that stored fifty-gallon barrels of auto paint and chemicals. They held his wrists up on either side of his face and tied them to the cage with rope. Next, they tied his feet. Once Jake was helpless, they took turns punching and kicking him. The cab driver walked up and kicked him in the crotch.

Jake stared at him. "I never forget a face. We'll meet again one day."

The man in charge stood in front of Jake and blew some cigarette smoke in his eyes. "My name's Yuri. One of Pavel's soldiers saw you running out of his building, went upstairs and found what you'd done."

"Maybe my dog and I were dancing in the club and then we got invited to a party and had to run."

"I've had all kinds of people on the street watching for you— taxi drivers, doormen, hookers and drug dealers."

"Why, do you want my autograph?"

"I'm going to make you suffer in ways you can't imagine."

Jake shook his head. "You'll be hunted down and exterminated by friends of mine. When does it ever end?"

"Where is Pavel's phone?" Yuri pressed the hot end of the

cigarette against Jake's chest, burning a hole in his shirt and singeing his flesh.

"The police have Pavel's phone. Maybe if you ask politely, they'll give it to you."

Yuri backhanded Jake. "Liar! I need that phone."

Blood trickled from the corner of Jake's mouth. "Call it. Maybe you'll hear it ring."

Yuri scowled. "You think you're funny? You won't be laughing when I get done with you. I'm going to wipe that smile right off your face."

Jake said, "You just quoted my high school algebra teacher, word for word."

Yuri picked up a rubber hose and began beating Jake about the chest, stomach and thighs. His temper flared as he swung the hose again and again. "You. Killed. My. Brother."

Jake took the beating, staring straight ahead without flinching.

CHAPTER 56

Terrell went inside the warehouse and found dead bodies littered everywhere, along with pallets stacked with plastic bags full of white powder. He smelled the sharp, pungent odor of exploded grenades and expended ammunition.

Beth and Roxanne arrived, along with a number of Black-and-whites, with lights flashing and sirens wailing.

Terrell patted Roxanne on the back. "Good work, Rox. This is a bust that will go down in SFPD history."

Beth gave Roxanne a fist bump.

Roxanne shrugged modestly. "I just got lucky."

Terrell raised an eyebrow. That reminded him of something Jake would say. He saw dog prints on the concrete floor and felt his heartburn flare up. "It looks like maybe everybody is dead."

"Let's search upstairs," Beth said.

They went into the offices with weapons up and ready for battle. Searching room-to-room, they found Abhay, Elena and Banks in the main office, hog-tied with a crazy number of zip ties, including one around their necks. Elena cursed at them.

Abhay gasped. "I'll testify against Banks in exchange for immunity, but I have favors to ask."

"Beggars can't be choosers," Beth said. "You'll be lucky to avoid the death penalty, or life in prison."

Roxanne was pumped up on adrenaline and working on zero sleep due to her endless computer-hacking work. She drew her pistol and pointed it at Abhay's face. "That's right, bitch-boy. I'll pop a cap in your head unless you give me one reason not to!"

Beth's eyebrows went up and she pushed Roxanne's hand away. Turning her back on Abhay, she whispered, "Whoa, girl. I'm only playing, to make him talk."

"Yeah, I knew that," Roxanne said, but the look on her face indicated otherwise. She stared at her pistol in surprise and put it back in her holster.

Abhay said, "The information I have will help you put Chairman Banks away for a long time. Can you offer me witness protection? But I don't want to live in Point Roberts."

"How about Sedona, Arizona?"

"I like warm weather. Do they have any Indian restaurants?"

"You wouldn't be allowed to go to restaurants, but maybe your handlers could get takeout."

"Now we're talking."

"Or, maybe they'll send you to Nome, Alaska, where you can eat whale blubber and seal stew while you freeze your ass off."

Abhay groaned.

Roxanne saw a purse on a desk, and gloved up to search through it, finding Elena's clutch wallet, Pavel's phone and a pistol. She tapped on the phone, nodded her head, and opened the wallet to check the driver's license. She looked from the license photo to Elena's face and back, making positive ID. "The owner of this phone was shot with a pistol that fired nine-millimeter rounds. You have his phone in your purse, along with what might be the murder weapon."

Elena shook her head. "Impossible."

Terrell officially placed Banks under arrest.

Banks scoffed at Terrell. "Where is all the cash, you fool?"

Terrell looked around. "Cash?"

"Yes, millions of dollars in small bills. It looks like the police have been robbed of a forfeiture fortune." Banks laughed heartily at Terrell.

Terrell scowled. "Go ahead and laugh it up, on your way to jail."

"Hardly. I'll live like a king in a federal country club prison. I'll bribe the guards to have gourmet food and liquor brought in, conjugal visits from beautiful women—anything I want. My life will be better than yours, with your low-income police paycheck and working-woman wife."

Terrell grabbed Banks by the upper arm and perp-walked him to his vehicle. "You weren't arrested by the feds. I'm with the SFPD. You'll be processed at the nearest police station and transferred to the San Francisco County Jail to begin spending quality time in a shared cell while you wait to be tried for murder."

"You can't be serious. I demand my rights."

Terrell shoved Banks into the backseat of his police SUV and locked him inside.

At the jail, two guards escorted Banks down a long hallway. He wore his orange prisoner clothing, handcuffs, and leg chains. Dozens of other prisoners yelled at him, whistled, ridiculed him, and made threats.

Banks tried to offer money to the guards, but they put him into a jail cell, took off his restraints, slammed the iron bar door closed, and walked away.

In the cell, a giant of a man sat on the lower bed. He had a nasty bruised lump on his forehead. He looked Banks up and down. "They call me Party Animal. We need to have a little talk."

CHAPTER 57

Vito drove to the Victorian house where Sarah rented a studio apartment, pulled up and parked in front. "Sarah, take Cody inside with you. Lock your door and keep your pistol nearby. I'll stay parked here and keep an eye on the street."

Sarah got out of the car. Police sirens wailed off in the distance. She shook her head at Vito. "No, Cody should stay in the Jeep and wait for Jake to call you. I'll be fine. My part in this is over." She walked away and went inside her building.

Vito said, "Well, Cody, I guess we'll guard Sarah's building."

Cody barked once.

Vito sat there in the car, reached for a cigarette and realized he'd left his smokes in the cab of the container truck. Maybe Jake had a pack of gum. He opened the glovebox and the center console, rummaged through the contents, and then stopped cold.

What was this? A U.S. Marshals badge? Was Jake working for the feds?

Vito felt a chill go down his spine as he put the badge in his coat pocket and sent a text to Anselmo.

Vito: *I have to talk to you. Alone.*

Anselmo: *My office. Leave the dog in the car.*

Vito: *Send someone to protect Sarah Chance.*

Anselmo: *ETA five minutes.*

A car roared up and stopped. Two men in dark suits got out. They spoke briefly to Vito. One stood in front of Sarah's building, the other went around to the back.

Vito nodded, satisfied that Sarah was well protected. He drove to the restaurant and parked. "Stay here, Cody, I'll be right back."

He walked into Anselmo's office, feeling a weight on his heart. If Jake was a traitor to his oath and to the Family, Anselmo would order a hit on him, and Vito would be the one who had to kill Jake the Knife.

Yuri swung the hose one last time, hitting Jake across the face, raising a red welt on his cheek and making his nose bleed. "Feeling funny now, wise guy?"

Jake stared straight ahead and didn't reply.

Yuri turned his head and gave an order in Russian, pointing at a two-wheeled cutting torch cart.

One of his men wheeled the cart close to Jake.

Yuri put on a pair of leather welding gloves with long cuffs. "I run an auto supply business. We steal cars, chop them up and sell the parts. Now I'm going to chop you up and drop your parts into a barrel of sulfuric acid."

He turned the knobs on the acetylene and oxygen cylinders, lit the torch, and held the bright flame near Jake's face. "What should I cut off first? Your ears? Your nose? Your fingers? Maybe put this torch up your ass? Oh, wait, I know the perfect thing."

He held the torch down near Jake's crotch, shooting the flame between his thighs, and then leaned his head in and sneered in his face. "Say *do svidaniya* to your manhood. I'm going to make you a eunuch."

When Yuri's face was close, Jake gave him the head-butt from hell, knocking him back on his heels.

Yuri staggered and fell down, raised his hands to his injured forehead and burned his face with the cutting torch.

For a moment there was chaos as Yuri screamed in pain and rolled on the floor. One of his men turned off the torch, another tried to help him get up, but Yuri punched him in the face.

Jake turned his head and bit into the square knot of the rope that held his right wrist. He loosened it, slipping his hand through the loop.

He reached behind his waist and drew his knife, cut the rope free of his other hand, and then squatted and cut the ropes around his ankles. He drew a pistol from an ankle holster and began to shoot the gang members, one by one.

A uniformed SFPD policewoman ran into the garage, firing a suppressed assault rifle. She shot the men at the same time Jake was shooting them, then dropped her weapon and walked over to Yuri.

Yuri groaned as he lay bleeding from the torch injury and the bullet wounds. He tried to draw a pistol from his waistband.

The cop took a straight razor out of her pocket, grabbed Yuri's hair and pulled his head back. She looked Jake in the eye as she slit Yuri's throat and tossed him aside. She then wiped the razor on the dead man's shirt, stood up and faced Jake.

Jake stared at the polished blade. "Are you *Razor?*"

She put the razor in her pocket. "Were you responsible for the deaths of dozens of foreign gang members tonight?"

They studied each other.

She waved her hand at the men she'd shot. "If it wasn't for me, you'd be dead now, or wishing you were."

Jake shook his head, holding up his pistol, keeping it pointed away from her. "I was doing all right, but thanks for the help. What's your real name?" He looked at the name on her uniform: *Martinelli.*

"Anselmo said you took the *omertà*."

"Yes, I took the oath."

She shook Jake's hand. "Tammi Martinelli. You can never tell Terrell Hayes about me."

"And you can never betray Terrell. He's my brother, and that makes him *family*."

"That black man is your brother?"

"Yes, we're blood brothers. Literally. He once donated his blood to save my life."

"I've never betrayed any of my police coworkers. The Family just helps me dispense street justice where I act as judge and jury."

"Understood."

"You owe me. I came to your defense. Keep my secrets and I'll keep yours."

"You're invited on a boat trip out on the Bay one of these days. I'd like to talk with you in private about some things."

"I have to go. I was never here."

"See you around, Razor."

She went out the door. Jake heard her car door slam. The engine started and she drove away.

He retrieved his pistol from the backseat of the cab, got into the driver's seat and drove toward Sarah's apartment while sending a text to Vito, saying he was on the way.

Vito replied that plans had changed. Sarah was at home. Cody was safe in the Jeep, which was parked at the restaurant.

When Jake arrived at the restaurant, Vito was standing next to the Jeep. Jake got out of the cab and looked in the Jeep window. Cody barked at him. "Did Cody behave himself?"

Vito nodded.

"I called Sarah when I was in the cab. She's doing fine," Jake said.

Vito nodded again.

"You're awfully quiet, Vito. What's going on?"

"Who hit you?"

"Pavel's brother, Yuri."

"And the taxi?"

"Stolen from one of Yuri's snitches."

"Are Yuri and his crew going to come here, shooting?"

"No, they're dead."

Vito tapped his phone. "I'll get rid of the cab."

"Thanks. Can you send someone out here with a few meatballs for Cody?"

"Sure."

"Not warmed up, no sauce, just plain and cold from the fridge."

Vito went inside the restaurant.

Jake watched him walk away. He had an odd feeling about Vito's mood.

A black sedan dropped off a young man. He nodded at Jake, got into the cab and drove away.

Jake opened the door of the Jeep and sat in the driver's seat. "Hey, Cody, did you miss me, buddy?"

Cody barked once, pushed between the two front seats and placed his front paws on the center console. He sniffed Jake's face and shoulder, then whined and licked his bloody cheek.

"Yeah, I had a painful detour on my way here."

Jake tapped on Elena's phone for a moment, scrolling through her contacts, texts and emails—and finding a hidden document listing dozens of passwords. It was fascinating. She had millions of dollars in offshore bank accounts.

A waitress came out to the Jeep and gave Jake a take-out container filled with several meatballs. "Just plain and cold, no sauce? Our sauce is legendary."

"These are for my dog."

She laughed and went back inside the restaurant.

Cody sniffed the air. Jake opened the container, set it down on the center console and held onto it. Cody gobbled the meatballs, then licked his snout and looked at Jake.

"That's all for now, Cody. Too many would upset your stomach."

Terrell drove up in his SUV and stopped with a screech of tires. He got out and walked directly toward Jake, frowning.

Jake had been hoping to avoid this confrontation, but Terrell appeared as if he was going to punch him.

Terrell stood next to the Jeep and started yelling as if Jake was in boot camp. He held his hand out with his fingers straight and chopped the air in between them with a "knife hand" gesture, like a drill instructor.

"Chief Pierce wants to know where the money went. He said my job is hanging by a thread. You're going to tell me—and you're going to tell me right *now!*"

Jake felt bad for Terrell. He hadn't counted on the police finding out about the money. "I'm sorry, my brother. I don't… I can't… I won't lie to you."

"Tell the truth, dammit," Terrell said.

"That *was* the truth. I can't say anything, ever."

Terrell reached into the car, grabbed Jake's right hand off the steering wheel and looked at it. He saw the cut on his thumb, and the bloodstain from when he'd made the imprint. He threw Jake's hand down as if it was poisoned. "You went and did it. You became a made man, and I thought we were brothers, both on the right side of the law."

"We'll always be brothers, and I'll always be on your side."

"Criminals are my enemies. You joined my enemies?"

"No, these are businessmen—capitalists who are willing to go the extra mile."

"They have no respect for the law, or for me and my fellow cops. They kill people as part of their business plan."

"I respect you and everyone in law enforcement; you know I do. Besides, how many people did you and I kill in combat?"

"That was different."

"Listen, I had to take the oath. I thought Sarah might die a horrible death. I was desperate to save her."

"Tell me where the money went."

"If I do, I'll be killed. Sometimes they kill your best friend too. In my case, that would be you."

"Pffft, those pussies can't touch me."

"I'm not going to take that chance."

"You want to go to jail, is that it?"

"I've been there before, and I'll go back if I have to. What other choice do I have?"

"What crimes are you going to be working on now, for the Family?"

Jake hung his head and sighed. "That's not funny, Grinds."

"I wasn't joking, fool."

"I don't work for them. I only took the oath of secrecy. Yes, I know where the money went. No, I can't tell you where."

Terrell gestured at the restaurant. "Well, you can inform Chef Boyardee that Chief Pierce will go after the drug money, under forfeiture laws, to help the SFPD fight crime in this city. Anselmo can hand it over immediately, or else we'll take it *and* every other dime they have."

"Do you know what you're saying?"

"Yeah, read my lips. Pierce said he'll start an all-out war on organized crime in Little Italy. The Amborgetti Restaurant will be closed—tomorrow. The entire North Beach area will be crawling with cops and informants—forever."

"And you want me to deliver this bad news? Thanks a lot."

"It serves you right. Don't ever call me again. You're no longer welcome at my house."

"Grinds, please don't do this."

"Goodbye, Jukebox, my former brother."

Terrell turned his back on Jake and walked to his car, then drove off and didn't look back.

Jake cursed and put his forehead against the steering wheel. Cody pushed his head against his shoulder.

Jake drew in a deep breath and slowly released it. "Sometimes I understand why Stuart used drugs to dull his feelings."

Cody barked twice and shook his head. He took Jake's hand in his mouth, not biting it, just holding it.

Jake nodded. "Don't worry, buddy. No matter how bad life ever gets, I'll never do that. You're stuck with me for the duration. Grinds will get over it, I hope."

Jake sent a text to Alicia. *Just now, Terrell said goodbye to me forever. But I can't survive without my brother. Please talk to him. Help us. Thank you.*

Alicia replied. *Oh no, Jake. I'll see what I can do.*

As he sat there thinking, Jake came up with an idea. The cops probably didn't know how much money had been in the warehouse. Jake's half of the four million take might appease Chief Pierce.

He sent a text to Terrell. *Tell the Chief I'll take the two million away from the Family and deliver it to him.*

Terrell replied. *Yeah, sure. In your dreams.*

Jake looked over at the restaurant. "Cody, we have to go take my two million dollars in cash away from the Family. Are you up for this?"

Cody barked once and growled at the nearby building.

CHAPTER 58

Jake and Cody got out of the Jeep, went inside the Amborgetti Restaurant and were greeted by the hostess.

He walked past her without comment and went into the kitchen, passing by the cooks, who all stopped what they were doing. They stared in recognition at Jake the Knife and paid him respect.

Jake sent a text to Anselmo.

I'm coming to your office for a meeting. Right now.

As he went to the back room, a bodyguard blocked his path, but Jake stared him down and said, "I have an appointment."

Anselmo called out from inside his office. "It's all right, Jake can come in."

Jake opened Anselmo's door, went inside and closed it behind him.

Cody stared at Anselmo's hands.

Anselmo sat behind his desk and showed no fear of Cody. "What's on your mind, Jake? Have some grappa. We have four million reasons to celebrate." He poured two glasses of the liquor.

Jake looked his friend in the eye. "I need my half of the money from the heist, right now, in a truck."

Anselmo laughed hard. He slammed his hand on the wood desk and shook his head. "Oh man, that's rich. I haven't had such a good laugh in ages. So, are you going to drive the truck to Vegas and throw a big party?"

"I'm not joking," Jake said. "I'll be driving it to the police station."

Anselmo's eyebrows went up at the mention of the police. He reached for his glass of grappa, drank the shot of fiery liquor down in in one gulp, and coughed hard afterward. "You're a lawyer now. Can't you fight the cops on whatever charges they have against you? What are they threatening you with? How many years?"

"I'm not being threatened—you are. I'm trying to protect you."

Anselmo looked skeptical. He tossed a U.S. Marshals badge onto the desktop. "Vito found this badge in your Jeep. Did the feds send you to infiltrate the Family, to betray us?"

Jake sat up straight, aware that his life was in danger. He held eyes with Anselmo. "No, they don't even know I'm here."

"But you're a Marshal, a fed?"

"Not exactly; I was deputized so I'd have jurisdiction to do a one-time job for the government."

"Let me guess. You killed somebody."

"Whatever it might have been, it's classified as top secret. I can't talk about it."

"The guy you put a hit on—did he deserve to die?"

Jake stared at Anselmo, held his gaze, and then nodded. He picked up the badge and put it in his pocket. "I'd never betray you, Mo, but I'd never betray my friends in law enforcement either."

"Do you think you can walk a tightrope between both groups?"

"I'm doing it right now."

"What are you, neutral? Like Switzerland?"

"I don't know what I am," Jake said.

"Honest answer. So, you're not a traitor to the Family?"

"No. I'm only trying to save my friendship with Terrell, and to protect you from financial ruin and life in prison."

Anselmo looked over at his wall of framed photographs. He appeared in pictures with celebrities, politicians, businesspeople … and some notorious criminals. "This I understand—loyalty to conflicting interests. Love versus duty." He opened a wooden box on his desk, handed a cigar to Jake, and then pushed a gold lighter across the desk.

Jake sat down in a leather chair, picked up the lighter and lit the cigar. He knew from experience this was a sign Anselmo might be willing to talk and negotiate. The two of them smoked in silence for a while, and then Jake said, "Chief Pierce wants all of the money from the warehouse, or he'll seize your bank accounts, real estate and businesses. I'm going to give him my half, and hope he believes that's all of it."

Anselmo pointed his cigar at Jake. "What do you have to offer in exchange for half of my money?"

Jake laughed. "Are you joking? It's all my money, not yours. I gave you half of it for helping me take it away from the Russians. I let you hold onto my half for safekeeping. I promised the cops I'd deliver two million, so maybe you should cough up one million as your share."

Anselmo shook his head. "No way, I'm not giving a million to the cops so they can use it against me."

"It's a cost of doing business, but feel free to keep two mil as my overpayment for services rendered. Unless you piss me off. Then I'll want my half, a million dollars, immediately." He puffed on the cigar and blew smoke toward Anselmo.

Anselmo smiled and poured himself another shot of grappa.

"Jake, you're crazy, fearless, and stupidly honest. I've always liked that about you, even though it might get you killed someday."

Jake picked up his glass of grappa. "It has to appear that you gave all of the money to the police, or there'll be a war. The cops have technology and endless tax dollars to fight you with. You can't win."

"We might win. It happened in Chicago when Al Capone was running the city."

"No, times have changed, and I don't want to live in a city run by the Family. There has to be a balance between you and the police. Working together, tonight, we got rid of a foreign gang of heroin-dealing kidnappers. The city is a better place to live now."

Anselmo set his cigar down on an ashtray and crossed his arms. "I was glad to see them go."

"The Chief is demanding the money immediately or the apocalypse begins tomorrow morning at sunrise. Your restaurant will be the first casualty. Seized under forfeiture laws and closed until further notice."

"Half of the cops in the city are on our waiting list for dinner reservations."

"Don't underestimate Terrell. I've seen him kill men with his bare hands."

Anselmo looked at his hands. A shadow crossed his eyes. "Terrell and I have something in common."

"Chief Pierce will have your house and bank accounts seized too. You'll be homeless."

"I don't take kindly to threats."

"This is business. I'll give my half of the money to the police, and you can keep the other half for the Family as a reward for helping me and Sarah. I get nothing. You're welcome."

"Any other demands? Maybe a statue of you in North Beach? Name a street after Cody?"

"Cody would like that, but for now I'd suggest you invite the chief of police to dinner and give him the royal treatment. Have Terrell and me there too, so Pierce knows it's not a setup."

"That's not a bad idea."

"Explain to him that you are *not* involved in addictive drugs, prostitution or weapons—only gambling."

"Betting on sports is legal in Nevada and in other countries, but here in California it's a crime. Why?"

"I have no idea. I've studied the law, and it often makes no sense."

"Some of the local cops come here and bet on baseball, football, basketball, golf—you name it."

"I wouldn't mention that to the chief."

"We used to make a fortune from the illegal numbers racket, until the government legalized it and called it the lottery."

"Sometimes I take the chief out on the *Far Niente* for fishing trips. You should come along next time. Talk with the big guy, in private, off the record."

Anselmo ran his hand over his jaw and then nodded. "I accept your invitation."

They drank their grappa. Anselmo coughed afterward. His face went pale, and he closed his eyes and held a hand against his chest.

Jake watched him, worried.

Anselmo studied Jake's face. "How is your mother? We all miss her here. Customers come from miles around because they love the lasagna we make with her recipe."

"She sends her regards. Now, about my truckload of cash."

Anselmo shook his head and made a phone call.

At police headquarters, Terrell finished a report, then stood up and grabbed his coat. After this crazy day of trying to maintain law and order, all he wanted to do was to go home and have dinner with Alicia and then curl up with her in bed. That woman kept him sane. She made his life worth living.

But he sometimes wondered if his life had any meaning. Even though he'd arrested scores of criminals and put them in prison, there were thousands more out there right now. He thought about the thin blue line that the police represented. They kept civilization from coming apart. Yes, what he did mattered, even though he got very little thanks or recognition.

His phone buzzed, and he saw that the call was from Jake. He let it go to voicemail. Next, he received a text message from Jake:

I have the money. Millions of dollars in cash. Look outside, my brother. My life is in danger every minute I drive this rolling bank vault. Tell your fellow cops to hold their fire.

Terrell looked out the windows of the Homicide Detail offices and saw a container truck flashing its lights on and off. It was heading straight for police headquarters at high speed. Several cars were chasing the truck, with men leaning out their windows and firing weapons at it.

Terrell shook his head. "Oh, hell. Jukebox can screw anything up, no matter what it is."

He alerted the SWAT team to deploy and asked a police sniper to take out the drivers of the cars in pursuit of the "police truck."

Next, he replied to Jake's text: *Sniper will provide support. Put on the Marshals badge. Stop the truck now. Do not get any closer to HQ, or I can't save your stupid ass.*

Jake replied: *Roger.*

Terrell saw the truck begin to skid as Jake hit the brakes. The rear tires smoked and shuddered. The truck fishtailed and planed half sideways down the street. Several parked cars were knocked out of their parking spots and a bus stop shelter was mowed down.

Terrell looked through binoculars at the truck cab and saw Jake and Cody in the seats. Cody was barking at Jake, but Jake stared straight ahead with a resigned look on his face. Terrell had seen that look in the past, overseas in the desert, right before Jake had nearly died.

"I should retire right now, before I have a stroke," Terrell said. He ran out of the room and down the stairwell, yelling at his phone as he went.

CHAPTER 59

As Jake drove the truck full of money, cars chased him and men shot at his tires. He wondered if somebody had talked, or if there was a spy in the Family.

He downshifted and applied the brakes. The truck shook and the tires squealed as he drifted to the side. The back end started coming around, and Jake fought to keep the truck from going into an uncontrolled skid.

The truck crashed into cars and parking meters, took out a fire hydrant, and then finally shuddered to a stop.

An armored SWAT vehicle roared up to the scene and the team disembarked and got into a shootout with the pursuing cars. The SWAT team blew the lead car full of holes, causing it to crash and flip upside down. The police sniper shot the driver of another car and the rest veered off and sped away, being chased by police vehicles.

Jake ducked down below the windshield of the truck to avoid being shot by an overeager rookie cop. He held on to Cody and kept him safe.

Sirens filled the air. Blue and red lights were flashing. A radio crackled, and an authoritative voice gave commands over a loudspeaker. The broken fire hydrant shot a plume of water high into the air, raining down on the scene. Car alarms wailed, dogs barked, and a news helicopter began to circle overhead.

Jake ignored it all, remaining down and out of sight. He patted Cody on the back. "We did good, buddy. Hopefully we'll survive our good deed."

He got an idea, took out his black phone and sent a text to Agent McKay. *FYI, I'm about to be arrested by the SFPD. My black phone will be taken as evidence and hacked by Sergeant Roxanne Poole. If you can keep me from being arrested, I'll do one mission for your POETs group.*

Somebody tried to open the locked door handle. Jake turned his head and saw Terrell. He lowered the window. "Grinds, is it safe for Cody?"

Terrell looked around at all the cops. "Hold on a second." He went to the nearest police vehicle, grabbed the mic, and spoke over its PA system. "This is Lieutenant Terrell Hayes of the SFPD. I am in command of the situation. There is no threat. Hold your fire. I repeat. Hold. Your. Fire."

Jake ordered Cody to stay down in the footwell. He then sat up in the driver's seat, feeling like a target. "Here's the key to the cargo doors."

Terrell grabbed the key and walked to the back of the truck. He opened the lock, drew his pistol, and swung open the doors. Inside he found two pallet loads of bottled water and nothing else.

He walked back to the cab and yelled at Jake. "Is that water your idea of a *joke*?"

"They hid the cash in the center, behind the bottled water. Cut the straps and shrink-wrap, and you'll see it."

Terrell walked back, climbed inside the trailer, pulled a knife and slashed through the straps and the shrink-wrap on one of the pallets.

The packs of bottled water fell away, revealing a hidden core of vacuum-bagged bundles of cash. He was no expert, but his experience told him the stash probably held a million dollars in small bills. He slashed the other pallet and found a similar amount of money.

Terrell took pictures of the cash with his phone and sent them to Chief Pierce. He closed and locked the doors to the trailer, waved to some cops from SWAT, and went back to the truck window. "Chief Pierce wants to see you in his office, Jukebox. Right now. Get out of the truck."

"All right, but I'm bringing Cody with me. That is nonnegotiable, unless I'm under arrest. If I am, Cody will take the bus to your house and hang out with Alicia."

Terrell sighed. "You're not under arrest, so far. Let's go."

Jake carried Cody in his arms as he passed by all of the heavily armed SWAT officers. One of the SWAT guys saw the Marshals badge and slapped Jake on the back.

When they arrived at the front door of the police station, Jake set Cody down and clipped a leash onto his collar.

They went inside to the lobby, where Terrell pointed to a bulletproof glass window. "You have to surrender any weapons before you can go inside."

"Understood."

The uniformed female officer at the window stared in surprise as Jake removed a pistol from a shoulder holster, another from an ankle holster, and his illegal KA-BAR knife from behind his back.

Jake and Cody followed Terrell through a door and walked

down a hallway. Jake turned to Terrell. "You know, technically, Cody is a weapon too."

"Shut your mouth."

"Yes, sir."

"I'm not a sir. I work for a living."

The door to Chief Pierce's office was open. Terrell walked in. "Jake Wolfe and Cody, here to see you, as requested."

Pierce looked up from some papers on his desk. He wore the SFPD dark blue uniform with a gold star badge pinned above his left shirt pocket and four small gold stars on both of his starched shirt collars. "All three of you Marine misfits come in here and close the door behind you."

Terrell gave Pierce a questioning look.

Pierce waved his hand. "Sit down." He looked at Cody. "You too, Marmaduke."

Cody barked twice when Pierce called him Marmaduke. One of his eyebrows went up and down.

Pierce scowled, took off his glasses, polished them with a cloth, and put them back on. "I want some answers from you cowboys. The unvarnished truth about what the hell has been going on in *my* city."

Jake and Terrell sat there in silence. This was a familiar situation to them. In the Marines, Jake had often been NJP'd, treated to nonjudicial punishment, for saying or doing something reckless. He and Terrell never said a word about what had happened. They'd experienced collective amnesia.

Pierce crossed his arms and looked at Jake. "Let's hear from you first, wannabe fishing boat captain. Say something, or go back to jail. I guess your former cellmate is asking where he can find you."

Jake nodded. "Speaking of the boat, that reminds me. You're way past due for another fishing trip on the *Far Niente*. Let's go out on the water this weekend."

"You're damned right I'm going fishing on the *Far Niente*. Tell me why I shouldn't just take your boat as forfeiture, now that you've joined an organized crime family that I'm dedicated to putting out of business."

"Because then I'd be homeless and I'd pitch a tent in your backyard?" Jake said.

"Not persuasive, try again."

Jake leaned forward. "I bring you a truck filled with two million dollars in cash, and you're not satisfied? You want to steal Dylan's boat too? No way, I'm an attorney. You can't just take my friend's boat without a court battle."

Pierce glared at Jake. "You never learned when to keep your big mouth shut, did you?"

Terrell raised his hand to his face, pinched the bridge of his nose, and shook his head.

Jake turned his palms up. "Don't ask me questions if you don't want to hear the truth."

"The truth is, I could lock you up and throw away the key for any one of the stunts you've pulled. I should do it, too, after that lawsuit you filed last month."

"That lawsuit wasn't against you or the SFPD, it was a municipality litigation lawsuit against the City of San Francisco for tortious acts by Sergeant Denton."

"If you want me to drop all the charges I have against you, you'll need to drop that lawsuit as a return favor."

Jake took a deep breath and let it out. "I'll think it over. And remember, I could file another lawsuit, against Kirby, but instead I delivered a truckload of money to the police department."

"Never file another lawsuit against the city or any of my cops."

"Meanwhile, Kirby goes unpunished."

"Kirby has been placed on paid administrative leave while the allegations are investigated."

"His so-called punishment is a paid vacation? Did you see my Jeep-cam video of the arrest?"

Pierce ignored the questions. "You'd better explain your membership in an organized crime group we've been trying to infiltrate—and make it good."

"I only took the Family's oath of *loyalty and secrecy*. That was so my friends could freely and aggressively seek out, find, and rescue my kidnapped girlfriend—and I would be bound to never reveal the details."

"And your friends were breaking every law in the book."

"Correct. The mission was similar to some work I've done for the US government. Against current laws, but morally justified and top secret."

Pierce shook his head and drummed his fingers on the desk.

Jake noticed the pale scarring on the knuckles of his right hand. Four tattooed letters had been removed with a laser, one near each knuckle. Jake thought about something Terrell had once said. When Pierce was a young man, he'd belonged to a violent criminal gang. It gave Jake a risky idea.

"Chief Pierce, are you trying to help me avoid going down the wrong path, because you did that in your youth? If so, I want to thank you, sir. I give you my word I won't become a gang member."

Pierce's face darkened with anger. He glanced at his right hand and made it into a fist. His neck turned red.

Terrell shifted in his seat.

Cody got to his feet and kept his eyes on Pierce's hands.

Jake felt Cody's change of mood. "At ease, Cody. This is Gunnery Sergeant Pierce. He's in command of us Marines right now. After this debriefing, we'll get some chow."

Cody relaxed his shoulders when he heard the familiar words, but he still kept watch on the unknown man who was challenging his handler.

Pierce stared at Cody for several seconds, then turned and glared at Terrell. "Is this a war dog?"

"Yes."

"Has he ever killed anyone?"

"Yes."

"Does he have PTSD?"

"Well … yes … sometimes."

"You brought an unstable military weapon into my office that might go off unexpectedly?"

Terrell sat up straight. "Your orders were to bring Jake and Cody here, and I followed those orders. Did I misunderstand you, or did you change your mind?"

Pierce scowled at Terrell. "You'd better not be picking up Wolfe's smart-mouthed attitude."

Jake put a hand on Cody's back. "Terrell knows Cody is nonviolent, as long as everybody else is nonviolent."

Pierce looked Jake in the eye. "Do you have him under control?"

"Most of the time, but he definitely has a mind of his own. I'd sit perfectly still and smile for a minute if I were you."

Pierce cracked his knuckles and then held a finger hovering over one of the buttons on his desk phone.

Jake shook his head at Pierce and said, "Please don't." He turned to Cody. "Be friends, Cody, and lie down."

Cody shook out his fur from head to tail, and lay down on the carpet next to Jake. He grinned at Pierce and let his tongue hang out.

Pierce nodded at Jake and took his hand away from the phone.

CHAPTER 60

There was a knock at the door. Pierce scowled. "I'm in a meeting."

Roxanne spoke from the hallway. "It's Sergeant Roxanne Poole. I want to join the meeting. I'm part of the investigation and I have something you need to see."

Terrell said, "Rox was indispensable, as usual."

Pierce waved his hand. Terrell got up and opened the door. Roxanne entered the room.

Jake stood up. "Here, Rox. Take my seat next to Terrell. These are police chairs, and I'm a civilian."

Roxanne sat down and held up a tablet. "I have some evidence you're not going to like, sir."

Pierce pointed at a TV monitor on the wall. "Put it on the big screen."

The TV lit up with an image of an office wall covered with photos, maps, and notes, along with a kill list. Chief Pierce and his wife were on the list. Terrell and Alicia were too. The list went on and on, featuring Jake and Cody, Beth and her son, Roxanne and many other cops, some FBI agents, and the mayor.

There were photos of faces, homes, schools, cars, and license plates. Lists of work schedules, weekend habits, and notes about the best way to kill each target.

Roxanne tapped on the tablet and zoomed in on a photo montage that showed Chief Pierce's house and his wife and children. There was a map with the driving route to his kids' schools.

Pierce's face darkened with blotches of red. He put both hands on the desktop and took deep breaths to control his rage. "Where did you get this?"

"At the heroin warehouse, in a meeting room."

"What else do you know about it?"

"The gang was preparing for a surgical strike against all their enemies in the city. They were going to blame it on a terrorist attack."

"Do you have any more evidence?"

"Yes, witness testimony. We arrested three people at the warehouse. They all required medical treatment. One of them was soon high as a kite on pain meds, and we talked him into answering our questions."

Pierce consulted a report on his desk. "I'm guessing this is the guy named Abhay, who gave the statement: *Jake Wolfe punched my boss in the face repeatedly, and the dog tried to bite his dick off.*"

Cody panted, Ha-Ha-Ha.

Roxanne held up a phone in a plastic bag. "In addition to the videos taken by Gene Stephens, we have Pavel's phone, full of incriminating evidence. He was one of the top bosses and heroin dealers in the Russian mafia."

"Was?" Pierce asked.

"He was gunned down in his luxury suite above the dance club he owned."

"What evidence do we have against Elena?"

"The USB drive has a video of Elena giving orders for her men to commit murder. She is also seen walking past pallets of heroin, stashes of assault rifles, and a dead body."

"Was she the ringleader?" Pierce asked.

"It appears that she and Pavel became partners in the drug dealing scheme," Roxanne said.

Jake said, "I'm glad Cody found the thumb drive for you, Chief. It was the key to everything."

Pierce glanced at Jake and exhaled loudly. "Jake, tell me your side of the story, and make it good."

"I'm sorry, sir, but I'll have to take the Fifth Amendment. However, I will say this much. We were all on that kill list—yet we're all still alive, and the killers are dead. Any questions?"

Jake saw that the threat to Pierce's wife and kids had awakened something in him—something personal. Pierce looked Jake in the eye, and the two of them reached an unspoken understanding. They would fight to the death to protect their loved ones.

Chief Pierce pointed a scarred finger at Jake. "Are you admitting you're responsible for that warehouse filled with dead bodies?"

"No, sir. I admit nothing, but I believe the cops have a phrase for this kind of situation: *public service homicides.*"

The desk phone rang. Pierce tapped the speaker button and answered, "I told you to hold my calls."

"The Secret Service is on the phone, and they won't take no for an answer. You also have a Secret Service Agent and a U.S. Marshal here to see you."

"Put the call through and send the feds to my office."

"You're connected."

"Chief Pierce."

"Chief, this is Secret Service Agent Shannon McKay."

"We've spoken once before."

"Yes, and I need to participate in your meeting."

"You're on speaker, McKay. I'm here with Terrell Hayes, Roxanne Poole and Jake Wolfe."

Cody barked at Pierce.

Pierce frowned. "And a dog named Cody."

"Sergeant Poole, can you hear me?" McKay said.

"Yes, I can hear you," Roxanne said.

"I wanted you to know that Jake Wolfe's black phone and his Jeep are property of the Secret Service and you are not to investigate or tamper with them in any way. Understood?"

Roxanne looked at Pierce. He nodded. "Understood," she said.

"Chief Pierce, I'm calling to ask the same favor I did the last time we spoke," McKay said.

"Regarding Wolfe?"

"Correct, I'm asking you to let Jake Wolfe go free and not press any criminal charges against him. He should have a letter with him, on White House stationery, that says he's not to be detained or arrested."

"I saw a copy of that letter once, but your troubleshooter seems to have lost it."

"One of our agents, named Easton, is bringing a copy to you now. He's being accompanied by the U.S. Marshal who recently deputized Wolfe."

Pierce looked at the badge Jake was wearing. He put his hand on the back of his neck and turned his head from side to side, cracking his neck. "If Wolfe is qualified to be in law enforcement, it means hell has frozen over."

There was a knock at the door and Pierce gestured toward it, irritated.

Jake opened the door and let two men into the room. "Chief Pierce, this is Secret Service Agent Easton, along with U.S. Marshal Garcia."

"We've met before, haven't we, Easton?" Pierce said.

"Yes, sir." Easton reached into his suit jacket and took out his badge, credentials, and a business envelope printed with the presidential seal. He displayed his creds and then handed the envelope to Pierce.

Pierce opened the envelope and removed a letter on White

312 MARK NOLAN

House stationery. He read the terse note, and said, "McKay, I have the document and it appears to be genuine."

"Are you on board with giving Wolfe a pass?" McKay asked.

"Although I'm sorely tempted to toss Wolfe in jail, I don't have any pending charges against him at this time. We're concluding a debriefing where he agreed to drop his lawsuit against Sergeant Denton, and the City of San Francisco."

Jake shook his head. "I only agreed to think it over."

"And he won't file one against Sergeant Kirby for false arrest, assault, battery, false imprisonment, and more," Pierce said.

Jake held out his hands. "How about this—I won't sue the city if Kirby agrees to get in a boxing ring with me."

Pierce scratched his chin. "Settle it the old fashioned way? With your fists?"

"Yes, a fair fight, with boxing gloves, a referee and you as a witness," Jake said.

"Win or lose, you agree not to sue Kirby or the city?"

"Yes, sir. That's my offer."

"All right, I'll tell Kirby you challenged him to a fight. His ego won't let him refuse," Pierce said.

"Fair warning, I'm going to knock his head off the way I was taught to in Marine Corps bootcamp," Jake said.

Terrell shook his head. "Kirby is *so* screwed."

McKay interrupted. "Chief, we currently have a situation brewing, and Wolfe might be needed to assist as an off-the-books asset."

"Is that why he's been deputized into the U.S. Marshals Service?"

"I can't say any more, only that it's a matter of national security. You'll get a briefing from Homeland."

"Understood … and, McKay, the next time you're in town be sure to stop by and have a cup of coffee."

"I look forward to it. Thank you for your cooperation."

"You're welcome. I'd also like to go on record that the Secret Service now owes a favor to the SFPD. Agreed?"

There was a pause. "Fair enough. Easton will give you his number. Take care." McKay ended the call.

Pierce looked at the letter on his desk. "Wolfe, your *get out of jail free card* is still working, I see. I'll need an authenticated paper-and-ink copy of that for my files."

"Keep that one," Easton said. He reached into his coat for another envelope and handed it to Jake. "Try not to lose this."

Pierce said, "Jake, don't ever put me in the position again where I'm forced to make a split-second decision about whether to let the police sniper shoot you in the head."

"Good advice. Thank you for not having me shot," Jake said.

Pierce stared hard at Jake. "Don't make me regret my decision."

Marshal Garcia spoke up. "Chief, we met once, when I deputized Terrell Hayes."

"When he was subpoenaed in a lawsuit?"

"Right. Somebody tried to dig into the secrets of a little-known ... *device*. We deputized Hayes, took your files to our offices, and that was the end of it."

"Are you here because of Hayes or Wolfe?"

"Because of Wolfe. As much as it pains me to say this, I deputized his ornery self, and that currently remains in effect. The request to deputize him came from the highest levels of the federal government."

Pierce glanced at the letter with the White House seal. His desk phone rang again. He punched the speaker button. "What now?"

"Congressman Anderson is on the line. He said he wants to put in a good word for Jake Wolfe."

Jake smiled. McKay was going all out on his behalf.

Pierce shook his head, tapped a button and connected the call. "Chief Pierce."

"Chief, this is Congressman Daniel Anderson. I'm a big supporter of the SFPD."

"Yes, you are. Thank you. We appreciate that. Now you're going to tell me what a great guy Jake Wolfe is, right?"

"Have you been getting some calls?"

"Yes, and visitors," Pierce said. "Don't worry, I'm going to release Wolfe from custody."

"Thank you. Even though Jake attracts trouble like a magnet, Kat and I owe him a debt of gratitude."

Jake spoke up. "Chief, please ask Daniel how his wife, Katherine, is doing."

Pierce asked, "How is Katherine? We all have her in our thoughts and prayers."

"Thank you. Her medical treatments are extra difficult when she's pregnant, but Dr. Brook says Kat and the baby are doing fine so far."

Jake nodded. "Thank God."

Pierce said. "Congressman, let's have lunch one day this week. You, me, and Katherine."

"Call me Daniel. Yes, let's meet for lunch. My staff will call back and schedule a time."

Pierce ended the call. "Jake, you're free to go, but I'll be keeping a close eye on you from now on."

Jake stood up. "Thank you, sir. It's always a pleasure to meet with you. The SFPD is an honorable organization, staffed with superb people dedicated to the protection of their city. The fishing trip on the *Far Niente* is this Saturday. You're all invited, and I hope you can make it."

Jake walked to the door, then stopped to look Chief Pierce in the eye for a moment, nodding his head.

Pierce met his eyes and nodded in reply. "Stay out of trouble."

"I'll try, sir—and you try to spend that two million dollars wisely." Jake left the office and went out into the hallway. As he closed the door behind him, he heard Pierce say, "Easton and Garcia, I have some questions for you."

In the hallway, Beth was arriving. "Jake Wolfe, you turn up everywhere."

"I'm like a bad penny, Beth. You'll see me again soon."

"That's what I'm afraid of."

They smiled at each other, and Jake walked down the hall with Cody by his side. He rode the elevator down, stopped at the front reception window and collected his weapons. He nodded at the curious cop behind the bulletproof glass, and exited the building.

Jake sighed as he and Cody walked down the street in the dark. "As Terrell often says, being a good man is a thankless job."

Cody barked once.

"Being a good dog is a thankless job too."

Cody barked again.

"Why do we do it?"

Cody had no reply.

Taxi cabs passed by, but Jake ignored them as he continued walking and mulling things over. Sometimes he just had to walk and think. Maybe he'd wander into a new pub and try a new beer. Maybe he'd cruise down the coast to San Diego. Right now he just wanted a shower and a shot of whiskey.

His black phone buzzed with a call from McKay. He answered, "Thanks for keeping me out of jail, McKay."

"You're welcome," she said. "Now I need you to do something for me."

"I'm afraid to ask what it is," Jake said.

"It's simple, just keep an eye on the Golden Gate Bridge, at dawn and at dusk, for the next several days."

"Go boating and fishing twice a day? Okay, if you insist."

"Keep your eyes open for trouble. If you see anything suspicious, call me at once," McKay said.

"You've got it."

The phone went dark. Jake put it in his pocket and continued walking.

After a while, a blue sedan pulled up next to them and stopped. The front passenger window was down and Jake saw a cute black woman behind the wheel. Alicia waved at him. "Come on, you two bad boys, hop in the car."

Jake opened the back door for Cody and then got into the front passenger seat. "Does your husband know you pick up questionable-looking hitchhikers?"

Alicia smiled. "Terrell asked me to give a ride to a pain-in-the-butt troublemaker, and a dog who's too smart for his own good. And to ask them to come over to the house for dinner tonight—along with Sarah Chance, who should know better than to date Jukebox. Did I get the right guys?"

"You did, indeed. Thank you, Alicia."

Cody pressed his paw on the window control, lowered his window and put his head out—sniffing the intriguing scents of the evening as the car drove along.

CHAPTER 61

Dmitry sat in his rental car near a restaurant, watching Wolfe's Jeep and waiting for him to show up.

A blue car arrived, dropping off Wolfe and his dog. They got into the Jeep and began following the car.

Dmitry sat there until the Jeep was several blocks away, then followed from a discreet distance, tracking it by a beacon he'd placed underneath.

When the beacon came to a stop, he saw its location on a map on his dashboard. He waited a few minutes and then drove slowly through a residential neighborhood until he spotted the Jeep parked in front of a house.

He found a spot down the street where he could sit in his car and observe the house while waiting for his target to show himself. There was no point in harming anyone else in the home. He was only being paid for the one target, and collateral damage wasn't his style.

He tapped his phone and sent a text to Elena. She didn't reply, again. It was as if she was ignoring him. Fine, so be it.

No matter; he would kill Wolfe tonight. Hopefully the man

would enjoy his last meal, and drink plenty of alcohol to slow his reflexes.

When Wolfe left the house, Dmitry would shoot him as he got into his car, or follow him and strike when he parked the car and got out.

How many men had he killed while they sat in the driver's seat, putting on their seat belt and not paying any attention to their surroundings?

Inside the house, Jake filled a bowl with water and set it on the kitchen floor. Cody lapped up half of the water in a hurry and then let out a wet cough.

Alicia cut a loaf of sourdough bread lengthwise into two long halves, spread some garlic butter on each half, and put them in the oven.

Jake grabbed a couple of beers from the fridge. He and Cody went outside, where Terrell was grilling steaks. He handed a beer to Terrell. "A cold one for the grill master."

The two friends studied each other.

Terrell drank from the bottle and then pointed his finger at Jake. "The Jake I know would never take money from LEOs and give it to criminals."

"I wasn't taking money from cops. You guys already have tons of tax dollars to work with. The Family took it from a foreign gang of heroin dealing kidnappers, and kept it as payment for putting the gang out of business."

"In other words, you put an Italian mob hit on the Russian mafia? And then stole the Russians' money to pay the Italians for the hit?"

Jake scratched his chin. "According to the media, the members of a Russian gang and a Serb gang killed each other, fighting over a fortune in heroin."

"A friend of yours at your former media job reported it first, saying she'd received a tip from an unnamed source."

"She's good. I'm sure she has lots of sources."

"Uh huh. When I got to the warehouse, a gang started shooting at me and the SWAT team. Then, an unknown individual on the second floor dropped a flash-bang grenade into the crowd on the ground."

"Great idea."

"After it went off, he got into a gun fight with the gang and fought them with what I'd call infantry Marine precision. One shot, one kill, over and over. Just like a MOS 0311 rifleman who'd been to SOI and was firing an M4 carbine in a war."

"Could have been anybody." Jake leaned toward the barbecue to give the steaks a critical look.

Terrell waved Jake away, and used tongs to lift a steak and look at the underside.

"Sorry I lost my temper," Terrell said. "My headaches have been worse lately."

"Sorry for putting you through hell so often," Jake said.

"Never a dull moment when you're around," Terrell said.

It seemed to Jake as if Terrell was wrestling with whether Jake deserved jail time or a pat on the back. Jake steered the conversation away from the warehouse. "Grinds, you never told me you were deputized by the U.S. Marshals."

"I've got a few secrets. Speaking of secrets, how did you know the cash was hidden among the six-packs of bottled water?"

"When I was a photojournalist, I saw a story about the Miami police finding drug money hidden that way when it was being transported in trucks."

Terrell turned the steaks. "Well, at least you squared things with Chief Pierce."

"Yeah, and it only took two million dollars to cheer up his grouchy ass."

"We need that money to buy the latest crime-fighting

technology. The city is having a budget crisis. Your donation could save the lives of my coworkers."

"I'm glad I could help my local cops. Let's do this again next week."

"Sure, I'll put that on my 'F' list."

"What's an 'F' list?"

"It's like a bucket list, but it starts with an F."

Jake's phone buzzed; Sarah was pulling in. He looked through the sliding glass door and saw her walk into the kitchen, getting a hug from Alicia.

Alicia said something and gestured at the refrigerator. Sarah opened the fridge, grabbed a beer, and joined them on the patio.

Jake hugged her and held her tight for a while. The bruises on his body cried out in pain, but he tried to ignore the hurt.

He looked over Sarah's shoulder and saw Alicia standing by the window and smiling at him. He smiled back.

Terrell saw Jake wince when he hugged Sarah, hiding his pain. He'd seen that before. When the hug ended, Terrell yanked on Jake's shirt and lifted it up, exposing the marks left from his beating. "Do you want to explain these injuries, Jukebox?"

"I tripped and fell down onto a pile of rubber hoses."

Sarah gasped when she saw the red marks, welts and bruises all over Jake's chest and stomach. "You need to see a doctor."

"It's all right, Sarah. I'll be fine. And besides, you're a doctor. Don't you have some liniment that's good for man or beast?"

She brushed aside his attempt at humor. "What happened?"

Jake looked off in the distance, thinking about Razor. "Ask me no questions and I'll tell you no lies."

"Wrong, you lie like a rug," Terrell said. He put the steaks on a platter and led everyone inside, where Alicia was tossing her famous Caesar salad.

A wine store employee rang the doorbell to deliver several bottles of Silver Oak cabernet.

Alicia looked at the fine wine in surprise. "Jake, you shouldn't have."

"No worries, those are from Dylan's locker at the wine company. He bought hundreds of top-rated bottles and then quit drinking. That's just wrong, but he gave me free rein to enjoy any and all of the collection. You *have* to drink this so it doesn't go to waste."

"Well, in that case, you might want to donate a few bottles to my empty wine rack, just to save your liver from undue stress," Alicia said, laughing.

Jake laughed with her. When her back was turned, he sent a text to the wine company, scheduling a delivery for the next day of a mixed case of wines she'd enjoy.

Outside the house, Dmitry continued waiting in his car. He ran a leathery hand through his salt-and-pepper hair. Various aches and pains in his body were telling him he was getting too old for this work. He was looking forward to going home on the next available flight.

The coughing fits came upon him then. He hacked violently into a tissue several times. When he took it away from his mouth, it was red with blood.

"Sweet lady tobacco, the one true love of my life." He lowered a window and reached into his coat for an unfiltered Russian cigarette, smoking while he waited.

He craved a shot of vodka too, but he would never drink before a job, only after. This would be over soon enough, and then he'd enjoy a celebratory drink on the airplane.

CHAPTER 62

The doorbell rang and Jake said, "I'll get it." He opened the door and let Beth Cushman in along with her little boy, Kyle.

When Kyle saw Jake, he asked his mom, "What happened to his face?"

Beth looked at Jake and shook her head.

Jake smiled at Kyle. "That's what my mom asked the doctor when I was born."

Kyle laughed. "Can I pet Cody?"

"Wait, I have to give him a talk first."

"I know!" Kyle said.

Jake smiled at the precocious kid. He saw Beth watching him. Kyle was her world—her reason to get out of bed every day. "Cody, be friends. You're off duty."

Cody shook his whole body, stretched his front legs and then his back legs, flopped his ears from side to side, and let his tongue loll out of his mouth.

Kyle knelt on the floor and petted Cody while Beth stood close by and kept her eye on them.

Alicia carried a basket of hot sourdough bread into the dining room and set it on the table. "Okay, let's eat."

Everybody took seats around the table. Terrell put a rare steak on a plate and set it on the floor for Cody, who attacked it, chomping on it as if he was worried that someone might take it away from him.

Jake sat with Sarah on his left. He held her hand as he tasted the wine.

Sarah looked at Jake with a bemused smile on her face and then glanced at Alicia. The two women grinned. Sarah said, "Jake, I'm right handed."

Jake turned to her. "What?"

"You'll have to let go of my hand if I'm going to be able to eat dinner."

"Oops, sorry. It's, uh, a new diet. Yeah, the hand-holding weight-loss plan."

Sarah tilted her head. "Are you implying I need to lose weight?"

"No, no, don't change a thing. Should I just shut my big mouth now?"

"Yes," Terrell said.

Alicia said, "Jake, this red wine tastes delicious."

"You should try it with some freshly baked chocolate chip cookies," Jake said.

Terrell savored a bite of steak and took a drink of wine. "I can't keep covering for you when you break the law, Jukebox. It's a full-time job. You need legal protection to keep your dumb ass out of jail."

Jake nodded. "I'm a lawyer now, so maybe that'll help my dumb ass."

Sarah stared at him. "So, it's true? You're a lawyer?"

"Yeah, I studied law online."

"Why didn't you ever mention it?"

"Lawyer haters would have tried to talk me out of it."

Terrell said, "What if you could carry that U.S. Marshals badge full-time? Get the creds to go with it. Maybe Agent

McKay could talk them into putting you on their payroll and making you an official manhunter."

"I'm not qualified to be a Marshal. They're highly trained and bad to the bone."

"You could go through their training."

"That would be an honor, but then I'd have to drive to the federal building every morning and report to my boss. No thanks. I'd rather just be a boat bum lawyer and spend most days taking the *Far Niente* out on the water."

"Good luck with that. The feds have their claws in you and they'll never let go."

"Thanks for being the voice of doom. I can always count on you."

Alicia said, "Jake, you should just say no. Tell the government to find another tool. Not that I'm saying you're a tool." She studied her fingernails.

"You're right, Alicia, I am a tool. I'm their blunt instrument. They use me to hammer on their enemies."

Sarah looked at Cody, and considered his wound that was healing up and scarring over. She crossed her arms and shook her head.

Alicia noticed Sarah's concern. "Jake, you have a family and a home now—Sarah and Cody and the *Far Niente*. You have to take them into consideration. Don't be reckless."

Jake nodded and stared at the tablecloth. "I need to learn to control my temper, but..."

"And think twice before you get deputized by the U.S. Marshals and become involved in some kind of dangerous task force."

Jake glanced at Terrell, who gave him a slight shake of the head.

"That's true," Jake said. "But it's usually a secret, so your family doesn't worry."

Terrell kept an innocent look on his face. "Sorry I mentioned that. But talk to McKay. Maybe your deputized status could be useful."

Jake nodded. "The law says if the threat that prompted the deputation is ongoing, the individual may qualify for a continuation of the Special Deputy U.S. Marshal status until such time as the threat has abated."

"There you go again with that legal mumbo jumbo."

"I think I'll ask them to deputize Cody instead. He can wear the badge on his collar and be in charge."

Cody stopped chewing his steak bone for a moment, let out a dog burp, and nodded his head.

After dinner, Jake said his goodbyes, then walked Sarah to her car and gave her a kiss. "Cody was hoping you'd join us on the *Far Niente* for an after-dinner drink."

"Oh, Cody was hoping that, huh?"

Cody wagged his tail.

Sarah smiled. "I'll be happy to come over later, after I check on a patient at my clinic. But no fooling around; you have all those bruises."

"That's just wrong. I think we should talk it over ... in bed."

"Unbutton your shirt—let me see your chest."

"Can I say that to you sometime? It would only be fair." Jake unbuttoned his shirt.

Sarah studied his injuries, touching him here and there. "Soak in a hot bath and drink some of that Irish painkiller you love so much. See you soon." She got into her car, and Jake and Cody climbed into the Jeep.

Both cars drove away in opposite directions.

Dmitry observed his target kissing a woman. Was she the girlfriend Elena had planned to kidnap? Did Elena fail, or did

Wolfe have more than one girlfriend?

He couldn't shoot Wolfe without putting the woman at risk and that was against his personal code.

He waited until Wolfe drove off and then followed him.

Now was the time to get him alone and finish this.

CHAPTER 63

Jake drove to a park where he stopped the Jeep and clipped a leash onto Cody's collar. They walked toward a fir tree in a dark corner and Jake went behind it, reached into a hedge, and removed a black trash bag.

They returned to the car and climbed inside, where Jake took a quick look in the bag. It held a vacuum-bagged bundle of cash. He'd hidden it there before delivering the truckload to the police, guessing they wouldn't miss this one small slice out of the multimillion-dollar pie.

Jake tossed the bag onto the front passenger seat and drove away.

Dmitry followed Wolfe to a park and saw him get out of his car and walk among the trees.

What was the fool doing? Was this a trap?

He used night vision goggles to keep an eye on his prey.

Soon, Wolfe came walking back toward his car. He had a bag in his hand. Dmitry considered trying to shoot him now, in this quiet place. However, it was too dark. If he drove past, one tap on his car brakes would turn on the red lights. If he tried to sneak up on foot, the dog would smell and hear him before he could get close.

Dmitry sat watching the man and dog get into the car and drive away. He waited a while, then began following, but not getting too close.

Jake didn't notice the car following him as he drove to the church where Father O'Leary held mass and gave confessions.

When he and Cody arrived at the old stone church, he grabbed the trash bag and went inside. Candles flickered in the dim light, emanating the aroma of beeswax. The polished wooden pews were empty except for one young woman, kneeling and crying.

A small sign said that Father O'Leary would be hearing confessions this evening.

Jake led Cody into a confessional booth, closed the door and knelt on the pad, causing the light to go out. In the darkness he said, "Bless me, Father, for I have sinned. So many sins, so little time. It's all a blur to me now. And Cody too—if he could talk, the tales he would tell you."

Father O'Leary chuckled in the dark. "Ah, Jake, how do you manage to sin more than anyone else, when there are only twenty-four hours in a day?"

"I make an extra effort, and I use one of those day planner things. Right now I want to partially atone for my sins with a donation to the soup kitchen."

"Good lad. We're going through a tough time. We'll be all out of food for the homeless folks in just a few days without a donation."

"This will buy some more meals."

"Where did you get the money? Did you come by it honestly, I hope?"

"Not exactly. A criminal gang got this money by hurting people. I took it from them, and now the cash will help those in need."

"That works for me. Are you trying to stay out of trouble?"

"Not really. Sorry, Padre."

O'Leary let out a sigh. "At least you're honest about your shortcomings."

"You'd never believe me if I wasn't."

"God bless you, son, and Cody too."

"Thank you, Father." Jake left the trash bag in the booth, said his goodbyes, and exited the church.

Dmitry found the Jeep parked on the street but there was no sign of Wolfe. He might be in one of the restaurants, or visiting someone at an apartment building. As he passed by a church, Wolfe came out the front door and walked down the steps.

Dmitry was on a one-way street and had to go around the block. By then, the Jeep was rolling. He cursed and followed the beacon signal.

Jake drove to the cemetery where Stuart was buried. He and Cody visited Stuart's grave and Jake went down on one knee.

"Hey, Stuart. It's me Jake, and Cody is here too. We miss you, buddy. I wanted you to know I'm taking good care of Cody, and he's taking good care of me."

Cody dropped to his belly on the grass next to the grave and let out a mournful howl.

"We got rid of the heroin dealers. Their drugs won't kill any more veterans. And they won't be trading AK-47s to terrorists who shoot at our troops."

Cody howled again. Jake patted him on the back for a while and then faced Stuart's grave. "Rest in peace, Marine. Fair winds and following seas, brother. We've got it from here. Semper Fidelis, until we meet again…"

When Jake tried to get up and walk away, he couldn't move. Once in a while his grief would overwhelm him and break out of the vault where he kept it locked away. He knelt there and wept, for Stuart and his family, and for so many other families who had lost someone in military service.

Cody whined and licked Jake's tear-streaked face.

The world seemed to stop for Jake as he knelt there like a statue. After so many of his friends had died so young, he felt both bitter for their loss and also grateful to be alive. He was painfully aware that each day was a gift. It could all end tomorrow—there was no guarantee that you or anyone you knew would live another day.

Jake wiped his eyes on his sleeve, then got to his feet and walked to another part of the cemetery. He stopped at the plain grave of a Russian assassin. The marker only listed his name and date of death, the day Jake had killed him.

Jake reached into a jacket pocket and took out a pint bottle of Russian Standard vodka and two shot glasses. He filled both shots, drank one down, and slowly poured the other one onto the grave.

"I wanted to tell you that Elena hacked your offshore bank accounts. Now she's in jail, and I've got her phone, along with your passwords. I have access to your accounts and the millions you were paid to kill people. Thanks for the money. I haven't decided what to do with it yet, but you can bet I'll put it to good use."

Headlights approached, and a dark sedan parked near the

Jeep. A broad-shouldered man got out and walked toward Jake in a non-threatening way.

Cody alerted and showed his teeth. Jake gave him a command, and Cody trotted ten feet away, then turned and circled behind the stranger.

The man stopped at the gravesite and looked at the name on the marker. "We had a mutual friend."

"Your voice … you sound just like him."

"My name's Dmitry. I heard that you killed my friend with a Marine Corps knife." He drew a wicked-looking blade.

Jake drew the KA-BAR knife from behind his waist. "Yes, I did. This one, in fact. He left me no choice. Are you going to force me to make the same decision?"

Dmitry nodded and tossed his pistol on the grass.

Jake drew his pistol and tossed it there too.

"When will this ever end?" Jake said.

"Maybe in one hundred years, when the world has all new people." Dmitry said.

Cody felt a threat from the unknown man. He sensed a change in Jake's body language and saw the stranger holding a shiny blade.

Danger.

Threat.

Protect.

Cody did what he'd been trained to do. He bolted straight at the threatening man, snapping his teeth at him to protect his handler.

CHAPTER 64

Dmitry ignored the dog's attack, lunged forward and tried to stab Jake in the chest.

Jake dodged the blade and slashed at Dmitry's throat, missing by an inch.

Cody ran behind Dmitry, then bit him on the back of his thigh, making him cry out in pain.

Jake leapt in and stabbed at his enemy. The tip of his knife grazed Dmitry's shoulder.

Dmitry grunted. He slashed at Jake and cut his jacket, barely missing his stomach. He then charged full bore into Jake, betting everything on his attempt to sink his blade into Jake's heart.

Cody snarled and leaped at Dmitry's knife arm, biting down and trying to disarm him.

When Cody bit Dmitry's elbow and pulled him sideways, Jake punched his opponent in the throat.

Dmitry staggered on his feet, stunned. He put one hand to his throat, and dropped his knife. Cody picked up the knife by the handle and carried it six feet away, dropping it before returning to the fight.

"I'm sorry it had to be this way, Dmitry," Jake said. "We might have been friends under different circumstances."

"Get it over with," Dmitry said, his voice hoarse. "I'm dying of lung cancer. You'll be doing me a favor."

"Are you working for Elena?"

"I was, until she kidnapped a woman named Sarah and was planning to kill her. That's against my code. I was going to take the thumb drive from you and talk Elena into letting Sarah go free."

Jake stared at him for a moment. "The police have the thumb drive, Sarah was rescued, and Elena is in jail. Her money is gone. You won't get paid."

"I don't care about the money. I earn plenty in Vegas," Dmitry said.

"Elena also kidnapped two children, and started dealing in large quantities of heroin."

Dmitry cursed. "In that case, I'm glad she's in jail."

"Go home, Dmitry. I have no quarrel with you. Maybe I'll visit you in Vegas sometime," Jake said.

Dmitry looked doubtful. "Are you serious?"

Jake put his knife away, then picked up his pistol and holstered it. He poured vodka into the two empty shot glasses and handed one to Dmitry. They both drank the shots.

Jake held out his hand. Dmitry hesitated, looked Jake in the eye, and then shook hands.

Jake and Cody walked to the Jeep and drove off. As Jake headed toward the Golden Gate Bridge, he felt a wave of exhaustion wash over him. He was looking forward to going home, having a drink and then going to bed with Sarah.

His phone buzzed with a text from Ray Kirby: *Chief said you wanted to fight me. Great, I'm at the 16th Street boxing gym, waiting to kick your ass. Get over here.*

Jake replied: *No, Kirby. Chief Pierce will decide on the day, time and location.*

Kirby: *You're stalling.*

Jake: *The fight was my idea.*

Kirby: *That was big talk, but now it's obvious you're afraid of me.*

Jake: *You think a combat veteran is afraid of a boxing match? Thanks for the laugh.*

Kirby: *I can't wait to get you in the ring.*

Jake: *The feeling is mutual. Until then, this conversation is over.*

Jake received several more texts from Kirby, but he ignored them.

Soon, Jake and Cody were on board the *Far Niente*. Cody pressed the lever on the water cooler to fill his bowl, taking a long drink.

Walking into the galley, Jake grabbed the bottle of Redbreast Irish Whiskey and poured himself a glass.

He felt a familiar post-combat depression setting in. Today he'd had to kill men—kill or be killed. Their deaths would haunt him now, weighing on his soul. Hopefully, the whiskey might help him forget about them for a while.

"Cody, stand post."

Cody trotted out onto the aft deck to guard the boat.

Jake carried the whiskey bottle and his glass into the master stateroom. He got undressed and took a long shower, letting the hot water ease some of the pain from the bruises and welts on his chest, stomach and thighs. Every few minutes, he opened the shower door and took a drink of whiskey. After the hot water and alcohol eased some of the pain, he toweled off and then put on a pair of faded jeans and a T-shirt. Walking barefoot and carrying the whiskey bottle to the galley, he poured himself another drink.

A beeping sound came from a security system speaker. Jake looked at his phone and saw a CCTV view of Sarah approaching the boat. Outside, Cody put his front paws on the aft rail, barking happily and wagging his tail. Sarah came on board and she scratched Cody behind the ears. Cody followed her inside, where Jake gave her a hug. When she hugged him tight in return, he grunted in pain.

"Did you soak in a hot bath?" Sarah asked.

"This boat doesn't have a bathtub, but I took a hot shower," Jake replied. He drank from his glass of whiskey.

Sarah stared at his face. "Jake, are you okay? You look like there's something weighing on your mind."

Jake tossed back the rest of his drink in one gulp. "I guess I'm feeling tired ... of life."

She looked at his jacket hanging on the back of a bar stool. "Why is there a gash in your jacket?"

"I stopped by Stuart's grave. Somebody tried to kill me."

She sighed and reached for his hand. "Come to bed."

"All right, but first I'm going to take us out on the water and get away from it all." Jake walked out the sliding door to the aft deck. He untied the lines, went upstairs to the bridge, and cruised out onto the Bay to a quiet cove where he dropped anchor. Looking around at the empty water on all sides, he once again felt grateful for being able to borrow Dylan's boat. He went downstairs to the salon. "Cody, you're on guard duty tonight."

Cody trotted out onto the deck.

Sarah took Jake by the hand and led him to the master stateroom. They got undressed and slid between the sheets of his bed. She ran her soft hands over his bruised chest and stomach.

To Jake, her hands felt like they had magical healing powers to soothe his battered body and soul.

"Where does it hurt, Jake?"

"Everywhere."

Her hands went everywhere.

Cody stood guard out on the deck and gave his two favorite people their privacy. Jake and Sarah were meant to be together as mates, he could tell that by their pheromones, but two-footed folks were overly complicated compared to four-footed.

His alpha was also a difficult man to be with—a Marine who couldn't seem to stop fighting. He could sense Sarah's frustration with Jake and her yearning for peace, but his alpha was a warrior and would always be a warrior. Sarah was a healer, maybe she could heal Jake's troubled heart.

He took in a deep breath of clean ocean air and let it out, shook out his fur and lay prone on the deck.

This life by the seashore was so much better than when he'd searched for explosives in the hot desert. All of his handlers had died so far, and he felt lucky to be living with Jake, the man who could "speak dog." Hopefully Jake wouldn't die like the others. He'd fight to protect Jake, and Sarah too, she was special to him. She looked into his eyes and understood him like few others could. He wished she would move in and live on the boat.

The moon shone down upon the *Far Niente*. Sea birds called, fish jumped in the sparkling water and the boat rocked gently on the waves.

Cody sniffed the salty air, gazed at the ocean and the stars, and then put his head down on his front paws. Nobody would get onto this boat unless he allowed them to. If there was any danger, he'd take action. Sometimes a dog has to do what a dog has to do.

CHAPTER 65

Epilogue:

The next morning, Jake woke up before dawn. He smelled freshly brewed coffee and … dog breath. When he opened his eyes, he saw Cody's face inches from his own. "Is it morning already?"

Cody ran out of the room. Jake followed, grabbing some clothes off the floor and pulling them on before closing the bedroom door behind him to avoid waking Sarah.

He walked to the sliding glass door at the aft of the boat and opened it. Cody went out onto the deck, to a spot off to the side, and peed on the small artificial grass lawn. Jake didn't remember closing the door last night.

In the galley, the preprogrammed coffeemaker was hissing. A fresh pot of coffee was nearly full. Jake poured a cup, added some Baileys Irish Cream, and went upstairs to the bridge.

He navigated the *Far Niente* through the water of the San Francisco Bay and dropped anchor near the Golden Gate Bridge. Agent McKay had asked him to keep an eye on the bridge at dawn and at dusk for the next few days. That was fine with him, it just meant more time out on the water, which he loved.

Jake went downstairs and stood on the aft deck to do some fishing. Cody sat next to him, like his shadow.

It was still dark out, but visibility was good. There wasn't much fog. Jake took a sip of coffee and enjoyed the ocean breeze on his face. "Let's try this again, Cody. Maybe this time we'll actually get to catch some fish without being interrupted."

Cody sat there and wagged his tail, and it thumped on the deck of the boat. Thump, thump, thump.

A while later, Jake got a call from Lauren Stephens.

"Good morning, Jake. The kids have been asking when you and Cody will be coming over for dinner."

"Good morning, Lauren. You're up early. Would tomorrow work for dinner?"

"Yes, tomorrow works."

"Can I bring my friend, Sarah? She's the veterinarian I mentioned who knows people at service dog schools."

"Yes, of course. I'd like to ask her advice."

"How are the kids doing?"

"Much better. Ben is talking constantly, mostly about how he wants to be a dog trainer when he grows up. Chrissy and I picked out a karate school, and she's excited about starting lessons soon."

"That's good to hear."

"And thanks for suggesting that I hire Paul. He's been a great help around here. Oh, and he didn't drink last night. He's giving sobriety a try."

"Tell him I said congratulations. My sister can help him with that."

"Nicole has been wonderful with the kids."

"I'm glad."

"Jake, is there any way I could convince you to work for me?"

"You mean through Levi's security firm?"

"No, directly for me as a consultant, so I can talk with you about ... situations. It's lonely at the top."

"You could retain me as one of your lawyers."

"You're an attorney? Yes, that would be perfect. How much is your retainer? I'll send it today."

"For you, one dollar."

She was silent for a while, then said, "That proves my instincts about you were correct. Thank you, Jake."

"You're welcome, Lauren. Call me any time, and our conversations will remain confidential under the rule of attorney-client privilege."

"See you tomorrow." Lauren ended the call.

Jake sipped his coffee and watched a motor yacht cruise under the bridge. It came to a stop and set anchor close to one of the towers—too close.

He suddenly felt a strange sense of impending danger. He could almost smell it, if such a thing was possible. There was a tingling at the back of his neck, and he heard the now-familiar little song in his head, similar to the way some people with epilepsy hear a tune just before they have a seizure.

Cody sensed the change in Jake. He stood up and let out a low growl as his eyes searched the horizon and his nose sniffed the air for threats.

Jake grabbed a pair of night vision binoculars. As he studied the yacht, his black phone buzzed. He took it out of his pocket and answered the encrypted call. "Go."

Secret Service Agent Shannon McKay spoke in the no-nonsense, controlled tone of someone who was directing a mission. "This is McKay. We have a situation. Please confirm that you are on board your boat, near the Golden Gate Bridge."

"Confirmed."

"Do you see a motor yacht anchored in unusually close proximity to the San Francisco tower of the bridge?"

"Affirmative."

"I'm sending photos to your phone. Compare them to the yacht and make a positive ID."

"Roger that." Jake studied the photos and then observed the yacht through night vision binoculars. "Yacht identity confirmed."

"Jake, are you ready, willing and able to assist the President's Operational Emergency Team in stopping an attack by foreigners on American citizens?"

"The POETs? Yes, I am. Give me a sitrep."

"How many people do you see on that yacht?"

"I see three men on board. One of them is wearing a large backpack."

"When you were a temporary operative in the CIA Special Activities Division, you wiped out a terrorist cell known for beheading hundreds of women who refused to be sex slaves."

"Correct."

"Those men on the yacht are terrorists from that cell."

Jake glared at the boat and clenched his jaw as he was reminded of his recurring nightmares from that mission. "That can't be right. I didn't leave any survivors, except for the rescued female hostages."

"These three terrorists were away at the time, trading heroin to arms dealers in exchange for AK-47s."

Jake's anger boiled to the surface. "Are these bounty hunters? Hunting for me or Cody?"

"No, there's still a price on your head, but those men are here for a different reason. That backpack contains a bomb. Their intention is to plant it on the bridge tower and detonate it by phone during commuter rush hour."

Jake cursed. "Your orders?"

"Terminate all targets. You'll find a sniper rifle in the cabinet where you store your shotgun."

"Confirm the order to take no prisoners."

"Confirmed. These are suicide bombers. If their boat is

boarded by law enforcement or the Coast Guard, they'll detonate the device, right on top of their boat's fuel tank."

"Acknowledged. What is the current status and proximity of LEO personnel?"

"The FBI bird and the SFPD boats are standing by at a safe distance, by request of Homeland Security. A Coast Guard cutter is heading in your direction. Once you've completed your mission, you are to leave the area at once, so they can arrive and take command of the situation."

"Have you ruled out collateral damage?"

"Affirmative. There are no other passengers on board the targeted yacht."

"Collateral intel acknowledged. Mission underway."

Jake opened a tall cabinet and found the sniper rifle. "Cody, *patrol*."

Cody walked on patrol in a circular route around the perimeter of the boat deck, protecting Jake's back, with his eyes and ears alert for any boats or scuba divers that might be approaching.

Jake got into firing position. He put an earbud into his left ear and connected the wire to the black phone. Looking through the rifle scope, he saw one of the men on the yacht using a dinghy crane to lower a rubber raft down to the water's surface. Next, the man wearing the backpack climbed down a boarding ladder and got onto the raft.

Jake drew upon his war experience with explosive devices as he judged the distance between the yacht and the bridge tower. His calculations included an additional explosion from that size of yacht's large fuel tank. He made a decision and focused his weapon on the man in the raft. He saw a device attached to the backpack. It appeared to be a detonator—the kind terrorists could shoot at if a cell phone jammer was blocking their call to set off the bomb.

Jake put the crosshairs of his rifle scope on the detonator and took careful aim. He inhaled and then let out a slow breath as he whispered a Bible verse.

"The avenger of blood shall put the murderer to death."

He squeezed the trigger and fired his weapon.

The backpack exploded, along with the boat's fuel tank, in a giant ball of flame that shot straight up into the sky instead of against the tower. The yacht was blown to pieces, creating a junkyard of burning chunks of wreckage, floating in a flaming oil slick.

Jake noted that the base of the bridge tower was scorched but remained standing strong. "Mission accomplished, McKay, but they didn't go quietly."

"I saw it on a surveillance cam. Son of a…"

"Your orders were to terminate all targets. An enemy boat is definitely a target," Jake said.

"Get out of there—now!" McKay said.

"Withdrawing from area of operation." Jake put the rifle back into the cabinet and walked quickly toward the stairs to the bridge. On his earbud he heard McKay take a deep breath and let it out.

"Wolfe?"

"Yeah, McKay?"

"Thank you for your service—and welcome to the POETs."

Jake didn't reply. He ended the call and climbed the steps to the bridge, where he took the helm. He maneuvered the boat away from the Golden Gate Bridge and turned the vessel toward Sausalito, pushing the throttles forward to increase speed. The twin engines growled in response, and the boat rocketed across the water.

Jake felt a strange sense of peace. Three terrorists had left this earth by his hand. He felt lighter somehow, from the absence of their weight on his shoulders and his tortured soul. Maybe those three who had escaped justice were the reason for his recurring nightmares. Perhaps now he could sleep through the night for once.

He opened the windows of the bridge and felt the salty sea breeze on his skin.

Hearing movement behind him, he turned to see Sarah coming up the stairs with Cody by her side.

Cody ran over to Jake, who got down on one knee, patted him, and whispered, "You did good, Cody. Thank you for protecting my back. We got it done, partner. Everybody is safe now. Semper Fi."

Cody wagged his tail and held Jake's hand in his mouth.

Sarah crossed her arms and kept her distance from Jake. She repeated a question from a previous time she'd had suspicions about him. "So, Jake, what were those noises I heard?"

Jake knew she was testing him. It seemed like women were always testing him. Maybe it was in their DNA. He felt bad that he had to lie to her. "A motor yacht's fuel tank exploded. Probably a tragic accident caused by an electrical problem."

"You're *lying* to me, Jake. I didn't just hear it—I saw it. When I woke up and went to the galley for a cup of coffee, I looked out the sliding glass door just as you fired your rifle."

Jake took a deep breath and let it out. "I'm sorry you had to see that. It's classified as top secret. You can't ever talk about it, or the government will come down on you like a ton of bricks."

"If you knew it was top secret, why did you invite me on board the boat with you?"

"I had no idea this was going to happen until I got a call from Washington a few minutes ago."

"So, Washington calls, and you kill people. Is that it?"

"*Duty* calls. You have no idea what those men were capable of, or the evil things they've done. I put a stop to that today, and I'd do it again in a heartbeat."

"Who was on board that boat?"

"Terrorists, serial rapists, and mass murderers who have killed scores of men, women and children. They were attempting to blow up that bridge tower at rush hour to kill a lot of Americans."

"Were there any survivors?"

"No. My orders were to make sure they all died. I followed my orders and killed every person on the yacht. And I did it with what the CIA calls *extreme prejudice*." Jake glanced back at the smoking wreckage.

Sarah stared at him, seeing the angry look on his face. "How can you be sure there weren't any innocent people on that yacht?"

"Because I asked. Those three terrorists were under constant surveillance. There was a careful accounting to prevent any possible collateral damage."

"I just—I don't know what to say. I can't believe you're an assassin who murders people in cold blood."

"They were enemy soldiers, out of uniform, engaged in an act of war against the citizens of the United States. I killed them the way I was trained to do. Infantry Marines do one thing—fight and kill the enemy—and we're damned good at it."

"Was this a one-time service for your country, or did you sign up for something I probably don't want to know about?"

"I might have to serve my country again someday in the near future. I'm sorry—I made a deal."

"Is Cody part of the deal?"

"Yes."

"He's an innocent dog!"

"That innocent dog attacked criminals to save your life."

Sarah looked at Cody and shook her head. "What about your plans to be a lawyer?"

"I'm still going to practice law, but I'll have to take the law into my own hands once in a while, at the request of my government."

Sarah looked back toward the Golden Gate Bridge. The sun

was starting to rise and smoke floated in the air from the burning wreckage. The police boat, *SF Marine 1*, had arrived on the scene and the SFFD fireboat, *Phoenix*, was firing her water cannons at the blaze. A black helicopter circled overhead, and a Coast Guard cutter was approaching the area.

Jake saw the conflicted emotions playing across Sarah's face. He guessed she might be thinking that if he hadn't intervened, there would have been a catastrophe with a high number of casualties. Instead, he'd destroyed a motor yacht and killed three terrorists. It was the right thing to do, but she probably wondered why her man had to be the one to do it.

Cody pressed his head against Sarah's stomach. She petted him and started crying. Jake went over to her and held her in his arms. She buried her face against his neck and wept.

Jake held her and let her cry it out. She'd been through hell lately because of him. He wondered if this might be the last time he'd ever hold her in his arms. She'd probably be better off with somebody else—another man who was far different than him. He couldn't change into that guy. He was way past that point. Maybe it was in her best interests if he let her go now so she could find someone who was better for her. That was probably the right thing to do. His heart felt heavy as he resigned himself to what was coming.

Sarah lifted her head and looked at him with wet eyes. "What does this mean for us? Do we have a future together?"

"That's up to you, Sarah. I haven't changed, but now you know the cold reality of my life. I've agreed to temporarily resume my black ops work as one of the government's assassins."

"I was so glad when you sent me that text message and called me your girlfriend, but now…"

"Today I was going to ask if you wanted to be in an exclusive relationship."

"Really? Are you sure?"

"Yes, I'm sure, but what about you? After what you've just seen…"

Sarah wiped her eyes on her sleeve. "Honestly, Jake, I don't know. I'm willing to continue dating you, but as far as an exclusive relationship is concerned—I'll need to think that over for a while."

"I understand. We can just take it day by day and see how it goes. Does that work for you?"

"Yes, I can do that. But please don't tell me about your missions. I don't want to know." She looked at Cody and bit her lip.

"Fair enough," Jake said.

The sun began to rise, painting the sky and water with streaks of purple and gold.

Sarah watched the sunrise, deep in thought.

Cody sniffed the morning scents from the Bay and the shoreline as he stood close to Sarah and leaned against her.

Jake navigated the boat across the water and headed toward the harbor, his body and soul feeling beaten and worn far beyond his young age.

The three of them didn't know what the future might hold, but they were going to face it together—one day at a time.

Ready for the next story about Jake and Cody? Grab a copy of book three! Tap here: Killer Lawyer (Jake Wolfe Book 3).

DEAR READER

Dear Reader,

I do plenty of research while writing novels for you, and I try to include interesting facts and technology for your reading entertainment.

Quite a few readers send emails asking me which things in my books are real. To answer that for everyone, I've put together a quick list pertaining to this book.

Note: The following list contains spoilers, so if anybody skipped to the back, I advise them to please read the book before reading this list.

First, what is *not* real:

As in every book, names, characters, places, events, incidents, and dialogue are all products of the author's imagination or are used fictitiously. Any resemblance to actual persons living or dead, businesses, organizations, events, or locales is entirely coincidental.

~

Second, what *is* real:

The following things really do exist, but are used fictitiously in this novel. Noted in order of appearance:

The Russian shotgun drone is a flying weapon that holds a magazine of 10 rounds and has a flight time of 40 minutes. It looks like an RC airplane and is controlled by an operator wearing a visor who aims the 12-gauge shotgun through a live video link and sighting system. It features "auto-follow" technology that, once zeroed in, allows the operator to continue shooting at the target without having to adjust course. You can see a photo and a video of the drone if you search Google for: Russia's shotgun drone is the flying nightmare you didn't know you had.

~

There really is an acoustic device that generates a combination of high-pressure sound waves and induces dizziness, imbalance and nausea. It can cover an area the size of a typical bedroom and have an affect on every person within range.

~

A wingsuit allows you to fly through the air by adding surface area to the human body with fabric between the legs and under the arms, enabling a significant increase in lift. A wingsuit flight normally ends by deploying a parachute, but if the character named Elena jumped off a skyscraper and flew above city streets, she wouldn't be high enough to use her chute. Stuntman Gary Connery safely landed a wingsuit without deploying his parachute, landing on a crushable "runway" built of cardboard boxes. Another method of landing without a parachute would be to drop onto one of those giant-sized inflatable cushions the firefighters deploy so people can jump from a burning building. YouTube features some amazing videos of wingsuit flyers.

Criminals infected the entire Georgia Department of Public Safety (DPS) network with spyware and crippled all of the laptops installed in police cars across the entire state. If it happened in Georgia, it could happen in your state next.

It's true that Russia emptied their prisons and sent thousands of criminals to America as "refugees."

The California Department of Justice Bureau of Investigation released a report stating, "The KGB emptied their prisons of hard-core criminals, much like Cuban dictator Fidel Castro did during the Mariel boat lift." The Lautenberg Amendment expanded refugee admissions from the Soviet Union to 50,000 per year. This was followed by provisions for legal immigration from the now independent states of the former USSR. Dubbed by Russian criminals as "the big store," the United States is now home to criminal gangs from all 15 republics.

The hub of Russian organized crime in the U.S. has been the Brighton Beach area of Brooklyn, New York, known as "Little Odessa." From this center of emigre activity, the *russkaya mafiya* spread their operations throughout the nation.

Russian organized crime groups have formed alliances with La Cosa Nostra and the Colombian cocaine cartels. The alliances allowed these groups to become a dominant wholesale cocaine and heroin distribution factor in California.

In this book, I wanted to point out that law-abiding Russian emigrants are afraid of these criminals released from Soviet prisons, the same way American-born citizens would be afraid of a mass escape from all US prisons. In my fictional story, Jake shuts down one gang in one city. In real life, law enforcement officers (LEOs) are hard at work, trying to investigate, locate and arrest thousands of "escaped" Russian mafia prison inmates. It's a dangerous situation and I wish our LEOs the very best of luck. Be safe out there, and thank you for your service.

JAKE WOLFE SERIES

Novels about Jake Wolfe.

Have you read them all?

Book 1. Dead Lawyers Don't Lie

Book 2. Vigilante Assassin

Book 3. Killer Lawyer

Book 4. San Diego Dead

Book 5. Deadly Weapon

Book 6. Key West Dead

Please subscribe to my reader newsletter at marknolan.com and I'll send you an email when I publish another book or give away a Kindle.

ACKNOWLEDGMENTS

First of all, I'd like to thank *you* for reading this book. I'm honored to have you as a reader. I wrote this for you, and I hope you were entertained by the further adventures of Jake and Cody. They'll be back soon, because they just can't seem to stay out of trouble.

Thank you to all of my family and friends who had faith in me and offered encouragement while I was doing the nearly impossible task of writing a novel.

Thanks to my early readers of the manuscript's first drafts who gave helpful feedback.

Thanks to my secret team of beta readers, editors and proofreaders who all worked hard on the story.

Thank you to the highly talented artist Elizabeth Mackey for designing the book cover. You were a joy to work with.

Thank you to John W. Pilley, retired psychology professor, for writing the book, *Chaser: Unlocking the Genius of the Dog Who Knows a Thousand Words*. In the book, Dr. Pilley proves that dogs can be incredibly smart and that we've underestimated them. This scientist and his beloved dog, Chaser, are redefining what we know about canine intelligence.

Thank you to Mike Earp, grandson of the legendary lawman Wyatt Earp, for writing the book *U.S. Marshals: Inside America's Most Storied Law Enforcement Agency*. Mike Earp served as one of the top three people in the Marshals Service. He reveals how the Old West tradition of deputizing citizens to form a posse and chase criminals has been updated and now enables the Marshals Service to form task forces. Unique in law enforcement, these fugitive task forces may include contributing officers from any local, state or federal law enforcement agency. Marshals are also empowered to deputize private citizens.

Thanks to the Northwestern California University of Law for providing information about their online Juris Doctor (J.D.) law study program. When completed, the online law degree is designed to meet the requirements for licensure and admission to practice law in the California State Courts and the United States Federal Courts as a California attorney.

Thank you to Lisa Rogak for writing the book *The Dogs of War: The Courage, Love and Loyalty of Military Working Dogs*. Rogak goes into detail about dozens of these dogs and their handlers.

Thanks to the dog handlers who served alongside my son when he was an 0311 infantry grunt in the Marines, on deployments overseas. Just knowing that you and your dogs were there with my son's platoon on patrols outside the wire helped me to get a few hours of sleep at night—very few, but infantry Marine parents will take any hours of sleep they can get.

Thanks to the folks who invented all kinds of unusual equipment that seems like science fiction but actually exists in real life. Feel free to look these up on Google if you'd enjoy seeing pictures and videos.

1. The Pneu-Dart CO_2 tranquilizer pistol that fires a disposable remote drug delivery dart.

2. The Coda Netgun that shoots a fifteen-foot knotless net into the air, with four bullet-shaped steel weights on each of the four corners.

3. The bulletproof black Jeep with all the extra protections (which anyone with plenty of cash money can buy if they want a Jeep like the one Jake Wolfe drives).

Thank you to Jim Slater, former K-9 cop and police dog

handler, for inventing and manufacturing the K-9 Storm Vest. These are Kevlar-lined tactical flak jackets with integrated cameras and communication systems. The jackets act as dog-sized bulletproof vests, armored with ballistic panels that can stop a bullet or a knife, to protect our brave four-footed police dogs and military working dogs from harm. Officer Slater's desire to protect his own police dog led to the creation of a vest business that has protected and saved the lives of countless working dogs who are dedicated to protecting you and me.

Thank you to Columbia Pictures for use of a brief quote by Tom Hanks from the movie "A League of Their Own," spoken by a character in this book as parody and commentary which is allowed as fair use under Section 107 of the U.S. Copyright Act. My compliments to the talented writers of the fantastic story and screenplay, Kim Wilson, Kelly Candaele, and Lowell Ganz.

Thanks again to the good people at bookstores, libraries, e-book retailers, Goodreads, Amazon, review blogs, and book-related websites of all kinds. Yours is a proud profession, and you make the world a better place.

EMAIL SIGNUP

If you'd like to be the first to know about specials and upcoming books, please sign up for my reader newsletter on my website: www.marknolan.com

ABOUT THE AUTHOR

Mark Nolan is author of the Jake Wolfe thriller novel series.

To be notified by Amazon when another book is available, visit Mark's author page and click on the gold "Follow" button under his photo:

Mark Nolan's page on Amazon.com

Sign up for his newsletter for specials and updates:

www.marknolan.com